Journey of an American Son

John Hazen

BLACK ROSE writing™

ISBN: 978-1-61296-446-1

PUBLISHED BY BLACK ROSE WRITING

www.blackrosewriting.com

Printed in the United States of America

Suggested retail price $17.95

Journey of an American Son is printed in Cambria

Dedicated to Stuart J. Hayes, my grandfather,
whose trip provided the initial inspiration for this book and to all
the others—my father, father-in-law, and Lynn's grandparents—
whose lives and stories helped to enrich the tale that follows.

And, as always, to Lynn, my constant inspiration.

Journey of an

American Son

1

Startled by a sharp pinch on his cheek, Benjamin Albert bolted upright from his fitful sleep. For the briefest of seconds, he blissfully did not remember where he was; but it did not take long for the nightmare that had become his life to cascade back over him. He brought his knees up to his chin and huddled on the corner of his straw-filled mat against the cool stone wall.

Ben didn't bother touching his grizzled cheek; he knew there would be a small trickle of blood where a rat had bitten him. When he received his first bite on his first night in prison over two months earlier, the bacteriologist in him envisioned the host of deadly diseases to which he was being exposed: the plague or typhus or leptospirosis or any one of hundreds of deadly infections. He idly wondered if one of these maladies was the cause of the fever he had been running the past three days or whether it was something more mundane like malaria. If it were a fatal disease, he had some consolation that he would at least depart this wretched place.

He briefly toyed with the idea of seizing an opportunity to "leave" two weeks earlier. A guard had taken pity on him and lent him a straight-edged razor to remove a month and a half worth of beard that had overtaken his face. It would have been so simple to slit his own throat and end it all for good. His mind weighed the possibility, but he lacked the courage to take such a step. He still had a modicum of hope that the truth would eventually emerge and he would be set free, although he did not know how this was to come about.

He also thought about the trouble the guard would be in for this simple act of kindness. Kindnesses should be promoted, not discouraged. So, he continued living with the backbreaking work, the malnutrition, the beatings, the disease, the hopelessness and, of course, the rats.

He had found that the best way to avoid being bitten while he slept was to scrunch up like a ball in the corner. This raised his head and exposed fewer areas of skin to tempt the hungry rodents. On nights like this, though, after a day of excruciating hard labor in a blazing sun—made even harder by having only one hand—with meager rations and sadistic overseers, he would crumple into his cot from sheer exhaustion, paying little attention to the position his body was in as he drifted off to sleep.

He had been allowed to send one telegram upon his arrest and one letter upon his conviction but there had been no other correspondence in or out of the prison. He was sure his wife, Catherine, had written numerous times but her letters were being intercepted. He was, after all, not the most popular inmate having been convicted of murdering a popular and influential member of the Indian National Committee.

Ben stared out into absolute darkness. The only sounds he heard were the occasional snores and movements of the four other men who shared his cell. In this regard he was somewhat lucky. Other cells of similar size throughout the prison housed as many as thirty inmates but imprisoned foreigners, especially white foreigners, were accorded a higher status and kept apart from the general population.

His cell was located at the far eastern end of the prison. This put it in the city's shadows as the afternoon progressed, making it relatively cooler even on brutally hot days. His cell also caught an occasional breeze off the Hooghly River, cooling the stone structure and replacing the fetid air that had gathered. After a long day of road building or whatever other task they had devised for him during the day in the relentless sun, he appreciated the chance to go back to a cool place.

He wished he could fall back asleep, but it was futile. At times like this, when his mind was most idle, he was filled with the most dread about his precipitous decline in fortune.

In 1916, he met and got engaged to Catherine Jackson, the

woman of his dreams. In 1917, at the age of nineteen he graduated first in his class from Rutgers University and promptly volunteered for the U.S. Army, serving with distinction in the Great War. In 1918, he returned to marry Catherine and complete his graduate studies, again graduating first in his class. In 1919, he landed a job doing scientific research, work he loved, with Langdan Textiles, one of the largest textile businesses in the country if not the world, and taught part-time at the Massachusetts Institute of Technology. In January 1920, Catherine gave birth to their son, Harry. In March 1920, Langdan sent him and three business associates on a trip to Calcutta, India to investigate why jute, the principal component of burlap and other rough fabrics manufactured by the company, was subject to a rotting, degenerative disease.

After growing up in meager circumstances, everything was coming together for him. Life was good; his prospects were bright.

Then, in the blink of an eye in August of 1920, he found himself rotting away in an infested Calcutta prison framed for a murder he did not commit.

At times like this, he would dredge up a memory from his past and then purposely flood his mind with the memory, hoping he could escape to that time and place. Even his most tragic and sad memories were preferable places to visit than his present reality.

His very earliest recollection was one that haunted him throughout his life. He was not even sure it was a true memory, that he actually experienced it, but it was an incident that played in his mind so often over the years that he was convinced it was true.

Three-year old Benjamin toddled through the house, looking for someone to play with. Finding no one, he sat down on his little three-legged stool in his corner of the overly warm kitchen and gnawed on a cracker. During the winter months, this spot was especially comfortable. It was midway between the large black cast iron coal stove and the somewhat drafty back door. On this day, though, the kitchen, as well as every other room on the first floor of the house in the Jewish neighborhood of New Brunswick, New Jersey, was packed with people. Some he knew, but most were strangers.

Although his spot put him out of the bustle of—and therefore kept him from being jostled and stepped on by—the numerous adults who filled the house to overflowing, he still felt closed in. The only things he could see from his particular vantage point were the legs and backsides of these strangers and an occasional glimpse of his mother sitting at the white kitchen table, periodically dabbing her eyes with a lace handkerchief.

He thought momentarily of going over to be with her, but she was crying and he did not know why. He was afraid he was the cause. She had been sobbing on and off for the past two days since she returned from her trip. Four days earlier, Ben's Uncle Sol came to the back door. Ben got all excited. Uncle Sol was such fun. He was always joking and laughing and playing and bestowing little gifts for everyone, but not on this day. He knocked on the back door, stayed outside with a very serious look on his face until Ben's mother came downstairs with her cardboard suitcase. They then departed without saying a word to anybody.

Ben was already concerned because his father had departed three days prior to that and had not yet returned. Before leaving, his Papa knelt down, gave Ben a big bear hug, and told him to be a good boy, to eat his vegetables and to listen to his mother. Ben said he would, but he wasn't sure why he was being given this advice. He pretty much always did these things as a matter of course.

But now his mother was leaving as well. His sister Bessie, who in all honesty Ben hardly knew since she was fifteen years his elder and was hardly ever home, was put in charge of the household. Ben would find that, over the following week, he would have to fend for himself or depend on one of his brothers, who were also substantially older than he, as Bessie was still never home except to sleep. He was therefore greatly relieved when his mother returned from her trip and walked through the door. Like his father had done, she knelt down and gave him a big hug, but he could sense no joy in her. Normally, if she went out even for a short period she would greet Ben with unbridled delight, calling him her "American Son". This time, however, when she returned she gave him a squeeze and said nothing.

Ben asked where Papa was and when he was coming home. In response, his mother just offered a weak smile, patted him on the head and then plodded up the stairs to her room to unpack.

Over the next two days, his mother moped around and did not say a word. When he ventured too close she would snag him, draw him close, wrap her arms around him, bury her head into his neck and burst into tears. She hugged him so tight that it hurt and he had trouble breathing. It was not an experience he wanted to recreate so he tried to keep his distance. It was his mother's job to comfort him when he cried, not the other way around.

Ben could not get a straight answer where his father was. If he were here, he would make her feel better; he was the only one who could put a smile back on his mother's face. He asked his brother Robert where their father had gone. Robert said something about a trip to North Carolina, wherever that was, on doctor's orders to get away from the winter, but in the end it did not do any good. That was all he would say as he walked away. Ben was more confused than ever.

Now there were people all over the house. Many would come up to him and tell him to be strong. He would say okay, he would be, but he did not know why they said such things.

So, he sat on his little stool. At one point, the crowd in the kitchen thinned a bit. Despite the previous unpleasant experience, he still desired the comfort of his mother. This seemed like an opportune time to go over and climb into her lap but two thirds of the way over, an elderly man with a long white beard and formal, wide brimmed black hat cut him off. Defeated, Ben headed for another part of the house.

Everywhere he went, strangers jostled him as they wandered sadly about. They talked to each other in hushed tones. Almost all of the men he encountered in his wanderings were like the man who had cut him off in the kitchen, many sporting beards of various lengths and dressed in dark clothes and broad-brimmed hats. The women were similarly formally attired.

He was getting very hungry; it was mid-afternoon and he had not eaten since early that morning. He could smell one of his favorites, stuffed cabbage, and this only made him hungrier. There were platters of food on the dining room table and keeping warm on the stove, but nobody was eating. All the chairs had been removed from the dining room and were lined up along the walls of various rooms on the first floor, occupied mostly by women who were chatting in the same hushed tones as the people who wandered about the house.

The dining room table was too high for him to reach without a chair. He was too intimidated to ask any of the strangers to help him get something to eat so he decided to go hungry. He continued his walk into the front parlor.

Like the dining room, this room had been completely changed from its usual décor. There was usually a sofa and two chairs as well as a coffee table and several small tables throughout the room. All of these pieces of furniture had been removed, replaced by a single large rectangular brown wooden box. The box had arrived at the same time his mother and Uncle Sol returned from their trip. His uncle and three other men whom he did not know struggled as they carried the box, angling it to and fro to finally get it into the parlor.

This was the only room with no people in it. Ben decided to go in for some peace and solitude. Looking around, the only familiar item was the full-length ornate mirror on the wall, but even this was rendered different as it was draped and covered with a large black sheet.

Ben did not know quite what to do in this room, but he liked the quiet and not being run over constantly. He had seen a group of about a dozen men enter the room earlier. He could hear them reciting something, but could not make out what they were saying from his spot in the kitchen. Their words sounded like what his father used to say the times Ben tagged along with him to temple on Friday evening, but he could not swear to that. The men had since dispersed to other rooms on the first floor and, a few who needed a smoke, to the porch.

Since it was past both his mealtime and naptime, Ben was understandably getting tired but he did not have any place to sit or lie down. So he did what any toddler would naturally do, he climbed up on the box and sat there. He liked the spot. It gave him a perch from which he could look out the window to the street below. It also provided a good view of the people milling about in adjacent rooms.

Ben was quite content until Yakov Zvi, a dour, humorless elder of the synagogue, spied him from the dining room. With purpose and resolve, Zvi strode over with an even more austere look on his face than usual. He stopped a few feet from Ben and spoke.

"It is not permitted." Zvi scolded the young boy in Yiddish.

Ben looked questioningly at the gaunt face framed by a medium-length gray beard. What was not permitted, he wondered?

"You must get down. Show your father some respect!"

Ben climbed down from the box and walked out of the room back into the crowd of people. All the while, Zvi glared at him as if he were a criminal. Ben's eyes started to well up. He did not know what he had done wrong. He knew he could not go to his mother in her condition and he still had no idea where his Papa had gone. He decided to return to his little stool in the kitchen, hopefully sitting there away from mischief.

A few hours later, he saw the box once again as six men, three on each side holding ropes, lowered it into a hole in the ground. He stood in front of his mother, who by this time had recovered her composure. His brothers and sister were arrayed on both sides of her. At one point his brother, Phil, reached down and put his hand on Ben's shoulder. Ben looked up at him and received a warm but shaky and tentative smile.

After the rabbi intoned a blessing, his mother kneeled down beside Ben, gave him a gentle hug and spoke to him.

"Benjamin, take a handful of dirt and throw it down on the coffin and say goodbye to your Papa. He loved you very much, you know."

Ben loved his Papa very much, too. He couldn't quite understand what his father was doing in that box and why everyone was heaping shovel after shovel of soil on it. He was slowly beginning to comprehend that he would never see his father ever again.

As he sat on the floor in his cell, Benjamin thought back to this event, nearly twenty-two years earlier. As time progressed, any memories of his Papa had faded into the background. In some cases, he was not sure whether his recollections were true memories or his own dreams and imagination. The image of the coffin, and the scolding he received by the elder for climbing up on the coffin, were always vivid in his mind, however, as was his father's passing away on a warm autumn day in 1901, leaving a widow alone to look after four children.

Ben closed his eyes and tried to go back to sleep.

2

Catherine

I first met Ben in the spring of 1916. Our initial encounter could have been disastrous. I worked at the Rutgers College library. It wasn't that I needed the money. My mother demanded that I work part-time to build my character. I'm still debating whether that worked or not. She was a close friend of Mabel Smith Douglass, who was leading the drive to open Rutgers to female students. Mother wanted me poised to enroll the minute that happened. She figured that physically working at the university gave me an advantage. She also paid for an apartment in the middle of New Brunswick for two of my friends and me. I felt quite the independent young lady.

Anyway, it was a Saturday afternoon on a beautiful day in late May. The library was practically deserted. I was wheeling a cart full of books I had to return to their shelves in the biology section. I turned a corner and saw him sitting alone at a table, surrounded by his notes and a number of volumes.

He didn't see me at first. He was studying very intently, but he wasn't staring at his books. He was concentrating on a dollar bill he held in his hand. I was fascinated by his catatonic state as he gazed at this bill. I found him to be quite handsome, too, with his chestnut colored wavy hair and penetrating dark brown eyes. He was dressed in what could best be called workman clothes, a blue denim shirt, black somewhat worn but still serviceable slacks and rubber-soled light brown shoes. He certainly was not the typical college student I ran into every day. I decided to walk over and speak to him.

"So, is that the first dollar you ever earned?" I airily asked as an icebreaker.

My voice startled him as he sat upright from his slouched position. I could tell he was weighing his answer. He later told me that he actually mulled over the possible responses he could make to this question. He was in a foul mood and his initial inclination was to say: "Just because I'm Jewish doesn't make me a miser!" But when he looked up from his seat in the library and saw (his words) the most beautiful hazel eyes he'd ever seen in his life, he quickly reconsidered. I had no idea at the time (nor did I really care) that he was Jewish and he made a wise choice in not responding in the way his original instincts guided him. I probably would have turned and stormed away, never speaking to him again.

Still, though, it wasn't in his nature to make a breezy, witty retort. Instead he said:

"No, actually it's the last dollar my father earned before he died."

I stood there a few seconds, uncomfortable and dumbfounded.

"I...I'm so sorry."

I turned to walk away as he called after me.

"No, wait. I'm the one who should apologize for my rudeness. Please, won't you sit down? I could use the company."

I slowly lowered myself into a seat across the table from him, but I still didn't know what to say after that.

Ben couldn't keep his eyes off of me. I have to admit I was rather a stunner back then. He said he especially loved the dimple that appeared in my left cheek when I smiled. I was hoping he'd be determined to do whatever it took to keep me smiling for a long time.

"My name's Ben Albert."

"I'm Catherine Jackson. It's a pleasure to meet you."

"Pleasure's mine, Catherine."

There was silence for a few moments more until I asked the question most on my mind.

"Is that really the last dollar your father earned?"

"Yes, one of them. He got sick when I was three years old. I never did get a straight answer what he had but from what I could gather I always suspected it was cancer. The doctor told him it would be best for his health to go to a warm climate for a while. He traveled to North Carolina, worked two days in the tobacco fields down there and then died that night. He made all of five dollars for his efforts. Each of his four children got a dollar as a remembrance. My mother has the other.

"My sister, Bessie, spent hers within a week. As far as I know, the rest of us still have ours. I carry mine with me all the time. Occasionally, when things are going tough I'll pull mine out and look at it. It puts things in perspective for me when I think of what he had to go through, immigrating to America with only about twenty words of English in his vocabulary, living in the tenements of New York before settling in New Brunswick to raise his family and build a new life. Then cancer cut him down before he could really get going. Looking at the dollar reminds me of my obligations and responsibilities. That's why you find me here in the library on a gorgeous Saturday."

"You said your father died when you were three? Do you have any memories of him?"

"Only very vague ones. As time goes on, I'm less and less sure which are real and which I've invented from the stories I've heard about him over the years. My mother's still going strong, though. I live at home with her. What about you?"

"Well, I live in an apartment with a couple of friends not too far from here on Church Street. I know it's very scandalous, three un-chaperoned females living on their own in the city. It was my mother's idea actually. She lives up in Westfield and she could not see me traveling every day back and forth. Besides, she wants me to be independent. Like she is. My earliest memories revolve around accompanying her to suffrage meetings. Hopefully, you're not one of those who wish to keep women from voting, are you?"

"No, not at all. Women can't do any worse at choosing leaders than men. You mentioned your mother. Is your father dead?"

"No, they divorced when I was young. He lives up in Boston. He's been very generous financially to my mother and me, but he's never wanted much to do with my life. It's okay, though."

The look on his face showed that it wasn't okay. He changed the subject.

"So, what's a nice girl like you doing in a place like this on a gorgeous Saturday afternoon? Shouldn't you be getting ready for a date or something?"

"Well, I work here. I have to work until 6:00, or at least be here until 6:00. I don't think my supervisor would exactly classify what I'm doing now as 'working' but she's nice. And no, no date. No nothing tonight, I'm afraid."

"I refuse to believe that a beautiful woman such as yourself does not have a line of men waiting at your doorstep on the off chance you'll honor them with your attention."

I laughed, but was very taken by the compliment.

"I'm sorry to disappoint."

"Well, as it so happens I find myself similarly unoccupied and uncommitted for this evening. Would you like to grab a bite, perhaps at Timothy's Pub, when you get off? Unless of course you don't want to be seen with a man who still lives with his mother."

"Well, when you put it that way, it does seem a lot less desirable."

He smiled back but then just as quickly got serious again.

"Or unless you'd feel funny about going out with a Jew."

"No, that doesn't bother me in the least."

"I'm glad to hear that. I like to be upfront to see where I stand. So, can I pick you up at your place around 7:30?"

3

Malka Abramowitz was the first to see it. She sprinted down the four flights of stairs, nearly tripping a half dozen times, to the hold of the ship where her husband Hirsch and their three children, Baila, Pinchas and Reuben, were still asleep. She shook Hirsch from his stupor while she shouted in Yiddish.

"I saw it! I saw it! I saw land! I saw America!"

Hirsch always slept with his pants on in case he had to move quickly in an emergency, and this was an emergency. He leaped up from his cot, threw his shirt over his back, pulled on his boots and wrapped the children in blankets. Together the five of them, along with six other immigrants who had been awakened by Malka's shouting, started the ascent to the upper deck.

It was late October and the sharp ocean breeze stung their cheeks as they stood at the front point of the SS Pennsylvania in the early dawn. They did not mind the cold in the least as they gazed out over the calm water. The skyline of New York slowly came into focus. Malka, holding Reuben in her arms while Hirsch held the hands of the other two children, glanced over to her husband and saw a tear tracing down his cheek. She gently squeezed his shoulder.

"Malka, my dove," he spoke to her in Yiddish, "we are going to make it. Our dreams will come true. We are going to be Americans."

Then, as if he had gone through a physical transformation, Hirsch switched to broken English.

"We learn English. We American. I talk with others who know things American. We to have American, not Yiddish, names. I not Hirsch, I is Harry. Baila is Bessie, Pinchas is Phil, Reuben is Robert. You is Molly. We not Abramowitz. We is family Albert."

Hirsch stood there, his jaw jutting out towards his soon-to-be-adopted land. Malka, now Molly, gazed up at him. She was proud of him and so transfixed by him that she completely missed the Statue of Liberty—a sight she had looked forward to since she was a girl—as the ship sailed by. Normally, he would not be so dictatorial, especially about something so momentous and life altering, but she did not mind. She had always disliked the name Malka. "Molly" had a nice ring to it; she could get used to it very easily.

She liked that Hirsch, or rather Harry, was being so self-confident as they sailed into the New World and a new life. Every time she thought about it rationally, she shuddered at the perils they were facing. They needed all the self-confidence they could muster. She shuddered even more knowing that in six or seven months they would have a new baby to name and feed.

She had not told Harry or anyone else that she was pregnant. She feared this could provide the authorities with an excuse to send the family back to Germany. Some people had been returned to their native lands because they were sick or deformed or for myriad other reasons. She was not sure whether pregnancy fell into one of these categories, but she was taking no chances. It worked out well that, when morning sickness began to regularly strike, she passed it off as seasickness.

Her baby would be born in the United States. He would be different. While Bessie and Phil and Robert worked at a very early age to help support the family, the new baby would go to school. He would be a learned man who would make his living using his mind, not his hands. A rabbi or a doctor or a lawyer, any of these professions would be fine. She would make sure that he knew Yiddish, but his first language would be English.

Molly wondered what name they would give the new arrival. Would Harry want to give him an old world name and then rename him like he did everyone else or would the new baby immediately be given an American name? If he were a boy, Harry would try, like he had with the previous two boys, to name him after his father, Abram.

Abram Abramowitz was killed in 1882 defending his family during a pogrom that swept through the shtetl near Warsaw. Hirsch was six years old when the pounding on the door began at around 1:00 in the morning. Abram held off the four assailants while his wife shepherded Hirsch and his three sisters out the back door and into the woods. For the rest of his life, he could still hear his father's wail that rang out into the night as a pitchfork pierced his chest.

Hirsch and his family ran the entire night, fleeing deeper into the woods and finally collapsing near a stream. Hirsch's mother woke in terror the next morning to find a young peasant looking down on them. After convincing them that he meant them no harm, the peasant brought the family back to his shack where he and his wife sheltered them for a month until the pogrom fever subsided.

In the meantime, Mrs. Abramowitz was able to get a message to her brother-in-law, Mordecai, who lived in Vilnius. He wrote back that she and her family were welcome to come and live with him until they could get themselves settled and find a new place to live.

After numerous thanks and blessings to their benefactors, the family set out on foot on a 250-mile trek through unfamiliar forests and towns. Three weeks later, they collapsed from hunger and exhaustion on the doorstep of Mordecai Abramowitz's modest house.

Once he regained his strength and acclimated himself to his new surroundings, Hirsch found he liked Vilnius and the bustle of a city. He apprenticed in his uncle's kosher butcher shop. It was not work he was especially fond of doing, but it was readily available. And after weeks of total hunger while on the run, he knew that at least he would not know hunger again if he stayed in this profession. He was such a good worker that Mordecai came to trust Hirsch to run the store by himself while he butchered beasts in back, went out to make deliveries or performed other duties.

Two things happened when Hirsch was sixteen years of age that were to change his life forever. The first was that he became enthralled with America. Mordecai's cousin, Sol, had fled Vilnius for America three years earlier, ultimately settling in New York City. He wrote letters back home extolling all the bounty of the New World. He started as a street peddler of home goods—pots and pans and the like—and soon had his own business. He wrote of far away places to which he would travel to sell his wares, places with exotic names like Poughkeepsie and Hackensack and Yonkers. He wrote of mighty buildings stretching to the sky. He wrote of Jews living free with no thoughts of pogroms.

The second event that changed his life was the day Malka Levy walked though the front door of the shop and ordered two chickens to make a soup. Although she was also only sixteen, the long dark hair braided in a bun on top of her head that made her look much older. She had pleasant looks, but was by no means a beauty. She could tend towards plumpness, but had an attractive figure that could be discerned through frumpy, unfashionable clothes.

Hirsch was manning the counter by himself on this day while his uncle was in back butchering a special lamb for the rabbi's son's bar mitzvah. In an effort to be friendly but no more than that, Hirsch struck a conversation.

"Hello, I don't believe I've ever seen you in the shop before. Are you new to town?"

"No, we usually shop at Mr. Feldman's butcher shop at the other end of town, but his wife passed away and the shop was closed. We needed some chickens for soup for the holiday so I came here."

"I'm sorry to hear about Mrs. Feldman, but I do hope you will continue to get your meats here. Between you and me, our meats are much better than Mr. Feldman's, and I'm completely unbiased in this appraisal."

Malka could not help but smile, but she said they would most likely have to remain loyal to Mr. Feldman.

"I understand completely. Loyalty, even if it's to an inferior product, is admirable. So, you want some chickens. How many can I get you? A dozen?"

"No, there's only my mother, my father and me, so I think two chickens will be sufficient."

"Only two? That's hardly enough to make strong soup for one person, let alone three."

"Two will be quite sufficient, thank you."

"Okay, how many feet do you want?"

"Feet?"

"Chicken feet, of course. You put them in the soup. It's the best thing to thicken it."

The disgusted look on her face told Hirsch that she never had heard of this trick.

"I tell you what, I'll throw six feet in, no charge. You go home, make your soup and then come back here and tell me whether or not this was the best soup you'd ever had in your life."

"You're just trying to get me to come back here, aren't you?"

"Who, me?"

With that, Malka paid for her chickens and left the shop. Three days later, she walked through the door and declared that it was indeed the best soup she had ever had. After that, she would come in once a week, generally on Tuesday afternoon. Each time she would ask Hirsch what was good that day or if he could impart any more cooking tricks. Although they never talked about anything more than what was good in the shop, Hirsch sensed that something else was going on. This was confirmed when he returned to the shop one day after making a delivery and Mordecai remarked about a young woman who had stopped by. She lingered around the shop for a bit, not saying a word. When he asked if he could help her, she implied that she might want some veal to make a stew, but she did not commit to buying anything. She stayed a little while longer, letting several women who had come in after her place their orders, but otherwise she stood around shifting from one foot to the other and generally looking uncomfortable. In the end, she did not purchase anything and left quietly. His uncle thought it quite strange; Hirsch was delighted. It was now clear that she was coming to the shop over and over again not because of the quality of the meats and poultry they sold but to see him.

After that, he made sure he was in the shop every Tuesday afternoon. If a delivery had to be made, he would come up with excuses to delay his departure. When she came in, Hirsch's face would light up, but he still did not want to push too hard for fear of scaring her away in her shyness. This had gone on for three months and he still did not know her name so one day when she ordered some beef and asked for it to be cubed, Hirsch spoke without looking up from his cutting.

"My name is Hirsch, Hirsch Abramowitz."

"I'm Malka, Malka Levy."

"It's a pleasure to meet you Malka."

Malka simply nodded in return. She took her package of beef and handed over some coins in payment. Hirsch made sure to brush her hand in accepting the money and again when handing her the change. Her head had been looking down the entire time but as she was turning to leave, she looked up and saw Hirsch gazing at her. She smiled demurely, said goodbye and left the store.

Hirsch had not seen his uncle come in from the back room. He stood and watched the scene unfold.

"Ahh, that explains it. When she came in a few weeks ago it wasn't that she was indecisive about what she wanted to buy; she was waiting for you to return. She seems like a nice girl and she's definitely in love with you. Have you known her long?"

"She's been coming to the shop every week for the past three months now. But today was the first time we ever spoke to each other about anything than chickens. I didn't even know her name until just now."

"Trust me, Hirsch, I can tell. She's head over heels in love with you. And if I'm any judge, which I think I am, you love her, too."

"Well, even if I am, that's too bad. I'm sure she has a match all chosen for her."

Hirsch said nothing more and set about cleaning the counter. Mordecai looked fondly at his nephew whom he had come to regard as his own son. He knew what he had to do.

That evening, he cleaned himself up, put on his only suit and went searching for the home of Malka Levy. But he only had a name. There were a fair number of Levys in the ghetto. From his nephew's description, she came for meat quite often, so he surmised her family was relatively well off. They also lived closer to Feldman's butcher shop. That narrowed it down considerably more. Armed with this knowledge, he went to the ghetto's version of the hall of records. He thought about going to the rabbi, who would know everybody, but the rabbi was a busybody. Mordecai wanted to be discreet about his intentions.

At the Hall of Records, he located four families named Levy who appeared to fit the description. He wrote down the addresses and proceeded to knock on doors. At the first two houses, there was no Malka. At the third, the door opened and there she was. He introduced himself and asked to see her father.

Mordecai was led into the study, which was an impressive wood paneled room. Mordecai made a nice living, but he quickly realized Mr. Levy was far richer than he.

When Malka's father walked in, Mordecai got right to the point. He was interested in arranging a marriage between Hirsch and Malka. Levy was not overly impressed. He candidly admitted he had higher aspirations for his daughter than a butcher's apprentice. Levy told Mordecai that he had already started to make arrangements for Malka to marry the son of a fellow merchant. What he did not say was that she had made it crystal clear that Hirsch was the man she was going to marry, with or without her father's blessing.

Levy considered ordering his daughter to marry whoever he told her to, but he could not bring himself to be that unkind to his only daughter. When Mordecai knocked on his door, he knew this marriage was fated to be, but he still had to put up a fight. If for no other reason, he could reduce the terms of the dowry by making it clear that Hirsch was a definite second choice. If truth were told, Mordecai was ready to agree to a marriage without a dowry. His only goal was the happiness of Hirsch.

Three months later, Hirsch and Malka were wed. Within a year of the wedding, Malka gave birth to their first child, whom they named Abram after Hirsch's father. Almost from the beginning, they could tell that there was something terribly wrong with the baby's health. He could not keep anything down. Instead of gaining weight, he had trouble keeping it on. Three weeks after Abram was born, a high fever burned his young body. Three days after that, the baby was dead.

In successive years after that, Baila, Pinchas and Reuben were born. Hirsch wanted to name one of his sons Abram after his late father, but Malka thought it was bad luck and would not allow it.

Under Mordecai's tutelage, Hirsch became a master butcher. He worked closely with the rabbi to learn the art of koshering meat. He also became adept at negotiating with the goyim who would purchase cuts of meat or entire animals that were not up to kosher standards. Mordecai was uncomfortable about this practice. He had lived through several pogroms. The gentiles did not need much of an excuse to turn on the Jews. Any illness that the gentile community suffered could be linked back to the Jews, even if there were no connection whatsoever. By selling them non-kosher meat that could potentially be diseased, Hirsch was handing them that connection on a platter. But the money was too good for Hirsch to think about stopping.

This allowed Hirsch to put some money aside. He had never forgotten about his other dream: going to America. All the money he made on this little side business was saved to make this dream a reality. Luckily, it was a dream Malka shared with him.

Despite realizing that losing Hirsch would be a severe setback for his business, Mordecai understood, and to some extent shared, Hirsch's desire to immigrate to America. The letters his cousin had written filled him with wonder as well, but he could not abandon his responsibilities in Vilnius. If nothing else, Hirsch's mother could not hope to go to America since she had developed tuberculosis. When she first contracted the disease, Hirsch at first gave up his dream and resigned himself to living out his days in Vilnius. It was Mordecai who came to him one day and told him that it was his duty to get on a boat and leave. He was the family's hope. Also, Mordecai convinced him that he could help his mother more from America, sending money to help pay for the medicines and care she needed. And so it was settled.

On October 12, 1897 Hirsch, Malka and the three children bid tearful goodbyes to all of their friends and family as they boarded a train at the station for Danzig on the Baltic Sea. From there they would take a steamer to Hamburg, Germany where they would ultimately board the steamboat to America.

Two steamboats, the SS Rotterdam and the SS Pennsylvania, were scheduled to sail out of Hamburg for New York. Despite being slightly more expensive, Hirsch chose to book fares on the Pennsylvania since a wondrous city called Philadelphia, Pennsylvania was one of the magical names he remembered from Sol's letters. Hirsch took it as a positive omen that the ship they were to take was named the Pennsylvania.

As the ship drew close to the dock at Ellis Island, Hirsch, now called Harry, stood with his arm around Molly and his three (soon to be four) children looking at the magnificence of New York. He felt nothing but hope for the future and pride in his soon-to-be new country.

Molly felt the first kick of her unborn son. She believed he was excited about being born an American citizen.

4

Catherine

I've made it a habit never to let on to anybody I dated who my father was. I wanted the boy to like me for myself, not because my father, albeit an absentee father, was one of the richest men in all of New England. To keep the separation from my father clear, at the age of sixteen I announced to the world that I was no longer to be known as Catherine Andrews but that I was adopting my mother's maiden name, Jackson. To assist me in this ruse, Mother went down to the county courthouse and legally changed both of our last names.

It only took Mother and Father a few months after their wedding day to realize that their getting married was a terrible mistake. Somehow during that time, though, I was conceived. I think he always categorized me as a mistake as well, but, to my father's credit, he was an honorable man who admitted his mistakes and was willing to take responsibility for them. So, after six months of wedded not-so-blissful life, my parents separated. I was still in the womb at the time. A year later the divorce was final.

My mother took me back to Westfield, New Jersey to be near her parents and we started our life there. My father set up a generous trust fund that I could access once I turned twenty-one. He also sent checks every month to support mother and me. I believe his accounting department automatically drafted and signed the monthly checks so he didn't even have to do that much. Though he'd never once laid his eyes on me, I liked to believe he thought he was being a good father by authorizing the release of these checks.

I did see him once when his father, my paternal grandfather, passed away. My mother had actually known Mr. Franklin Andrews, Sr. longer than she did my father, Mr. Franklin Andrews, Jr., having worked in the older man's office. That was where she met my father. She would often tell me what a wonderful man my grandfather was. When she first met my father, she assumed that the 'acorn not falling far from the tree' would apply to his son, but she soon found she was sorely mistaken.

After the separation she wanted to keep in touch with her former father-in-law but my father strictly forbade it. I believed he was acutely aware of his shortcomings relative to his old man and did not want to be reminded of them. I think he was afraid that his father would love his former daughter-in-law more than his own son. He was probably correct.

To emphasize his point, my father made it clear that he would only set up the trust fund and provide support payments if my mother agreed to sever all ties to everyone in the Andrews family. My mother can be very headstrong, but she was also very practical. A part of her wanted to tell my father to go to hell and that she would associate with whomever she chose. But she was aware that a pregnant woman on her own needed to eat. She wanted an education and nice things for me. In the end, discretion won out and she agreed to all my father's conditions.

My mother kept her part of the bargain and never directly contacted my grandfather again, but she did exchange monthly letters with a friend of hers with whom she worked in the old man's office. This went on for years until one day there was a knock on the door. It was a Western Union man delivering a telegram from my mother's friend advising her that her former father-in-law had passed away and when and where the funeral was to be held.

My mother had already determined she was going to go to Boston to pay her respects, but then she came up to my room and asked if I would like to go along with her. I was thirteen at the time. Over the years, she had thoroughly explained the situation with my father and she realized it could be a shock for me to actually see him, but she felt I was old enough to make the choice on my own.

Even if I did not choose to go to the funeral, she told me she would enjoy my company for the train ride north. We would tour Boston and see all the sights. I told her I'd love to accompany her but I remained uncommitted about attending the services.

It was my first ride ever on a real train. I'd taken the trolleys that crisscrossed Union County, but the thought of being on a genuine steam locomotive-drawn train for the eight-hour ride into New England filled my skin with goose bumps. I felt so grown up, making a trip like this with my mother, but I also felt like a little kid heading out on a first-of-a-kind adventure.

By the time we passed New York City and were heading into Connecticut, the novelty had worn off somewhat. Also, the reality of what I was heading into started to dawn on me. I was hurtling toward seeing, and perhaps meeting, a man I hated but at the same time a man who had given me life. He was a man I desperately wanted to love but, more importantly, whom I wanted to love me.

My mother could sense my dilemma. She told me it would be perfectly fine if I stayed in the hotel room while she went to the funeral. I didn't respond one way or the other and sat staring out the window the rest of the trip.

When we arrived in Boston, we stayed at the Lenox Hotel. It was a beautiful place. Our room overlooked the bay. I was back to being an excited kid again but it was time for me to make a very adult decision. I told my mother I would accompany her to the funeral. My mother hugged me and told me how proud she was of me.

I'd always had an inkling of how important men my father and grandfather were but it was confirmed for me when I overheard my mother ask the hotel clerk to get us a carriage to go the Old North Church. Normally, mother would walk or trolley anywhere she wanted to go, but here she was ordering a carriage. Also, I'm sure that ordinary people have funerals at the Old North Church, but I was impressed that we were going to the venerable old church of Paul Revere fame. We piled onto the carriage and headed to the church.

The trip was longer than we expected and we arrived at the

church just as the service was beginning. The sanctuary was packed but we were able to find seats in the very last pew on the right hand side as you looked at the altar. I have a feeling this would have been where we would have sat even if the church were totally empty. As we were sitting down, I cast a glance over the audience but there were too many people for me to make a guess as to which one was my father.

It was a beautiful service, the minister telling of undying devotion to his city, his country, his church and his family. I was struck that family was listed last. My mother dabbed tears away on a few occasions but otherwise kept her composure. We stood and sang all the hymns. At the conclusion, six men rose in unison and proceeded to the casket. I recognized my father in an instant. He was a tall, dashing man, slightly graying at the temples but otherwise fit and youthful looking.

The six men grabbed the railings on each side of the casket, three men on each side. My father was in the front on the casket's right side. They lifted the casket and solemnly escorted my grandfather's body down the center aisle towards the church's rear exit. About three quarters of the way he happened to glance over in our direction and saw my mother. A sad smile bent his mouth. He gave her the slightest of nods to thank her for coming but as he did this, he noticed me sitting there beside her. At first, I don't think he made the connection. He probably thought I was one of the many, many people who knew and respected his father. But almost immediately I could see his eyes shifting back and forth between my mother and me. I could not discern the look on his face. Was it anger at my mother at having brought me here? Was it was befuddlement at the overall situation? Was it distain and contempt? Was it simple curiosity? I cannot say. I only knew it was not the look I wanted my father to have as he gazed upon me for the first time in either of our lives. I needed to get out of there.

We never did see the sights of Boston. As far as I was concerned, the train could not leave soon enough or travel fast enough to get me back to the safe, familiar confines of Westfield, New Jersey.

5

Benjamin Albert was born at 6:40 AM on October 3, 1897 in Ward C of St. Benedict's Hospital located on the Lower East Side of Manhattan. Molly would have preferred to have her baby at home with a midwife in attendance, the same way she had delivered her other children, but Sol was insistent that she deliver her baby in the hospital. Since Sol was their benefactor, not only paying for the hospital stay but for the rent of their two-room apartment over a haberdashery at 250 Ludlow Street, she did not feel she had the right to argue. She also sensed that delivering a baby in a hospital was a very American thing to do.

Molly was determined that her baby be an American citizen. By having her baby in a hospital, she knew there would be no question that he or she was born on American soil. If she were to have the baby at home, questions could be raised as to the timing. She wanted a piece of paper from the hospital to prove to the world that her son or daughter would be the first American in the family.

When the Albert family first arrived in New York, an immediate priority was for Harry to find work. Sol had contacted all the kosher butchers he knew, but none were hiring at the moment, so he hired Harry to work in his home goods store located on Delancey Street, a few blocks away from the apartment. As he had with his Uncle Mordecai, Harry showed himself to be a model worker and a master salesman. Sol found that goods that had been unsold gathering dust on his shelves for years were now moving out the door quicker than he could restock them.

Sol was walking through the store and he noticed a vacant spot on the shelf where some apple peelers/corers were supposed to be. Curious, he went to Harry to see if he had moved them somewhere.

"No, they're all sold," explained Harry.

Surprised that any of these items sold, let alone all on the shelf, he was a little exasperated that Harry had not taken the initiative to restock the shelf from the back. If there was one thing that Sol hated, it was a blank space on a shelf that could be filled with a product that could catch a customer's eye. When he last checked inventory about a month earlier, he still had seven in the backroom in addition to five on the shelf. Although it was his own fault because he had transposed some numbers and seriously over-ordered the gadgets five years ago, he expected more out of his prize employee.

"Well, can you please go get some more from the back to fill in?" he asked.

"There are none."

"None?"

"I sold the last one this morning. I was going to ask you what you wanted to fill in there until we get more in."

"Harry, I've had those for five years. I've sold two, maybe three in all that time. You sell the remaining fifteen in the course of five months?"

"I was able to convince the ladies who come in that their lives would be made so much easier if they had one of these contraptions. In fact, I swear that a couple of women became convinced they could not live without one. One woman bought three so that she, her mother and her daughter could all peel and core apples together."

Sol looked at Harry with amazement. On the one hand, he hoped his customers never caught on that they were being duped. While this was certainly a welcome quick sale that moved product he had conceded could not be moved, it could be disastrous long-term if the women or their husbands felt that they had been flimflammed into buying something they did not need. These women and their families did not have a great deal of disposable income. They accounted for every single cent as they struggled week-to-week and day-to-day in keeping food on the table and a roof over their heads. Most did not have the wherewithal to buy one of these devices, let alone three.

On the other hand, Sol could not argue with results. He could hardly tell his young protégé to stop selling things. He himself had made his way in America in a very short time by being aggressive and resourceful. He often overlooked long term implications in his drive to close a deal and make a sale. How could he ask Harry to do anything different?

In the end, he told Harry he was doing a great job and told him to put some tin bowls on the shelf to fill the empty hole. Sol had a feeling that whatever it was that they put there, Harry would sell it in short order.

Sol came to the conclusion that Harry was too talented and ambitious to keep him unless there was opportunity for advancement. Sol had been very successful in securing customers for his goods all the way from Philadelphia up to Albany, but they had been wholesale customers to which goods were shipped. Sol had always dreamed of opening a new retail outlet outside of New York, but he needed someone he trusted implicitly to run such an operation. He had not located that person, until now. Harry would jump at this opportunity and would thrive.

New Brunswick, New Jersey was a bustling college and industrial town with a growing Jewish population. Sol visited there a few times and noticed there were not many home goods stores. It would provide a perfect opportunity for a new store. The Alberts were cramped into a tiny apartment. In New Brunswick, they could afford a full house and that would be good for the children.

Ben had just turned one when the family settled into their new home on Commercial Avenue. He was just beginning to walk and took to exploring everywhere he could possibly get to.

Molly was looking forward to managing a household in a real house. She had achieved the American dream. There was still hard work ahead of them—they realized that the joys of being an American were not handed to them on a silver platter—but they could see opportunity out there in the distance for the taking. In the old country, dreams were just dreams, no more.

Not all their children were turning out exactly as they had envisioned. When they moved to New Brunswick, Bessie was a wild sixteen who thought she was thirty-five. She had a tendency to leave for long stretches of time without letting her parents know where she was. They had hoped that the exodus from New York City would have a positive influence on her, but instead her negative behaviors only intensified. Neither were they pleased with the types of boys she chose to date. Harry was especially frustrated and tried grounding and scolding his daughter, all to no avail. Both parents knew that it was only a matter of a very short while before Bessie left for good. They could only hope that they had imparted, and she had absorbed, enough good sense to help her get by as she entered adulthood.

Phil was fifteen and seemed to have some intelligence about him. He was inquisitive about finding out how things worked. He loved taking machines apart and then putting them back together again. Harry had developed a special bond with his oldest son and wanted him to learn the business and help around the store. Using the images of Mordecai and Sol, who both quickly realized that they could leave the running of the store itself to Harry while they pursued other ventures to expand the business, he hoped Phil would naturally assume this role. Harry was sorely disappointed. Instead of waiting on customers and moving the product, Phil would spend hours examining gadgets and small appliances such as toasters to see how they worked. It did not take long for Harry to come to the realization that Phil would be much happier as a repairman or a mechanic. That left Robert as his hope to carry on the family business.

The family had been onboard the Pennsylvania when Phil turned thirteen. While Harry appreciated the efforts of his fellow Jews onboard to put together a makeshift bar mitzvah to celebrate Phil's entry into manhood, Harry felt guilty he was unable to offer more to his eldest son. He was determined to make up for it by providing Robert with a proper bar mitzvah in a synagogue with a fine reception to follow.

Harry was sensitive to Phil's feelings and offered to make it a dual ceremony in which Phil could participate as well, but Phil was past that and declined. In addition, he did not want to have to relearn any more Hebrew than he already had. He told his father that he was very happy for his younger brother and would enjoy his bar mitzvah. Harry only wished that he could enjoy it as well.

Robert was not what one would call slow, but he was no great intellect either. Moreover, he was supremely lazy. Getting a rise out of Robert on anything was considered a major accomplishment. He was definitely not the one to count on to eventually take over any business. Harry and Molly thought that if they could transfer just a little bit of Bessie's unbridled energy and a modicum of Phil's intellectual curiosity to Robert, they would have three normal, productive children to work with. But it was not to be.

Ben's arrival was a surprise to everyone, most especially his thirty-eight year old parents. Molly had thought that her childbearing years were long done. Robert's birth had been especially long and hard. She was in labor over twenty hours. The midwife had to shift the baby, who was extremely large, several times to get him through the birth canal. The pain was excruciating and Molly told Harry she believed there had been some damage in the process, rendering her incapable of conceiving again.

She and Harry continued to have intimate relations, but she did not become pregnant. So it came as a shock when, after going through all the tests and paperwork at Ellis Island and they first stepped foot on the American mainland, Molly leaned over to Harry and quietly whispered in his ear that she was pregnant.

"Are you positive? It's been twelve years since Robert. I'd given up hope of having any more children? You're sure?"

In response, Molly demurely nodded her head and smiled.

In contrast to Robert, Ben's delivery was quick and relatively painless. As the doctor held the crying baby out to the nurse, Molly could see that this child was special and would be especially dear to her. She would never admit it to anyone, but she knew immediately that she would love this child above others.

Like the story of Jacob in the Torah, her new child was to be named Benjamin. Like the Benjamin of old, who was born after

Jacob and Rachel arrived in Canaan, this Benjamin would be a symbol to the world of the Albert family's arrival in America. Harry agreed that Benjamin was a good name, especially when he learned that one of the founding fathers of his new country was also named Benjamin. After seeing the new arrival and making sure that his beloved wife and new baby were both healthy, Harry, with Sol at his side to act as translator, set off for the hospital's administrative office to complete the necessary papers to obtain the birth certificate for his son.

Harry's hopes were rekindled with Ben's birth. With the one-year old in his arms, Harry accompanied Sol to inspect the retail space that Sol was renting for the new store. Harry hoped that the infant would soak everything in, even at this early age.

The space itself was serviceable, but Harry envisioned infinite possibilities in the location as he looked through the plate glass onto George Street and saw the endless foot traffic that passed by. The store was right next door to a popular butcher shop, which would result in a constant stream of customers coming to the block. Harry's eyes welled over with nostalgia when he thought of Mordecai and his butcher shop. By Vilnius standards, Mordecai's shop was grandiose and well stocked, but this little neighborhood butcher dwarfed it all respects: size, variety and quality of meats, equipment. He made a mental note to send Mordecai and his mother letters as soon as he got settled in.

Harry assumed the new store would be named Sol's Home Goods, just like the parent store on the Lower East Side. When Sol told him he thought it should be named Harry's, Harry nearly broke down in gratitude. Sol had to explain that it wasn't entirely altruistic that the new store be called Harry's. He was not going to be in New Brunswick much and he thought it better for business that the customers have a face that went with the name of the store. People would not be loyal to some absentee owner but they would be to the personable, winning Harry with whom they did business everyday. And so, Harry's Home and Dry Goods was started.

From the very first day of its opening, the store was a fabulous success. New Brunswick was busting at its seams with new immigrants—Hungarian, Jewish, Poles, Irish—arriving daily. Along with all this cheap labor, the rail lines and docks on the Raritan River made the city a perfect location for a number of factories producing everything from shoes to healthcare products to heavy machinery. These people needed to outfit their houses and apartments and Harry was willing and able to help them out.

Harry would arrive to open up his store at 5:00 AM and would be there until 7:00 or 8:00 in the evening, except on Fridays when he would close at 5:00 or 6:00 depending on when sunset was. It was not that he was religious and needed to be home for the Sabbath, but many of his clientele were. It would not be good for business to remain open.

On some days he took a lunch break, but most not. The store would be open five days a week, Monday through Friday. He would have loved to be open all seven days, but he would not do much business on Saturday and the City's blue laws precluded him from being open on Sunday. He did not mind; the money was pouring in hand over fist. People could not get enough apple peelers/corers and the other odd gadgets that Harry convinced them they absolutely needed. If truth were told, what the people came for was Harry himself, not the latest device.

Within a year, Harry was able to buy out two thirds of Sol's interest in the store. He wanted the business all for himself, but could not quite raise the capital to purchase the entire business. It was doubtful that Sol would be willing to sell his entire interest anyway. He wanted to keep somewhat of a hand in the business. It was a sure money-maker and he did not want to divest himself of this stream of revenue for which he did not have to lift a finger. Harry was content with this arrangement.

It was at this point that the stomach pains started.

Harry would get home in the evening complaining of nausea and some cramps. He joked that affluence had adversely affected Molly's cooking ability. He would take some bicarbonate of soda, feel better and go to bed. Steadily, though, the pain increased. Molly tried to get him to back off on his schedule, attributing the discomfort to stress, but she was fully aware that he would never do this. She also tried to convince him to go to a doctor, but he always had an excuse for not going.

One morning she walked in the store and Harry was not at the counter. There were several people waiting to be helped but he was nowhere to be found. That was very unlike him and she started to worry. After helping the customers, she locked the door, put up the closed sign and went into the back. There she found her husband doubled over unconscious on the floor. He had just vomited and there was blood in his vomit.

Panicked, she flagged down a boy roller-skating on the sidewalk in front of the store and asked him to get the doctor. She returned to the back room to revive Harry.

The doctor conducted a number of tests, but could not determine the root cause of Harry's affliction. Both Harry and Molly kept up a good face for the children, but there was no way of hiding the facts. He started to lose weight so that his clothes hung on him like a scarecrow. His skin, which had always looked clean and healthy, took on a grayish hue. Dark circles developed around his eyes. Even Bessie noticed that her father was not well and stayed at home to help her parents out.

Despite a distinct lack of energy and drive, Harry went to the store every day and put in his twelve to fourteen hours. The difference was that he now needed occasional naps to revive himself. Then one day he could not bring himself to leave the house. The doctor was called again. He told Harry and Molly that he suspected it might be a cancer in his stomach area. His recommendation was that a warm climate for a few months might work wonders for him. To Molly's surprise, Harry said he would try it.

Sol had a friend who owned a tobacco plantation in North Carolina who said he would love to have Harry come down for a month or two to recuperate. Harry said he would do it only if he could work, either in the office or even better in the fields, figuring the physical labor and sun would help him. On the second day in the field, the foreman found Harry on the ground, dead.

Like many Northeast cities at the turn of the century, New Brunswick was growing at a steady pace. To accommodate this growth, construction projects—office space, residential, commercial, industrial, new roads, trolley tracks—were in various stages of completion throughout the city. These projects often made getting around the city an adventure or a longer journey than expected.

When Ben was seven years old, he was in second grade at the Lord Stirling Elementary School. The school was named after William Alexander, an American major general during the Revolutionary War who claimed the disputed title of the Earl of Stirling and hence became known as Lord Stirling. Since much of his life was spent in New Jersey, naming an elementary school in his honor seemed fitting. It was widely believed that not a single student, at least while they were in attendance at the school, had a clue about who the school was named after. At least, no student other than Ben Albert.

Ben and Molly had their routine down to the minute on school days. After breakfast, they would leave their house promptly at 7:20; walk the three blocks to the school so that Ben would be at his homeroom desk by 7:45. Molly would then walk back four blocks so that she would be at her job, which was now behind a butcher shop counter, by no later than 8:15. Their neighbors joked that they could set their watches by the sight of the two of them hurrying along. When they turned the corner onto New Street from George Street they knew it was precisely 7:33. After work, Molly would pick up Ben and the evening walk would reverse the process on a similarly punctual basis.

It was therefore disconcerting when, on Monday, November 7, 1904, Molly and Ben set out on their usual route only to find George Street totally blocked for construction. Molly shook her head, took Ben by the hand and proceeded to go another route down an unfamiliar side street. They were a few minutes late but otherwise fine. At four o'clock that afternoon, Ben came down the stairs to his mother and they began their trek back along that same route.

Ben was excitedly relating his report on Lord Stirling as they walked along. He knew all about the general and his exploits during the war that made America. The teacher was very impressed and said that Ben had told him some things he did not know. They were so wrapped up in the story that they did not notice they made a wrong turn and found themselves on a street where nearly all the black, or colored as they were known those days, folk of the city lived.

Molly reached down and grabbed Ben's hand, holding it very tightly. With her other arm she clutched her purse close to her breast. She glanced from side to side as she quickened their pace. There were a couple of colored children playing on the sidewalk and three men sitting on a stoop talking. The men did not seem to notice Molly and Ben hurrying along, but that did not comfort Molly. By the end of the block she was nearly running, pulling Ben along behind. When she turned the corner and recognized it as being more familiar territory, she slowed down and stopped to get a breath. Ben looked up at her. Molly said nothing as she tried to get her heartbeat back to normal.

"Mama, what's wrong?'

"Benjamin, my darling. You must always watch out for yourself around the schvartes, the coloreds. They will steal everything you have if you give them a chance. Promise me you won't ever go down that street alone. Promise me."

She was gripping Ben's arm so tightly that he exclaimed and started to cry a bit.

"Okay, Mama. I promise."

Ben never went down that street ever again. The next day, their path to and from school went the other direction, through predominantly Jewish and Italian neighborhoods although it added considerable more time and distance to their travel.

In later years, Ben would learn about how Sol was beaten up by a "colored" man in his store in Brooklyn. The neighborhood had started to change from Jewish to African American. Many of Sol's neighbors and fellow merchants moved on but Sol was stubborn and held on. He saw this as an opportunity to reach new clientele.

One night he was working late taking inventory in the store when he heard a noise in the back. When he went to investigate, a pipe flew out of the darkness hitting him on the head, knocking him unconscious. Although Sol never saw who it was, he was sure it one of the youths who had taken to congregating outside the store. He told his suspicions to the police, noting that one of young men in particular had especially been watching the store. The man was arrested. Nothing from the store was found on this man or in his home. He also had an alibi for where he was that night. Despite all this, the man was convicted based on Sol's testimony alone He was sent to prison for five years.

After the conviction, Sol's troubles really began. Shoplifting, broken windows, animal feces on his doorstep, and other acts of vandalism became a constant occurrence. After six months, Sol had had enough and he sold the property at a fraction of what it was worth. He was happy to be out of there.

Through the entire ordeal, Sol would keep Harry and Molly abreast of what was happening and warn them about letting any schvartzes into the store. If one did happen to come in to shop, he said, follow them incessantly to make sure they were not stealing anything. When he first starting imparting these warnings, Sol's head still had a baseball size welt from the beating. This made a big impression on Molly. Then, after Harry died, she was especially fearful and mistrusting especially since she would often be walking the streets alone. She truly believed that she and Ben came very close to receiving the same type of beating as Sol's when they made a wrong turn on the way home from school. The vice-like grip she had on Ben was intended to ensure that the message was passed on to her son. It was.

In school there was one colored boy in Ben's class with whom Ben would sometimes play. After the incident, or rather non-incident, with his mother, Ben ignored the boy completely. The boy asked Ben if he would like to throw a ball with him at recess. Ben walked away, saying nothing and leaving the boy standing there dejected. Throughout the rest of his schooling, Ben would purposely avoid any interaction with the few 'coloreds' in his classes.

Noah Charney enjoyed what he did. Each morning, he looked forward to walking five blocks through the center of New Brunswick to Lord Stirling Grammar School so that he could teach six graders about a host of subjects. He saw himself as opening young minds to the limitless possibilities of new ideas and to a lifetime of learning. He took this responsibility very seriously and with passion. In turn, the children responded to his passion and enjoyed taking his classes.

He especially liked teaching six graders. They were at a point in life where they were open to the idea of learning, but not yet old enough to think they knew everything. He was not especially thrilled with having to teach a steadily increasing number of foreigners as wave after wave of immigrants poured into the city, but he accepted this as part of the territory. At times, he had to remind himself that his maternal grandparents, Hyman and Libba Hoffman, were themselves recent immigrants to this country.

In sixth grade, students still stayed with one teacher the entire day. In seventh, as the subject matter became increasingly specialized and complex, they would move from class to class to be taught by teachers who had deep knowledge in a particular subject matter. Mr. Charney thought he would go crazy if he were forced to teach math all day. He loved being able to shift gears several times during the school day, starting with math, then American History, then grammar, then biology, and so on.

Ben came under Mr. Charney's tutelage in September 1909. As he did for all of his students, Mr. Charney sat down with Esther Wynne, the fifth grade teacher, to review Ben's record, personality, interests, etc. He liked to know as much as he could possibly know about his students before they entered his class.

"Benjamin Albert is brilliant but extremely undisciplined," said Miss Wynne.

"There are times I could swear he did not hear a word I said but when I would ask him, he would recite what I had told him back to me, for the most part verbatim. It was most extraordinary. But I never could discern what he was interested in or whether he was interested in anything at all. He doesn't seem to participate in any school activities but instead heads straight home to help around the house. He has very few what I would call close friends, but as far as I know no one picks on him or bullies him. Perhaps it is because he is always very willing to help any other student who asks for help with his or her homework, but once he helps them there's little additional interaction. It's all most interesting, Noah."

Noah Charney found it thrilling when Miss Wynne used his first name.

Mr. Charney imposed very few rules on his classroom, feeling that too structured an environment stifled learning and expression of ideas, but the one rule he insisted upon was that his students pay attention. Sometimes it was a challenge, especially since his classroom was directly across the street from the stables for a local livery service. When the horses were out, being harnessed for their next job or washed down after they returned, it was difficult for some of the children not to look out at the magnificent creatures. He had to admit there were times he had to exert substantial self-discipline to keep his gaze from wandering to one of the larger draft horses. But he did exert this discipline on himself and he expected his charges to do so as well.

School had been in session for three weeks and Mr. Charney had not seen any of the negative qualities in Ben that Miss Wynne had described. He was indeed very intelligent but he was engaged and attentive in class. Maybe she had read him wrong.

It was a warm, sunny late September day, a time when the students (and many teachers for that matter) would much rather be outside playing. It was tough keeping the attention of any student focused on class work, but they seemed to be coping quite well. After the lunch period, however, Mr. Charney noticed Ben gazing out the window at a team of horses being groomed and harnessed for an affair that night. He decided to test whether what

Miss Wynne had said was true.

Mr. Charney was telling the class about General Washington and his stay at Valley Forge. He continued his discourse for about ten minutes, all the while noticing Ben's attentions were elsewhere. Then he turned to Ben and asked him a question about something from the previous night's assigned reading.

"Mr. Albert. Can you be so kind as to describe for the class what happened at Bunker Hill?"

Ben turned his eyes away from the horses and toward his teacher.

"Me, Mr. Charney?"

Charney was very disappointed. He would now have to make an example of Ben in front of the class; otherwise no one would bother doing their assignments. He was sorry he had asked the question for he truly liked Ben and did not want to treat him in this manner.

"Yes, Ben, what happened at Bunker Hill?"

Ben stood up.

"Yes Mr. Charney. The Battle of Bunker Hill took place On June 17, 1775. It is one of the most important colonial victories in the U.S. War for Independence. Fought during the Siege of Boston, this battle made both sides realize that this was not going to be a short war, decided by one quick and decisive battle. The Battle of Bunker Hill started when the colonists learned about the British plan to occupy Dorchester Heights overlooking Boston. The colonists were understandably shaken by this news. They had to protect their land and freedom. In order to preserve low supplies of ammunition, the leader, General Prescott, issued his famous order, "Don't shoot until you see the whites of their eyes." This battle lasted for approximately three hours and was one of the deadliest of the Revolutionary War. The British technically won the battle because they took control of the hill, but they suffered many more losses than the colonists. The British had more than one thousand casualties out of the 2,300 or so who fought while the colonists only suffered about 400 casualties from an estimated 2,500 men.

"Is that what you wanted to know, Mr. Charney?"

Dumbfounded, Mr. Charney said nothing as he settled back into his chair. Slowly he opened the textbook to the section on Bunker Hill. Using no notes or the text, Ben had recited the text verbatim. Ben spoke up again.

"Mr. Charney? Was that okay?"

Noah Charney looked up at Ben, who was still standing beside his desk.

"Yes, Ben, that was very good. Class, that's enough American history for today. Let's move on to math. Ben, while you're still standing, why don't you solve an equation for me."

"Sure, Mr. Charney."

"How much is four fifths plus five ninths? You can come up and work it out on the board if you would like."

"I don't need to, Mr. Charney. The answer is one and sixteen forty-fifths."

"Ben, what is the speed of sound?"

"1,125 feet per second, Mr. Charney."

"Ben, please recite for me the Longfellow poem *The Village Blacksmith.*

"Under a spreading chestnut tree
the village smithy stands;
The smith, a mighty man is he,
With large and sinewy hands;
And the muscles of his brawny arm
Are strong as iron bands."

"Very good, Ben. That'll do."

For the next fifteen minutes, Noah Charney drilled Ben on a host of subjects, everything he had been taught, or been asked to read, over the past three weeks. In every case, Ben's response was perfect. The other students, having pulled out their mathematics primers, were thoroughly confused at the stream of questions plucked from every subject matter. Ben placidly stood there, answering the questions.

Ultimately, Noah Charney conceded defeat; he was not going to be able to stump this sixth grader. He told Ben he could take his seat. There was only fifteen minutes left in the class day and Mr.

Charney knew there was no point in continuing, so he dismissed the children. As Ben passed his desk on the way out, the teacher asked him to remain behind for a minute.

"Ben, how do you know so much?"

"I don't know, sir."

"But you were able to recite the entire passage from the book on Bunker Hill. Did you study hard on this section?"

"I read it like you asked, Mr. Charney. I usually like to read things twice to make sure I understand, but I was tired last night and only read it once. Did I do something wrong, Mr. Charney?"

"Wrong? No, on the contrary, Ben. You did everything perfectly. I was just curious, that's all. You can go now."

"Okay, goodbye, Mr. Charney."

That night, Noah Charney had dinner with his college roommate, Dale Pearson. Dale had moved up the ranks at Rutgers and was now Associate Dean of Admissions.

"Dale, I tell you, reserve a spot for this kid right now. You're going to want him. His family is not very well off, so you're going to have to ante up some scholarship money as well."

"You can tell that in sixth grade? Aren't you jumping the gun a little bit?"

"Not at all. Sometimes you can just tell. Ben Albert is something special. I feel like a philatelist who gets a letter and on it is the rarest stamp in the world. A child like this only comes along once in every hundredth teacher's lifetime. If you don't grab him, he'll be at Harvard or Yale or MIT. Mark my words. I'm going to do my best over the coming years to sell him on Rutgers, home field advantage and all that."

Dale Pearson just smiled. He always appreciated his friend's earnest passion about his avocation. Early on after they had graduated college, Dale had tried to persuade Noah to become a college professor but he eventually conceded that teaching sixth graders was exactly where he belonged. As a matter of fact, Dale personally had interviewed a number of incoming freshmen who cited Noah Charney as the best teacher they ever had and he was the reason they ultimately decided to go to college. Looking fondly at his former roommate, he fully anticipated interviewing this Benjamin Albert in a few years for a spot at Rutgers.

The next day, Noah Charney returned to spreading his attention to all of the students in his class. He especially focused his attention on two others who were also very bright—albeit not on a par with Ben—to make them feel that he was not playing favorites. However, as the class day ended, he asked Ben to stay behind once more.

"Ben, what do you like to do when you're not in school?"

"I don't know, Mr. Charney. I like helping my mother in the garden."

"Do you know what you want to do when you grow up? I know it's early for you to make a decision like this but I'm just curious."

"My mother wants me to go to college. She wants me to do something that uses my mind. Maybe I'll do that."

"I'm happy to hear that. I'd like to help you. There are so many things to learn and study. The trick is to find something that you love doing. I love teaching, for example. There's nothing else I would rather be doing. I'd like to help you find what ever it is that is your passion, if that's okay with you."

"Okay, Mr. Charney."

With that, Ben and Noah Charney would get together two to three times a week after school for two to three hours. Generally, Mr. Charney would bring in a book from his home library, Ben would read it over the course of one or two nights and then they would discuss it together.

The one thing Noah came to realize was that, while Ben had a seemingly infinite ability to absorb information, he had not yet developed the ability to question that information. He took what he read or was told on its face value. Also, Ben was not yet at a stage where he could interconnect two or more ideas that on their surface seemed disconnected but deep down were related. Noah knew he could be invaluable to Ben in these regards.

They met in the classroom but after two weeks, Ben asked Mr.

Charney if he would come over to his house to do the work. Noah said he would be happy to. When they arrived, Molly eyed him suspiciously at first but as she watched the two of them working together, her attitude visibly changed as she realized that he truly cared for her son and was solely interested in helping him to succeed. She quickly invited him to stay for dinner. He accepted. After that, he became a regular dinner guest.

6

Catherine

I finished work at the library and went back to my apartment to shower and get ready for my date with Ben. I had definite misgivings about going out with him. I found him quite handsome with his wavy dark brown hair, dark eyes and beautiful deep cleft in his chin. And I found him personable and charming in a disarming and at times self-deprecating sort of way. But (there's always a but, isn't there?) I was extremely nervous about dating him all the same.

For one thing, he was so defensive about his Jewishness. He had a right to be proud of his heritage but he didn't have a right to make assumptions about my feelings about the subject without even knowing me. I guess it was a defense mechanism with him; it was easier to get it all out on the table right away than to get hurt later on by an anti-Semitic comment by someone you thought you knew.

I never had any problem with Jews, not that I had much contact with them in my life before meeting Ben. I hadn't ever dated a Jew before. In all honesty, and somewhat ashamedly, I can't say I'd ever be attracted to someone who looked too stereotypically Jewish. Ben certainly did not "look" Jewish. If he had told me he was Italian or Spanish or any other nationality, I would have believed him.

It wasn't anything about Ben that generated my misgivings. No, he did not play a role in it at all, although one of the things he said struck home with me. He asked why I didn't have a string of men waiting at my door on the off chance they'd be able to date me. He meant it as a compliment, but the truth of the comment stung me. I'd often asked myself that question, and the answer that resoundingly comes back is: me. My friends have often told me I put up barriers that keep men from coming close. They knew men would grow to like me if they got to know me but I never gave them that chance.

When I arrived at the apartment and told Sarah and Margaret that I was seeing a boy I met in the library, they were more excited than I was. They helped me with my hair and makeup and clothes. They wanted me to look just so. They had me try on about a dozen dresses, both mine and theirs, until I threw on the first one I had tried on and said enough is enough.

Finally, I was ready to go. There was a knock and Sarah answered the door. When she came back to get me she gave me a "are you crazy for not being thrilled to go out with that beautiful man out there?" look. I guess I was thrilled, but (there's that word again) I still had a sense of dread as we walked out the door together. Looking back, I suppose it was that I based my view of all men on my feelings about the one man I had had the least dealings with in my life and whom I loathed: my father. I expected they would treat me the way he had.

The date went well enough. We had dinner at one of the traditional places for first dates near the Rutgers campus, Timothy's Pub. We talked about typical topics one talks about on a first date: ourselves, our likes, our dislikes, our families.

Ben exuded self-confidence, yet it was difficult to get him to reveal much about himself. When he talked about his family, you could not stop him. I envied him that he could go on and on about his father, whom he didn't even remember. He told me a story about him climbing up onto his father's coffin before it was buried and how that still haunted him years later.

He asked about my mother. He was impressed with how progressive she was, and how she pushed me to live on my own. He liked my stories about accompanying my mother to suffrage meetings. He was pleased she was using her connections to get me in line to be in the first class of students to enroll at the New Jersey College for Women, which was slated to open its doors in 1918. I told him there was no way I was going to ever take a science course. He said he had taken enough for the both of us.

He seemed especially impressed that I knew as much as I did about world events, notably what was happening in the war. All of Europe had been engulfed in a war that was beyond our comprehension for over a year and a half. He said most women with whom he was acquainted had an idea there was a war going on, but beyond that could not converse on the subject. His mother, for example, was worried about her family, friends and in-laws in Vilnius but had no clue as to whether they were anywhere near a battle zone. He then asked me a question.

"Do you think the United States will enter this war?"

"I don't think so. President Wilson is doing everything he can to keep us neutral. He has done his best to maintain good relations with both sides, although the Germans do make it difficult sometimes."

Even I was impressed with the depth of my knowledge on the subject. Ben evaluated my opinion for a second and then gave his.

"Perhaps you're right and we can ride this out, but I personally don't think so. I believe President Wilson is biding his time. He's content to let England, France, Germany and all the rest punch themselves out for a while. Then there will be some incident that will turn public opinion and he'll tell the world that we are going to war reluctantly. That way, we'll be there at the end of the war on the winning side and can take part in dividing the spoils. There will be a lot of spoils when these colonial powers are weakened. Look how we virtually stole the Philippines from Spain in 1898. There's a lot more for us to get and I think Wilson wants his cut, but not at too high a price."

For someone who claimed his true passion lay in doing research in the laboratory, he seemed extremely passionate on the war. Trying to gauge my feelings on the subject he asked another question.

"And if we chose to go to war, would you support it?"

"Yes, if the President declares war, I would support it. And you?"

"The day after war is declared, I will be down at the army

recruiting center to enlist."

I couldn't believe the feelings that were coursing through my body after he said this. I barely knew this man and here I was worried to death about the danger into which he would be putting himself. I couldn't help but to react rather strongly.

"Why would you enlist? You're not a trained soldier; I'm sure there are many others who could take your place. What about your studies? You have to get your degree, don't you? Otherwise they'll take back your scholarship."

He regarded me for a second and then smiled.

"If I didn't know any better, I'd say you were worried about me."

I said nothing in return so he continued.

"I don't see Wilson sending us to war for at least six months or so. I will have completed my coursework by that time."

"You're going to be done in three years?"

"I'd have finished sooner if it weren't for the damn Greek I'm required to take. I hear they're about to eliminate it as a requirement, but not soon enough for me. I put it off as long as I could. I'm absolutely no good at languages. Even my Yiddish is no good, and that's what I speak at home with my mother when she's tired and can't concentrate enough to speak proper English. I was worrying about my Greek course when you first saw me in the library staring at my father's dollar bill."

That was the first and probably last time that he would concede there was a possibility he could not do something. I pressed on about the war.

"But why do you feel you have to go to war? There's plenty to do here."

He gave me a very warm look.

"I'll have to go because my country needs me. Let me tell you a little story. My parents came here with only one thing: the dream of America. They gave up a lot to come here. My mother was pregnant with me on the boat over and she was scared to tell anyone for fear they would not let her enter and would send her back. But there was something more that I only just learned about a few years ago.

"My brother Robert is the closest in age to me and he's twelve year older. His was a very rough birth. My mother almost died from it. After that, my mother told my father that the birth must have damaged her somehow and that's why she couldn't have any more children. When I came to be, she proclaimed it to be a miracle. My father was satisfied with that explanation.

"A few years ago my mother, partly out of shame at having lied to the man she loved and partly out of a need to provide me with the truth about myself, told me what really happened. After Robert's birth had nearly killed her, she was determined not to have any more children but, knowing my father's wish to have a big family, she couldn't tell him to leave her alone. Plus, my parents were in love and wanted to express that love as often as they could.

"So instead she went to a local apothecary and bought some herbs that would prevent her from getting pregnant. She took these without telling my father for eleven years.

"Then, when coming to America started to become a reality, she decided she wanted another child. She wanted an American child, one that would be born in this country. She timed it perfectly so that she would be a couple of months pregnant when the boat docked at Ellis Island. I was delivered in a hospital in New York, a bona fide American citizen. With a background like that, how can I not answer when my country calls?"

"I guess you can't. Your mother never told your father the truth, did she?"

"No, she said she was hoping to confess one day as they sat in rocking chairs in their old age, but of course that wasn't to be. Don't feel too bad about my father not knowing, though. A few years after his death, my mother learned that he got her back but good with a secret of his own."

I could tell from Ben's demeanor and mischievous smile that it was not some scandal of epic proportion. Whatever his father did not diminish his saintliness in the eyes of his son.

"What did he do?"

"Well, she learned that my name is not actually Benjamin."

7

A month after Harry passed away, Molly sat down with Sol to review the family's finances and to discuss the future of the store. Molly was not surprised to learn that Harry had done a good job of saving money. Both of them had always been extremely frugal and Harry's business acumen had amassed a tidy sum in a very short time. He was able to pay off their mortgage, so she now owned the house outright.

She was surprised to learn that Harry had also made some very smart investments in the stock market. Sol told her that the stocks she held were very solid and would provide her with dividends for years to come. She did not know what a dividend was, but from Sol's reaction she assumed it was a very good thing and did not bother asking.

Molly knew the family would be secure at least for the next couple of years but after that they would need some sort of steady income. One would have assumed that a successful store would fit this bill, but, without saying as much to each other, both Molly and Sol believed the store would eventually fail.

After Harry died, Molly, Phil, Robert and even Bessie pitched in to keep it running. At first, the customers that Harry had cultivated over the years came in out of loyalty but Molly could see that their visits became fewer and farther between. And when they did come in, many just browsed without buying anything.

The final nail in the coffin was pounded in when a new Woolworth's Department Store opened two blocks away. People could purchase many of the same items Harry's sold for a much cheaper price at Woolworth's. They could buy these items at the same time they were buying clothes for their kids or hardware to fix a broken back door. Not only that, but they could have lunch and a banana split at the shiny new lunch counter.

If Harry were still alive, his drive, personality and chutzpah would have been enough to keep customers coming back. But nobody else in the family possessed any of these qualities. Molly glanced at four-year-old Benjamin playing on the floor over in the corner. My American Son could do it, she sighed. If only he could age fifteen years overnight. We don't have the luxury of waiting for him to grow into a man to take over, to lead us. But no, she thought, she must resist these thoughts. Benjamin was not going to spend the rest of his life running a store. He was going to be a learned man with a profession. Nothing was to stand in the way of that goal.

So, the store limped along for a year more. Molly tried various things—sales, leaflets, events—to get people in the door, but she could not undersell Woolworth's. Many of her neighbors would avert their eyes if they passed her on the street. She could not blame them, though. They all had their own families to take care of and needed to stretch their dollars as far as they could.

Phil and Robert helped in the store after school but it was obvious they would rather be elsewhere. Eventually, Phil got a job with the gas company and Robert left to work in a florist.

Molly fully expected that one day Bessie would announce she was leaving town on the next train to find her fame and fortune. She had too much of a gypsy spirit in her. So it was not a shock when Bessie came to the dinner table one night and said she was heading for Texas in three days. Molly knew she would be wasting her breath trying to talk her daughter out of it. Neither would she get a straight answer if she asked whom she was traveling with. Molly was sure it was the no account boy Bessie had been seeing over the past few months. The best Molly could do was give her a little money, wish her well and let her know that the door was always open if she needed to come home, which she was sure would happen sooner or later.

Ben was better able to comprehend his sister's departure than when his father had died a year earlier. Even though he hardly knew her, he would miss her. He cried and asked her not to leave.

Bessie promised that she would write him letters every week and that mollified him somewhat. Molly figured that this promise would be kept for three days, and then a weekly letter for the next two, maybe three, weeks and then the letters would stop coming altogether. That was Bessie.

Molly saw her to the train station but Bessie was insistent that her mother leave before the train pulled in the station. Bessie claimed it was because she did not want any tearful farewells. Molly knew the truth: she did not want her to be around when the boy came. That was fine with her, anyway. She was not one for prolonged, teary bon voyages either.

As expected, Harry's Home & Dry Goods closed its doors. Molly went to work for the butcher shop next door owned by Louis Bress. Molly was pleased that someone was following in her husband's footsteps. She thought back to the first time she laid eyes on Hirsch when she walked through the butcher shop door and knew then and there that this was the man she was going to marry. It seemed strange to be on the other side of the counter.

Ben was growing by leaps and bounds. As he was approaching five, Molly started the process to get him into school. She contacted the school officials and was advised that she needed to bring in his birth certificate or other form of identification.

All of the family's important papers were kept in a metal box on a high shelf in the kitchen. Their immigration documents, the deed to the house, documents showing ownership in the store, stock certificates and other vital pieces of paper were all contained there. Harry had put Ben's birth certificate in the box immediately after coming home from the hospital and it had remained there since.

Molly had seen the birth certificate only once when she was looking through the papers after Harry passed away. While her command of oral English had steadily improved since arriving in the states, she still could not read much English. The certificate was only a confusing jumble of foreign words.

She dug the document out of the box, put it in an envelope and asked Phil to accompany her down to the administrative offices. He would act as her translator to clarify anything she did not understand.

The two of them walked up to the counter and spoke with a young woman there.

"Good afternoon. I'm Mrs. Conway. How can I help you?"

"My son. He should go to school when it start in September."

Mrs. Conway looked at Phil, who had just turned nineteen and looked back at Molly questioningly.

"He's a little old to be starting school, isn't he?

Molly stared back confused. Phil realized the miscommunication and spoke up.

"No, Mrs. Conway, not me. We are here to enroll my young brother. He's going to be turning five soon."

Mrs. Conway laughed.

"Well, we could probably find a place for you as well if you care to join your brother."

They all joined in the laughter. Mrs. Conway resumed.

"We'll just have to fill out some paperwork to make it all official and he can start in the fall. All I will need is the boy's birth certificate and we can get started."

Molly pulled the envelope out of her bag, took out the birth certificate and handed it to Mrs. Conway. She examined the certificate.

"Abram. That's a good name."

Molly looked confused anew.

"Abram?" she replied, "His name is Benjamin."

"Yes, it says it right here: Abram Benjamin Albert."

She pointed to each name as she said them. Molly took back the birth certificate as Phil confirmed for her what it said. Molly's perplexed look slowly gave way to merriment and eventually to a full belly laugh. Both Phil and Mrs. Conway gazed on her with a mixture of their own puzzlement and concern. When Molly had composed herself, she looked up and said something in Yiddish.

"Hirsch, you old fox. You got your way, didn't you?"

Mrs. Conway looked to Phil who roughly translated what his mother had just said. Molly then reverted back to English and explained her husband's desire to name a son after his father, Abram. After the first baby, whose name was Abram, died in infancy, Harry tried to convince Molly that one of the succeeding boys should be named Abram. She insisted that it was bad luck and forbade it. When Ben was born, Harry knew enough not to ask but instead went to the hospital administrator and filled in the name himself. It was only now, five years later, that Molly finally uncovered the subterfuge.

Mrs. Conway thoroughly enjoyed the story. She also had gathered that Harry had passed away.

"Your husband must have been quite a man. I bet you miss him."

Both Phil and Molly answered nearly in unison.

"Yes he was. We miss him very much."

"Well let's get this paperwork going. What say we put down your son's name as A. Benjamin? Otherwise, when the teachers get the roster it will list Abram as his first name. We don't want confuse him right off the bat, do we."

Molly greatly appreciated Mrs. Conway's kindness.

From his very first day in school, Ben's teachers could tell that he was different from his classmates, that he was their intellectual superior. Whether it was learning his ABCs or learning to count or add or anything else, his teachers sent home notes to Molly about how "gifted" he was. Molly was not exactly sure what "gifted" meant, but she had a feeling it was very good.

8

Catherine

War was declared on April 6, 1917. We'd been dating for nearly seven months at that point. Ben didn't march down to the army recruiting office on April 7 as promised. When I jokingly called him on it, he sheepishly replied that he was so close to graduating that he could wait a month or two before enlisting. He said it would take the army that long before it would know what it was doing anyway. The truth was he did not want to take any chances on missing his graduation, which was scheduled for June 2. I laughed at his reasoning but deep inside I was terrified because I fully realized that the only thing that would keep him from going to the recruiting office the minute graduation finished was that it was being held on a Saturday. On Monday, June 4th, he would be at the office as soon as it was opened. If nothing else, the President had announced that the announcement for the draft would be made on June 5 and Ben would enlist rather than suffer the indignity of being drafted.

As he predicted, Ben graduated in only three years. It turned out that he actually liked Greek and his trepidation was unwarranted. He was to graduate first in his class.

He invited me to his graduation. I wasn't so sure I'd be invited. Each graduate had been given six tickets. His mother, his two brothers, his uncle Sol and Mr. Charney were the people he was definitely going to invite. When his sister Bessie arrived back home a month before the graduation, I resigned myself to the fact that she would be getting the sixth ticket and I would not be attending. I was disappointed, but I understood. Family meant so much to Ben.

When he got his tickets about two weeks prior to the event he came over to my apartment and handed me one. I told him I didn't think he'd invite me. He looked at me like I had two heads.

"Of course I'd invite you. Why wouldn't I?"

"Well, I know you only got six tickets and between your family and the two men you've told me about that have been so important to you throughout your life, that would leave me odd man out. It's okay."

"Why would you think I'd invite my sister?"

It was my turn to look puzzled.

"Because...she's...your sister?" I ventured.

"Well first of all, Bessie has never had any time for me in her entire life. When my mother ran down to North Carolina to retrieve my father's body, Bessie was put in charge of the family. Even then she was never there. I would have starved to death if it weren't for Phil and Robert. She's only home now because she left Texas after the guy she was staying with ran out on her. She didn't come back for us; she had nowhere else to go.

"I have absolutely no qualms about not inviting Bessie. If a spare ticket comes my way, I probably will invite her but, until that happens, the people I love the most will be there. And let me tell you one more thing."

By this point Ben was more worked up than I had ever seen him. He wasn't angry, just passionate.

"If I were only allotted five tickets, then Phil would be staying home. If four, then Robert would be. You get the picture? If I were only given one ticket, then I would have a dilemma, you or my mother, but in the end she would be at home and you would be attending.

"My mother tells me stories all the time about my father and her life with him. She said one time she was serving food at the dinner table and there was a cut of meat that Phil really craved. He let my mother know in no uncertain terms that he had his eye on that particular piece of meat. But when it came time for doling it out, my mother put it on my father's plate. Phil started whining about how she always favored my father over her own children. My mother shot him one of her looks that shut him up immediately. Very calmly she explained the nature of the situation."

At this point Ben went into an imitation of his mother's heavy accent.

" 'Phil, my dahling, I love you. For you I vould give up my life but dis man, he I choose.'

"Phil knew from that day on that if it ever came down to a competition, my mother was always going to come down on the side of the man she chose, not the one she ended up with. Phil never pushed it again. Even Bessie who was also at the table was smart enough never to go there after than.

"Catherine, what I'm trying to say is: You're the one I choose. No one or no thing will ever come above you as far as I'm concerned."

I didn't know what to say. In all the time we'd been together, Ben had never spoken in such a manner. I knew I was falling in love with him, but I had no clue if he felt the same. Now I knew.

At the graduation, I finally got to meet Mrs. Albert. We had been dating nearly seven months but in all that time I had never met Ben's mother. I had heard so much about her and her amazing life that I felt I knew her. But every time I suggested meeting her, Ben would change the subject or come up with some excuse. After awhile, I stopped asking.

Now, as the time approached that I was actually going to meet her, I was very nervous. What if she had made it clear to Ben that she did not want him seeing a shiksa, a goyish girl, like me? My mother was less than thrilled when I first started dating Ben, but he'd since won her over. I had no idea what Ben's family's reaction to me had been or would be now that they were to meet me.

My fears were allayed when Mrs. Albert grabbed me and gave me a huge hug and kisses on both cheeks saying she was so glad to finally meet me. She said she had heard so much about me. She welcomed me to her family. She had me sit beside her during the ceremony, one hand holding a handkerchief, the other my hand.

Ben delivered the valedictory address to the graduating class. Instead of the usual themes of calling on the graduates to use all that they had learned over the past few years and applying it to future life, he instead issued a call to arms. He made it clear that he thought it the duty of every member of that graduating class to heed the call of their country. As he progressed, I glanced around the graduates. There was a lot of fidgeting and casting of eyes downward. I did not get the sense that many of his comrades were going to be accompanying Ben to the recruiting office the following Monday.

When he was done, the audience gave Ben a rousing ovation. He received at best a tepid applause from the graduating class, most of whom I would imagine had no thought whatsoever of joining the armed forces.

I was so proud of Ben as he stood there accepting the applause. At one point as he glanced about the auditorium, he located me in the audience and smiled. I smiled in return, and it was then I realized that I truly loved this man and that I wanted to spend the rest of my life with him. I suddenly burst into tears. Within a few short months he could be sent thousands of miles away to be on the front lines of a barbarically brutal war. It could well be that these next few months might be our only time together...ever. I couldn't bear that thought and tried to refocus my thoughts on this happy day. As the tears ran down my cheek, Ben's mother gripped my hand tighter. It was as if she could read my mind and was as frightened as I about what the future held.

9

When Ben walked into the U.S. Army recruiting center the following Monday morning, the place was already packed with the willing, and many not so willing, prospects. The Selective Service Act had been enacted in May and it had officially been announced that the following day, Tuesday, June 5, 1917, the first selection of potential inductees would be made. Whether it was out of patriotic fervor, like Ben's, or whether many of these men thought they could get a posting more to their liking than if they were to be drafted, it seemed as if every able-bodied male from New Brunswick and the surrounding towns were there.

Ben recognized a number of his classmates and some undergraduates among the crowd. Just as he was speculating if his speech had kindled the patriotic fire in any of these men, one walked over to him. Ben didn't know him personally but had seen him in classes and around the campus over the years. He was a strapping lad with short-cropped sandy colored hair. If he didn't know that this man had just graduated from college, Ben would have sworn he was a farmhand. He got around three feet from Ben and stopped short, his face turning redder by the second.

"Ben Albert. I was wondering if you'd have the guts to show up or whether you were all talk," the big guy bellowed as he glowered down at Ben.

It was obvious the bigger man was used to intimidating people. He expected Ben to naturally back away. Knowing this, Ben instead took a step forward and was right in the man's face. In addition to the element of surprise at doing the unexpected, Ben figured his adversary would not be able to get a full swing if he chose to do so. The best he could do at this close range was to give Ben a giant bear hug, which would hurt, but would not send him into the next county.

"Ya, I'm here and so are you. What of it?"

If anything, Ben was moving closer and could at this point give the guy a kiss on the lips if he were so inclined.

"Well, I wouldn't be here if it weren't for you. My Pap was in the audience at graduation and after the ceremony he comes up to me and says you was right. He says I wouldn't shame him by not volunteering to serve our country. I tell him I don't want to go to war and he calls me a lazy coward. My Pap never talked to me like that in my life, but here he is saying all these things and all because of you. I oughtta strangle you."

"Be my guest, and then you'll be nice and safe spending the duration in prison."

Ben continued to stare the other man in the eye, neither of them blinking, but Ben knew he had him. It was just a matter of time before he backed down.

"Well, you just watch your back out there on the battlefield."

Ben recognized a threat when he heard one, but it would infuriate the guy even more if he didn't take it as a threat. So Ben very calmly replied.

"I thank you for the kind advice, friend. And you watch out for yourself as well."

With that the guy, still shaking, turned and walked away. Ben stood his ground until the giant had left and then he went and leaned against the wall, waiting for his name to be called. Ten minutes later a sergeant walked into the waiting area and called out "Benjamin Albert." Surprised at having his name called before at least fifty men who were there before him, Ben followed the sergeant through the door into an office. Behind a desk was an officer, a captain. He rose when Ben walked in.

"Benjamin Albert?"

"Yes sir. That's me."

"I'd tell you at ease but since you're not officially a soldier yet, you don't have to listen to a thing I say. But why don't you have a seat."

Ben warily sat down, unsure as to what was going on. The

captain continued.

"I'm Captain Mark Harris. I sort of run this little shindig here. Gonna be a busy day, all these men to process. They think they'll get a better deal, enlisting instead of being drafted. Surprise is going to be on them though; we treat everybody like shit no matter how they got here."

Ben liked the captain's manner.

"Before I tell you why I asked you to come in, I'd like to ask you why you're here."

"I would have been here earlier but I decided to wait until I graduated, which happened on Saturday."

"A Rutgers man, eh?"

"Yes sir."

"Me too. Class of '09. But you only partially answered my question. You said why you're here today, but I want to know why you're here. To beat the draft?"

"Well, in a way, but only because I thought it would be a discredit to my father's memory if I had to be dragged here instead of coming on my own. My parents gave up a lot to come to this country. The least I can do when my country calls is to volunteer to serve."

"Good answer. You know, as an officer there are two things I trust without question: my sidearm and my sergeants. Take Sergeant Jones here."

Ben had not noticed that the sergeant who led him in had not left but was standing quietly off to the side.

"On days like this, I ask the sergeant to stand unobtrusively and observe the quality of enlistees the Good Lord has provided us. Sergeant Jones reported to me about a potential altercation in which you were a participant. The other participant—and I do forgive the sergeant for exaggerating somewhat here—was reported to be three times your size yet you adroitly defused the situation. He indicated that you turned the tables and intimidated him in turn. Is this an accurate rendition of the events?"

"You are correct that Sergeant Jones may have a slight tendency to exaggerate, but in general it is an accurate retelling of the story.

Am I in some sort of trouble, sir?"

"Trouble? No not in the least. The fact that you are here indicates that you are at least somewhat aware of world events and even may have read a newspaper once in your life. So, as you are well aware, the Limeys and Frogs have gotten themselves in a terrible mess and are counting on us Yanks to come in and kick the Kaiser in the keister all the way back to Berlin. My job here is to pull together some men who can be whipped into fighting shape in the course of a few months and then sent over to get in the action. America has never been known for maintaining much of a career army between wars so when we do go to war it's the job of men like me to be on the lookout for men who will not only make good soldiers but more importantly, who can make good leaders."

The captain paused here to let what he had said sink in. Ben responded.

"Well, I came here to be a soldier, sir, and am ready to sign the papers as soon as you can get them ready."

"I appreciate that, but I don't think you heard the second part of my eloquent dissertation. You're a leader, Mr. Albert. I am only recruiting part time to amass a company that I will in turn lead in France. I need to round up men very quickly, men I can trust. When I mentioned about counting on and trusting my sergeants, I wasn't blowing smoke. I want you to be one of those sergeants."

"Me, sir? On the basis of one little brush-up in a waiting room? That can hardly be enough to qualify anyone for such an honor, can it?"

"Probably not, but I do have to admit I wasn't entirely straight with you when you walked in. One of my many duties is as a military instructor for officer candidates in the Rutgers program. Since several of my men were in your graduating class, I was at graduation on Saturday and I heard your speech. I was impressed, but not nearly as impressed as when I interviewed no less than five of your classmates who came in here because of your speech, and the day's only a quarter done. In some cases, such as the oaf who was ready to pop you out there, they came in out of shame or because their daddies made them. In others, you awoke some dormant patriotic spirit in them. Whatever the reason, they're here because of you. And then, when it came down to one-on-one, you handled yourself splendidly.

"Lastly, after the graduation I looked up some of your professors to see what they thought of you. I only wish my mother was so glowing in her opinion of me. So, no, the incident here today by itself didn't convince me but, taken with everything else, I think I know what I'm getting."

"I guess I'd be a fool to say no, wouldn't I?"

"That's a good way to say it. So can I be the first to welcome you to the company, Sergeant Albert?"

"Yes, sir. Thank you. What exactly will I be doing, if you don't mind me asking?"

"Certainly. The one thing we are all deathly afraid of is the German's use of gas: mustard gas, chlorine, you name it. I need someone with a scientific background who can understand what it does and how to treat the men if there is an attack. We leave for training in three weeks. I expect you to become an expert on all the gases the Germans are using, on how to train our men to protect themselves if we are attacked and how to help their comrades if one of them is exposed. Can you handle that?"

"Yes, sir."

Ben had no idea if he could learn all this in three weeks.

"Okay then. Sign here and you belong to us for the duration."

10

Catherine

Ben came straight to the library to see me immediately after leaving the recruiting office. We sat down at a table in the far corner of the first floor reference section. He was so excited as he described the experience. After some summer-session students who were studying admonished us to be quiet, he suggested we go for a walk; he had so much to talk about. I asked my supervisor if I could take a short break and we headed out into a beautiful sunny late spring day.

I listened intently to all he was telling me. I held it together when he said he needed to report in three short weeks. I did not let it outwardly bother me when he apologized that we would not be able to spend as much time together as we would want over that time because he had a lot of work to do. I even kept my composure when he mouthed the words 'poison gas'. But then when he asked me if I wouldn't mind looking in on his mother every once in awhile, I broke down completely. He patiently waited for me to regain some semblance of self-control.

"What's wrong, hon?"

"What's wrong? What's wrong? You're going off to war! You're going to be thousands of miles away hunkered down in some trench! You're learning about poison gas! You're entrusting your mother, whom I've met only once in my life, to my care! And you have the nerve to ask me what's wrong?"

I felt sorry about my outburst as the words were leaving my mouth, but I couldn't help myself. I knew it was not the frame of mind I should be putting him in. He had important work to do; he shouldn't be spending his time worrying about silly old me.

Ben didn't say anything. He slowly reached into his pants pocket and pulled out his wallet from which he extracted the wrinkled old dollar his father had left to him.

"I've had this dollar with me every single day since I was seven when my mother decided I was old enough to be responsible to take care of it. As you know from the first day you met me, it's my most cherished possession. It's always given me a feeling my father is watching over me but I've realized something recently. I think he wanted me to have it so he could watch over me until something else replaced it. Well, something else has replaced it."

"What's that?"

"Your love."

With that he put the dollar in my hand and kissed me.

"I'll reclaim this when I get back. That should prove to you that I will be back, given how Jews are about their money."

He smiled his most radiant smile and I melted into his arms.

I had anticipated seeing very little of him as he had so much work to do in an extremely short three week span. I was mistaken. First, he had me search with him throughout the library for every single book on poison gas we could find. We found volumes on identifying them, on their chemical makeup and nature, on the individual toxicological effect of each gas, on how they are typically deployed, on antidotes or treatments that may be used in case of exposure, on how they react to atmospheric conditions. In all, we found thirty-seven volumes. He had me arrange these in small piles on a table by these broad categories. Then I saw Ben go into action. I had never observed him academically, so what I saw truly amazed me.

First, he leafed through each book in turn, scanning every tenth or twenty page. After getting about halfway through the book he had a clear enough idea as to whether the book would be useful and informative. Those he thought would be helpful he put aside; those he didn't he gave to me to return to their respective slots on the shelves. In the end, before him sat six thick volumes on the various aspects of poison gas.

Then he told me that I was welcome to stay around, that he

would enjoy my company, but he warned me that it would be mighty boring as I sat around watching him read. He estimated that it would take two days for him to read through the six volumes. I decided to stick around to see him in action. I could not believe my eyes, or more precisely I could not believe his eyes.

He opened the first book to the first page and thirty seconds later he was through page ten. His fingers meandered in a wavy motion down each page, his eyes following closely behind as they frantically darted back and forth. After forty-five minutes he put this tome, which was about 550 pages, to the side and picked up the next. I had to ask him.

"You couldn't have actually read that book, could you?"

"Well, yes. To make sure I absorbed it, I'll go through it again tomorrow. That's why I said I'd be incommunicado for two days. If I were reading this for pleasure or just for a test, I'd only read it once through. But this is too important to cut corners."

I didn't know what to say. I was still in shock at the thought of anyone being able to read through six extremely dry, technical texts of 500 pages or more in a day, and then doing it all over the following day. I asked him what he was planning to do the rest of the three weeks.

"Well, for two days after that I want you to pick up any of the texts at random, open it to any page and read to me. I want to make sure that the words all securely etched on my brain. I should be able to recite the rest of the page to you after that."

I initially thought he was bragging, showing off for me, but I quickly realized that wasn't the case. He said this matter-of-factly, as if he were telling me the weather. I was simply getting a glimpse at how his magnificent mind worked. He continued.

"I also need to be able to master all this information out of the context of the textbook. Men's lives could depend on my ability to dredge up the appropriate facts at a moment's notice."

"Well, that takes care of four days. You said you would need the full three weeks to do what you had to do. What about the rest of the time?"

"That's where I really need your help."

I liked the sound of that.

"I'm very good at the theoretical. It's the next step, applying what I've learned to a real world setting that I'm afraid I fall somewhat short. You have a much firmer grasp on what would work with actual people, for example in developing a training program. I have some ideas but I need to work them through with you to make sure they can pass muster and are realistic. Can you help me?"

Even if he asked me to do the impossible, I could not say no to this man.

Over the next three weeks, much to my chagrin I became an expert on poison gas. Phosgene, mustard gas, chlorine, chloromethyl chloroformate, you name it; I could tell you whether it was toxic when breathed or whether it was a skin irritant. I could tell which gases tended to cling close to the ground and which ones dispersed more readily into the atmosphere. I could tell you their colors and smell, not that you ever wanted to be close enough to smell any of these. I could tell you any known antidotes and remedies in case someone was exposed.

I was still frightened beyond all belief that in no time Ben would be heading off to war and may be exposed to one or more of the gases I was reading about as well as numerous other horrors. In a strange way, however, going through this exercise did offer me some level of comfort. While many wives, fiancées, girlfriends (I'm not exactly sure what I would categorize myself at this point in time) can never be sure that their men are as prepared as they can be, I was receiving this assurance each moment we worked together.

As he predicted, I could open any of the six books at random, read a passage and then Ben would flawlessly take it from there. I did point out to him that he made a grammatical error when he said "a ester", but when I looked back at the text I noted that it was grammatically incorrect in the book, not in Ben's recall.

I wasn't at all necessary for this exercise, he was so perfect in his recall, but I think it helped him in a security blanket sort of way. He was able to access this knowledge out of the context of a chapter in a book.

It was during the following phase of our work together that I began to feel useful. Ben had gotten copies of the various Army manuals that guide the training for dealing with poison gas, or chemical warfare as they bureaucratically referred to it. Time after time he would read about a procedure and remark in exasperation that it would work for one gas but not another. He was frustrated over the 'one-size-fits-all' approach the manuals took.

Starting with the manuals as his base, we went gas by gas, delivery system by delivery system, input the variables of weather and atmospheric conditions to come up with a set of action plans for any contingency. My job was to provide my opinion as to whether the plans we came up with were realistic, that they could actually work not just on paper but in the real world. I was proud of the suggestions I made and so was Ben.

As the days went by, I began to worry that we would not complete our task before he had to leave. Then, two days before he was to get on the train, Ben announced our task was done. He was satisfied that he had done as much as humanly possible to protect the men. I breathed a sigh of relief. I had been so immersed in our task that it had not occurred to me that we had been moving inexorably toward the day that Ben was to leave. I do think that he valued my assistance and counsel but I also think that he was trying to occupy my mind sufficiently that I would not worry the entire time. It worked.

Now, however, as he walked me back to my apartment, my mind began to wander to this worrisome truth. He sensed my anxiety and held me close. I loved the warmth of his arms. As we approached the doorway to my building, I expected him to kiss me goodnight, wait until I had gone inside and then head back home. Instead, he asked me if he could come inside.

"But my roommates aren't here, they're gone for the weekend,"

I replied as a lady should to let a young man know that it would not be proper for him to enter without an appropriate escort or third party.

"I know," was all he said.

I took his hand and led him inside, closing the door behind me.

The dreaded appointed day finally came and Mrs. Albert and I walked with Ben the five blocks from his house to the train station. No words were spoken the entire time as he walked between us, holding our hands.

As we waited for the train to pull in, he went over some details of managing the house with his mother. These were things like paying the bills that he usually handled. He was fully confident that his mother could manage, but he had asked me to check on her to make sure she was doing everything she was supposed to do. I assured him I would. He continued ticking off things to his mother, ignoring me as if I weren't there until at one point he spoke up in a voice he was sure I would hear.

"And Mama, while I'm away once a week I want you to make Catherine a proper Jewish meal, your brisket or stuffed cabbage. I will be marrying this woman when I get back, if she'll have me, and I don't want her to be skin and bones when I put the ring on her finger."

He turned to me.

"Will you have me when I get back?"

"You know I will. I love you so much Abram Benjamin Albert. I will always love you."

"And I love you, too, Catherine Anne Jackson. I will come back to you."

"If you don't, I'll go out and spend your dollar, and it will be on a bottle of schnapps no less."

"And I will drink it with her," Mrs. Albert defiantly interjected.

Ben laughed.

"I've created a monster putting the two of you together. I admit defeat. I have to return if for no other reason than to keep schnapps from passing my mother's lips."

The train whistle blared as it approached the station. Ben hugged his mother tightly. She took his face in her sturdy hands and kissed him as only a mother can. I could hear her tell him to be safe and keep his head down. She then took both his hands and looked him in the eye.

"Your Papa. Your Papa, he would be so proud of you, our American boy."

Ben was exerting his full will to maintain his composure. He could not respond but nodded his appreciation and love. Then he turned to me and drew me close.

"Catherine Albert," he whispered in my ear, "I like the sound of that."

11

The train ride from New Brunswick to Camp Devens in Massachusetts took about eight hours. Ben had heard the Army was constructing a new training facility in New Jersey, which would have been much more convenient, but that camp would not be ready until early 1918. Oh well, c'est la vie, as he would soon be saying in France.

As Ben climbed down the stairs to the train platform in the town of Ayer he heard a sergeant standing off to the side barking orders for recruits to form into ranks. The training had begun already and Ben was excited.

About thirty other men joined him in front of the sergeant who quickly put them in four rows of seven and a couple others in the rear. Ben stood at attention in the middle of the second row. He appraised his comrades and found them to be pretty similar in height, weight and build as himself. He thought he could pick out the various ethnicities and nationalities.

The sergeant introduced himself as Sergeant O'Malley. His thick brogue gave him away as either an immigrant or at most first generation American. He had a bushy dark brown mustache and wore a khaki uniform with boots and spats and a broad brimmed scout hat. He held a clipboard and read off the names in alphabetical order, checking off whenever anyone answered. He never once looked up from his paperwork even on the three occasions when his recitations did not elicit a response. In these cases, his only reaction was a 'tsk' and then he moved on to read the next name. It was not his job to get to know these men; he only was responsible for collecting whoever showed up and delivering them to the camp, where some other gruff sergeant would take over. Ben was wondering how he would be as a sergeant, whether he would be as impersonal as this man or whether he would be a more empathetic type.

Sergeant O'Malley then marched the men over to three horse-drawn jitneys patiently waiting at the siding to the station. He berated those men who fell out of step and even a few who were perfectly in step if he felt they were too sloppy in their initial approach to soldiering. Ben felt lucky to be spared a barb. As they approached the jitneys, the sergeant dictated which one each soldier would get on. Ben climbed onto the second one and soon they were underway. He was rather surprised that they did not use motorcars, thinking that no expense would be spared for soldiers who were about to devote years, and perhaps their lives, serving their country.

It took about twenty minutes to get to the camp. After an extremely bumpy ride over pock marked roads sitting on hard wooden benches, everyone was ready to jump down to begin their soldiering career but Sergeant O'Malley ordered them to stay in their seats as the sergeant to whom he was to turn them over had not yet appeared. They sat like that for fifteen minutes until the new sergeant, whose name was Willets, walked out of an adjacent tent to relieve O'Malley. Finally, the men were ordered to disembark and each man in turn was told the unit to which he was to report. Ben received his orders to report to Company D of the 16th Infantry Brigade in the First Division. His company came to be known as the Special Gas Company for the Division. He was to report directly to Sergeant Jones.

Named after Civil War General Charles Devens, Camp Devens was a sprawling collection of row after row of tents that had been hastily constructed to become one of the training facilities for soldiers from the entire northeast. Thousands of soldiers would call this camp home for six weeks prior to boarding steamships for Europe.

Ben was given the tent number and general location of where to find Sergeant Jones but, since every tent looked exactly alike, it took him nearly a half hour before he finally peeked into a tent to find the sergeant sitting behind a makeshift desk, actually a board stretched across several soapboxes piled on each other.

"You're late," was all the sergeant said upon seeing his newest charge.

"I'm sorry, sir," Ben responded.

"Sergeant," Jones corrected him, "save the 'sirs' for officers. And second, never ever apologize. Just say it'll never happen again, and then make sure it doesn't."

"Yes, sergeant," Ben responded, correctly this time.

"Let's go, Captain Harris wants to see you immediately."

Ben could feel the adrenaline flowing through his veins as they exited the tent to head over to yet another tent. He had learned his lessons on poison gas well over the past three weeks and was ready for any question the captain threw at him. He had the training regimen he developed with Catherine's assistance down pat and he was ready to proudly lay it out and defend it like a dissertation if the captain offered any resistance or had qualms about what he was about to propose. He was certain the captain would be impressed.

The distance between tents was about one hundred yards. For the first eighty of those yards, Sergeant Jones was silent. As they approached the command tent Jones spoke up and offered a short bit of advice.

"Albert, whatever you think you may want to say, just respond 'yes sir' or 'no sir' no matter what. Do not say anything else. Understood?"

Ben was confused as he looked at the sergeant but he said nothing.

"Do you hear me?" Jones was more forceful this time and Ben said yes, he understood. He was confused as to why the sergeant would make this request and why he was so adamant.

Sergeant Jones announced Ben to the Captain who in turned called out that they had permission to enter. Jones indicated to Ben for him to enter, who did. Jones walked in and greeted the captain with a salute. The captain was sitting at a much more substantial and real desk than Sergeant Jones had. Captain Harris looked up.

"You lied to me, Albert," Harris snapped.

"I did, sir?"

"You never told me you were a fucking Jew, did you?"

Remembering Sergeant Jones' advice, despite wanting to answer back in kind, Ben simply responded: "No sir."

"Do you really think that the men are going to obey commands from a Hebe?"

Realizing it was a rhetorical, not to mention demeaning, question, Ben said nothing.

"Albert? That certainly is no Jewish name. You trying to fool people with that name, boy? Make 'em think you're a regular guy, a Christian instead of a Christ-killer?"

Captain Harris looked rather pleased with himself at putting together this clever (at least in his own mind) turn of phrase.

"No sir."

"I would certainly not think that the men would obey the commands of a Jew; I know I wouldn't. I will not have a hook nose in a position of authority under me. Do you understand that, Private Albert?"

Ben had been here many times before. Captain Harris was trying to goad him into a rash answer, into a violent response. Then he would have just cause for court martialing him. That would be some kind of record, getting thrown in the stockade only fifteen minutes into his tour. So Ben remained silent as the captain continued his tirade.

"I'm just glad I caught onto you in time. You have anything to say in your defense?"

"No sir."

"You are going to report to Sergeant Jones. You're probably a lazy Jew and didn't do anything except make money over the past three weeks but I do know how bright you are and I want you to do exactly what I told you to do and make the men prepared for poison gas. Sergeant Jones will keep a close eye on you. Dismissed."

Ben saluted and exited the tent. Sergeant Jones was standing outside waiting for him. They walked together for a while in silence. Ben was ready to burst but he assumed Jones was of like mind as his captain so he did not say a word. After they were a safe distance from the captain's tent, Jones spoke up and uttered one word.

"Shameful," was all he said.

Ben wasn't sure to whom or what the sergeant was referring, so he pretended he didn't hear what Sergeant Jones said.

"Pardon me, sergeant."

"That scene back there. Shameful, that's what it was."

"But I did exactly what you said to do, sergeant."

"Not you. Him. He acted shamefully and without honor."

The sergeant stopped and looked directly at Ben.

"Look, I totally disagreed with what Captain Harris was doing, offering you sergeant stripes on the spot. It took me years to earn my stripes and I'm mighty proud of each and every one. Moreover, the men under me respect me because I earned their respect. You may very well make a fine sergeant, but you don't get that honor on the basis of a speech and how you handle yourself during a brush-up at the recruiting center. You earn it."

"Then it sounds like you agree with what the captain just did, so I can't understand your reaction, sergeant."

"While I totally disagreed with the captain offering you those stripes, still he did it. A man of honor keeps his word. He doesn't renege. He acted shamefully and disgraced our unit and the Army."

"You don't care that I'm Jewish and I report directly to you, sergeant?"

"I wouldn't be honest if I told you it was my preference, but, no, it doesn't bother me. You can be a goddamn Hindu as far as I'm concerned. Just do your job, that's all I care about. And there's another thing."

"What's that?"

"I was at your graduation, too. Nobody could be as convincing as you if you didn't really believe what you were saying. And I think you can save a large number of men in our company if we're faced with gas. I don't know you real well but I consider myself a pretty good judge of character. I'd bet a week's pay that over the past three weeks you've studied your ass off to learn everything you possibly can about the poison gases they're using at the front lines. Am I correct?"

"Yes, you are."

"I hope you won't keep all of what you've learned to yourself, just because our captain is an anti-Semitic jerk."

Ben considered his options for a moment. In a fit of pique and more than a little bitterness, he was indeed contemplating not working with his fellow soldiers to help keep them safe. He could do so with a clear conscience, blaming it all on Captain Harris.

"No, sergeant," he relented, "I can't do that."

"Good. Let's get you situated and get down to work."

12

Catherine

As promised, I stopped in on Ben's mother to make sure she was getting along. Initially, I was only being polite, but by the time I left on that first day to head back to my apartment, I was on a first name basis with her and looking forward to returning as soon as possible.

It was a Thursday afternoon around 4:00 when I knocked on the door. Mrs. Albert gave me a big hug and kisses on both cheeks in the European style. It was a little awkward, me being around five foot eight and she barely five feet, but we managed. Her graying dark hair was pulled back into a bun on top of her head and she wore a rather blousy blue dress with a flower pattern. She was not fat; rather, one would perhaps term her chunky. I could see, however, that she probably had a nice figure in her youth.

She walked me through the house to the kitchen located in the back. I was impressed with her walk. It showed a confidence and bearing, making her appear much taller than she was.

When she invited me in, I felt like I had already been in the house many times. Ben had described it so vividly; I could readily envision each room as we walked through. As it would be normal for people to receive guests in the living room, I was a bit surprised to be led back to the kitchen. But after the greeting I received, it would not take me long to realize that I was not considered a guest. Rather, I was family.

As we headed toward the rear of the house, I glanced into each room we passed. I looked the living room, or parlor as Ben had called it, and, in my mind, I could see where Ben's father's coffin would have been. Now, it was full of furniture: a sofa and loveseat, several small end tables with knick-knacks and lamps on them. The seats all had a definite worn, used look to them, but everything was well maintained and clean.

As we walked down the hallway I noticed a large oval framed photograph of a man and woman, it was their wedding picture. The frame was ornate but not garish with a greenish tint and gold highlights. The glass over the photograph was rounded and curved like a lens. The photo itself had been retouched to add some color and to make it appear more a painting than a photo.

"Mrs. Albert, is that you and your husband? You make a handsome couple."

She looked at it a few seconds and then spoke.

"Yes, that is my Harry and me. At the time, he was known as Hirsch and I was Malka, Hirsch and Malka Abramowitz. We change our names the day we step in America. I carry Benjamin but nobody knows but me. I did not want that they return me to old country because I was pregnant. I was foolish young thing.

"Wasn't my husband the dashing man? With him by my side, he could make even me look pretty. He had that way. He made everyone feel good when they were with him. And please, call me Molly.

"This picture was taken on our wedding day at the Beth Shalom Synagogue in Vilnius. The frame, it is bought here in the United States. But the picture was taken there, in old country. My Harry, he brings it with him on boat to America. It is with us ever since."

She gazed at the photo a few seconds more, sighed, and then said it was time to get to work as she guided me into the kitchen. We opened the door and, like the other rooms, I felt at home because of Ben's descriptions and stories. I could see the exact spot he described where he would sit on his three-legged stool halfway between the stove and back door.

Molly immediately put me to work cutting some vegetables. She was making a lamb stew for dinner. I apologized to her for my atrocious cutting skills and my lack of expertise in the kitchen. My roommates often joked that, if it were possible, I would burn water; my cooking abilities were that bad. Molly was very patient and gently instructed me on what to do.

All the while, she kept up a running monologue about her first meeting Harry in Mordecai's butcher shop and how she fell in love with him at first sight. In those days, especially in the old country, it was not permissible for a young woman to be too forward. Many of her friends growing up had to marry someone they did not love —and in some cases did not even like—because marriages were arranged by the families. Love did not enter the picture as a prerequisite for marriage. She was determined she was not going to suffer the same fate. Even though there was a shop much more convenient to where she lived, she kept coming back to Hirsch's butcher shop until, as she said, he got the hint. With a little arm-twisting of her father, a match was eventually made.

Although Molly already knew the story, she asked how Ben and I met. I related my nearly disastrous opening line and she smiled. She said she thought it extremely rude of Ben to answer the way he did but I assured her I did not mind. In fact, I appreciated his honesty. All too often I've found that those relationships that start with pleasantries and careful responses are not the deepest and don't last.

We continued to chat as we prepared dinner. After a bit, I finally asked her the question that was most on my mind.

"Molly, do you mind that I'm not Jewish?"

"At first, when Benjamin came home and told me of you I asked him, 'So, there are no nice Jewish girls you could find?' He got very mad, said some nasty things and left room. It was only time I remember we fight. My mind was still trouble because I want him to find nice Jewish girl but I no want to fight with my American boy so I say no more after that to him. But that is why I think he never brings you to see me.

"I talk with a friend of mine, a lady I met on ship coming over and tell her my troubles. She say I am a fool. She asks who I hurt by feeling this way. She says Benjamin will do what he feels in heart. I can be mad the rest of my life, but that would hurt me not him. After I talk with her, I look at Benjamin. I see how happy he is after seeing you. He is like me after I go to butcher shop and see Hirsch.

It was true; I was old fool. The only thing that matter is Benjamin is happy.

"And then I meet you and I look into your eyes. I see this is good person. This is person my American son loves. This is woman who loves my American son. How can I not love her, too?"

At first, I dropped by once a week, on Thursday evenings. Then it became every couple of days and finally I would drop by at least three to four times per week. The more I got to know Molly, the more I came to love and respect her. It soon became apparent that we were kindred spirits in many ways. She relished her role as a pioneer, coming to a new land with little but the clothes on her back and a dream for a better life. Then, when it looked like they were going to be successful in their chosen country, her beloved husband dies. Instead of wallowing in despair, she carried on as a single mother working two jobs and protecting her family the best she could, which wasn't bad at all if you ask me.

I so wanted to be a pioneer as well in some field or venture. In February 1918, I received a piece of mail advising me that I was going to in fact become the pioneer I dreamt about. While there were a number of colleges and universities around the country that had opened its doors to women, none of these were in New Jersey. For over a decade, my mother's close friend, Mabel Smith Douglass, had been leading a crusade to open Rutgers University to women. After years of stonewalling—and at times denigrating— her efforts, in late 1917 the announcement was made that the New Jersey College for Women would commence operations. It would be a separate college but would be adjacent to and affiliated with Rutgers. Mrs. Douglass would be named the college's first Dean.

It was an exciting time for my mother. It appeared that her lifelong goal of amending the United States Constitution to give the vote to women was going to become a reality. And now, educational opportunities were going to be expanded for women as well. My mother was absolutely beaming, but little did I know that she wasn't done yet.

Unbeknownst to me, my mother had petitioned Mrs. Douglass to include me in the College's inaugural class, which was scheduled to begin in September 1918. When the letter arrived in February advising me that my application had been accepted, I was at first mystified. I had not 'applied' for anything. But then my mother's connection dawned on me. I wanted to rush home and throw my arms around her and dance a giddy jig with her. It was a Wednesday when I got the letter, though, and I had to work the rest of the week. Since I didn't have an automobile at that time and it would take hours to make all the connections to get to Westfield, my jig would have to wait until the weekend. I had to share this great news with someone and the next person who came to mind, even before my roommates, was Molly.

The reaction I received when I told many people about my plans to enter college in 1918 was discouragement and doubt. They'd tell me to forget college and concentrate on finding a husband, setting up a home and giving him children. Although she was old world in so many ways, I instinctively did not expect this reaction from Molly. I was not disappointed. She was so excited for me when I announced my intentions you would have thought she, not I, was the one going to start school. She was thoroughly convinced that everyone, men and women, should get as much education as they possibly could. She said she was sorry her other children had not gone further in school, but getting started in a new country took everybody's help. It wasn't until much later, when Ben was born, that they could even dream to have a child who finished high school, let alone go to university.

I was surprised when she said she thought that Bessie was bright enough to have done well in school. She said Bessie's problems were a feeling of entitlement and a most definite lack of discipline. It was somewhat natural she was this way as she was the oldest and the only girl. Molly blamed herself for allowing Bessie to be this way, but she blamed Harry even more. Bessie could wrap Harry around her little finger and exploited this power to the maximum whenever she could. She and Harry should have put their foot down from the start, but they didn't and Bessie turned out the way she did and that was that. Molly did a fatalistic sigh and moved on.

I found that even when she was criticizing and castigating Harry, there was such love and longing in her voice that it broke my heart. I was looking forward to such a lifelong relationship with Ben. I didn't know what I would do if our time together were cut short like theirs had been.

I came to realize that I may be the only one Molly had ever confided in on certain things. She had friends in the neighborhood, but her relationship with each of them was purely superficial. On a couple of occasions, I arrived at the house and a friend was visiting. Molly would always introduce me as her daughter-in-law, which made me feel special since Ben and I were not yet married. I would sit down and they would continue their conversation, including me whenever possible. Generally, out of politeness, they'd switch from Yiddish to English (although they would sometimes slip back into Yiddish out of habit). Even when they were talking in Yiddish, I could tell that the conversation was about mundane, everyday things. They'd talk about what everyone in the family was doing, but only the positive, never about problems; about gossip in the neighborhood; about letters they'd received from the old country.

When she talked with me, however, the conversation was much deeper and more complex. We were washing dishes together when she revealed that she had had at least one suitor since Harry passed away.

"Sol, he is very kind when my Harry died. Two years after he ask me marry him. I refuse. Every year since then he ask me marry him. I like Sol; he very good to us but I no love him. He not Harry. No one is. Sol, he understand, but this time every year he ask again. Maybe I change mind one day. It is sweet."

It was sweet. She was flattered by the fact that someone still desired her, but she was content to be alone the rest of her life because she had known true happiness already. Nobody could ever surpass that for her.

I was flattered, too, that she was taking me into her confidence like this. If she ever had any trepidation about me becoming her daughter-in-law, that certainly wasn't the case now.

Of course, we'd compare notes about Ben. We would read the letters each of us had gotten from him to the other. Since he would write to Molly in Yiddish, it would be a rather slow process with her translating into English to me, but we muddled through. A few times he would write rather personal things in his letter to me that I probably could have skipped over, but Molly was so hanging on every word from her son that I read them anyway. We would both blush a little, but then laugh at our prudishness.

In December 1917, Ben came home unannounced for a three-day leave. He thought he would surprise us but he was the one who was surprised at how close we had become in the few months he had been gone. He walked through the back door into the kitchen around 5:00 in the afternoon and found us in our usual spots preparing that night's dinner. Molly was seasoning a chicken and I was preparing an au gratin sauce for our potatoes when we looked at each other as the outside storm door creaked open.

When Ben walked into the kitchen, we both squealed in delight and ran to him. He was in full uniform, buttoned up to the neck and complete with the spats and scout hat. We showered him with kisses, Molly on his left and me on his right. Unfortunately, his uniform got totally smeared with chicken fat and grease since, in her excitement, she neglected to wash her hands before flying to him. Ben didn't care in the least.

After the wave of hugs and kisses, Ben stepped back and looked at the two of us, trying to figure out the tableau.

"Mother, when I asked you to cook some good Jewish meals for Catherine, I didn't realize you were going to make a Jewish cook out of her!"

Molly blushed a little. I had realized long ago that this was exactly what she was doing. But because she did it in a subtle, not heavy-handed, way and because we used these times to chat and get to know each other, I wouldn't have traded the experience for anything in the world. In addition, it was working. I was becoming a pretty good cook. To allay her embarrassment that she had imposed herself on me against my will, I answered Ben in the thickest imitation of Molly's Jewish accent I could muster.

"So, becoming a Jewish cook is a bad thing?"

Molly burst into laughter, easing the tension. It was at that moment that I noticed what a fine specimen of manhood Ben had become. He had put on at least fifteen pounds, but every single one of them was sculpted muscle. I already ached for the want of this man; now I knew when he left it was going to be unbearable.

The three days passed much too quickly. It did his heart good to see that Molly and I had gotten so close. He could go into battle knowing we both would take care of the other. While Molly had Phil and Robert, Ben was aware of their shortcomings and that his mother needed someone close to depend on. He saw in an instant that I was that person.

Molly and I saw him off at the train station yet again, telling him to be safe and come home to us. Not one of the three of us dared shed a tear, fearing that once we started we would not be able to stop. As the train faded down the tracks, Molly turned to me.

"Come. We not cook tonight. We go to restaurant like important people. We order some wine and toast my brave American boy."

She took my hand and we started toward an Italian restaurant that was near the station. I'd been there several times over the years. It was inexpensive but good and authentic. I pointed out to Molly that the restaurant wasn't kosher. She said she kept kosher mostly out of habit but not out of any beliefs.

"If God is angry at me for breaking kosher, my Harry will talk to Him and make it all right."

The thought that Harry could charm God the same way he had everyone else on earth was priceless. From all the stories I'd heard about him, I believed she was correct.

I asked Molly the last time she had been in a restaurant. She thought for a moment and then said that it was when she was a girl in Vilnius. It was her fifteenth birthday and her father took her to a kosher restaurant near her home. She could have had anything but she ordered stuffed cabbage, something her mother made quite often at home. What she remembered most was ordering a fountain soda, or sarsaparilla as they called it in those days. It was the most wonderful drink she had ever had in her life. She said that in addition to some wine, she was going to order a sarsaparilla as well. I told her I wasn't sure they would have that but they might have root beer or another pop.

After our diversion for that day, we went back to our usual routine of making dinner together. It was over the next couple of weeks that I got to see how much Ben meant to everybody in the family. We knew that we might not hear from Ben for long stretches of time once he got oversees, especially when he went to the front. Both Phil and Robert dropped by a lot more regularly for dinner now. While their outward excuse was that they missed their mother's cooking, it was very plain they wanted to see if either of us had gotten any news from their little brother. There was concern on their faces. Molly said she had even received a letter from Bessie asking after Ben.

It was during this period that I came to understand how Ben developed his love of plants and his decision to pursue botany as his course of study and career. In addition to helping Molly around the kitchen, I spent time with her in her massive garden. She grew both vegetables and beautiful flowers. There were rows upon rows of squashes, cucumbers and tomatoes as well as gladiolas, irises and peonies.

She had never gardened in the old country but after Harry passed away she found gardening to be very therapeutic as well as providing food for the family. I couldn't comprehend how she could work full-time, cook and clean and take care of her family and still have time for a garden, but she did. Her garden soon became the envy of the neighborhood.

Since Ben was so young when Harry died, Molly would naturally bring him out with her as she worked around the grounds. At first, Ben would simply play by himself but as he got older, he would help her with planting, weeding and other necessary tasks. Molly related how distraught he would become if a single plant looked sickly or started to do badly. He would stay up all night trying to nurse it back to health and would take it personally if his efforts were to no avail and the plant died. But, as

Molly proudly noted, very few plants perished when they were under Ben's care.

Four weeks to the day after Ben left I was working in the Rutgers library when Martha Hughes, a student who also worked there and with whom I had become friends, came up to me in the Ancient History section.

"Catherine, there's a short middle-aged woman waiting for you down at the front desk."

At first I thought it was my mother, surprising me with an offer to take me to lunch. She had done this in the past on several occasions. But then Martha continued.

"She seems very upset and it's hard to understand her with that thick accent. I came to get you right away."

I knew then it was Molly, and she had to be upset to come here in the middle of the day. She was supposed to be working at her job in the butcher shop. I wasn't sure she knew where the library was. Every time I'd seen her over the past months it was always at her house. I thanked Martha and ran down the two flights of stairs to the front desk. I found her there, shaking.

"Molly, what is it? What's wrong."

She hugged me and handed me a telegram.

"A man deliver this to me at butcher. My reading English not good. I read but no understand. Mr. Bress, the butcher, he offer to read it to me but I say no. I must go to my Catherine. Please, tell me everything is good with my Benjamin. Please tell me."

I wished I could tell her everything was going to be fine but in my experience, telegrams were never good. I took the telegram from her. My hands were shaking as well. The message, as with most telegrams, was terse and to the point.

MRS. ALBERT STOP BENJAMIN WOUNDED IN FRANCE STOP HURT BADLY STOP SENT TO HOSPITAL IN ENGLAND STOP PRAY HE WILL SURVIVE STOP WILL WRITE WHEN MORE NEWS STOP SERGEANT JONES

"Oh Molly."

It was all I could say as we sagged into each other sobbing.

13

After his short leave, Ben reported to Pier B in Hoboken, New Jersey to board the ship to Europe. The troop ship, named the *Alberta*, carried one thousand men when it departed on January 7, 1918. As it sailed out of the harbor past the Statue of Liberty, Ben felt a rush of pride fill his chest. He silently noted that this was his second trans-Atlantic sailing, although he could be forgiven for not remembering the first since he was in his mother's womb at the time.

He had been pleasantly surprised at the lack of anti-Semitism he encountered in the company. After his encounter with Captain Harris, he dreaded the worst as he started training camp. These attitudes had ways of trickling down from the command to the common soldier. He had found that many people harbored anti-Semitic feelings and if those in power created an atmosphere in which these feelings could be freely expressed or acted upon, they would be.

Instead, he was accepted as a fellow soldier, no more, no less. There were a couple farm boys in the company who seemed more wary and skeptical of being in the same company as a Jew, but they did not say anything offensive. After awhile, some of his comrades felt comfortable enough to make some off-color or inappropriate remarks, but Ben discounted these as the usual soldier banter.

He had several theories on why the anti-Semitism was non-existent, or at least not expressed. He did not think it was because they all became close friends. Ben's usual style was to remain aloof; he did not make many close friends. Rather, they all knew about his work on poison gas and how being on his good side may someday save their lives. Over the past three years, story after story had been splashed across the newspapers of the use of gas on the battlefield. While it was true that the actual impact of the use of gas had been relatively minimal, the psychological effects on the troops had been great. However, even in the face of these stories, the U.S. Army had done little to train the men on how to cope. The troops in this company were appreciative that they had an expert on hand to fill in this training gap.

Another possibility was that Sergeant Jones made it clear from day one that he was not going to tolerate any behavior of this kind in his unit. Throughout training, Ben came to appreciate the sergeant's penchant for order and discipline in himself and in the men who served under him. He was not going to allow anything that got in the way of that order and discipline. It would not be a surprise if Sergeant Jones had nipped any inappropriate behavior in the bud at the very start.

Whatever the reason, he was thankful he was not subjected to abuse. He would have been forced to fight back and, given Captain Harris' predilections, Ben doubted the end result would have been positive for him.

The trip across the Atlantic was uneventful, although there were constant reports of German U-Boats infesting the waters. Sleeping was an adventure as men had to climb into hammocks that were arranged floor to ceiling in groups of five throughout the hold. At 2:00 one morning there were screams when one of the ropes holding an upper hammock shredded and broke, sending its occupant onto unsuspecting fellow doughboys below. Despite a lack of culpability in the affair, a brief fistfight broke out, but the skirmish quickly fizzled as everyone was shouting to go back to bed.

After eight days at sea, the ship arrived in Liverpool. Ben's unit was toward the back of the ship and it took nearly two hours before he could disembark. Soon after, they were directed to hastily constructed barracks where they would stay for two weeks as they awaited orders.

The men wanted to go into the city and out into the English countryside to tour a bit, but they were kept on constant lockdown in case they received orders to head for France. Ben put the time to good use as he worked his way through a set of French grammar and reading books that Catherine had "borrowed" from the library. It probably would have been wise for the two of them to work together on studying French since she had taken it in high school, but neither thought of it until their last day before he left for training. It turned out absolutely no one in his unit could speak a word of French and he was sure that by studying books alone his accent would be atrocious but it would be better than nothing as he tried to communicate with their allies. In high school and college, Ben had studied Greek and German. The former language he was sure he would not have to use while he was overseas; the latter he sincerely hoped he would not have to.

Finally, the orders came through. They boarded a steamer and docked in Le Havre. At the harbor, they were immediately herded onto a train ready and waiting on a siding. Once the train was loaded, it started lumbering east. It all happened so quickly the men hoped their duffel bags had also made the trip. Once out of the city, the trip consisted of mile after mile of farmland, dotted with small villages. Occasionally, Ben could see a farmer out in his fields tending his crops or a young girl walking though town, carrying bags of produce. It was all quite pleasant.

The only city of note they passed through was Rouen. Ben could feel his jaw physically drop as he looked out the window across the river and saw the Rouen Cathedral dominating the entire city. He had read that just a short thirty years earlier, the cathedral had been the tallest building in the world. He didn't know it was so ornate. He had been to New York and seen St. Patrick's Cathedral. Maybe it was because nothing in Rouen could compare in size or style, but in his estimation Rouen dwarfed St. Patrick's. He mentioned to the soldier sitting beside him that he wanted to come back to Rouen and visit the cathedral the first leave he got.

After Rouen, it was more pastoral countryside and picturesque villages. Ben was settling into a bit of a nap when the train ground to a halt and the order went out to disembark. They were in a small hamlet of no more than 600 people called Tartigny. Word was that the train would have kept going but the tracks on the eastern side of town had been hit by a couple of artillery shells. They were within a few miles of the front.

As the soldiers disembarked the train, they could hear a low constant rumble. If it were not for the crystal clear sky, one would have thought that the distant thunder was the harbinger of an approaching storm. Everyone knew, though, that this was no harmless cloudburst. Rather, it was the French artillery doing its utmost to halt the German advance on Paris, which was about 75 miles to the south. By all accounts, the French were having a bad time of it and were being drubbed in battle after battle. The troops from Ben's 1st Division were there to provide needed reinforcements to repulse or at least slow down the German advance.

Ben and his colleagues were curious as to how they would be welcomed by the French. Nobody in the company except Ben knew French, and his fluency was sketchy, having been acquired on the trip. Moreover, many Frenchmen who had been slogging around in trenches for nearly four years viewed the Americans as soft upstarts who would probably run at the first inkling of trouble. Many of the doughboys themselves did not know how they would perform in battle. The most recent battle of note America had been in was the Spanish American War, and that was nearly two decades ago against purposively inferior opponents. Now they were to face the battle-hardened German Army. Would the Americans turn and run? Would they stand shoulder to shoulder with their French brethren and drive back the Huns to the Rhine? Only time would tell.

Ben's train was the fourth to transport American troops into Tartigny that day. In all, more than 4,000 Americans would arrive in the small hamlet over the course of three days. Once the Americans had all amassed, they would begin their march to the front line at Cantigny, a more substantial town twelve miles to the east.

News from the front was dire. They had to get up there without further delay. Each soldier carried his own rifle and each officer had a sidearm but until supplies caught up with them, the Americans would have to count on the French for machine guns, flamethrowers and other heavy arms.

The march began. Ben was heartened by the townspeople who lined the sides of the road leading out of town to cheer them on. Cries of *Vive' l'Amérique!* could be heard a good mile out.

The American command was determined to make the march and get the troops situated during daylight. Even though the terrain was relatively flat in this part of France, each man was carrying fifty to sixty pounds on his back and it was a bright sunny day. There were no major rivers that had to be forded but there were a number of smaller streams that they had to wade through. The column would slow considerably at each watercourse as the soldiers bent down to fill their canteens, not knowing how soon the next water source would be. The officers wanted to keep moving, but they understood this desire to have a full canteen.

They trudged on. Occasionally, Ben would spy an officer weaving in and out of the column to urge the men on but, as usual, it was the sergeants who did the majority of the cajoling, insulting, pleading and whatever else it took to keep them moving forward. Sergeant Jones got in his face on more than one occasion to admonish him that he was lagging and slowing down the rest of the unit. Like most foot soldiers, Ben had learned in basic training not to take anything personally.

Finally, they could see and smell the acrid smoke from the artillery. The din had steadily increased with each step they took but the reality had not totally set in that they were heading into battle until their nostrils were filled not with clean country air but with the rank stench of battle.

It was not until it was too late that the American officers realized the route they had chosen was a mistake. They looked at a map and chose a road that went straight as an arrow into Cantigny. What they should have done was to have sent a messenger to the French to ask where the field hospitals were located and then planned the route to avoid passing by those facilities, even if it added a couple of miles to the march. The one thing they did not want was for a bunch of untested troops—men whose only view of blood in their lives may have been from a steer they had slaughtered—to march by a field hospital on their way into battle. You don't remind men of their mortality before they enter a situation where that mortality may be tested.

The pace of marching visibly came to a crawl as men gaped in sickened wonder at the hospital. The converted farmhouse was bursting at the seams with wounded and crippled soldiers. Bandages covered every conceivable part of the human anatomy. Men with only one leg hobbled around on crutches or sat in wheelchairs. A group of five men with bandages around their eyes sat against the outside wall of the hospital. The collective educated guess was that they had been gassed.

To compound matters, traveling on the road in the opposite direction was a steady trickle of freshly wounded soldiers. Some walked on their own, holding compresses or bandages to their wounds. Others had a buddy helping them limp along. Stretcher-bearers transported the more seriously wounded. A few arrived by ambulance, both horse-drawn and mechanized.

Colonel Musgrove, who was leading the column on horseback, immediately sensed the problem as his men took in each wounded veteran. He feared mass mutiny if the troops were allowed to sit around, perhaps for days as they awaited orders to deploy, and stew over the carnage they had just witnessed. He had to get his men to get into action immediately.

The Colonel dismounted his horse and called out for anybody who could speak French fluently. Ben raised his hand as did about a half dozen other men who heard the colonel's question: a couple of privates, a corporal, two sergeants and a lieutenant. The colonel called the lieutenant over and, after the obligatory salutes, issued this order:

"Lieutenant, I want you to take my horse and rush up to the front and find someone—anyone—nominally in charge. I want you to tell them that our men need to get into action, immediately. There is obviously heavy fighting going on. Ask where we would be most effectively deployed. I do not want these men sitting around for days. Got that straight? Good. Now go. We'll keep marching."

The lieutenant leapt up on the horse, gave it a couple hard heels and off he went. Ben was relieved the colonel did not select him since he had been on a horse only a couple of times in his life but could not by any stretch of the imagination be termed a rider.

A half hour later, the lieutenant came galloping back down the road. He advised Colonel Musgrove that the fighting was especially intense in the center, but that the Americans would do best to position themselves on the right flank, about a mile and a half away, to keep the Germans from mounting an action to overrun that end of the line. The colonel ordered the column to veer right and to march at the quick step. The men were already exhausted from a day's marching, but adrenalin would kick in once they got into action.

A half hour later, Ben and his infantry squad reached the fortified trenches a mile southeast of the town of Cantigny. They were to deploy to the furthest trenches away from the town. There was no action in this sector at the moment they arrived.

Rather than being a continuous single trench that ran for a mile or more as Ben had been led to believe, there were a series of unconnected holes, each about thirty feet long, fifteen feet wide and ten feet deep. Sergeant Jones ordered Ben to ask one of the French soldiers about the situation. When he came back, Ben advised the sergeant that there were seven soldiers in this particular trench but the dugout area fifty yards to the southeast was, to the best of their knowledge, abandoned after a previous German assault. Sergeant Jones, realizing that that trench was the furthest reach of the right flank and therefore strategically important, began barking assignments to deploy seventeen of his twenty men to the furthest trench. Corporal Fleming was placed in charge of those men.

In order to be more readily available for communication with the main force, Sergeant Jones stayed in the next trench with the seven Frenchmen. He kept three of his men, including Ben, with him, making for a total contingent of eleven men in this location. They descended into the trench, awaiting the signal to go over the top and charge the German lines.

Ben was impressed with the design of this hole in the ground. While the floor was earthen, solid thick timbers lined the length of the trench. The trench extended back a further ten feet with a timber and earthen roof. This was where the soldiers could huddle in case of rain or heavy artillery shelling. There were a couple of bedrolls and a small butane camp stove under the overhang. Some coffee was brewing on the stove. It was all the comforts of home.

The seven French soldiers eyed the Americans coming down into the trench. Three were out in the open area, four sat in the roofed area waiting for the coffee to finish. They nodded in the direction of the Americans, but made no more greeting than that. The Frenchmen looked as if they had not emerged from the earth in years. There was no real rush to welcome the newcomers; rather they had a blank look on their faces that perhaps betrayed a fatalistic attitude.

Ben did not smoke, but he knew enough to have bought a couple of cartons of American cigarettes before he shipped out. He knelt down to his knapsack and pulled out a pack of cigarettes. He looked up and offered the pack to the Frenchman with whom he had spoken earlier. Through the sweat-streaked dirt on the Frenchman's face, Ben detected a smile of appreciation. Ben held up the pack, intending to tell him to keep the whole thing when the explosion shook the entire trench. A mortar shell had landed on the lip of the trench, just on the other side of the timbers.

Just before he was thrown on top of Ben, the smile on the Frenchman's face was immediately replaced by a look of astonishment as the back of his head burst from the impact of the explosion. For the most part, in his crouching position Ben was shielded from the blast. The dead Frenchman flopped on top of him.

After he had rolled the body to the side, Ben was not surprised that he no longer had the pack of cigarettes in his right hand. He saw the pack, looking somewhat damaged but otherwise intact, off to the side. In his stupor, for some reason he felt the need to retrieve the cigarettes but as he did so he noticed a foot or so away from the pack what appeared to be a thumb. Poor bastard, Ben thought as he looked back at the dead Frenchman. But when he reached down to pick them up, he quickly realized that he could not grasp the pack. That was his thumb crying out to him. He looked closer at his hand to confirm this and saw blood pumping out of his hand onto his sleeve.

He was amazed at the lack of pain he was feeling, but that would come. The most immediate objective was to stop the bleeding. He took off his shirt and wrapped it around his hand and raised it high in the air. Using his left hand only, he pulled item after item out of his backpack until he found what he was looking for: a ball of thick twine. He cut himself a length of it, and using his one good hand and his teeth, he made a loop and proceeded to wrap it around his right wrist. He pulled it taut, but the twine snapped. He cut himself a new length and this time doubled it around his wrist. By now, the pain had started to intensify and he wondered if he would pass out as he applied the pressure of a tourniquet. He felt woozy, but he managed to maintain consciousness. He checked and the tourniquet appeared to be working as the blood from his hand had been reduced to a mere trickle.

He gazed around the trench to see what the damage was and whether there were any survivors. The smoke and dust were thick but he could still see large objects. He heard a few moans. The timbers lining the side of the trench were intact but the ones providing the roof for the "living room" section of the trench had collapsed. The four Frenchmen in that area must have been killed instantly. Even if they were still alive, it would have been impossible for him to move the timbers with only one hand and steadily diminishing strength.

The first person he came upon was Sergeant Jones. Ben felt for a pulse in the sergeant's neck and found one. He groped around for wounds but did not find any; the sergeant had been knocked unconscious by the blast but seemed otherwise intact. He moved on to the next fallen comrade. It was Private Knowles, someone from his unit whom Ben knew only in passing. When Ben felt for a pulse, all he found was a pool of blood from a gaping hole in his neck where some shrapnel had passed. He moved on. A Frenchman was lying right beside Knowles. He was unconscious but alive with wounds in his left shoulder.

Another Frenchman over next to the wall started to come to. He rose up to his knees but then just as quickly slumped back down as the exertion was too much for him.

Then Ben heard a thump. He hit the deck, expecting another explosion. When none happened, he went to investigate. He came upon a canister, which he recognized immediately as one designed to dispense a gas, probably phosgene. There were three choices. The canister could be a dud and would not detonate. The canister could be on a timer and it was only a matter of seconds or minutes before the noxious fumes spewed forth. The last possibility was that the mechanism had jammed, meaning that it could release the gas at any moment. Because of the last possibility, Ben could not attempt to grab the canister and heave it out of the trench. Any new movement could activate the mechanism and all would be dead.

He had to get out of there. He took two steps toward the exit at the rear but then stopped and turned around. He squatted beside Sergeant Jones, grabbed him by the back of the collar with his one good hand and started to pull. Making periodic heaves of the sergeant's inert and unresponsive body, he inched his way along. All the while he kept an ear alert for the hiss of the canister. Ben would have to do better to get the sergeant up the stairs and out into the open. He winced and almost passed out as he slid his bloodied hand under Sergeant Jones' legs so that he could pick him up the stairs.

Using all his strength, Ben hoisted the sergeant up and carried his dead weight up the thirteen steps to the outside world. He staggered about ten feet away, gauged that this spot was upwind from the trench and dropped Sergeant Jones with a thud on the grass, muttering 'sorry' as he did so.

His head was getting cloudy but he had to see if he could make one more pass to pull out any other survivors. He made his way back to the entrance to the trench. Explosions and gunfire were all around him now as the combined French and American forces poured over the top to drive back the Huns. In the mayhem, nobody seemed to notice Ben or what was going on in this little corner of the war.

Slumping down the stairs, he found the one Frenchman who had previously regained but then lost consciousness on one knee, trying to regain his wits, his bearings and some strength. Ben knew that he should be looking out for his own, the other Americans, but he did not know how much, if any, time he had. The canister was unobtrusively and innocently laying there, but it could become deadly in a matter of seconds.

He tried to get the semi-conscious Frenchman to help him carry his unconscious countryman out, but it would have taken too long to communicate his intentions. So Ben slid under the armpit of the man and they started to walk together up the stairs. As they reached the top step, Ben heard a pop followed by a hissing sound. Gas was being released. Because of the confined space, it was only a matter of moments until anybody who may still have been alive would die.

Ben and the Frenchman staggered over to Sergeant Jones. The Frenchman crumpled beside the sergeant. Ben went down on his knees. His head was spinning out of control by now from the loss of blood. Any adrenalin that had been coursing through his veins was spent.

Four soldiers from other units finally caught on to what had unfolded in Ben's trench and rushed to assist. Two headed for Ben, who was on his knees over his two unconscious companions. The other two peeled off and headed toward the trench. In one final act, mustering his fit bit of strength, Ben pointed at the trench entrance and shouted one word: "Gas." Then he fell forward, landing on top of the sergeant and the Frenchman.

14
Catherine

Molly and I were beside ourselves with worry. All we had to work with was Sergeant Jones brief telegram. We did not know how Ben was wounded or the extent of his injuries. We didn't know which hospital he was in. For all we knew, he may have died already. We felt so helpless.

I tried to get some answers from the Army. The captain I spoke with was very solicitous, but he was not very helpful. He kept spouting the usual army lingo about the difficulties of getting news from the front, about how word should be coming shortly about Ben's condition, about how he was receiving the best care possible, etc. He seemed somewhat surprised and a little alarmed that Sergeant Jones was able to send a telegram from the front the way he did. I could see him making a mental note to investigate how a breach of security like this could have happened.

I looked into the possibility of making the trip myself to London, but it would have been impossible. All passenger travel across the Atlantic had been suspended for the duration. My mother exercised the final veto of this foolhardy plan. I still had one more year before I could access the trust fund set up by my father. Even if I were able to find some form of transport across the sea, she refused to lend me the money to pay for it. So I sat, day-by-day, minute-by-minute, waiting for any news, hoping it to be positive.

Two weeks after we received the initial telegram Molly came to the library, this time with a letter from Sergeant Jones. I read it aloud.

Dear Mrs. Albert,
I would have written you sooner about Ben but I only recently

was released from the hospital myself. I hope you received the telegram my corporal sent on my behalf. I apologize for the lack of detail. At the time I did not have much information on his condition but I felt you had a right to know about your son.

I wish I could give you further details, but I am still in France while your son was rushed to London where he could get better medical care. I have received word that he is alive but that his condition is still very much critical and day-to-day. I have been told that if I divulge too much about the injuries he sustained or how he sustained them, this letter may be intercepted. For some reason that is unclear to me, I cannot even divulge the name of the hospital he's in. If I hear of any further developments on Ben's condition or prognosis, I will contact you immediately.

One thing I can tell you is that you can be very proud of your son. The actions he took were heroic. I would not be alive today if it weren't for Ben.

Sincerely,

Sergeant Walter A. Jones

We were relieved to hear that Ben was still alive but the lack of specifics about what happened and how Ben was doing was driving us crazy. We appreciated the sergeant telling us what he knew, but I was wondering if it wouldn't have been better to be kept ignorant rather than this constant feeling of helplessness.

As I read the letter, Molly would ask me to explain or clarify a certain word or expression she did not understand. When I came to the words 'critical' and 'day-to-day' I had to choke back tears to explain to her that there was a chance that Ben might not survive. We both nearly burst out crying when I read about his heroism. We were indeed proud.

And so it went for another two weeks. We received another letter from Sergeant Jones during that time, but he had no additional news to impart. I spoke with the captain once more. He was less cordial than the first time I met him; in essence he advised me not to bother contacting him and that he'd contact us if he heard anything.

I returned to my apartment after work. I had been staying with Molly all this time but I told her I needed one night to myself. She said she understood. My roommates had taken a trip to Philadelphia for a couple of days so I had the place to myself. I unlocked the door and on the floor was a small pile of mail that had been pushed through the slot. I leafed through the mail and stopped cold at a letter from St. Albans Hospital, London.

It was a standard beige colored envelope. The postmark was a week earlier. The writing was not Ben's; it had a definite feminine flourish to it. My hands started shaking as I imagined all the different messages that could be contained inside. I was tempted to tear it open but then I stopped. I owed it to Molly to let her share in whatever it was, good or bad. I needed her to either cry or celebrate with me. I put my jacket back on and rushed over to her house. She was just sitting down to dinner and when she saw me come in she automatically set another place.

"Molly, I have a letter. It's either from Ben," I stifled a sob, "or it's about him. Either way, I wanted to be with you before I opened it."

I could sense Molly was momentarily upset or jealous that this letter had been sent to me, not her, but it passed as she took my hand and we sat down at the table. I opened the letter and started to read.

My dearest Catherine,

Those were the three most beautiful words I have ever read in my life. He was alive! It was not the words of some nurse expressing her condolences to me for the loss of my fiancé. I continued.

I am so sorry I had not written to you earlier. I have been very sick and this has been my first opportunity. As you can see, I am not writing this letter. I am being ably assisted in this endeavor by a pretty young nurse named Emily (I made her swear that she would write down everything I dictated word for word and now she is blushing a beet red.)

Sergeant Jones sent me a note telling me that he had written to my mother, whom I assume is with you right now (hi Mama!), telling you that I had been wounded but also that he could not get into detail because of the censors. They are not as strict in London as they are at the front so I can tell you more.

First off, I am fine. They tell me that I ran a very high fever and was delirious for over a week. Nurse Emily said at one point in my delirium, I grabbed onto her calling out your name. But the fever is gone now and I am feeling much better.

My memory of what happened to me is rather fuzzy at the moment. Sergeant Jones thanked me for saving his life, but I honestly cannot remember doing that. I received a letter from a Frenchman, Louis D'Anton, also thanking me for saving his life. No memory of that either. All I remember is going down into a trench. Then there was an explosion. I recall the look of terror on another French soldier as he was dying in the blast. I remember putting a tourniquet on my arm. After that, everything is a blur.

There were a dozen or so of us, French and Americans, down there. Only three of us made it out alive. They tell me my battlefront experience lasted all of about ten minutes. I hope you are not too ashamed of me because I did not do more.

There is one part of the ordeal that has stuck in my memory. I originally thought it was a dream but then the doctors confirmed it for me. I vividly remember digging a ball of twine out of my pack and fashioning myself a tourniquet. The pain was excruciating as I pulled it taut around my wrist. The doctors praised my quick thinking in that situation. One of the doctors who had spent some time at the front actually saved the twine for me, thinking I might appreciate a battlefield memento. In a strange way, even though it is only an ugly, blood-soaked piece of string, I do appreciate having it.

All this leads me to my other news, my other memento of the war that I will carry the rest of my life. I am telling you so you will be prepared and not shocked when you next see me. The reason I am not writing this letter myself (other than the pleasure of watching Nurse Emily periodically blush) is that in order to save my life, the doctors had to amputate my right hand. Since as you know I have always done absolutely everything with my right hand, I will have to learn how to use my left hand. I remember how good a team we were in my studying before we left. I look forward to your help in this venture as well.

They tell me I will probably be ready to travel in about a month and they will be shipping me back to the states at that time. I cannot wait to see you and Mama. Tell my mother to have some stuffed cabbage ready for me when I get back. The hospital is quite fine but the food is, well let's just say there's a war on.

Well, Nurse Emily needs to change my bandages now. I will write again soon. One last thought, at one point while I was lying in bed I mentioned that I had to live so I could get my dollar back. The doctor who was there at the time thought I was slipping back into delirium but I just laughed so he knew I was okay. You better not have spent it while I was away.

I love you.

Ben

We were drained, a mixture of joy at learning he was alive, of sadness over what he had gone through and his disfigurement, of exhilaration at the thought that he would be back to us soon and a host of other emotions thrown in as well. It worried me that he thought I could ever be ashamed of him and that he himself was feeling some misplaced shame.

Molly hadn't said a word the entire time, not even to ask me to explain a word. She smiled when her son said hello to her and the fact that, although it had been addressed to me, Ben knew full well that he was writing to both of us. But other than that, she displayed no emotion whatsoever. When I finished, she got up and walked into the kitchen to carve up the chicken she had roasted for dinner. I remained seated in the dining room to give her some privacy. I heard the sharp scraping as she sharpened the knife but then it abruptly stopped. I got up to see if I could help her but when I reached the kitchen, I found her leaning against the counter, holding a handkerchief as she quietly wept into it. She looked over at me, her eyes moist and reddening.

"My son, my American boy, your husband. He is alive. Praise God."

It did not surprise me that she referred to Ben as my husband, even though we had not officially been wed. Like me, she had come to view the ceremony and the piece of paper as mere formalities. In her eyes, as in mine, we were already husband and wife. What did surprise me was the last exclamation she made. She had never shrunk from her identity or pride as a Jew, but I had never heard her, or Ben for that matter, ever make a statement that betrayed a belief in God or in any of the religious part of Judaism.

I walked over to her.

"Yes, Molly. Praise God indeed."

We stood there hugging and crying for several minutes.

15

Although the fighting on the fields of France was still intense, the ocean wartime activity had diminished sufficiently that Ben's ship was not entirely occupied by troops. Pleasure travel would not fully resume for another three or four months but Ben could spot a number of businessmen who had crossed the Atlantic to buy and sell their wares. He doubted any of them had volunteered for service, leaving the fighting to protect their way of life to others. Feeling morally superior, he made sure that his stump was prominently displayed whenever he ran across one of them on deck.

His wound had healed by this time, but it was still quite tender. It was also rather red and angry looking. The doctors told him that the redness would dissipate as time went on. He wore a bandage over it for protection and to hide it from others. There was one businessman, an American named Fremont, who was especially smug. Ben took an instant dislike to him. If Ben were up on deck and he saw Fremont walking toward him, he would be sure to hike up his sleeve, pull off the bandage and then assume a position of looking out to sea with his red, handless wrist prominently displayed on the railing. Ben had no idea if this had any impact of Fremont, but he liked to think perhaps the businessman was somewhat disgusted by the sight. It was one of those petty enjoyments that he could savor as he made the ten day trip.

As the tugs gently moored the ship into its berth, Ben surveyed the crowd waiting to greet passengers as they disembarked. It did not take long for him to spot Catherine and his mother. They were standing there holding hands. Catherine had written how close the two of them had become while he was away. Watching the two of them, it was obvious they had really become mother and daughter.

He had written to warn them about his wound so they would

be prepared when they first saw it but he knew it would be quite a blow for his mother. She would react with tears when she saw it, no matter how well prepared she was. It was simply part of her nature. Catherine would, on the other hand, look him in the eyes and not take her gaze away. Outwardly, she would have no reaction that a part of him was missing.

His reception was everything he expected. When he got home, everybody – Phil, Robert, Sol, Mr. Charney – was waiting to give him a proper welcome back. His biggest surprise was when he opened the door and Bessie was standing there. She was actually showing signs of settling down. She had taken to California wonderfully. She met and married a good, solid and employed man and was expecting their first child. She had taken the train cross-country just to be part of the family welcome. Molly, a little nervous that her daughter would move back in when she received Bessie's telegram that she was coming home, had to control her exuberant reaction when Bessie broke it to her that she was only staying for two days. She had to get back to her loving husband in sunny California.

16
Catherine

Ben could not help but notice how subdued I was during his welcome home celebration. I sat off to the side and did not participate in any of the conversations or listen to his story telling. He attributed it to all the excitement of the day, but after most everyone had gone home he asked me what was wrong.

"Ben, my mother's very sick. She has the influenza. She caught it at a clinic she volunteers at in Newark. They're not sure she'll make it."

With that I broke down, crying softly on his chest. Normally, he would raise his right hand to pat my hair to comfort me. Since he didn't have a right hand anymore, he had to consciously tell himself to use his left hand.

"Why didn't you say anything?"

"I didn't want to ruin your homecoming. They tell me there's nothing they can do. She's not even conscious right now. Her fever is so high. She wouldn't know if I were there or not."

I looked up into his eyes.

"I'll go in a few minutes. But I had to be here for you. I chose you after all, didn't I?"

"Yes you did."

And then we kissed.

"Before I go, I have to remember to give you this."

Whereupon I pulled the dollar bill out of my purse and slid it into his hand.

"It was close. There was this nice blue blouse down at Newberry's, but I resisted temptation."

"I'm glad you did."

Ben fingered the dollar in his hand. He saw me to the door and kissed me goodbye as I headed to the hospital to be by my mother's side. He volunteered to go with me but I told him to stay to catch up with his family and friends. He said he'd drop by the next day. I said that would be wonderful. I had lots to tell him about my first days of class at the New Jersey College for Women, which started its inaugural semester just two weeks earlier. I'd missed the past couple of days of classes because of my mother's illness and Ben's return but the instructors. Dean Douglass had been very kind, letting me make up the missed classes in the near future when things returned to normal.

17

Molly came up to Ben and handed him two envelopes.

"These came this morning," she told him.

He looked at the return addresses on each. One was from the Massachusetts Institute of Technology. He opened that letter. It was an offer of admission for graduate studies and a scholarship to cover his tuition and all educational expenses. He would be on his own for living expenses, although the letter did indicate that employment opportunities were available to help him pay those costs.

He was a trifle confused. He had not sent an applications to this school. How could he have? If things had gone according to plan, he would have still been in Europe for the duration. Yet here was one of the top schools in the country, if not the world, courting him on his first day home. Word must have spread that he was heading home.

The second letter was from Langdan Textiles. It read:

Dear Mr. Albert:

I am writing to offer you a unique opportunity. First, however, I have been advised by a mutual acquaintance, Dr. William Fowler, that you have recently returned from serving your country in Europe. Thank you for that service and for making the world "safe for democracy."

I also understand from Dr. Fowler that you have been offered admission in the prestigious Massachusetts Institute of Technology, where he currently teaches. I hope that you take advantage of this once-in-a-lifetime opportunity.

Dr. Fowler has noted to me that already at your young age you are approaching the pinnacle of the fields of horticultural pathology and bacteriology. He says your dedication to research is second to none. He has provided me with several of the articles in prominent journals you have authored and co-authored. I have read these articles and I must say I was most impressed. I can only imagine what new discoveries you will make as you enter into your graduate studies and your professional life, which brings me to the reason for this letter.

As one of the leading textile manufacturers in the world, Langdan Textiles can only stay at the forefront of the industry through constant innovation and new product development. This is possible only through maintaining a robust and progressive research department. This involves not only the emerging field of synthetic fiber development but also the constant research on natural fibers, protecting their health and increasing their strength and productivity. After reading your papers, I came to the conclusion that you could be an invaluable asset to this company.

I apologize for constantly digressing, but I hope you find it understandable for me to get carried away. This business has been my life, as it was for my father before me and for his father before him. I am writing in the hope that it can also become your life, too. I would like to offer you employment in the Langdan Textiles Department of Research and Development.

Understandably, you would start in an entry-level position and the hours would be adjusted to accommodate your school workload, but we are ready to welcome you into our firm. This may seem a bit rash on my part, hiring someone sight unseen. I must admit that it is rather out of character for me, generally being a cautious individual. However, I implicitly trust any recommendation from Bill Fowler, a man I've known since childhood. Second, the scholarship and thoroughness of the research in your articles bespeak a brilliant scientist that I am confident will be heading a research department somewhere in the future. I can only hope it will be at Langdan.

The one thing that ultimately persuaded me to leave my comfort zone and act out of character was your war service. Dr. Fowler told me that you volunteered to serve when millions of young men sat back and waited to be called. Do not get me wrong, I am not disparaging the service of those brave men who are over there now, but your action denotes character and an inner integrity of the highest order. Those are the types of individuals that I want working at Langdan. That is what convinced me that I was not taking any risk here.

I do hope that you seriously consider my offer and come to work in this exciting company. I would be happy to meet with you in person to discuss any details of the offer that I have not made clear. I look forward to your response.
Sincerely,
Franklin T. Andrews, Jr.
President

Bill Fowler, Ben's mentor and friend at Rutgers who had moved on to MIT, wanted his protégé to follow along. He certainly had done an excellent job of laying out all the inducements.

Ben instinctively reached into his pocket and pulled out the piece of twine he now carried with him at all times. It was an ugly thing, soaked with dried blood. It had formed into the shape of his wrist. If it were not so hideous, he probably would wear it as a bracelet. He kept it in a little cloth sack in his right back pocket.

It was almost like fate itself was calling out to him. He had indeed as a lowly undergraduate gained a substantial reputation in the fields of horticultural pathology and bacteriology, mostly because of a course he took freshman year with Bill Fowler. Fowler's dynamism and passion for the field captivated Ben. Then, when his initial attempt to save his own life almost ended disastrously when the twine he was using for a tourniquet snapped, he became fascinated with the scientific characteristics that led to a weakening in the fibers and how they could be strengthened. This offer from Langdan Textiles, one of the world's largest manufacturers of burlap and twine, came to him like manna in the wilderness, feeding an insatiable part of him. It was almost as if Andrews had known.

Ben dreamed his whole life of attending a prestigious school like MIT, and here they were handing it to him on a silver platter. He had grown somewhat tired of Rutgers, quite frankly thinking that he knew as much as the professors there. He needed a fresh approach to academia to expand his mind and the breadth of his knowledge.

All the elements were there. He would be a fool to turn down such a deal. And yet, he knew instantly that he would have to say no.

There was one part of Mr. Andrews' letter that he knew could never apply to him. When Andrews said, *"This business has been my life,"* that would never be the case for him. His academic and professional pursuits would always be important to him, but he knew exactly where his life began and ended: Catherine.

Catherine's mother, by all accounts, was not going to survive. She had contracted the especially virulent strain of influenza, known as the Spanish Flu, that was devastating the world. Over the course of two years, it would kill more people than the Great War.

If Ben went to MIT, he would either have to desert his fiancée at a time when she needed him most or she would come with him, deserting her mother. He could not countenance either of these possibilities.

In addition, Catherine had just started her courses at the New Jersey College for Women. Ben was so proud of her and wanted her to stick it out. When her mother took ill and was still conscious, Catherine contemplated dropping out but her mother would not hear of her doing such a thing. She was the one who got her daughter into college; she would not be the cause of making her quit. Mrs. Jackson made Catherine promise she would not quit. With all this, Ben could not leave her. He would remain at Rutgers. He was sure to get a similar deal he had received from MIT.

The more he thought about his decision, the more content he became. All that he loved was right here in New Brunswick. His mother was not an old woman, but she had aged considerably in the short time he had been away. Granted, going off to war was a little more taxing on his mother than going off to school in a different state would be, but now she would not have to be separated from her "American son" for extended periods of time.

He sat down and wrote letters to MIT and to Mr. Andrews

apologizing that he would be unable to accept their generous offers. He framed his response so that if the situation changed in the future, he hoped they would be open to reconsideration. He put the letters in the mail and headed over to the hospital to join Catherine in her vigil.

18
Catherine

One day, my mother was just fine; three days later, she was comatose. The doctors appeared helpless as they could not stem blood hemorrhaging from her nose and ears. Each visit, she looked worse. There was nothing I could do. It was made harder because the doctors had to place all influenza patients into quarantine and I could only view her through a window. I couldn't hold my mother; I couldn't stroke her hand; I couldn't talk to her and tell her about my day. Even though she couldn't hear a word I was saying, it would have been good therapy for me.

I planned to quit school. I couldn't study; my mind was not on anything but my mother. In addition, Ben was back and we were to be married. He deserved a proper wife, one who would take care of him and his needs. He did not deserve a wife who would put him off while she crammed for an exam.

I announced my plans to drop out of school. Immediately, three people vehemently objected. First, Dean Douglass pleaded with me not to leave. There were many men throughout New Jersey, and throughout the country as well, who were hoping that the college would fall on its face. She needed the inaugural class to stay as intact as possible all the way through to graduation. Inevitably, there would be women who would not be able to keep up with their course work and would drop out for scholastic reasons. That was to be expected. In fact, if every single woman who entered the curriculum made it all the way through, it would look as if the school was too easy, not a rigorous academic atmosphere. The courses were extremely tough, but I was thriving on the work. Dean Douglass could see this and implored me to stay on.

I don't want to give the impression that Dean Douglass was a heartless creature, only focused on her objective of keeping her lifelong dream of a college for women alive. She was one of my mother's best friends and I could see the pain in her face as my mother's health steadily deteriorated. And I knew she was concerned about me, wanting me to continue school for my own sake. She fully believed that a cadre of educated young women was not only good for society but for the women themselves.

She alone would not have been enough to deter me from my plan. The second assault was by Molly. She made it clear that she thought my quitting to be a terrible mistake. She said she would not trade her life with Harry for anything on earth, but still she longed for something more. For someone who led such an insular existence and was so traditional in many respects, it was strange to hear her longing to explore new ideas and to learn about far away places and cultures. She wished she had been given the opportunity I was afforded. She didn't say as much but she implied that it would be an insult to her if I quit.

Ultimately, the coup de grace came from a source that was both expected and unexpected: Ben. When I told him I was going to quit to be a better wife for him, he calmly told me I wasn't making sense. He said that one of the main things that first attracted him to me was my intelligence. The best wife I could become, he argued, would be through my realizing my potential, not through keeping a tidy house or through ensuring that a hot meal was on the table the minute he got home or by having a bunch of his children. Although he conceded that all of those qualities would be nice, he'd gladly give them up if they came at the price of limiting me and my future. He wanted a wife with whom he could discuss things, bounce ideas off of and conduct a learned conversation. Those were only obtainable through education.

By the time he finished, I was in tears. I was convinced not to quit. He also told me at that time that he had been accepted into the Rutgers graduate program. They had offered him a full scholarship and employment on campus to help with his living expenses. He said they probably could have offered him housing as well but they did not have any housing for married students and he wanted us to marry as soon as possible. So did I.

If my mother had been conscious, we would have held the ceremony in the outside waiting room. She would not have been able to participate but she would have at least observed the service through the window. But unless there was a miracle—despite my lack of religious upbringing I was praying for a miracle—my mother would never look upon her daughter taking her vows.

We had to start planning our lives together. The immediate issue was where we would live. Ben's stipend would not be sufficient to afford an apartment near the campus. I told Ben that within a year I could pay for our housing. Besides the modest inheritance from my mother, a fact neither of us acknowledged but realized was an approaching reality, in a year I would be attaining twenty one years of age and would therefore have access to the trust fund set up and steadily augmented by my absentee father. I had never seen a statement of how much was in the account, but my mother had advised me that it was in the "seven figures" category. My father had done right by me at least in this respect.

I wasn't certain how Ben would react to my proposal. Like Molly, he could be a complex mixture of tradition and new ideas. I didn't know whether he would take kindly to living off his wife's money for any period of time. When I suggested it to him, he did not seem to mind. I think he was confident that, with his talents, it would not be too long before he was commanding a generous salary himself and he was not going to let pride stand in the way of us living together as man and wife. However, there was the question of where should we live in the meantime.

The first place we considered was my house, or rather my mother's house that I feared would soon be my house, in Westfield. We would have had the privacy of newlyweds and it was a beautiful home, just off the center of town. Several things kept us from considering it. First, I would have been very uneasy about moving into there. It would appear that we were taking advantage of her condition, in essence waiting for her to die. I don't think I would have the heart or stomach to move in after she passed away either. In any case, it was too far from New Brunswick to consider. We did not have an automobile. Since there was no direct rail connection between the two towns, taking the train on a daily basis with all the connections we'd have to make would have been exhausting.

That left us with only one alternative. When he first suggested it, I was adamantly opposed but the more I thought about it, the more sense it made. I had come to love Molly as a second mother, but would it be a case of absence making the heart grow fonder? I feared that if we lived under the same roof, nerves would get frayed, each of our idiosyncrasies would annoy the other and we'd ultimately detest each other. I only got along with my roommates because they were away three quarters of the time. I did not want my relationship with Molly to be poisoned. I also did not want to be in a position where Ben might have to take sides between the two of us. It was very romantic for him to state that he "chose me" but it was also rather rhetorical. I did not want to risk testing this proclamation in actuality; I was afraid what the result might be.

Until I could get access to my money we did not have much choice in the matter so we planned to move into Molly's house. Luckily, the living space could be divided and a separate entrance constructed.

The first thing we had to take care of was the marriage itself. This presented some difficulties. Neither of us were active members of our respective congregations. Ben approached the rabbi at the synagogue nearest his house and the rabbi would only perform the ceremony if I agreed to convert to Judaism. Ben jokingly asked when he should start scheduling the classes.

Likewise, the minister at the Methodist Church at which I was baptized many years previously outright refused to sanctify a marriage between a Christian and a Jew. So, in the end we went down to the New Brunswick City Hall to find ourselves a justice of the peace to perform the ceremony. Ben, Molly and I were heading out of the house when Ben's brother, Robert, happened by. He asked what was going on and when we told him, he insisted on accompanying us and being a witness. He said he was very proud of his little brother and wanted to be a part of the special day. We were stunned. We had never heard Robert so much as express a feeling, never mind show much in the way of affection. We told him we'd be happy to have him along and off we went.

I can't say the wedding was the type I'd dreamed of growing up, but it was a happy event. Everyone knew a part of me was with my mother in the hospital and my joy couldn't be complete, but it was quite a day nonetheless. Afterwards, Molly took us all out to a nice lunch. I felt honored to have been present at the only two meals she had eaten in a restaurant since she was a girl in the old country.

Then it was back to the house for Ben and me to begin our lives together, but we had to make a stop at the hospital first. We got to my mother's ward but her bed was empty. A nurse calmly walked up to me and informed me that my mother had passed away just ten minutes earlier. The last thing I remembered was fainting into Ben's arms.

19

Eric Wilhelm, PhD. was a giant in his field. His doctoral dissertation on diseases affecting alfalfa and how to breed new plant strains that would resist these diseases became an instant must-read classic. His dissertation, and the resulting acclaim of that work, earned him an immediate invitation for a tenured position in the Rutgers Botany Department. The school did not even require him to teach many courses. He would concentrate on research and lending his name and prestige to the university.

The problem was that Dr. Wilhelm earned his doctorate in 1897, the year Ben was born, but he had ridden on his reputation ever since. Unlike the plants he studied, he really had not grown much from then to the time that Ben entered the program. As an undergraduate, Ben read Dr. Wilhelm's thesis and, like the rest of the world, found it to be brilliant. However, as he read later works by the doctor, he found that there was not much in the way of advancements or new thought. In comparing him to many other plant pathologists at other universities, his work had been surpassed over and over again. Still, however, students and faculty alike bowed in reverence as they passed the doctor walking around campus.

Many questions ran through Ben's mind about Dr. Wilhelm's initial work and his subsequent writings. They would occasionally cross paths in the lab, but Ben could not get as much as an acknowledgement or greeting since he was only a lowly graduate student who was not in the doctor's circle of fawning sycophants. Ben decided to make an appointment with Dr. Wilhelm to ask his questions.

The meeting was cancelled three times, but Ben kept rescheduling. Finally, he walked into Dr. Wilhelm's office. Wilhelm looked up.

"Albert, isn't it?
"Yes, Dr. Wilhelm. I'm Benjamin Albert."
"Have a seat."
"Doctor, I have a few questions."
"Certainly, what's on your mind?"
Ben proceeded to ask a dozen pointed questions about various aspects of plant pathology. The answers provided by Dr. Wilhelm, many of which were superficial or evasive, in turn generated additional inquiries. The doctor squirmed in his seat. It was as if Ben were the professor grilling an unprepared student during an oral defense of his dissertation.

After a half hour, Dr. Wilhelm announced that he was late for a meeting and asked to be excused, again as if he were the student. Ben, silently realizing there was no more for him to learn here, responded that he himself was late for a class. As he shook the doctor's hand, Ben swore to himself that he would never let himself get to the point where he was like this, complacent and intellectually lazy.

20
Catherine

Ben fought his way through the crowd to get to me.

"Catherine, I'm so proud of you. You did it. You're a member of the first graduating class of the New Jersey College for Women. I knew you could do it. I'm so proud."

Ben looked at me with such love and pride that I almost broke down right there. When Molly grabbed me with hands on both cheeks to give me a proper congratulatory kiss, I did start to cry.

"Well, I wasn't first in my class like some people I know."

"It's highly overrated, let me assure you," he responded.

During the time I struggled through my curriculum to get my Bachelor's, Ben had breezed through his graduate studies and had earned his doctorate in near record time. His graduation was to be on the same day as mine so he opted to skip the ceremony. The President of Rutgers himself pleaded with him to attend since he was to give the valedictorian address. Ben refused. He said the only way he would attend was if Rutgers changed the date for the commencement. This was to be my day; he was not going to let anything detract from my accomplishment.

After the ceremony, Dean Mabel Smith Douglass held a reception for us graduates and our families and friends at her home. She likewise spoke of her pride. She thanked us for making her dream a reality. After a number of tearful farewells and promises to keep in touch with my classmates, Ben, Molly and I headed home.

Despite our original intentions, we did not move out of his mother's house, even after I obtained access to my trust fund. Molly so enjoyed having us there, but she never interfered with our lives. It became our home. That night we had a pleasant dinner. Robert and his girlfriend and Phil and his wife joined us.

While we found ourselves to be very comfortable here, we knew that eventually we would have to strike out on our own. Even so, I was totally unprepared for the bombshell Ben dropped regarding our future.

We had just awakened and had come down for breakfast with Molly. It was a Sunday morning and, not having to hurry off to the butcher shop, she was still in a housecoat and slippers. We were not much better dressed or prepared for the day. We had just poured ourselves some coffee when Ben broke the news. He told us that he was offered a job, in fact his dream job doing botanical research. (I personally could never fathom that this would be anybody's dream. My dreams were always more ethereal: a wonderful husband, children, a nice home. I wanted to do something with my life but I never really had much in the way of professional ambition.)

The first shock Ben revealed was that we would have to move to Massachusetts. That's where the job was. I immediately looked over to Molly to gauge her reaction. Sadness flashed across her face. I don't think Ben caught it because she did a magnificent job of immediately replacing this emotion with happiness and excitement for her son.

It wasn't until the second part of Ben's announcement that my emotions were exposed.

"I've been offered a research position at Langdan Textiles," he announced.

I let out an audible gasp at the mention of his future employer and then whispered: "Oh my God!"

Ben took my reaction as an aversion to pulling up stakes, leaving my friends to move to a new state.

"Darling, I haven't said yes. I can always thank them for the offer and find a job here. Rutgers has made it very clear that a position on the faculty is mine for the taking if I want it. It's just I think I can accomplish more with this job if I were to take it. I've also been given an offer to teach part time at MIT. Everything would be coming together for me. But if moving away is going to make you unhappy, nothing is worth that."

I don't know why I couldn't tell him the real reason for being unsettled and distraught. I could not tell him that it would at best be extremely uncomfortable for him to work for my absentee father. I was toying with the idea of selfishly avoiding that subject but at the same time getting him to reject the position when he told me something that made it impossible to do this.

"I do have a confession to make," he told me.

He disappeared for a minute and ran upstairs. When he came back, he was holding two envelopes. One was from the Massachusetts Institute of Technology and the other was from Langdan Textiles. I noticed both were dated November, 1918, nearly three years earlier.

I stared at them blankly. Rutgers was a fine school; he received an excellent education there. He was already nationally-recognized in his field. But, MIT is MIT. There was no way around it.

I knew exactly what this meant. My dear husband had given up a chance to attend MIT for me. He didn't exactly suffer, but he had sacrificed—or rather postponed—attaining two dreams at once so that I could chase mine. There was no way I could stand in his way now. We would move to Massachusetts.

It also became clear to me that I could not let on who my father was. First, I did not want my feelings for the man who had abandoned and rejected me to influence Ben's decision. He was so thrilled at the prospect of his new position. It would have been cruel of me make him reconsider. Second, he would be better off not knowing. During every waking moment of my life I pictured the look of loathing on my father's face when he laid his eyes on me nearly a decade earlier. If he were to discover that he had hired the husband of his despicable offspring, it could affect Ben's chances and future.

There was one last reason I would not stand in Ben's way. I was pregnant with his child. We would have to move out of the two rooms we occupied in Molly's house anyway. The money he was being offered, which was a fortune in those days, would help to support our new family without tapping my trust fund. I resolved to make this into an adventure, a new beginning, not a problem.

21

Ben's immediate supervisor, Joe Smithers, stuck his head into the laboratory. Ben and two other researchers were in the lab.

"Albert, Mr. Andrews wants to see you immediately," Smithers called out.

"Me?" Albert Fogg replied as he started to get up from the stool at his station.

"No, the other guy, Ben Albert. Mr. Andrews says to come get you right now. Better move your ass."

Ben was peering into his microscope, heavily focused on examining individual strands of three different varieties of jute that had been exposed to acidified water to determine if there was any difference in how the cells from each strain reacted to the acid. He did not notice Smithers' arrival, or the order aimed at him. He kept his head down, concentrating on the specimens before him.

"Albert, Ben Albert!" Smithers shouted, "Get moving."

Ben lifted up his head for the first time.

"Huh?"

"Mr. Andrews wants to see you. Immediately."

"Me? Why would he want to see me?"

Ben's tone betrayed the lack of regard he had for Smithers.

"How the hell should I know? I got orders to go collect your Hebe ass and get it up there. For all I know, you're being canned. You better move it or that might just happen."

Smithers walked away as Ben rose from his station. As he was walking out, the third resident of the office, Frank Cosolito, called out to him. "Good luck, Ben," he shouted.

Ben smiled. For every anti-Semite at Langdan Textiles like Smithers, there were good decent guys like Frankie who made life bearable. Ben hardly noticed the Hebe, Kike or Jewboy slurs anymore. Growing up on the streets of New Brunswick, he had to fight whenever a slur was thrown his way. It was the only way to gain respect. Some of his best friends were ones he had originally fought after such a comment.

Once he entered the real world, however, he could not fight everybody. Furthermore, he would find himself in jail if he had. In the nine months he had been with the company, he had become inured to the anti-Semitic comments, asides and slights. What made his palms clammy and his heart race was the fact that Mr. Franklin Andrews, the president and owner of Langdan Textiles, had summoned him. Even though Andrews had actively recruited Ben freshly out of college and then again after he received his PhD., they had never met in person. All contacts were made through intermediaries. Ben could not figure why he was being ordered to appear in Andrews' office on the fourth floor.

It did not take long for Ben's mind to latch onto what seemed to him to be a logical worst-case scenario. Mr. Andrews was only now realizing that the company had a Jew on its payroll. The company had about three hundred employees at this facility in Wayland, Massachusetts, all of whom were white and, by Ben's reckoning, at least ninety percent Protestant. Langdan Textiles could tolerate the occasional Catholic, but somehow the Personnel Department had let one Christ-killer slip through. Ben believed Franklin Andrews was about to remedy that situation in short order.

These were the thoughts that swirled around Ben's mind as he opened the door leading to Mr. Andrews' fourth floor office. A handsome middle-aged woman looked up from her desk and smiled. She looked to be about Molly's age but did not have the wear and tear a harder life had inflicted on his mother. He couldn't help but notice this woman's beautiful green eyes. She wore a stylish navy blue cotton dress with a big white collar. Her light brown hair was impeccably arranged in a bun on top of her head.

"May I help you?"

"I think so. I received word that Mr. Andrews wanted to see me."

"And you are?"

"Oh, I'm sorry," Ben stammered, "My name is Benjamin Albert."

"I actually knew that, but I wanted to see if you were nervous. And you are, but don't be. I have it on good authority that you've been asked up here for a good thing. You'll see. You can go in. Mr. Andrews is waiting for you."

She smiled again. Ben smiled back, thanked her and knocked on the inner office door. After hearing a voice telling him to enter, he walked in.

Four men were arranged in various seats around the mahogany paneled office. Ben not only had never met Franklin Andrews before, he didn't even know what the man looked like. He only recognized one of the other men seated there, Herbert Williams, who was his boss's boss. His immediate thought was that he would embarrass himself by greeting the wrong gentleman as Mr. Andrews. Luckily, the slim, tall man with a mane of flowing gray hair got up from behind the desk and introduced himself.

"Mr. Albert? Welcome. I'm Franklin Andrews. This is Mr. Herbert Williams, Mr. Frederick Gill and Mr. Alexander Searles."

Mr. Williams and Mr. Gill both rose out of their respective chairs and shook Ben's hand when they were introduced. Neither of them seemed to notice or react to Ben's having to shake with his left hand. Mr. Searles remained seated and only nodded in Ben's direction. Andrews continued.

"Mr. Williams you may know since indirectly he is your boss. He's our Director of Product Development, Research and Quality Assurance."

"Yes, our paths have briefly crossed a number of times since Ben has been on the company payroll," Williams noted.

"Mr. Gill is our Director of Overseas Marketing and Mr. Searles our Director for Government Relations. These three gentlemen will be your traveling companions."

"Traveling companions, sir?"

"You didn't think you'd be making a trip of this magnitude on your own, did you?"

"Sir, I have no idea what you're talking about. Am I going on a trip somewhere?"

"Why, of course you are. Why did you think I asked you up

here?"

"I have absolutely no idea. I was ordered to report to you, and here I am."

Andrews looked around the room at the three gentlemen.

"Do you mean to tell me that none of you bothered to advise this boy that he is leaving for India in three days? This is unbelievable!"

Andrews glared at the other men sitting there. Williams and Gill both squirmed in their seats while Searles sat impassively with a slight smirk on his face.

"India, sir?"

"Yes, India. The jute we've been receiving from India over the past year has been basically worthless. Our Calcutta packaging plant vouch that the jute is of perfect quality when it is processed, baled and laded on the ships. But by the time it gets to our manufacturing plants, much of it is rotting away. I've seen your report identifying the disease afflicting the fibers, but nobody has been able to come up with a way to prevent it or to explain how seemingly healthy fibers may be developing the disease. I want to send a party to evaluate the jute growth and processing to see what's going wrong. You've quickly become our top research scientist. I understand that in the few short months you have been here, you've demonstrated a far better understanding of the physical and chemical properties of jute than anybody else in this company, including me. That's why I need you on this trip.

"Today was supposed to just be a recap to make sure everything was set to go and whether there was any special equipment we needed to order before you left. It was not supposed to be a grand announcement that you were going! I gave specific orders over two weeks ago that you be briefed. It's unbelievable that you know nothing about it. I do not like my orders ignored, gentlemen. This is entirely unacceptable."

Ben glanced at the men seated around the room. None of them were looking up at Andrews. One of them was supposed to have advised him, but did not. When it did not appear Andrews was going to give up on determining which of the three was recalcitrant so he could be raked across the coals, Ben spoke up. If the trip did come off, it would best to ingratiate himself with these men right up front since they were going to be traveling together for months.

"Mr. Andrews, I think there may have been some miscommunication. Now that I think about it, Mr. Williams did come to me to tell me about the trip a few weeks back. I sometimes have a tendency to get overly absorbed in my work and what he was telling me didn't really sink in. He asked me to come up to his office but, like I said, I was in the middle of a project and when that happens, everything else has a tendency to slip. I apologize. I should have gone to Mr. Williams' office as directed."

"Yes, you should have."

Andrews still cast an angry eye at his subordinates but seemed to be somewhat mollified.

"Well, you are scheduled to leave in only three days. Can you go or not?"

"Yes, sir. I have a passport. My wife and son will be fine for the few months I'll be away. You tell me the boat or train you want me on, and I'll be on it."

"That's the spirit. Over the next couple of days Williams can fill you in on what we're looking for. You can gather your tickets, petty cash advance and other documents you'll need from Mrs. Epstein on your way out. Enjoy your trip, but not too much. I need work out of you."

"Thank you, sir."

Ben said goodbye to the men as he left the office. Williams gave him a nod of appreciation for throwing Mr. Andrews off the trail of looking for someone to blame. Ben stopped at the desk in the outer office.

"You're Mrs. Epstein?"

"Yes, I am. Is there a problem with that?"

"No, not at all. In fact, I was beginning to think I was the only Jew in this whole company. It's nice to know I'm not alone."

Mrs. Epstein looked surprised.

"Albert? That's not very Jewish sounding."

"My father changed it from Abramowitz the day he stepped

foot on Ellis Island."

Mrs. Epstein laughed.

"Now Abramowitz, that I would have recognized. We are a select few in this company, to be sure. I've been with Langdan for over twenty-five years. I first worked for Mr. Andrews' father. Now, there was a mensch."

Ben found it curious that Mrs. Epstein did not ascribe the same quality to the son as well, but he did not feel it proper to inquire.

"I understand you have some tickets and other nice things for me."

"Yes, it sounds like a wonderful, exciting trip."

She pulled an envelope from her desk and handed it to Ben. He thanked her and started for the door. As he opened the door, Mrs. Epstein called him back and whispered out one piece of advice.

"Mr. Albert. Watch your back around Searles. He's an anti-Semitic sorry piece of work, that one."

Ben nodded and departed.

22

Catherine

"I can't believe you'd do this to me! I can't believe you would abandon me like this! In case you haven't noticed, there's a two-month old baby—your son, Harry—sleeping in the next room. How am I going to be able to take care of him myself?"

"I'm not abandoning you," was Ben's meek reply.

"I didn't say a word when you marched off to get yourself blown apart in the war. I was the good wife and dutifully followed you up to Massachusetts when you got this job offer. I haven't said a peep all those nights you worked 'til 10:00 on one or another fool research project you just 'had to get done.' Now you blithely come home to tell me that in three days you're going away for the next six months. If that doesn't qualify as abandoning us, then what does?"

"Please, hon. I have to go."

"Why you? There are two other men who work in your lab, neither of whom have wives or children or commitments. You do remember that word, right? They could go off on this jaunt without missing a beat."

"But I'm the expert in this field. They will not know what they're looking for. The president of the company, Mr. Andrews, personally asked me to do this. I couldn't turn him down. It will be good for us in the long run. And he offered to have, at company expense, a woman to come over during the day to help you out. You won't be alone."

"I want nothing from that man. You work for him, that I have no control over, but I don't want him in my life any more than that!"

I surprised myself by the venom that dripped from each word that escaped my lips. He was about to say something when I got up and told him I had to look in on the baby even though we both knew he was sleeping peacefully. I left Ben sitting there helplessly.

After my outburst, I wouldn't say another word for the next two days. Ben tried to engage me but I was too hurt and too angry; I turned my back on him every time.

He was scheduled to board a train at 2:00 on May 27, 1920 out of North Station for Montreal, the first leg of his journey. By 10:00 he was all packed and ready to go. He asked once again for me to come down to the station to see him off, but once again his entreaties were met with stony silence. He kissed the top of my head, went in and kissed Harry goodbye and started to gather his trunk. I felt sorry for him trying to manage with only one hand, but I was not going to relent. He still had a chance to back out and stay home. Even if Langdan fired him, he'd land another job in a heartbeat. I was determined that no matter how much I softened and bent, I would not break.

Finally, the door closed and I heard his trunk thumping down the stairs to the livery waiting at the curb. I put my head on the table and sobbed. I was like that for about an hour when there was a knock on the door. Forgetting that it was unlikely Ben would knock on his own door, I flew to it to announce how sorry I was. I opened the door and there was Molly, cardboard suitcase beside her. She had taken the train up to surprise Ben and wish him a bon voyage. Her train was scheduled to get in much earlier in the morning but there had been delays around New York. She knew his train left at 2:00 and thought she was still in plenty of time so she was shocked that Ben was not there. I broke and explained what had happened the past three days. She didn't say anything but just occasionally shook her head and tsk'd a few times.

"Catherine, you know I love you as if you were my own daughter. There have been times when I take your side against my own son. But now, you are a silly fool. You run to your husband. I look after Harry and get to know my grandson. When you get back, we pack your bags. You and little Harry come to New Brunswick with me until Ben returns. You go now."

I was through playing the proud wronged party. I gave her a big hug and ran out the door and down the steps. A trolley was pulling up to the corner a block away. I ran for it shouting and jumped on just as was pulling out. The conductor contemplated giving me a lecture on proper trolley etiquette but decided to just take my money and move on. A half hour later we were at North Station. I checked the board for Ben's train and saw it was leaving from track 4. I went down the steps and saw him sitting on his trunk, leafing through a newspaper.

He hadn't seen me so I walked up behind him.

"Excuse me, is this the track for silly fools?"

Without turning he responded.

"I sure hope so. Otherwise I'm on the wrong track."

He whirled around and enveloped me in his arms.

"I'm so sorry Catherine. It was thoughtless of me not to consult with you before agreeing to make this trip. I just got caught up in having the owner of the company personally ask me to make this trip."

"Ben, I'm sorry, too, for the things I said and for almost letting you go without a simple goodbye or telling you how much I love you. I'm so proud of you and all you've accomplished. You would have been an idiot to say no to this trip. It's a once in a lifetime chance. I was proud of you all along. I want to explain why I acted the way I did."

"I understand, darling. You don't have to explain anything."

"Believe me, you don't understand. I have to tell you everything.'

Ben nodded and I commenced.

"My vehement reaction had nothing to do with you. Yes, I would have liked to have been consulted before you made the decision you did but I understand why you couldn't. Like I said, I'm so proud of you and I know in my heart you would never do anything to hurt Harry or me. In the end, it all goes back to my father."

"I do understand. You were reliving being abandoned by your father all those years ago."

I was beginning to lose patience but I didn't want to snap at him.

"Ben, please let me say what I need to say all the way through. It's not what you expect. Being abandoned is only part of it; it also had to do with who abandoned me. I know you lost your father at a very early age, but you can at least dredge up a couple fond memories about him. You know how much he loved you.

"My father was generous financially to my mother and me but in terms of all the other things that go into being a father, namely love, he didn't provide. Technically, I never lied to you but I did lead you to believe that I never knew who it was. But I do know who my father is.

"I never actually met my father but I did see him one time. When I was thirteen I accompanied my mother to his father's, my grandfather's, funeral. My father was one of the pall-bearers. We arrived late and sat in the last pew off to the side. As they were carrying the casket out he happened to look up and saw my mother standing there. It pleased me to see a sad smile on his face. But then his glance shifted to me beside her and it only took an instant to figure out who I was and the melancholic look changed to revulsion. The only image I have of my own father is that he detested me. He loathed my very existence.

"You may remember my initial reaction when you told me you had been offered a job with Langdan Textiles. I think I gasped. You took it as a reaction to having to move so far from home. That wasn't it at all. In my mind, wherever you are is home. You wouldn't have conceived that I would be reacting to the company you were going to work for. Langdan may be one of the biggest companies in the country, but they are hardly a household name. You'll find plenty of things in Newberry's that are made from Langdan cloth, but the Langdan name isn't splashed around everywhere. But yes, I was reacting to Langdan Textiles. I grew up knowing, and reviling, the name Langdan because, because, Franklin Andrews is my father."

Ben sat there ashen. As I had predicted, there was no way that he could have guessed the secret that finally exploded from me.

"Why...why didn't you tell me? I never would have accepted a job here if I knew."

"Well, first it was the shame I carried around with me. As a kid, I would ask my mother what is wrong with me that my father doesn't like me. She would of course assure me that there was absolutely nothing wrong with me; the fault lies with him. I also think that she tried to raise me to be independent so I could stand on my own two feet to stand up to the Franklin Andrews of the world. It worked, I think, to a point.

"You may not think it, but you are a determined man who is guided by your obsessions. I count myself as extremely fortunate that I am one of your obsessions. But I know you have others that will not be denied. The dollar you carry around drives you to be a man your father can be proud of, if not striving to be your father himself. You volunteered for war because an obsessive love for the country in which you were born. You even attacked re-learning how to write with your left hand with such passion that your penmanship is better now than when you had two hands!

"Your professional life is driven by that little piece of blood-soaked string you carry around with you, the one you credit with saving your life but almost didn't because the first length broke. Somewhere in your mind, you're obsessed with improving that twine so that it will never break. When this job came along, it was a perfect opportunity for you to strive to meet that obsession. I couldn't take that away from you. I knew I'd find a way to cope.

"I also have to admit that, despite the independence my mother tried to instill in me, in many ways I'm a traditional woman. You were exactly the man I dreamed about marrying someday. I was more than willing to be the dutiful wife and follow you wherever you wanted to go.

"There's one last thing and I hope you don't get mad at me for what I'm about to say. I'm am indeed grateful that I am one of your obsessions, but I did not have the confidence in myself to want to put that to the test, by making you choose between your obsessions. I don't know what I would do if I lost in that competition."

Ben smiled.

"You would never lose. I'm glad you told me all this. I can

imagine the strain it must have been to keep this locked inside you."

"I must admit I do feel better. I'm going to miss you so much."

"And I'll miss you and Harry."

At that point he sat up with a shot.

"Harry! Where's Harry?"

He knew I would never do anything to jeopardize our son but it was a reflexive reaction when he realized the baby wasn't with me.

"He's fine. He's with your mother."

"My mother?"

"Yes, Molly came up by train to surprise you and bid you a bon voyage, but the surprise was on her when she'd found you'd left already. She practically threw me out the door to come to you."

"I'm glad she did."

"Me too. And she also said that as soon as I get back home I am to pack Harry's and my things and we'll go back to New Brunswick with her. That way, I won't be alone and she can spoil Harry rotten."

"That's wonderful. I'll write every day."

"You better. Now, we have about twenty minutes before your train gets in. Since I've been so pigheaded the past couple of days, you haven't had a chance to tell me about your trip. Why don't you tell me now."

He proceeded to tell me about his trek, starting with a train from North Station to Montreal and then across Canada to Vancouver. There he would get on a steamer across the Pacific to Japan. If Ben had his way, he would have made direct connections and go to Calcutta, India as soon as he could to get down to work. Two things worked against this plan. First, he'd have had to wait until the growing season and harvesting of the jute plants to observe and experiment on them. This would not happen until the end of July or beginning of August. Second, his traveling companions factored in both work and touring of the various places they would be visiting. Langdan Textiles had suppliers and customers in each of the countries they would be visiting along the way. Andrews wanted his people to drop in on them to give the personal touch. Ben would be idle most of this time, which he hated, but he resigned himself to his fate.

He would tour a few Japan cities and then take steamers to Shanghai, China followed by Canton, China and then Hong Kong, Singapore and Penang before finally alighting in Calcutta. He would spend two months in Calcutta conducting his experiments and then they would head back home but instead of coming back the same way they would go across India through the Suez Canal and up through Europe. This way his traveling companions could conduct more business as they traveled along. Ultimately, his last leg would be a steamer out of Liverpool into Boston. It all sounded so exciting. I wished I could go along with him but, with a two-month old infant to look after, that was an impossibility.

We sat for a few moments, holding hands and enjoying each other. The mood was disrupted by the piercing sound of a train whistle as the old steam locomotive chugged into the station. Ben gave me a big kiss and held me close. There was no need for us to say how much we loved the other, we knew. Ben motioned for a porter to come and help him with his trunk and bags. I pulled some change out of my purse; I knew Ben would not think to tip him. This reminded me of one last thing I could needle Ben about as he was leaving.

"You do realize that India is full of coloreds, don't you? You'll be okay with that?"

"Oh, the British know how to handle their coloreds; they keep them in their place. I'll be just fine."

I could not tell whether he was joking or not.

As the train started to slowly pull, Ben surprised me by jumping off. He gave me a big kiss and stuffed his dollar bill in my hand. As he hopped back through the train door, he looked back at me.

"Now you can be sure I'll come back to you! Goodbye my love."

As the train chugged along, gaining speed out of the station, I blew him one last kiss, tears of joy and sadness streaming down my cheeks.

23

Ben departed Boston in a lot better mood than he originally thought he would. Getting Catherine's send off gave him back his confidence. He would have been upset and anxious the entire time if things had been left the way they were. Now, he was looking forward to this trip. He was going to miss Catherine and Harry but he did not think he would mind missing six months of changing diapers, wiping up spit or waking up at 3:00 A.M. as Catherine got up to feed the infant. While he would never admit it to anyone, he did not find babies—even his own baby—all that interesting. Six months of maturation would definitely make his son much more appealing.

As Ben and a porter were working their way back through the train, he noticed his traveling companions, who had boarded at a previous stop, seated at a table in the dining car. He was tempted to join them but there would be plenty of time for socializing over the next six months. He did not feel he was one of them. Other than the difference in faiths, they were all company managers in their upper forties while he was a new employee in his twenties. Mr. Gill and Mr. Williams both seemed to be decent sorts but he definitely did not trust Searles. Mrs. Epstein had confirmed his initial impression. He would most definitely watch his back. He did not want to sit down with him right away and he was sure the feeling was mutual. He had the porter direct him to his seat.

He was put into a first class compartment that seated four. The porter pulled open the sliding door and directed him to the seat against the window facing forward. The other seats were empty. He was not sure whether they were for his corporate colleagues or other people.

The porter took Ben's jacket and hat from him and hung them on a coat rack. The seats were heavily upholstered in brown leather. The walls were covered with a strong, masculine mahogany paneling. The porter asked him if there was anything else he needed and, after Ben replied there not, the porter retired from the compartment. Ben surveyed the scene and decided he could easily get used to traveling in this manner. He was sure that most of the trip would not consist of first class accommodations, so he was determined to thoroughly enjoy them when they happened.

His luggage and the trunk containing his lab equipment had been stowed in the baggage car. He threw his smaller travel bag on the rack above his head but before he did so, he pulled out a volume to start reading Richard Wolff's Classic "Die Jute. Ihre Industrie und volkswirtschaftliche Bedeutung" ("Jute, Their Industry and Economical Meaning"). His German was a little rusty so he was appreciative of the time to work slowly through this classic volume on the uses of jute in modern society.

He was only a couple of pages into Mr. Wolff's complex analysis when the compartment doors opened and Williams and Gill entered.

"Albert," Mr. Gill intoned, "You made it! Too bad you didn't join us for lunch. Exquisite pork chops with a reduced sherry sauce. Delicious."

Then Gill stopped, realizing he may have made a faux pas.

"Sorry, Albert. You probably don't eat pork, do you?"

Ben appreciated that Mr. Gill had the sensitivity to ask.

"Mr. Gill," Ben responded with a deadpanned expression, "my wife knows that she can get anything she wants from me by making me a bacon, lettuce and tomato sandwich. One smell of that bacon and I'm like putty in her hands."

Gill laughed.

"I'll have to remember that if there's something we need from you."

The two men took their seats. Williams sat across from Ben and Gill beside him. That meant the other seat was for Searles.

"So," Ben asked, "where is Mr. Searles?"

Both men fidgeted a bit.

"He was going to enjoy a cup of coffee in the dining car for a bit," Williams finally responded but then he sighed.

"Albert, I have to be honest with you. Searles did not want you along on this trip. As a matter of fact, he was the one who was to have informed you of this trip a month ago."

Ben had suspected as much. Williams did not seem like the type who would not perform a task asked of him.

"So, Mr. Searles is jealous of my youthful good looks, huh?"

Williams smiled.

"I only wish. When we left him, he was flagging down a conductor to see about getting a different seat, either for you or for himself. He wasn't clear on that point. Searles is a harmless windbag, but then again, I'm not the one who has to put up with his prejudiced attitudes. I personally did not want him along but his overseas contacts and his know-how about oversees governments will be invaluable to our success. One thing I can assure you is that I am the senior officer and, for purposes of this trip, he reports to me. If he gets too out of line, let me know."

"Thank you, sir."

"Now, this is going to be a splendid voyage. Albert, I realize you're going to have a lot of idle time. We won't need your services for two months or so. We had to structure it this way so that Gill, Searles and I can do business in cities along the way. We have clients and vendors in Tokyo, Kobe, Shanghai, and Hong Kong that we need to drop in on. There is nothing better in business than the occasional personal face-to-face meeting. Makes the people you're dealing with feel like they're important and worthy of your time. We could have sent you to handle our jute-rotting crisis all by yourself but we decided to use this as an opportunity. Some of these clients we hadn't visited in years, so we built in these little side trips. What you choose to do with your time while we're off glad-handing is your business. All we ask is that first you don't catch any diseases in the geisha houses and that you're ready to spring into action when we need you to. I can see from your light reading material that I don't have to worry on the second count. I'll leave the first up to you."

"I'll do my best, sir."

"Good."

Williams and Gill both pulled out newspapers that they perused while Ben returned to his German volume. Looking for some small talk, Gill idly stated:

"So, Albert, Williams, Searles and I have made a few trips abroad over the years. You ever traveled overseas?"

Ben held up his handless right stump.

"Only once."

Gill turned beet red with shame but Ben's immediate hearty laugh put him at ease. Gill had a sort of gullible innocence that Ben immediately liked.

"Sorry, Mr. Gill. That was thoughtless and rude of me."

"Nonsense. I should try thinking before speaking sometimes. Other than the obvious, was it rough over there, Albert?"

"To tell you the truth, I really couldn't tell you. My battlefield experience consisted of no more than a half hour or so. We arrived at this small French town and were immediate dispatched to the front lines. I would've loved to have spent more time in that town. We were marching in and I received the biggest smile from this petite mademoiselle. Très belle, if you know what I mean. Anyway, we were sent out to the trenches. We were in this hole, which wasn't connected to any other of the trench networks. There were three of us and five French soldiers. We were starting to get acquainted with each other. As a gesture of international goodwill, I ask one of the Frenchies if he wanted a smoke. He said yes and I kneel down to pull out a pack of cigarettes out of my knapsack.

"As I'm reaching up with the pack, it hits. An artillery shell explodes right on the edge of the trench. I'll never forget the look of astonishment on the face of the Frenchman as the back of his head blows apart. If I'm standing, I'm a dead man, but I'm kneeling so the blast passes over my head. Unfortunately, my hand was reaching up. It, along with the pack of cigarettes, took the full impact."

By this time, Williams had also put his paper down and was hanging on Ben's every word as he progressed through the tale.

"I remember seeing my thumb laying in the dirt and not fully comprehending it was once attached to me. I then looked at my own hand, or what was left of it, with a kind of third-party dispassionate disinterest. The next thing I did was very relevant to Langdan Textiles. I pulled out a ball of twine, jute twine no less, and proceeded to fashion myself a tourniquet. When the first length of twine snapped, I cut a second one and that one worked. I vowed at that moment that I was going to find out why it snapped and how it could be made stronger. After that, everything is a blur. They tell me I was rather heroic and saved my sergeant and a French soldier before passing out. I got a couple of medals for my efforts, but since I don't recall anything I did to earn them, they don't mean a hell of a lot to me. As I said, I have no memory after putting on the tourniquet. Next thing I knew, I woke up in an English hospital two months and a whole bunch of operations and infections later. Jute became my life, or as my wife would put it, my obsession."

Ben pulled the piece of jute out of his trousers' pocket.

"Even though I've gotten quite proficient at telling my tale, I always pull this out for dramatic effect. For some reason, the doctors saved this for me as my battlefield memento. Rather morbid, but I carry this with me wherever I go."

Williams and Gill both eyed the dirty old piece of string as if they had made a pilgrimage to a religious relic. Williams was fascinated, but was just as happy to change the subject.

"So, you have a wife. Any kids?"

"My son Harry. Two months old," Ben proudly responded.

"Two months? You sure you're okay with going away right now?"

"Oh. it's okay. Catherine and Harry are going to stay with my mother for the duration."

"With your mother?"

"Yes, they're crazy about each other. Sometimes I suspect my mother likes Catherine more than she does me."

"Count your blessings, Albert. If I ever wanted to get rid of either my mother or my wife, all I'd have to do is lock the both of them in the same room for an hour or so. When I came back, one or both of them would be dead. My money's on Mom; she's a feisty old lady."

Gill piped in.

"In my case, I don't think it would come to actual deaths but there would be plenty of bruises and broken bones. Your injury there, Albert, would not be entirely out of the question."

They all laughed and went back to their respective reading matters. That night, Ben wrote letters to Catherine and his mother, noting how lucky they all were. He smiled to himself as he recalled her comment that his penmanship had improved since he learned to write with his left hand.

The train weaved its way up through the hills and valleys of New England. The only stop it made along the way was Concord, New Hampshire. It is often difficult to make an accurate assessment of a place through the window of a train, but Ben liked the look of the White Mountain State's capital city. He spied the gold dome of the capital as the train rumbled on its way to Montreal and decided it might be nice to visit the quaint city with Catherine and Harry one day.

The train pulled into Montreal at around ten o'clock that night. Ben still had not exchanged one word, not even a greeting, with Searles. Searles had not been able to secure a different seat on the packed train so he spent the entire ride in the café car. Ben wondered whether this was what it would be like for the next six months, not that it really bothered him one way or the other. Ben was not going to allow himself be insulted by the likes of Searles.

Because of all the trunks and luggage the four men were hauling, they hired three taxicabs to take them to the Windsor Hotel. Ben traveled with Williams while Gill and Searles each took separate cabs. In addition to his personal luggage, Ben had packed a separate trunk with a microscope, scales, beakers and other equipment necessary for him to conduct his experiments. Langdan had arranged for this trunk to be loaded on the train separately and Ben was relieved to see that it had actually made it. He originally toyed with the idea of having the company ship the trunk directly to Calcutta but then he got nervous. What if it were lost or damaged in transit? The entire reason for him going to Calcutta would be nullified if he did not have his equipment. He could not take any chances. He would simply have to travel with it the entire time.

There appeared to be some sort of festival going on throughout the city, creating a joyful atmosphere even late at night. Williams hoped aloud that their rooms would be available when they got to the hotel. He said the telegram they received acknowledged that, even though the party would be arriving late at night, there would be no problems. However, Williams noted that on previous business trips he had taken to various cities around the world he had received similar assurances only to find that the rooms had been booked to other customers who had arrived earlier or paid more. With a festival in town, hotel rooms would be at a premium and, either through a mistake or through an exchange of cash, the reserved rooms would suddenly find themselves occupied by others. Williams did not relish the idea of spending the night in the hotel lobby.

Ben was starting to get to know the personalities of the two traveling companions with whom he was speaking. In many ways they complemented each other well. Gill had a certain optimistic naiveté that could be very appealing but could also lead to foot-in-mouth comments. Williams was personable and a good conversationalist but tended towards a pessimistic outlook about things that had not yet happened.

As it turned out, the rooms had been held as promised. While Langdan was generous in how it treated its managers, the company still exhibited a New England penchant for frugality and therefore the four men had to room together throughout the trip. Ben shared a suite with Williams while Gill roomed with Searles in a more modest but still nice room. As Williams had noted, he was the senior member on this voyage and, much to Searles' consternation, would claim the premium accommodations for himself. Ben was glad that Williams chose to pair with him and not one of the others.

At times, Ben often felt rather lost in this company, being the member of the group with the most modest background. He was the only son of immigrants. Williams, for example, could trace his lineage back to Roger Williams, the founder of Rhode Island. Gill was the nearest in Ben's class but even he was used to headwaiters and room service.

The Windsor was the preeminent hotel in all of Montreal and perhaps in all of Canada. In the past, luminaries such as Sarah Bernhardt, Mark Twain, Rudyard Kipling and various members of the British royalty had frequented it.

Ben's mouth dropped as they entered the front door and he gazed up into the ornate rotunda. The suite was no less grandly appointed. He woke early the next morning to explore the rest of the hotel. He pulled out his camera and took numerous photos of the famous "Peacock Alley", located in the North Annex, which had been constructed after a fire devastated the hotel in 1906. It was so named after the peacock designs in its stained glass windows.

As agreed the previous evening, Ben met his colleagues for breakfast in the Grand Dining Hall at 7:30. Gill called out in greeting as he entered. He walked over to the table near one of the twenty-five foot tall marble pillars adorning the hall. He was surprised to see Searles sitting there with the others. He was quiet and sullen. From what Ben could gather, Williams had given Searles an ultimatum. If he wanted the company to pay for his food, he would have to dine with the others. He was welcome to eat by himself, but it would be on his own dime.

The breakfast was cordial enough. Ben, despite still feeling somewhat the outsider because of the age difference, participated in the conversation. However, even when he made a remark in response to something Searles said, Searle's subsequent response in turn would be directed to Gill and Williams.

After breakfast, Williams invited Ben to accompany him on a hike up to the top of Mt. Royal. Mr. Gill, a rather corpulent man, begged off the strain of a steep climb up the hill. Williams did not think to invite Searles. Along the way, Williams talked about his family. His wife was descended from Boston blue blood aristocracy, one of the Lodges, but unfortunately not from a line of the family that had a lot of wealth. Still, though, they lived a comfortable life in Quincy with their two daughters, Emily and Penelope. They were obviously the apples of their father's eye as he dug photos out of his wallet to show Ben. He was going to miss them sorely over the next months.

They lingered for an hour or so at the top of the hill, enjoying the fine view of Montreal and St. Lawrence valley. Ben could see that Williams wanted to be alone with his thoughts, so they both sat in relative silence for that time. Contemplation and reflection were not things that Ben was very used to, but after a short time he found it was rather therapeutic. Eventually, Williams announced it was time to head back.

They arrived in plenty of time for the train. After checking in and ensuring his bags were taken care of, Ben ran to a post office near the station and sent off several post cards to Catherine and his mother. He was determined to keep to his promise of writing every day; the trick would be finding places to post his cards and letters on a timely basis.

He then settled into his seat and gazed out at the passing countryside. He found the scenery interesting with long, narrow oblong farms and rows of wheat planted in shallow ditches.

As the young man in the entourage, Ben accepted his assignment to an upper berth for the weeklong trek across Canada. He did find navigating his way up the ladder with only one hand to be somewhat awkward, but he managed. The berth was cramped and claustrophobic, but he eventually got acclimated and enjoyed a decent night's sleep.

The train ride across Canada was uneventful, ranging from scrub wood, much of which had been ruined by forest fires, to a long series of small lakes to Manitoba, where the land was as flat as the sea.

As the train passed through an Indian reservation near Cluny, Alberta, Ben looked out the window with some distain upon a few ill-kempt specimens living in tents. He had been told that the government provided houses, which the native population did not use except in winter. He could not fathom how in this modern era people could still live in such a primitive state. He chalked it up to the 'coloreds' not being ready for civilization.

His first view of the snow-covered Rockies, hidden in low gray clouds, took his breath away. Successively, one sight after another filled him with awe: Albert Canyon and its gray-green slit in the rock with a turbulent little river at the bottom; Mount Stephen, most imposing and beautiful in the bright sun; Thompson Canyon with its clean cut rocks and green glacial stream; the rugged Fraser Canyon and its whirlpools that appeared a coffee color in the stream. Sunrise colored the snow tops of mountains a bright golden yellow while the slopes were shaded a green-purple. The railroad passed through many tunnels and reached Vancouver right on schedule.

The four men were put up in a three-room suite with two baths in Hotel Vancouver. Ben was pleasantly surprised when Searles did not put up a fuss at this arrangement. Searles had become progressively less surly, but Ben still expected histrionics at his having to share a suite with a Jew. None happened. While one would not characterize Searles' demeanor as pleasant, neither was it unpleasant.

Ben treated himself to a nice luxurious bath and a shave. This was the first he had truly enjoyed in over a week as the water on the train was very hard, making it difficult to work up a lather. He had hoped to spend the rest of the day touring Vancouver but he found that some necessary duties occupied him all afternoon. First, he had to oversee the transfer of his trunks from the train to the steamer. It was a good thing he did as the trunk with his lab equipment and supplies had been temporarily lost somewhere on the train. He hounded the steward until it was found and then personally escorted it to the steamship.

At dinner, Searles was most talkative, expounding on what he saw as loose Canadian morals. He carried on, much to the other three men's amusement, about how short and narrow the skirts were and how extremely low the necklines were. Many wore summery white things that were translucent in sunlight. To top it all off, he had seen several girls smoking at lunch. This would not do back in Boston, opined Searles.

The next day Ben called on Mrs. Dobson, an Irish woman Molly had met on the ship to America. Her name was originally O'Brien. She met her future husband, Mr. Joseph Dobson, upon stepping off the boat. They got married and settled in Vancouver where Mr. Dobson owned a thriving business exporting native Canadian products. Ben was not exactly looking forward to calling on someone he had never met before, but his mother made him promise he would contact her. Hoping she would not be home when he telephoned, she answered and insisted he join her for lunch at the Grandview Hotel the next day.

Expecting to have a quiet, boring lunch alone with Mrs. Dobson, he was greeted by the entire family: Mr. and Mrs. Dobson and their two children, Gordon and Marion. Mrs. Dobson surrounded him with a huge hug as if she had known him all her life. Ben could see why she had gathered herself a husband straight off the boat; she was quite a handsome woman. He imagined she must have been quite a red-headed, freckled stunner in her youth. But even more than that, she projected such an exuberance and life force that would be impossible for any man to resist if she set her sights on him.

Mr. Dobson, for his part, was a pleasant but quiet man. He obviously enjoyed letting his wife dominate conversations. He was an inch or so shorter than she and had a receding hairline and pince nez glasses. While it would be natural for him to appear the henpecked husband, their relationship did not come off as such. They were simply two people who enjoyed each other's company.

Both children, Ben was happy to note, were well-behaved. Gordon was about eleven years old and was beginning to take himself seriously as a young man. Ben was especially taken by Marion who, at eight years old, was by far the prettiest child he had ever laid his eyes upon. She had black eyes and hair and a round rosy face. She was not conscious of her looks, but was shy in the presence of company.

"So, how is Molly?" Mrs. Dobson asked in the remnants of a

thick Irish brogue.

"She is very well, Mrs. Dobson. Thank you for asking."

"Please, call me Hazel. To this day I still remember your parents on the ship to America. I'm not really sure why we hit it off, to tell you the truth. They spoke very little English at the time, but they were very eager to learn their soon-to-be adopted language. I used to like sitting with both of them, but especially Molly, and teach them English words. I'm surprised your mother doesn't speak English with an Irish accent!

"I can still see Molly as she ran down the stairs to announce to all of us that she had seen America in the distance. We all stood at the railing, focused on the New York skyline as it became clearer and larger. I still can feel the tear running down my cheek as I first laid eyes on the Statue of Liberty. It was then your father announced to everyone that they were from thenceforth to be known as Harry and Molly. They were being reborn in their new country right before our eyes."

"Did you know I was there, too?"

Hazel Dobson looked puzzled.

"I remember the other children who were older but I don't remember a baby."

"Well, I was partially there anyway. My mother was pregnant with me. She hadn't let anyone know, not even my father, until after they were firmly on U.S. soil. I was born in a hospital in New York, my mother's "American son" as she loves to call me."

"What a wonderful story. Did she ever tell you how I came to be on their ship out of Hamburg?"

"No, she never did."

"Well, ever since I was a little girl I dreamed of coming to America. My parents both died when I was little and there was nothing keeping me in Ireland. I scrimped and saved every penny I could get my hands on. The day I reached legal age, I made my way to Belfast to book my fare. I paid this man who gave me a ticket and directed me to the boat. I boarded all excited as get out. After a bit, though, I thought the afternoon sun should be in a different direction so I went to a sailor and asked him how long it was going to take to get to America. He looks at me like I'm crazy. "America?" he says, "Dis boat ain't agoin' t'America. We're on our way t'Hamburg." Well, I nearly fainted right there but I'm never one to dwell on such things so I settled in Hamburg, working in a bar for a couple of years and scrimpin' and savin' all over again. I went down to the port once again, but this time I made sure I got on the correct boat. It all turned out well. I got to meet your lovely parents and then when we docked in New York, Mr. Dobson was waiting for some goods that were in the hold of that ship. I prefer to think that he was waiting for me."

Hazel reached across and held the hand of her husband who looked back at her with profound affection. They then ordered lunch. Hazel said grace, which was a relatively new experience for Ben.

After lunch, Mr. Dobson piled everybody into his Chevrolet for a beautiful drive around Stanley Park, which was noted for its many huge cedar trees. Then they drove through Shaughnessy Heights, where the new rich, including the Dobsons, had their residences. He thanked the Dobsons for a lovely afternoon when they dropped him at the hotel.

The next day, Thursday, June 4, 1920 was the King's Birthday, a national holiday and all the stores were closed. Ben used the time to write a letter to his mother, recounting his lunch with the Dobson family and all the stories they shared. He also wrote to Catherine, telling her about the wonderful family and hoping they would be able to have as nice a family.

Ben and his companions went down to the harbor and claimed their staterooms on the steamship, the Canadian Pacific steamship *Monteagle*. The four men were put into in a two-room suite and private bath. Williams and Searles occupied the rear room, with a brass bed, a davenport and an imitation fireplace while Gill and Ben took the forward compartment with an upper and lower berth.

Boarding the ship just in front of Ben and his party was the actress Elsie Ferguson. Gill, an avid devotee of the moving pictures, recognized her in an instant. He had seen all the films of Chaplin, Keaton, Pickford, Valentino, the Gishes and a host of other stars of the silver screen. This was the first time he had ever come face to face with one of his heroes and he was beside himself.

When Ben expressed ignorance about Miss Ferguson, Gill launched into a recitation of all her pictures. His favorite had been *Barbary Sheep*. This 1917 work was set in Algiers. Elsie (Gill spoke of her as if they were on a first name basis) played the heroine, Lady Katherine Wyverne, who leaves her neglectful sportsman husband for a charismatic Arab chieftain named Benchaalal. A scandal brews as Lady Katherine's reputation and social standing plummet but at the last minute her husband intervenes and rescues the heroine from disgrace. It was most thrilling and entertaining. According to Gill, Elsie displayed fine acting talents. Ben muttered something about making it a point to see it sometime, although he knew he never would devote his time to such drivel.

Gill also knew all about the personal and professional life of the eminent thespian and how she had the power to hold several studios at bay, each of which wanted to lock her into a contract. Ultimately she signed to an eighteen film, three year contract by the famous producer and director Adolph Zukor. She was commanding an unheard of amount of $5,000 per week. When Ben professed to have never heard of Mr. Zukor either, Gill threw up his hands, bemoaning the paucity of his young colleague's cultural experience. Ben simply smiled in return.

Miss Ferguson was accompanied by a traveling companion, a Mr. McKinstry. Once on the steamer, Gill worked hard to exude considerable charm and ingratiate himself into their presence. Soon he found himself in their company most of the time they were on board the boat. They spent hours with another woman playing bridge. Ben did not play bridge nor did he have any interest in learning but, even with his lack of knowledge at the game, he could see that Gill was a terrible player, often resulting in cries of exasperation from his partner. Despite continually losing money, Gill persevered.

Ben was amused by Gill's infatuation with Elsie Ferguson. For her part, the actress seemed to enjoy Gill's company but Ben could tell that her true affections were saved for Mr. McKinstry. Ben hoped that Gill would not be too devastated when he and Miss Ferguson parted company upon reaching Japan.

The ship set sail from Vancouver exactly at 9:30, too dark to see the shores of Puget Sound at all clearly. After a week on board a train, Ben felt the trip had finally begun as the steamer set out for the open sea.

24
Catherine

I eagerly ripped open the letter from Ben. As he had promised, he had written everyday but up until now they had been predominantly postcards with a 'wish you were here' note scribbled on it. This letter was different.

Ben has never been what one would call effusive or demonstrative. This letter, however, showed a side of him that few people see. In it he described a lovely get together he had with an old friend of Molly's. He described how the warm family life really meant something to him. He apologized again for running out on me the way he did and promised never to leave me again. Once he got back, he wanted to have a full family life, giving Harry some brothers and sisters along the way.

I smiled, but was unsure on how large a family I myself wanted. We could discuss that when he returned. I was just happy to hear how much he missed Harry and me.

He went on to tell me about his traveling companions. Mr. Gill was the funny affable one with a penchant for speaking before he thought, sometimes with hilarious results. He had a crush on an actress who was on board; Ben thought it was cute. Mr. Williams was a warm-hearted family man who could sometimes be a little too thoughtful and overly pessimistic. He had taken Ben under his wing.

There was something in his description of Mr. Searles that made me worry. He told about how standoffish and downright rude he was at the beginning of the trip but that he had since softened somewhat, although they still weren't on what one would call speaking terms. Ben attributed his attitude to blatant anti-Semitism, but he noted that neither of the other gentlemen was overly friendly with Searles either. In general, he was a disagreeable human being to everyone.

As expected, Molly had been my lifesaver. During the first two months of Harry's life when we were living in Boston, I was never able to get away. Once we moved down to New Brunswick, Molly would on occasion kick me out of the house. She said she wanted to be alone with her grandson, but I knew she was giving me some time to myself. She also got me a part time job working on the books for the butcher shop.

While in school, I was forced to take primarily liberal arts courses, but Dean Douglass made sure we were also taught some more practical courses such as accounting and finance. I found I had somewhat of a penchant for these subjects. When I mentioned this to Molly, she had an idea. After her husband's store failed, Molly went to work for a butcher, Mr. Louis Bress. Mr. Bress was a fine butcher but a terrible businessman. He could not manage his finances and the books were in disarray. Molly suggested I help him to improve his accounting system. At first he was reluctant; I was a woman, after all. But even he had to admit that things were a mess and something had to be done. Furthermore, he trusted Molly, so he agreed.

It was exciting to have my first real job. It was also perfect because much of my work could be done from home while still watching over Harry. I gathered all of Mr. Bress's receipts and sales slips and any other relevant pieces of paper I could lay my hands on. It took me five full days just to catalogue everything. Then I gradually started to make sense of it.

He had a very successful business and should have been generating a far greater profit than he had. Something was not right. The first thing I discovered was that over the course of many months, he had been double paying one of his main suppliers. For some inexplicable reason, he had created two different bank accounts and was paying the vendor twice, once from each account, for the same items.

When I pointed this out to Mr. Bress, he hit the roof. At first he said I must be mistaken; these were people he had dealt with for over twenty years. They were honest people and, if he had been doing this, he was sure they would have pointed it out to him. I knew I was absolutely correct, though, and I proceeded to show him all the records. After that he was more embarrassed than anything that he had stupidly let this go on for so long. Then he vacillated between wanting to string his supplier up and just moving on without any fuss. I suggested a middle road.

I thought he could at least outwardly give his supplier the benefit of the doubt. Maybe they were as oblivious as he was that this was happening. He should approach them, point out the error and suggest that he be reimbursed over time for the overcharges while maintaining their business relationship. If not, he would look for another vendor. This way, he would recoup his losses and the vendor could save face by having the appearance, whether it was true or not, that it was inadvertent. Mr. Bress appeared content with this approach.

I also found that Mr. Bress had a tendency to wait until the last moment to order essential supplies such as the paper to wrap meats. He would notice he was down to his last roll and call frantically to get some rolls delivered. Often, he would pay a premium to get them delivered the next day. I took over managing his inventory, ordering what he needed in bulk at reduced prices and ensuring that he had what he needed when he needed them

Over time, Mr. Bress was not only comfortable with having a woman in this role but came to rely on me more and more. I was in the shop one time with Harry, actually buying some chicken for soup, when a gentleman came in soliciting business from Mr. Bress, seeing if he would be willing to put a display of kosher canned goods in the front of the store. Mr. Bress heard him out and then told him he would have to see what his "business manager" thought of the proposal, whereupon he turned to me and asked what I thought. I don't think I was ever prouder of myself in my life than I was at that moment. I personally thought Mr. Bress could get a bigger percentage of the sales than the man was offering and I told him so.

The man scowled at Harry and me when Mr. Bress went back to him asking for an additional ten percent. I thought an additional five percent would have been fair but I told Mr. Bress to press for ten and negotiate from there. It was far more important for this man that the deal be struck than it was for Mr. Bress, so I thought we were operating from a position of strength. Eventually, the two men arrived at a seven percent increase. They shook hands and the man departed. Mr. Bress gave me a big wink and a smile.

I sat down and wrote all of this in a letter to Ben. Before he had left, he told me to send all my letters to a Mrs. Epstein at Langdan who in turn would forward them along with other correspondence to the traveling party.

In my letter, I joked that this was a twist. Generally, the stereotype is that the gentiles look to the Jews for financial assistance but here I was, a shiksa, managing the business operations of a Jewish butcher. I was hoping Ben would be excited about my foray into the man's world of business but I could not be sure. Most of the time he was so supportive of my initiative and independence but on occasion he could revert to a traditional view on men and women's roles in society. Especially after his observation that he wanted a large family, I was nervous that I was going to become a stay at home wife the rest of my life. I wanted more.

25

Like the long train ride before it, Ben and his associates settled into a routine during the steamship cruise. The main difference was the seasickness that each of them felt during the initial phase of the excursion. As Mr. Williams eloquently put it, "We heard a calling; yes, we heard it true. We have donated our supper to the Pacific Ocean. No hard feelings. Much better thanks."

The bond between Williams and Ben strengthened as the trip progressed. Ben was appreciative of the attention Williams gave him, but he could not quite figure out why this man who was twenty years his senior was doing so. They were different in so many ways. Williams was a devout tea-totaling Methodist; Ben a non-observant Jew who liked to imbibe on occasion. Williams could be at times be rather dour and pessimistic; Ben was generally a light-hearted optimist. Williams had only a high school education and had achieved everything in life through hard work and dedication; while Ben was no slouch when it came to hard work, he was a college-educated man for whom most things came rather easily. In spite of these differences, they were becoming close friends.

Williams' only observable vice was his love for fine cigars. Ben did not smoke but he would accompany Williams to the smoking room. It was the most beautiful room on the ship, finished in oak with deep leather chairs and writing desks. There was also a bar where they dispensed hard and soft drinks. Ben was rather surprised to see three attractive young women smoking cigarettes and drinking small yellow cocktails. He even ran across Gill's fair actress as she came in just before lunch looking for a place to smoke. Ben did not find it as scandalous as Searles had but he was taken aback somewhat as he had never seen women smoke before.

Ben would use the time in the smoking room to write letters or to read a book but sometimes he and Williams would just chat.

"Mr. Williams," Ben began.

"Please, after all this time I think you can call me Herb."

"Okay, Herb. I just wanted to let you know that I appreciate the friendship you've shown me. As the youngest and least senior of our group, I definitely can sometimes feel the odd man out. You and Mr. Gill have made me feel very welcome and included. Thank you."

"You're most welcome, Ben."

"Can I ask you one question, though?"

Williams nodded.

"Why?"

"Why what?"

"Why did we become friends? I am the first to admit that I am a rather dull young man. I don't share a lot of interests with any of you. In fact, I can't say that I have a whole lot of interests at all. My wife once told me that I am a man guided by, and even consumed by, my obsessions and one of my main obsessions is my work, my research. There are very few other people who would count this as a shared interest. I don't mean any offense, sir. I'm just curious, that's all."

"No offense taken, son. First off, you're a far more interesting character than you give yourself credit for. But let me tell you what made me want to get to know you."

With this he looked around to make sure no one was listening.

"It was your service in the war. You see, I was a Rough Rider."

Ben sat up straight up in his chair.

"One of Teddy Roosevelt's Rough Riders?"

"The very same."

"I didn't know."

"No one does."

"Why not? That's one of the most famous units ever in our military. Your charge up San Juan Hill is the stuff of legend. I would think you'd want your kids and someday your grandkids sitting on your knee hearing about your exploits!"

"For about ten years after I came back I was that way but as I got older and the world slid towards the Great War, I got to thinking over how silly it all was. My war was simply America puffing out its chest, showing the world that we were a force to be reckoned with. When the real fighting started in 1914, fighting that determined the future of the world, it made me a little embarrassed about my little war. When you started to work for the company, I heard you lost your hand in the war and I really felt embarrassed but I also felt very proud to have you working under me."

"I don't see why you should feel embarrassed or ashamed. You did what you were asked to do at the time. That's about all any of us can do."

"In my mind, I know you're right. I should be proud, but I just can't bring myself to be that way. I do hope you will keep my little secret to yourself. I just want to go through the rest of my life without that bit of notoriety."

"Your secret dies with me, Herb. Still, someday I suspect you'll be bouncing a grandson on your knee regaling him with your Rough Rider exploits."

Williams smiled.

"Perhaps. But until then we'll just keep it between us. Thank you."

The days on the ship bled into each other. Many of the passengers lost themselves in marathon games of bridge and draw poker in the smoking room. Gill, Elsie Ferguson and their respective partners were usually playing bridge. A group of French people played a game Ben did not recognize but he enjoyed listening in their French discussions and arguments. He was proud of the amount of French he had retained from his cramming on his trip across the Atlantic heading toward the war.

Searles made friends with a sprightly female who ironically smoked cigarettes in a long green cigarette holder. Ben first saw them together in the smoking room, each holding a brandy and laughing at some obviously witty comment Searles had just made. The way they were giggling, Ben figured they must have been on their second or third brandy. Ben claimed one of the upholstered chairs on the far side of the room, hoping to read a book he had found in the ship's library. This became impossible, however, after the two of them and another woman got extremely loud during a hectic and loud game of craps at a nickel a point. Searles was losing but he did not seem to care. Several people got up and left the room, disturbed by the commotion, but Searles did not seem to feel in the least rebuked.

As the ship passed the Aleutian Islands, the passengers all rushed to the starboard side to look at several whales jumping out of the water. Ben tried to get pictures but he doubted his lenses were good enough to make it out. Searles also took a couple with his camera, which had much more expensive lenses, but Ben was certainly not going to ask him for a set of prints. They saw a flock of small birds in the afternoon. There must have been a hundred of them. Gill said they usually follow pretty closely to the whales. The passengers tried to make out the Aleutians on the horizon, but only with a set of binoculars could they make out a long line of snow-capped mountains.

One day, Ben was sitting in a deck chair enjoying the sun and reading *The Portygee* Joseph C. Lincoln's new novel when an old man passed him as he walked around the deck. He had a piece of rope in his hands. Every time he passed Ben he stopped and made a knot in the rope, indicating he had finished another circuit. After the fourth time of doing this, Ben had to ask him what he was doing.

"Oh, about 3 knots an hour, I figure."

Ben burst out laughing.

"You were hoping that some stooge would ask you that question, didn't you?"

"Yes, and I thank you kindly for finally asking. I was getting tired."

And off he went back inside the cabin.

At 5:00 in the morning of Monday, June 14, 1920, ten days after they had left Vancouver, Ben woke from a sound sleep. He had not set an alarm for that time but just woke naturally. He found that, even without his traditional first cup of coffee, he was alert and ready to start the day. He quietly dressed and, without disturbing the others, went up on deck. The sky was clear and the air was cool and clear.

Standing on the ship's bow, he peered out in the distance as the dawn's light began to illuminate the horizon. He could first make out a layer of low-hanging fog but slowly and surely that gave way to a sight of the Japanese coast. It was very hilly, each hill looking like a cone. The mountains came to the water edge. Here and there were villages squatted in a little cove or wherever there was a flat place. The hills were terraced in many places, providing flat places to grow crops.

Ben later wrote of this experience to his mother, telling her that it gave her at least a little of the feeling she must have experienced being the first on the S.S. Pennsylvania to view the outline of the American coastline as the ship approached. Unlike Molly, however, Ben did not run below deck to wake his traveling companions to announce that land was approaching. He could just imagine the looks of consternation aimed in his direction if he did so. Instead, he stood at the rail and soaked in the sight and the feel of the cool breeze on his face.

The ship passed many fishing boats and a few eastbound steamers in the early morning. By noon, the *Monteagle* was steaming down the coast between islands. The passengers had a good view of fishing villages, curious sails on small crafts, and terraced hills. At one point, Ben looked over and saw Gill standing at the rail with Elsie Ferguson. While they were not holding hands, Ben could tell that there was some level of affection between the two. Given Gill's infatuation with the actress, Ben had to smile but he was also worried about his friend's mood—not to mention his effectiveness at doing his job—when they went their separate ways.

About four o'clock the ship approached the fortifications that guarded Tokyo Bay and passed through the harbor's narrow entrance. As the ship passed a Japanese battleship, Ben recalled his reading about Japan's convincing victories on both land and sea in the Russo-Japanese War of 1904-05. This had whetted Japan's imperial appetite. They had participated in the Great War on the side of Great Britain, France, Russia and America to expand their influence in China and throughout eastern Asia. He quietly speculated that their imperial ambitions may not have been sated, but it was certainly not something to which he was going to devote a lot of thought or worry.

They anchored outside the Yokohama breakwater for the Customs and Immigration officers to come aboard. The passengers and crew had to assemble in the dining room and file out as their names were called. The count was correct; Ben was relieved that no one had either stowed away or dropped overboard. An incorrect count could have resulted in hours of delay as the authorities tried to straighten it all out.

After that the passengers went up to the smoking room and stood in line to get their passports stamped and to be issued a police pass to go ashore. They then proceeded to the deck as the boat pulled into dock. Ben surveyed the scene as they moored. Yokohama harbor was a broad bay with a seawall across the mouth. A red and white lighthouse marked the entrance to the enclosed area. Small boats entered and exited the harbor through an opening at either side also. The port was bustling; there were many steamers in port, some of them from the United States.

As soon as possible everyone went ashore. On the wharf, their hand luggage was inspected and marked with a piece of chalk. Over to the side was a line of rickshaws waiting for fares. Each man took a separate rickshaw. The drivers spoke only a little English but they were able to understand that the group was to go to Yokohama's Grand Hotel. Ben had never been in a rickshaw before and he felt very conspicuous and decidedly foolish perched up in that little buggy. He also received his first lesson in Asian economics. The man asked 50¢, and Ben gave him a Canadian half, which he said was at a discount, and asked 10¢ more. Ben gave him 5¢ more, thinking he had been shrewd. Once he got inside the hotel, he found the fare was 30¢ at the most and 25¢ if you drove a good bargain. Ben learned right there that, with the exception of postage stamps and railroad tickets, one must dicker and haggle down to about two thirds the asking price throughout all of the Far East.

The party had good rooms at the hotel. Williams and Ben shared a room with two single beds. The room had very high ceilings and was big enough to easily fit two more beds. It opened out on to a wide alcove with four very wide high windows looking out on the boulevard and the harbor. There was also a huge balcony. The room occupied by Gill and Searles was similar, except no balcony. The four of them decided that, rather than venturing out that first evening, they would have dinner on the balcony. Despite having very broken English, a Japanese waiter, who Ben thought to be rather effeminate, served a sumptuous meal of local fishes that had been roasted over an open fire.

To Ben's surprise, Searles was affable and chatty during dinner, even directing a few friendly inquiries in Ben's direction. Searles revealed he had once been married but his wife, Edy, had passed away many years previously. He missed her still. Ben found himself actually having some sympathy for the man.

A little business was discussed during the dinner primarily because the first client visit was scheduled for the next day. Williams indicated that Ben was free to join them for the meeting but he knew he would have nothing to offer so he politely declined.

The next day, Ben's first chore was to change some money for the group. For his American and Canadian dollars, he received an assortment of Yens and Sens and a handful of little nickel coins the size of a cent and a few big copper discs. To Ben, the stuff did not look like money, feel like money or smell like money, but as he noted, it had the international habit of saying goodbye very readily. He got back to the hotel lobby just as the other three men were coming down. Their meeting was not until later in the afternoon so they all decided to tour the city in the morning. Ben distributed the money. He noted that Searles was back to being his usual surly self.

The four men hired rickshaws at a yen an hour at the stand back of the hotel. The drivers took them to the main street, where they saw the banks and post office, then through a market where the streets were ten feet wide but the smells were also ten feet high. They saw all kinds of raw and cooked meats, grain, meal, cakes and bread for sale in the open front shops.

Then the rickshaws took them to Sinyskiwara, in the segregated or red light district. In the short time they had been in Japan, Ben had observed that the Japanese geisha were very widely advertised and spoken of in general conversation. In his experience, it was not considered good form to discuss the professional prostitute of America, nor the coquette of France, in public. However, the segregated districts were found in all the large Japanese cities and had government blessing.

The rickshaws took the group across the end of town to an area near the canal that teamed with life and was full of picturesque native sampans. They went along a road by the canal, looking into the shops along the way. All the stores were electrically lighted, so there was no trouble seeing. The streets were crowded with people of all ages in various Japanese costumes and also in European clothes.

The trio had a follow-up meeting the following morning so Ben spent the day touring Tokyo after catching the 8 o'clock train out of Yokohama to Tokyo. The seats on the train ran the length of the car and were very wide and rather low. They were fairly comfortable but it was rather tiring to ride sideways all the time. Many of the native Japanese got around that by shedding their shoes and squatting on their feet. Ben found the whole sight rather amusing.

Ben spent the afternoon walking around Tokyo, observing Japanese life. He went to the American quarter up on a hill overlooking the city after which he came down a side path by an old Buddhist temple and then some more very crooked narrow streets back to the canal, which crossed very near the hotel.

By the time he got back to the hotel, the other three had returned and they all had tea together. They all then went to the famous Benten-dori, the best place in the east to buy silks and ivory. Ben picked a few items for gifts including an enameled mother of pearl cigar holder for Williams to thank him for his kindnesses on this trip. Williams picked up a beautiful heavy black brown silk kimono for his wife. Gill got a black, gold and silver damascene pin. He did not say for whom he purchased it, but Ben got the sense that he was going to send it to Elsie Ferguson.

They came back to the hotel, had a special early dinner, and then went to the train for the next leg of their trip, Kyoto. This time, they purchased tickets on the train for what they termed a "first class' car, although Ben and his companions could not determine what made it "first class." They had three extremely narrow upper berths. Williams was able to procure a lower berth by tipping the conductor, but he could not get any more lowers. It was hot, and stuffy. Because of a constant rain, they could not open a window.

The train reached Kyoto at 7:30. The rain had only intensified. They found an officious hotel porter with questionable English who put them in a shuttle to the Kyoto Hotel. They then rented a Hudson and went into the city. They saw the imperial palace grounds and a beautiful temple on a hill. They toured the cloisonee works, where they make pots, urns and other things by making designs in metal, filling the scratches with fine wire and then filling the open surfaces with enamel, with many successive firings.

The following morning it was on to Kobe for the next leg of the journey. This train was only 2nd and 3rd Class. One Japanese woman sat with five big bundles arranged around her. She spread a square of silk on the seat, shed her shoes and squatted down on the cloth with her feet under her. She smoked cigarettes all the way to Kobe, and was still on the car when they got out. Next to her was a man in a silk kimono but on top of his head was a panama hat. He shed his shoes promptly, arranged his nest and curled up on it. There was a very old couple in their car, too, who were seen off by a large and clamorous family. They shed their shoes, of course, squatted on the seat and took great interest in everything that went on.

It was raining all the time, so the people were out in straw raincoats, big conical straw hats and big Japanese oiled paper umbrellas. It looked to Ben like a bunch of sheaves of straw walking around.

The train reached Kobe and the group took rickshaws to the dock. The ship was just coming down the harbor, having been delayed by fog. They boarded and claimed their rooms but the ship was not to depart until the next day.

After spending nearly a week in Tokyo and Yokohama, the travelers had only a day to see the sights of Kobe. Williams begged off because of a stomachache and Searles, being his usual contrary self, declined to go along. Ben and Gill set off on their own as soon as the ship docked in the port. They flagged down a rickshaw, negotiated a price, and went off to explore the city. The man spoke passable English and promised them a "top-notch" tour of the city. The first stop was the Nauko Temple, the main sight of Kobe.

At one point, the rickshaw man stopped in front of a nondescript door in the middle of a block, pointed and said: "Bath-house, have look-see?" It sounded interesting, so Gill and Ben went in. A withered but spry old woman who spoke no English beyond a few words greeted them.

Beyond a little entryway there was a back room that had a sooty stove and a series of glazed earthen pots in a ring. The pots were filled with water into which heated stones would be dropped. The clientele could then either bathe in the water or toast in the steam. The room had one very small window and a tight door, so it certainly made a good steam room.

Instead of being guided into this room, the woman said "upstairs", so up they went where they found four small square rooms. The rooms had sliding paper screens and floors covered with straw matting, just like they had read in the tour books. Instead of more bathing apparatus, the two men found four Japanese maidens in full geisha dress, hair and makeup sitting on a mat in one of the rooms. They spoke varying degrees of English. One of the girls, the most dainty of the quartet, spoke perfect English with an American accent.

Ben's initial impulse was to flee, but there was something about the girl that intrigued him so he remained. Gill obviously was ready to tarry for a while. The girls invited them to come in and sit down.

This was Ben's introduction to the world of geisha. When he had shipped over to France in the Great War he had wondered if he would succumb to the French women and maybe even experiment with a brothel or two. However, his stay in that country was so abbreviated he never found out. Now, he was married and, remembering Catherine and his son back in the States, he did not know what he was going to do in this setting, but he decided to stay and see what happened.

The women offered to dance individually or collectively in any desired state of dress or undress for 10 yen. Ben and Gill had been in Japan long enough to know that it would have been impolite not to haggle the price down, so they politely declined. The price was promptly reduced to 8 and then 6 yen. When they said that 5 yen was the lowest they could go, Ben nodded. Gill immediately followed suit.

Ben took the hand of the English-speaking geisha and led her to one of the adjoining vacant rooms, leaving Gill with a huge grin on his face as he contemplated being alone with the other three. Ben sat down cross-legged on the floor as the geisha began to disrobe.

"No, hold on for a bit," Ben told her, "I'd just like to talk first, if that's okay."

The geisha nodded demurely and sat down facing Ben.

"What's you're name?"

"Kiko," she responded.

"It's a pleasure to meet you, Kiko. My name's Ben. How did you learn such good English?"

"I grew up in Kearney, New Jersey. My parents immigrated to America before I was born."

"Kearney? Talk about a small world. I grew up in New Brunswick."

Kiko seemed neither amazed nor impressed by the coincidence.

"If you were born in America, why are you here in Japan?"

"My parents first settled in California, near Sacramento, where there were plenty of Japanese. For some reason that they never explained to me, they moved to Kearney where we were the only Japanese family in the entire city. My father tried to run a small grocery store but he could not make a go of it. After the store failed, he tried several other things but they never worked out. Then, after years of me coming home from school crying because I was picked on, they decided we would come back to Japan. I was eleven. When I was thirteen, a train derailed and twenty people were killed. My parents were two of those people. I lived with my mother's brother for a few months until he raped me and threw me out of the house. I was sitting on a park bench when Madame Yakamori found me. She's the old woman who led you up here. With my English, I was very valuable to her. I've been here ever since."

"How long is that?"

"Six years."

Kiko told her story with such detachment and casual disinterest that she could have been reading a shopping list. When Ben failed to say anything more, Kiko asked him a simple question.

"Do you want me to take my clothes off now?"

Ben nodded his assent.

She stood up and untied the sash around her waist opening her kimono, which she then let slip to the floor. At this point, she glided into her role as she smiled coquettishly at Ben. She then hid her face except for her eyes behind a blue and yellow fan decorated with an assortment of birds. Ben had not seen her pull the fan out of her kimono so he was surprised when it opened to its fullness with a simple flick of her wrist.

She proceeded to undulate her hips, slowly swaying before taking a few graceful steps along the floor around him. She had a wonderfully lithe, athletic body. Ben wondered what her face looked like behind the paint. He imagined her to be a cute girl.

He could feel himself getting aroused. He was still unsure what he wanted to do or what he would do. His mind raced from Catherine, Harry and his mother at home to the delectable creature dancing before him and back again. He tried rationalizing that geisha was a revered profession; these women were accorded great status in Japanese society. He could justify his actions as taking part fully in Japanese culture. As he was ruminating and imagining himself making love to the young woman, Kiko stopped dancing.

"If you want to make love to me, that will be 5 yen more," upon which she smiled mischievously, "or as the other girls here say: 'fuckee, fuckee, five yen.' "

The starkness of the sex for money offer, not to mention the crude vernacular, brought Ben quickly out of his reveries. He politely declined and thanked her for the fine dance as he stood up. Kiko put back on her kimono. He pulled out his wallet and extracted a fifty yen note, which he handed to her.

"Wait here while I go to the madam to get you change," she said as she started for the door.

"No, you keep it."

Ben then pulled a five yen note from his wallet.

"Here, this is what you can give to the madam."

She smiled and kissed him on the cheek. Ben detected her eyes welling up. Most likely the girls were required to turn over all the money they made to the madam and then received a pittance in return as their share. Or even more likely, they did not receive any payment, instead having to be satisfied with room and board as their recompense. Fifty yen was probably more than Kiko would make in several months or maybe a full year.

She thanked him, making a little bow.

Ben smiled back and headed out the door, leaving her standing there in her kimono, which was still slightly open. He went downstairs and asked the old lady if Gill were still upstairs. He thought she said, "He upstairs yes," so he sat down and waited in the vestibule. A half hour later Gill clamored down the stairs, a broad smile etched on his face.

"My, that was something, wasn't it, Ben? When you left, they gave me a choice of one or two or all three of them. I figured you only live once so what the hell, I went with all three. I never imagined there were so many possibilities and combinations, eh Ben?"

Ben said nothing, but hoped that Gill would not get into any further vulgarities. Fortunately, Gill just walked on with a stupid satisfied look on his face, lost in his own little world. When they exited the bathhouse, they found their rickshaw driver right where they had left him.

"You have good time?" he asked.

"Oh yes, yes indeed," replied Gill.

Ben said nothing as he climbed into the rickshaw.

They proceeded out to a wide alleyway and passed by many shops as they wound their way back to the ship. As it had poured rain for the last hour of the trip, the rickshaw man was soaked. Gill sheepishly admitted he did not have any money left and asked Ben if he would pay for the rickshaw. Ben laughed and gave the man 4 yen instead of the 2.70 yen they had negotiated at the beginning. The man was very pleased, bowing numerous times as they headed up the dock to the ship.

As they were walking up the gangplank, Gill turned to Ben.

"Ben, our little side trip today, no one else needs to know about that, okay? Williams can sometimes be a stick-in-the-mud and Searles is, well Searles is Searles. We'll keep it between us, agreed?"

Even though he had done nothing—at least in comparison to Gill's activities anyway—Ben had no intention of ever telling anyone anything about that day.

"Mr. Gill, I don't know what you're talking about. We took a rickshaw ride all around town, saw a few temples, bought a couple trinkets and generally had a very congenial time. I can't imagine why you would want to keep this to ourselves, but if that is your wish, then I shall be more than happy to accommodate you."

Gill let out a hearty laugh and slapped Ben on his back.

"You're alright there, Mr. Albert, quite alright indeed!"

The ship was scheduled to depart Kobe for Nagasaki at noon the next day. Before they left, Ben wanted to be alone with his thoughts and went for a walk in the morning.

At around 10:00, he decided it was time to return to the ship. In his wanderings, he had worked his way to the other side of the bay from the ship. As he was deciding whether to walk back or hire himself a rickshaw, he saw several small boats go by that looked like water taxis. Deciding that was the way to go, he went to a nearby pier and caught one of these launches back to the steamer.

As the small craft was bobbing its way through the choppy water, Ben noticed a similar launch heading in the opposite direction. In the boat was a petit, pretty young woman wearing a grey kimono. Her shoulder length hair blew in the breeze. Unlike many women Ben had seen, she was wearing no makeup or jewelry. It was not until the boats were nearly side by side did she happen to look in his direction. In an instant they both recognized the other. It was Kiko.

Ben was under the impression that the girls were not allowed to venture far from the bathhouse so he wondered what she was doing out on this launch. The only possibility was that she was leaving, or more precisely, escaping.

She nodded in his direction and smiled, but it was a sad smile. Then she turned her gaze forward. As the boats receded from each other, all Ben could see was the back of her head and her flowing hair in the breeze. He hoped she was heading out to find herself a new life. He silently wished her Godspeed.

26
Catherine

Harry was getting big. Ben had been gone nearly three weeks now and in that time our son was becoming quite the little man. I could be with him all the time if I wanted, but Molly loved to have her time alone with him as well so I'd leave for a few hours to go downtown or to visit some of my old classmates.

Mr. Bress was amazed at how his business was growing now. He didn't have any additional customers than he did before, but he was able to save money and pour it back into the business to make more money. He was very pleased and he never hesitated to give me ample credit for his success.

I hadn't heard from Ben in awhile, but he had warned me that there may be times when it would be difficult to drop his cards or letters in the post. I figured one day the mailman would show up and hand me a stack of accumulated mail that Molly and I would eagerly sort through.

On that last day at the train station, the day I finally deigned to talk to Ben (what a fool I was and how much more of a fool would I have been if I hadn't rushed to the station to see him off), he sketched out a rough itinerary for me. Right now, on June 20, 1920, he would be, let me see, at sea between Japan and China. He had said he wouldn't have much to do yet. His traveling companions would be meeting with clients along the way in Japan and China and Hong Kong but he wouldn't be busy until he got to Calcutta. This would give him time to tour.

He said he was going to take lots of pictures, but I remember his previous attempts at photography as being dubious at best. We'd better count on the postcards he would buy.

I'd written him every day and sent weekly packages to Mrs. Epstein. I hoped she was forwarding them. She seemed like a very nice person so I didn't doubt she was sending them on.

It's probably noticeable by the way I'm rambling on that I'm sort of at loose ends today. It happens to me occasionally when I get into a mood where I really miss Ben and wish he were here right now. I'll get over it soon; I always do. For now I'll go play with Harry. He's looking so much like his father now. Everyone says so. His Uncle Sol says he looks just like Ben did when he was a baby. There are worse things.

27

Nagasaki, Shanghai, Manila, Hong Kong. Ben enjoyed the sights and soaked in the culture, albeit a somewhat primitive culture to his way of thinking, but what he really wanted was to finally get to work. Accompanying the other three men, who all seemed accustomed to idle time, must have been a good idea when it was first conceived, but he could not understand why he did not remain home for another month at which time he could have gone directly to Calcutta as the jute harvesting season approached. Idleness was not something he ever wanted to get used to.

Williams sensed Ben's discomfort and tried to include him in meetings whenever possible but it was not always practical since those meetings involved sales, marketing and other such matters. Such was the case when Williams went alone to a meeting at the Bank of Hong Kong, the primary agent for Langdan in the city. When he returned, the four got together for lunch in the hotel restaurant.

"When I arrived at the bank this morning," Williams advised the others, "there was a telegram waiting for me. It was from the head of operations in Calcutta giving us a heads-up that there was an accident. An electrical transformer exploded. Five men were killed."

Gill was especially taken aback by the news.

"Five men? Seems rather strange. In my experience these transformers are generally located in small buildings or sheds away from the main building. Tough cramming one man in there let alone five."

"The telegram didn't give much detail. They just wanted to let us know. Because the men were natives, the town is in a bit of an uproar. They anticipate the situation to be calmed by the time we arrive, but, in case it isn't, we'll know what we're walking into."

It was Searles' turn to make his thoughts known.

"Natives? That's good. They can be more easily replaced than the skills Americans or English offer."

While Ben agreed with Searles in concept that a white man was worth more than a colored man, he was still appalled that someone would articulate such a thought out loud. He offered his two cents.

"I hope they didn't have families."

Searles just shrugged and affected a 'who cares?' attitude.

"That's none of our concern," was all he said.

Before anyone could respond further, Williams, a religious man who valued all life, was uncomfortable with the direction the conversation was heading.

"Like I said, no details. No good speculating on what might have happened or what the consequences are. I just trust that the authorities will have the situation well under control by the time we get there."

Ben thought about his response to Catherine the day he departed: "Oh, the British know how to handle their coloreds. They keep them in their place. I'll be just fine." He still believed this to be true and order would be restored.

The men headed out to a restaurant recommended by the hotel. They walked along the Hong Kong waterfront to the Chinese restaurant district. They passed a number of Chinese lying around, smoking, drinking and eating, warily eyeing the Caucasian quartet. There were also numerous Chinese prostitutes looking for customers. While the Japanese had raised prostitution to an art form in the form of geisha; these were simply whores. Ben could only imagine the various exotic diseases they carried with them. He was relieved they were not allowed to approach Europeans or Americans.

Most of these restaurants did not admit whites, but by invoking the hotel concierge's name, Williams was able to gain entry for the group. The restaurant had an orchestra that made a terrific racket. There was a horn that sounded like a bagpipe, several kinds of cymbals and drums. They all seemed to go without any concerted plan except to generate plenty of noise, at which they succeeded.

Ben noticed that Williams did not eat much at the restaurant and in fact had not been eating much for the past week. He passed it off as Williams not wanting to put on too much weight during the trip.

Once the entourage had reached Hong Kong, the bank arranged for a personal servant to be assigned to each of them throughout the day. Ben found that he could get very used to such an arrangement. At 6:45 in the morning, he would ring for his "boy" to draw him a bath, shine his shoes and prepare his shaving water. Throughout the day, the servant would be asked to perform similar such duties. This servant would remain with him until he got to Calcutta. In Calcutta, another servant, known as a bearer would replace the "boy".

On Tuesday, June 29, 1920, they took the hotel launch out to *Kwai Sang*, a 3,000 ton freighter that would, after several stops along the way, take them to their ultimate destination, Calcutta. The ship had five staterooms, one large room in each corner in front and three in the middle of the starboard side. These staterooms would comfortably accommodate five to seven passengers. Another three to four hundred people, primarily Chinese, were traveling down in the hold of the ship.

In addition to Ben and his colleagues, an English Army major was booked for a large stateroom. He brought his two Javanese servants on at about 2:00 and left them there while he attended to some last minute business in town. At 6:30, when the ship had left its moorings and was headed out for quarantine, the major was nowhere to be seen. The ship captain had connections to make so he pulled up the anchor and set out without the English major.

The ship's crew was composed of a mix of Chinese, several Indochinese and two Sikhs, but none of them could communicate with the Javanese servants. For their part, the Javanese sat huddled on deck, distrustful of everyone save for their wayward major. The first mate expressed worry to anyone who would listen about the food they would eat and what to ultimately do with them. In the meantime, they were housed in the hold with approximately 400

Chinese, who had been let on board after they were inspected. The immigration doctor detained an old woman, blind in one eye and diseased in the other. She and her son were sent back to the dock. The rest were allowed to board and the ship proceeded on its way.

It was a fine cloudless evening with a cool breeze. The group enjoyed dinner and a pleasant evening on the small upper deck by the captain's quarters. Williams occupied a large stateroom right beside the first mate's quarters, Searles moved into the suite that was to have been occupied by the English major. Ben and Gill each had small but very satisfactory rooms nearby.

The boat would take 18 days to reach Calcutta by way of Singapore and Penang. On the second day, Ben was heading up to the deck when the captain offered his hand, saying "Congratulations." Ben shook it, but had to ask why the offer of congratulations. He said it was on its being "your day," meaning the American "violent celebration about beating the British." Ben thanked the captain for the July 4th wishes and then spent the day studying some typewritten sheets on the essentials of Hindustani that Gill had picked up. By the end of the day, Ben had learned to count to 20 and knew some rudimentary phrases.

The captain was so enamored with the Fourth of July that he threw a celebration for the Americans. An excellent dinner was prepared and liquor flowed freely. The only one who did not drink was Williams. Ben could not help but be amused by Gill. All he needed was two drinks to start giggling and get extremely silly, for which he was always quite ashamed the following morning.

The ship passed by Horsburgh Light, which marked the entrance to the straits leading to Singapore. The scene was enhanced by a beautiful sunset in garnet and crimson. The Malay shore and the palm trees stood in silhouette against the sky. The sky was crystal clear and one could clearly see the Southern Cross. The *Kwai Sang* slowly sailed into Singapore's outer harbor and anchored in seven fathoms.

The lights of the city showed prettily against the horizon. As they sailed along, they could just make out dozens of sampans with straw roofed deck houses, tightly packed into a river that ran through the lower end of the city. Before the passengers could disembark, the port doctor had to certify that they were without disease. He was not scheduled to come on board until 6:00 the following morning so everyone settled in for the night.

The group had reservations for rooms at the Hotel de l'Europe, the "best hotel east of Suez" at least according to the brochure. Ben looked back at the places he had stayed at thus far: The Grand at Yokahama, the Palace at Shanghai, the Manila at Manila and the Hong Kong at Hong Kong. It was quite an imposing list of hostelries. Growing up in New Brunswick, he could never have imagined going on a trip like this or staying in first-class hotels such as these. He wistfully wished he had taken a spoon or towel at each place as mementos. The Hotel de l'Europe would not get off so easily, he was quite sure.

After a prolonged and extremely bureaucratic examination of each passport, the Singapore officials finally allowed *Kwai Sang* to be hauled to the dock. Ben was taken aback as he and his traveling companions were met by a very dark skinned man who would shuttle them to the Hôtel de l'Europe. As they had gotten closer to India, the complexion of the people he encountered was steadily getting darker, but this man was definitely African, not Indian or Asian.

The man, whose name was Barak, chatted the entire ride, telling about how excellent the accommodations were at Hôtel de l'Europe. He told of how lucky he was to have a job with such a fine company after growing up poor in Senegal. However, he had absolutely no practical information to impart such as whether or not rooms had been reserved for the group as requested by wireless. In fact, when they arrived they found that there were no reservations, but fortunately the hotel was not fully occupied and they got rooms for one night.

Ben had only the following morning to tour Singapore so he hired a rickshaw to pull him around the city for a couple of hours. He had heard there were 25,000 registered rickshaws in

Singapore, and that each one was a robber. There was a fee they could legally charge, but generally they would ask as much as they thought the fare could be bled for. After seeing some impressive Buddhist shrines and wandering through the old part of the city, Ben was more than ready to get back on board the ship to continue on toward Calcutta, and he directed the rickshaw man to bring him back to the hotel. Ben paid the driver 30¢, which he believed to be a decent rate. The rickshaw man raised an awful howl and followed Ben into the building. Ben gave him 10¢ more to get rid of him, but that did not work. Finally, he shed himself of this pest by flagging down a Sikh policeman.

At about 4 p.m. Ben and his companions, along with numerous Chinese and Malaysians heading to Penang and some Indians going to Calcutta, made their way back to the ship. At the last minute, two ambulances skidded to a halt on the concrete pier, moist from the spray of the sea. Startled stevedores, crew and passengers jumped out of the way, eyeing the vehicles with a mixture of contempt and curiosity as the back doors of the converted Hudsons flew open. Two Malaysian guards with holstered sidearms hopped out and immediately conscripted six dockworkers to unload the ambulances. The dockworkers helped fifteen people, each of whom had filthy rags draped over what was left of his or her body, from the vehicles.

Once unloaded, the ambulances hurried off as quickly as they had arrived. The wretched creatures huddled together on the pier, awaiting instruction. Ben asked a crew member what was going on.

"Lepers. We take Pulau Jerejak, leper island," he casually noted, as if transporting fifteen lepers was an everyday occurrence (maybe for him it was), "What? You no see leper before?"

Ben told him he had not, and he noted to himself that he could have lived a very full life without ever seeing one. Now, here he was, about to spend two days and two nights on a ship with fifteen of them.

The lepers were in various stages of the disease. Some had white sores on an arm or leg. A few required stretchers, others crutches, for transport. The worst was missing one leg, half of one hand, parts of fingers on the other and the remaining foot was bandaged. His ears were deformed, too.

They trudged up, or were carried up, the gangplank to be placed in a hold under the fore deck, fenced off by themselves and under guard. Almost unnoticed, a solitary man walked solemnly behind them. He was a tall, thin, extremely dark Indian dressed in a Western-style black suit. The crew member identified him as the doctor who would care for them until they were deposited at the leper colony on the outskirts of Penang.

Ben surveyed his traveling companions for their reactions. Concern and sympathy for the plight of these poor unfortunates could be detected on Williams' face. Gill looked on with fascination at something new that was spicing up what had thus far been an uneventful trip. Searles viewed the scene with obvious disgust. Incredulity and anger completed the tableau on his face when the steward approached and advised him that, because he had a suite with an extra bedroom that was not in use, he would have to share his suite with the doctor who had a first class ticket.

"I will not share my accommodations with a colored," Searles indignantly replied.

It would have been difficult for the physician, now only a few feet away, to not hear this statement. However, he gave no indication or reaction as he passed. Ben sensed the steward, who likewise was "colored", was about to make an angry retort when Gill stepped in, hoping to defuse the tension.

"I can move in with Mr. Searles and the doctor can have my room."

Searles glared at Gill; he did not want to room with anyone, regardless of their color. The doctor, whom they had not noticed return, spoke up.

"It is quite all right. I will sleep with my charges. If you could please have a cot and blankets brought down, I would most appreciate it. I shall be quite comfortable."

With that he turned and left. It was clear the steward wanted to respond to Searles, but since the physician had resolved the situation, he let it drop.

A half hour after the lepers boarded, the ship was towed out of the quay by a tug. While the ship idled, a man and a little boy came off in a canoe to dive for pennies and dimes that the passengers and crew threw for them. They did wonderfully, the man staying down unheard of lengths of time before finally coming up, always with a dime between his teeth. Ben and Gill were at the ship's railing, enjoying watching the father and son as the captain started to pilot the ship out between the high green islands. They had only been there a few minutes when they heard a soft voice behind them.

"Thank you."

They turned around and there was the doctor.

"Thank you for your attempts to assist me."

In response, Gill simply nodded. He had previously confided to Ben that his gesture had nothing to do with the doctor; rather, he was simply trying to shut Searles up. If allowed to continue, Searles was fully capable of embarrassing himself, all of them and Langdan Textiles.

The doctor continued.

"I was educated at Oxford. I have a thriving practice and teach medicine at the University of Singapore. I have a beautiful wife and two beautiful children. I spend a week every two months working with the lepers, giving them a little comfort. Yet in one simple sentence, your friend reduces me to one thing: colored. In the end, it turned out well. I am with people I know and care about, not with him."

He said no more, but gazed out on the water, his sharp features silhouetted against the reddening sky. They didn't know how to respond so Ben asked him a question most on his mind.

"Do lepers know any happiness in their lives?"

The doctor turned to them and smiled.

"They are people, just people. Their problem is that the only function society gives them is for them to die, preferably out of sight and mind. Unfortunately, there is not much happiness in this endeavor. I shall tell them that you were asking. It will please them that someone inquired about them in this manner."

Ben looked in his face for irony, to see if the doctor was mocking him and his question. There was no irony, only sincerity. He truly felt they would appreciate the inquiry.

The doctor bid them good night, shook their hands and said goodbye. Ben and Gill went to their cabins; the doctor went to his charges.

28
Catherine

Ben wrote to me about an extraordinary experience he had. It involved lepers. When I first saw the word 'lepers' I couldn't believe it. I suppose there are still lepers here in the states, but we probably have fewer because of our advanced medicine. Or maybe we just do a better job of hiding them away than most of the world.

What truly amazed me about Ben's recounting of the story was the description of the doctor who was attending to them as they were being shuttled to a leper colony. The doctor was a very dark Indian. Ben found him fascinating. He was highly educated, Oxford no less, and had a thriving practice and taught at a university. He volunteered to work with lepers every couple of months. Ben was quite taken with him.

I don't think I can ever remember Ben ever saying anything positive about anyone with a skin color darker than his. It wasn't that he disparaged them at every turn, but, if asked, his opinions on the subject were clear. Encountering someone like this was surely an eye opener.

Perhaps my husband was growing up a little.

I've been worried about Molly. She doesn't seem to have her old get up and go. As a matter of fact, she stayed home from work one day; it was perhaps the first time in her life that she didn't go to work. I tried to get her to go to the doctor, of course to no avail. I accompanied her out to her garden. Many of her plants were sorely in need of attention. Under her tutelage I had attained some level of competency in the kitchen but my gardening skills had not significantly improved. I thought perhaps if I got her out of the house among her plants, she would come alive once she saw that they needed her help. But she simply shuffled out, sat on the bench and watched me do some weeding. After about a half hour, we headed back inside.

29

Ben was up at 6:30 to see the entrance to Penang. The lepers were put on a steam launch with their guard and doctor to be taken down the harbor to the leper colony. He freely admitted he was glad to see them go, although he had to admit he did find the Oxford-educated colored doctor intriguing.

At about 10:30 the shipping agent came onboard and, after conferring with the captain, took the Langdan contingent ashore in his launch. They went to the Eastern & Oriental Hotel, where they sat on the big tile veranda as they consumed iced drinks and watched the boats in the harbor. During the conversation, Gill related what the doctor had said. Searles only harrumphed.

They were in Penang for a little over a day and then took a sampan back to the ship. The water was brilliantly phosphorescent. Ben found it very spooky to be rowed in a sampan across the black harbor with the oars dipping silver and a bearded dacca at the helm looking like the engravings of Arab sheiks. They enjoyed the picturesque trip across the harbor but were relieved to get back to the deck again to sail the next morning.

Five days later, the ship reached the pilot lightship offshore of Calcutta. After some cruising, they found the pilot boat some 14 miles off his station. After weeks of beautifully hued ocean, this water was the color of pea soup. They anchored at Sagar Island and expected to go ashore the following afternoon.

Ben was looking forward to his upcoming work. He would never admit it to anyone but when they were back in Boston, he had had a pretty good idea of what caused the jute rotting problem and the steps the company should take to solve it. He could easily have designed experiments from the security of his own lab to test his theory, but he was not going to pass up an all-expense paid trip like this. Neither was he going to pass up the opportunity to personally view jute growing and processing. That hands-on information, not just reading about it in books, would be invaluable to his research for years to come.

In the meantime, there was so much to find out and so little time. He envisioned using every single daylight hour over the next couple of months through October 15, the day they were scheduled to start back by way of the Suez Canal. Allowing two weeks for Williams et al. to transact some business in London and Dundee, they ought to get back to New York the week before Christmas. He was looking forward to Harry's first Hannukah/Christmas.

He hoped his bacteriological supplies arrived intact. Whenever possible, he had personally checked to make sure the trunk was transferred from one vessel to the next, but he did not have access to the loading process on this current ship. Given the abilities he observed in the average stevedore, he would not be surprised if the trunk were sitting on a dock in Singapore or Hong Kong.

On the Hooghly River, the ship lifted anchor and made up stream with the tide. The lower reaches of the river were lined by flat low land, much of it partly under water and sparsely inhabited. Farther up the stream it narrowed to perhaps a quarter mile and the channel became very crooked so that the boat was close first to one bank and then the other. The water was very muddy with a few nondescript crafts sailing up the stream.

Finally, the ship moored. Passports were again examined. The police held them up to the light to detect alterations and to ensure that the watermark of the State Department was on the paper. Everyone then had to file Customs declarations before going ashore.

The passengers were to be loaded onto small launches for transport to shore. Meanwhile, the top executives of Langdan's Calcutta operations, Messrs. Colby, Sherman and Henderson, came out in their own launch to greet the American contingent. Williams and Searles went with them but Ben and Gill had to remain behind for lack of space. The launch was to come back for them, but it failed to show up. After a long wait, Ben and Gill hired their own dinghy and went ashore.

They chartered a taxi and went to the Great Eastern, the best hotel in town. To their relief, William had reserved rooms for all of them. It was then 7:30 pm. Gill and Ben were the only ones in sight without dinner dress, either black or white.

The next morning, Ben's bearer arrived promptly at 6:30 AM, bringing his new master tea, toast and bananas. In India, most whites appeared to have servants or bearers, a general factotum who brushed clothes, acted as a chambermaid and an interpreter, and did basically anything asked of him. He sent out laundry to a dhoby who cleaned it by hammering it on a smooth stone. He drove bargains with the native merchants, nipping a small commission on all payments, but in the end saving money. The amount of money saved would be determined by his haggling skills. The bearer would receive from 18 to 25 rupees a month from which he would feed and clothe himself and his family. The hotels assumed its guests would have a bearer; the only way to get your bed made was by your own servant or by tipping one of the hall porters.

Ben's bearer, a six foot tall Muslim, had worked exclusively for Langdan executives staying at the hotel for the last few years. He was very attentive, but he soon got on Ben's nerves by being around all the time. However, he spoke good English and handled a lot of details that Ben would rather not have to deal with.

Ben asked him his name, but even after he repeated it several times Ben still failed to comprehend it. In the end, the bearer said everyone called him Ram, and so Ben started calling him that, too.

Ram accompanied Ben out to the provision stalls in the market. All kinds of wares from chicken livers to flowers and from perfume to golf clubs could be purchased. Ram warned Ben to do no buying himself, saying he could save him over a half if he did the purchasing. Ben had to acknowledge that Ram was very good at haggling prices down.

Ben did have some difficulty getting used to having a bearer do things he normally did himself such as picking up his dirty clothes and putting them in the hamper, or laying out clean things or putting in studs or changing his belt. Ram squatted outside the room while Ben was away, and opened his door with an air when he returned. Ben thought he was a smooth operator. He would not have been surprised if his bearer were a thief, though nothing ever was missing.

Ben went with Williams to the main office and learned they had arrived ahead of the jute harvest by about two weeks. It was perfect timing; the jute had not yet begun to come in yet and the baling mill had not yet opened. This would give Ben plenty of time to examine the plants and to design his experiments. He also needed to locate several volumes—Burkill & Fenlow's "Races of Jute", Chaudhuir's "Jute in Bengal", and Royle's "Fitre Plants of India", as well as several bound committee reports of the Calcutta Jute Association—in the local library to complete his research.

It was at this point that Ben noticed his instruments were not with the rest of the luggage. He went back to the ship with Ram. They rented a sampan, but not until after a significant shouting match between Ram and the boat owner, which Ram explained was part of the necessary bargaining process.

Ben was greatly relieved when they found the trunk still sitting in the hold, untouched. Three young men quickly volunteered to help carry the trunk. Ben had made some observations about porters throughout their trip. In Japan, one shrimp of a porter would toss an old trunk on his shoulder and then trot off with it. In China, two would take it between them. Here in India, however, everything involved a squad. Two lifted the trunk up, and two or three got under it and carried it with a little wad of curled up rag on their heads.

From the ship to the hotel, at least ten men would at one point or another carry or at least touch the trunk. Each man expected to be recompensed for his labor. Additionally, another ten men had done nothing but had hopes of gleaning some pocket change from an unsophisticated sahib. For a full three quarters of an hour, Ram bickered with the men over who was to be paid and how much each would receive. At first it was a free for all but finally, one of the men, using scattered kicks, curses and slaps, asserted his authority over the others and reduced the mob to comparative silence. Then he and Ram haggled one on one, starting at 10 rupees and 2 rupees respectively. Ram was planning to pay four rupees but time was passing so Ben called it off when he got to 5 rupees for the crew. Once the trunk was loaded into the hotel, a new row broke out with other drivers and coolies who thought they had been cheated. As far as Ben and Ram were concerned, the negotiations were concluded, and they walked into the hotel lobby to the din of curses and invective.

Ben made it a habit to go out to the jute fields on a regular basis. Gill joked that his trips must be as exciting 'watching the grass grow'. Ben never quite grasped the meaning behind this saying because when he sat down to observe grass—or jute—growing, he could picture in his mind the complex operations (osmosis, photosynthesis, etc.) that were taking place. There was nothing boring about observing the jute first hand to determine where the internal processes were going wrong.

The jute plants varied in height from 5 to 15 feet. In a normal season, they would reach maturity in about four months from the time of sowing. The stems of jute plants were generally green or pink, and were straight with a tendency to branch. The leaves alternated on the stems, 4 to 5 inches in length, and about 1-1/2 inches in breadth with serrated edges. Pale yellow flowers sprang from the axil of the leaves, and there was an abundance of small seeds in the fruit. While many attempts had been made to cultivate jute plants in various parts of the world, the conditions for the successful cultivation of them were best met in the Bengal area.

He observed the farming operations in India to be rather simple; there was no need to extensively work the Indian soil. In addition, there were few horses in this part of the world. Ploughs were made of wood and faced with iron. Oxen, in teams of two or more, may be harnessed to the plough but just as often the plows were pulled by human labor.

After the soil had been satisfactorily prepared, the jute seed was sown by hand. The usual sowing time was from February to the end of May, and as late as June in some districts. The plants were cut down by hand with homemade knives. In general, these knives were quite crude, but they were suitable for the purpose. The operation of cutting a field of jute plants was a daunting piece of work since it required about 10 to 14 tons of the green crop to produce about 1 to 1.5 tons of clean dry fiber.

Bacterial action caused disintegration of the structural part of the plant, during which a gas was given off. The farmer, or ryot, and his men knew what progress the action was making by the presence of the tiny bubbles or air bells, which rose to the surface. When the formation of air bells ceased, the men examined the plants daily to see that the operation did not go too far. Ben's theory was that the bacteria, which normally would cease acting and rendered inert, somehow were being reactivated later on in the process. He had to figure out how and why this occurred.

If the fibrous layer were injured, it would render the resulting fiber weak. The stems were tested to see if the fibrous, or bast, layer, stripped off clean from the wood or stem. When the ryot considered that the layers were separated from the core sufficiently easy, the work of steeping ceased, and the process of stripping commenced immediately.

The men worked in the water, breaking up the woody structure of the retted plants by means of mallets and cross rails fixed to uprights in the water. Others broke the stems by hand; while in other cases the stems were handed out of the water to women who strip off the fibrous layer and preserved intact the central core or straw to be used ultimately for thatching. The strips of fiber were all cleaned and rubbed in the water to remove all the vegetable impurities, and finally the fiber was dried, usually by hanging it over poles and protecting it from the direct rays of the sun. Then it was pressed. A press was capable of turning out 130 bales of 400 pounds each in one hour. The fiber was compressed into comparatively small bulk by hydraulic pressure equal to 6,000 lbs. per square inch, and each packed bale was no bigger than 11 cubic feet after it left the press.

Ben spent considerable time looking at jute, feeling it and smelling it to get a good idea of the bulk fiber.

Three days after the group had arrived, a formal reception was held to welcome the American contingent to India. The reception was in a catering hall a few blocks from the main office. When Ben arrived around 7:30, the hall was packed with about 150 people. Every Langdan manager was there as well as anyone who actually was, or thought they were, a dignitary. The British provisional government was well represented. As Ben looked around, the one thing he noted was that the only dark faces in the crowd were the service and wait staff.

As he scanned the room, he saw Williams waving him to come over.

"Major Highsmith, I'd like you to meet another member of my team. This is Mr. Benjamin Albert. Mr. Albert is a research associate. He's the one I was telling you about who's going to solve our jute rotting problem. Ben, Major Highsmith is the commander of His Majesty's provisional security forces in Calcutta."

"It's a pleasure meeting you," Major Highsmith said as he shook his hand. He didn't react when Ben held out his left hand to shake.

"Yes, Mr. Williams has been telling me about how much of a problem the rotting has been for the company. Losing millions I understand. You seem mighty young to have such an awesome responsibility placed on your shoulders."

"Well, jute has been my life for some time now. I have a few ideas on what to do, but I need to conduct some experiments first to give me some data to work with and then I'll have a surer idea."

"Ah yes, I remember conducting interminable experiments while I was at university. I knew then and there that science was not for me and so I chose a military career. How have you liked Calcutta so far?"

"I'm afraid I haven't seen any of it so far. The only things I've seen are a couple jute fields and the inside of my laboratory."

"We'll have to get you out and about before you leave, won't we?"

"If I can accomplish my tasks, I'd love to see the city."

"That's the attitude! Very American of you, I must say! No pleasure before business."

"How long have you been posted in Calcutta, Major?"

"Six years now. It has been a good posting. There's never too much trouble that we can't handle. We try to let the Indians have some level of self-government," and then he added in a conspiratorial whisper, "but not too much self-government, if you know what I mean.

"I would much rather be stationed here than the posting my brother has. He has been in Palestine for the past five years. He says he has to shower day and night after being sullied by constant contact with that many Jews. He does his best to turn shiploads of them away, but they keep on coming."

Ben pretended to need a drink and excused himself.

30

Catherine

Now that he was in Calcutta, Ben's letters arrived regularly. Initially, he was posting letters directly to me but now that he's in Calcutta, he's routing them through Mrs. Epstein and they seem to get to me much quicker. Whatever the reason, I'm glad they come more frequently than they had over the past couple of months.

I do have to note that the tone of Ben's letter's have changed over time. His early letters would have an occasional reference to 'coloreds' or 'schvartzes'. Then as he got to Japan and China, the references would be of Japs and Chinks. That seems to have calmed down somewhat.

I was upset when he wrote me that Mr. Williams had taken ill. He'd been experiencing stomach problems throughout the trip but then once they reached Calcutta the pain became excruciating. He had no choice to go to a local hospital. Ben wrote that he would have full confidence if the leper doctor was looking after Williams but he did not trust any of the local witch doctors, as he called them.

The last he had heard, Mr. Williams had stabilized and was preparing to come back to the states to be treated. It was a shame; Ben had grown very close to Williams. The way he carried on about him, it was also like he was the father he never knew. I have a feeling they'll be close when Ben gets back here where he belongs.

31

He had been in Calcutta for nearly two weeks and Ben had seen very little of the city. Generally, in the morning he would walk a couple of blocks from the hotel to post letters to Catherine and his mother, and then walk the few more blocks to the lab. That was the extent of his wanderings.

His only excitement had been when he ran across a naked youth of about 10 chasing three cows along the sidewalk. They were sacred cows, he was told. They wander all over the city. The theory is that a man dedicates a cow to his god as a thank offering and turns it loose to furnish milk to the poor. It is branded so that its sacred use is plain for everyone to see but whether the poor get the milk is questionable.

Ben would devote the last two weeks of August touring the jute area, getting all the possible samples of jute he could: growing and ripening them. He would occasionally be joined by Mr. Cecil Tibbets, a distinguished, middle aged three quarters white Eurasian who would escort Ben in a company car miles out of Calcutta to sample jute.

Ben would then put in a month to review the drying process. He joked that he would be wasting his time, standing around watching the jute dry. But he knew this was a crucial stage when he believed the bacteria that promoted the rotting were doing their worst work. He would need all this time just for observation before he could even think of coming to any conclusions about how to reduce the rotting. Every day during this period he would take samples, glue his eye to the microscope and count bacteria. It was tedious but essential work.

His days were split equally between the laboratory, the field and the office as he gathered data, conducted experiments and wrote an endless number of reports memorializing his findings.

Then, much to his chagrin and definitely contrary to his loner persona, many evenings he was required to dine and socialize with company executives and local officials, who by and large were English.

In order to keep himself from going cross-eyed and insane from constantly peering into a microscope, he forced himself to take time off during the heat of the afternoon, preferably away from the lab. He religiously made a daily 3:00 visit to a nearby teahouse where he would sit over a pot of tea for exactly one half hour.

He had discovered the teahouse not far from the lab on his first day in Calcutta. It was located on Kanai Dhar Lane, not one of Calcutta's major thoroughfares. It was far away from the city's boisterous markets, which suited Ben just fine. Ever since he left Boston two month ago, he had a persistent feeling that everybody he encountered was out to cheat him out of his hard-earned money. In his mind, a rickshaw ride for a certain distance should cost a certain amount; arriving at a fare should not involve a battle of wits. Ben found the constant haggling in these cultures to be tiresome, but if one did not do it, the rickshaw puller, the merchant, the servant, would have the upper hand.

The teahouse was a typical affair for the city. There was one on practically every block. Some were frequented by natives, others by the English, others a mix. They all boasted large heavily designed doors that always seemed to be open to the street, beckoning the masses to come in to refresh themselves for a bit. A perpetual layer of cigarette-created haze hung over the patrons. An ornate teak counter dominated the far end of the room, behind which were six huge urns from which a variety of teas would be dispensed. The floor was crammed with a dozen small round wooden tables with cast iron legs. Around each table were two or three wicker chairs.

The one characteristic that especially drew him here, and kept him coming back, was how spotless the teahouse was. The owner was evidently as obsessed with cleanliness as he was. Someone was constantly scrubbing the counter and tables, even if there had been no evidence of a recent spill. This made him at ease, especially after all of the filthy places he had visited over the past few months.

Another quality he liked was that, because it was off the beaten path, there were usually plenty of seats to choose from. He was therefore surprised and somewhat annoyed when he arrived one day that the teahouse was so bustling, and on a Wednesday afternoon. He briefly weighed walking out and going back to his hotel, but he decided to stay. His dedicated half-hour here had become too much a part of his routine; giving it up would throw him off for the rest of the day and evening, and he had more work to do.

Waiters strained as they reached over people to deliver scalding pots of tea. Numerous expletives in both English and Hindi were hurled back and forth between workers and patrons when a bit of the brew sloshed out of the pot onto an unprotected head or arm.

Just as he resigned himself to standing at the counter to sip his daily Earl Grey, a diminutive dark-skinned middle-aged man wearing rounded glasses and a somewhat out-of-date (at least by American standards) suit and tie motioned to him, inviting him to join him at his table. Even though it meant having to make conversation with a colored stranger, Ben had been on his feet all day. A seat would be welcome. He nodded and worked his way through the crowd.

"Please, please join me," the man implored in proper, clipped English.

"Thank you very much. I believe I shall."

"Oh, an American!" The gentleman seemed thrilled at this chance encounter. "We meet so few of you in India. It's always very exciting to hear what's happening in the States. I did have a very close American friend when I lived in England some years ago. We were in law school together. We kept in touch after we went our separate ways. When the war came, he joined your army despite his somewhat advanced years. He survived the Battle of the Argonne in 1918 but then died of the influenza a year later. I miss him very much."

Ben's face took on a somber cast. He held up his right stump

"I was in the war, too. And then I lost my mother-in-law to the influenza. So I guess I know what you're talking about."

The man did not catch Ben's melancholic mood but instead excitedly pressed on, looking to build on what may be a commonality between the two.

"You were in the U.S. Army, too? My friend's name was Jack Brooks. He was from New York. Perhaps you knew him?"

Ben suppressed a smile. This wasn't the first person he had met during the course of his trip who assumed all Americans knew each other.

"No, I'm afraid I never met him."

"I didn't think you would have known him, but I'm constantly amazed at the number of seeming coincidences I run across every day."

The awkwardness of dredging up uncomfortable memories of the war dissipated as Ben could not help but to be taken in by the man's warm smile and infectious enthusiasm.

"Where are my manners," he continued. "Here I am your host and I have not introduced myself. My name is Mohandas."

"And I'm Benjamin, Benjamin Albert. It's a pleasure to meet you, Mr. Mohandas."

The man let out a strong laugh.

"Mister Mohandas. Very funny; very funny indeed! Mohandas is my given name. My surname is Gandhi."

"I apologize, sir. I've only been in India a couple of weeks and, in all honesty, I have yet to get used to your names here."

"No offense taken. Our names can get rather long and involved. Between you and me, I think we do it just to confuse the rest of the world."

Ben laughed.

"Well, it works, at least with me!"

"If it's any consolation, I never before met a Benjamin. So, Mr. Benjamin Albert, what brings you to our beautiful country with the confusing names?"

"Jute."

"Jute? The plant?"

"Yes, I work for Langdan Textiles. We're one of the major manufacturers of burlap in the world," Ben was obviously very proud of his affiliation with his employer. "This is about the only place in the world that grows jute. Lately, many bales of jute shipped to our manufacturing plants are unusable because of rot. I'm a bacteriologist and was sent here to examine how the jute is being cultivated, handled and processed to see why this is happening and what we can do to stop the rot."

"That is a fascinating line of work you are in. You delve into an invisible world that is unknown to most of us. Yes, fascinating indeed."

Knowing that people's usual reaction to his profession was a yawn and glazing over of the eyes, Ben appreciated the man's comments.

"I've always liked it."

"I am somewhat familiar with Langdan Textiles, as I am with many of the large concerns who do business in India."

Ben's interest was piqued but he said nothing at this point.

"Langdan employs a lot of native Indians, doesn't it?"

"Yes, I believe we do, but frankly I've been too busy to meet many of the other employees. I deal mostly with the Americans and English managers who oversee operations."

Gandhi looked as if he was expecting this response as he gave Ben a paternalistic smile.

"My son, I don't know you very well but I believe that you must lift your eyes up from your microscope once in awhile and look around to learn about the people around you. The little creatures you look at may be fascinating, but the human experience is even more so."

Ben was a little insulted at the lecture, no matter how well-intentioned it may have been.

"You said you knew about Langdan, Mr. Gandhi. Perhaps you could be so kind as to teach me about my company."

Ben realized his tone was a little superior, but he was finding the little man a bit presumptuous. Gandhi seemed not to notice and proceeded to lay out his expansive knowledge of Langdan Textiles, Inc.

"Well, Langdan Textiles employs nearly 900 Indians in Calcutta but, to be blunt, you are one of the worst employers in the region. The wages you pay are not enough to support a man by himself, never mind one with a wife and several children. There is an attitude that for each worker that leaves, there are 100 who can take his place. Your management is entirely English and American; not a single Indian helps to run the company. The jute you produce costs approximately 1 rupee per 500 linear feet and yet when the burlap and other products are produced, you can sell it for as much as 1 rupee per 5 linear feet. That is quite a profit margin, I must say. Your company can afford to send you and your companions half way around the world but they put little in to improve the safety and working conditions for the workers. There are many, many accidents reported at your facility; I am sure there are a far greater number that go unreported. Some of these accidents result in death. If fact, five men were killed just last month. I may be incorrect, but I do not believe that Langdan did anything for the families of the deceased other than a few token rupees they may have thrown their way. There have been, in fact, rumors that these deaths may not have been quite as accidental as the company has let on, but the authorities quickly determined that it was an accident so that was the end of that."

Ben sat there dumbfounded. Mr. Gandhi indeed did know far more about the company than he did, but there was something more. What astounded Ben was that this discourse was delivered without a trace of recrimination. It was like a father giving patient guidance to his son.

"I had heard about the accident before I arrived," Ben advised Gandhi, taking special care to use the word 'accident' while knowing that there had been rumors about the circumstances under which the men died.

"And what exactly do you do, Mr. Gandhi? Are you a union organizer?"

It was Gandhi's turn to closely examine his companion as the waiter arrived to take Ben's order of a pot of tea and a pastry. Likewise, Gandhi found Ben to be sincere; he had no idea who Mohandas Gandhi was.

"I guess you could say I am an organizer, but don't worry, I'm not here to shut down or strike against your company. I am here for a conference, a meeting of the Indian National Committee. You must have heard of the conference, haven't you?"

"No, I'm afraid I haven't."

"Representatives from all over India have gathered to discuss the fate of the Indian nation and the role Indians will play in governing that nation."

"That sounds impressive. From how you describe it, I would guess that you want more of a role than the English are willing to give."

Ben thought it prudent not to mention his belief that he did not think Indians capable of self-government.

"Mr. Albert, you are a very quick learner! See, once you lift your eyes up from your microscope you can actually see all the peoples of the world. We do hope some day that the English will leave and we can learn to govern ourselves. But, as was displayed at Amritsar last year, this is not going to happen overnight nor will it occur without some pain and even death."

"Amritsar?"

Gandhi looked mildly annoyed as he issued his admonishment.

"Mr. Albert. You really should read up on the history of a place before you come to live there for a period of time. I am sure that the massacre at Amritsar of over 150 men, women and children by British machine guns must have been carried in your newspapers."

As Ben sat there looking sheepish, Gandhi reverted from his lecturing persona back to the paternalistic one without skipping a beat.

"Yes, this is a very important conference that starts tomorrow. I have been in deep preparations for a month now and I have not had a minute to myself that whole time. I doubt that it will get any better in the future either. I just had to get away for an hour or so. I had to go to a place where no one knew me or wanted something from me."

He chuckled a little bit. "I am sure they are frantic, wondering where I am. Search parties are scouring the city as we speak. They probably think I am lying in a ditch somewhere, my life ebbing away."

Gandhi was very pleased with himself at the subterfuge he was pulling.

"Normally, you would not see me in a suit such as this. I have been a proponent of Indians wearing the cloth that they themselves make, our homespun we like to call it. But if I showed up here dressed that way, I would not have had a moment's peace. I have owned this suit since my days as a lawyer in South Africa, and I did not think I was straying too far from my basic beliefs to put on this old friend of mine one last time."

Gandhi eyed Ben in a conspiratorial manner.

"You won't tell on me will you? At least not until after the conference is concluded. Especially do not tell my wife that I was here instead of being with her."

Ben looked down fondly on the odd little man who thought he was so famous. Ben may never have heard of Amritsar, but he could not imagine of someone like this being such a notable figure. It was not like he was sitting down with Black Jack Pershing after all.

"No, Mr. Gandhi, your secret is safe with me."

"I knew I could trust you."

The two men ordered another pot of tea and chatted about nothing in particular for another twenty minutes. Ben showed him picture of Catherine and Harry. Gandhi remarked how beautiful they were and apologized that he did not have pictures of his family.

Ben was reluctant to leave, but there was still some daylight and he had to check on one experiment that was at a critical stage. Gandhi realized he had to get back as well.

"Well, Mr. Albert, it certainly has been a most enjoyable afternoon. I thank you for your company."

"As it has been for me as well. Good luck in your endeavors for your country."

"Thank you. And remember to look up from your microscope occasionally. There's a wondrous world for you to see but even more so, there's a world out there that needs your help. Good bye, Mr. Benjamin Albert."

On his way back to the lab, Ben picked up an English language newspaper to learn about the Indian National Committee Conference.

Ben went back to the lab but every time he sat down at his microscope, he could hear Gandhi's admonition in his ears: Lift your eyes from your microscope. The bacteria, formulas, pieces of jute and much of his life's work somehow seemed inconsequential. He tried to focus on his work for an hour or so but it was futile and he decided to call it a day.

When he arrived at his hotel room, Ram was waiting there as usual.

"Good evening, Ram."

"Good evening, sir. May I get you something to eat, sir?"

"No thank you, Ram. Actually, what I would like is to talk with you a bit. Why don't you have a seat?"

Ram regarded Ben with great apprehension as he guided himself to the sofa while Ben sat in the armchair. He was expecting the worst when Ben started to speak.

"It occurred to me that we've been together for weeks and I know very little about you. Do you have a family? Where do you live? How long have you been associated with Langdan? Things like that."

Ram's apprehension had lifted somewhat but now he was confused as to what was behind these questions. Still, he thought it better to respond.

"I have a wife and two children, one boy and one girl. I live three miles from here. I have been working with Langdan Textiles executives for four years now."

Ben noted how precise Ram was in his answers to each of his question in turn.

"Four years, that's a good length of time. You like it?"

"Yes, I am treated well."

"I'd heard about an accident a few months ago where five men were killed. Did you know any of these men?"

Ram's expression hardened and his body stiffened at this question.

"Yes, one of the men was my brother. His wife had just had their first child. They live with us now."

"Ram, I'm very sorry about your brother."

"Thank you, sir."

"Please, stop calling me sir. Call me Ben. It makes me feel so old when I hear the word 'sir.'

A hint of a smile creased Ram's lips.

"Very well, sir, I mean Ben."

"There, that's better. I was talking to a man in the teahouse today who knew about the accident. He seemed to think there was more to it than was in the official report; that perhaps it wasn't as accidental as everyone seemed to believe. I assume you've heard the same things."

Ram felt he was between the proverbial rock and a hard place. He had heard more, but no one had ever asked his opinion about the accident. Moreover, he was talking to a representative of the company. How free with his feelings could he really be? Ben sensed Ram's hesitancy.

"Ram, you can speak freely. I give you my word that anything you say here will be for my ears only. I will tell no one else, ever."

Ram looked at him once more and decided yet again that he was being sincere and honest.

"Yes, I have heard things. My brother was very popular with all the Indians that worked at Langdan. He was working to improve their safety conditions and increase the pay for their labor. He was negotiating with the managers and he seemed very happy about how the talks were progressing. Then the managers, Mr. Colby and Mr. Sherman, sent him word that they had heard all they needed to and the talks stopped. Two days later he died in the explosion.

"I did not know three of the men who died. They were mechanics and it was logical they could be in the building that housed the transformer. But my brother was not a mechanic. He knew nothing about electricity. Neither did the last man, his name was Ranesh. He assisted my brother in the negotiations. There was no reason he should have been there either.

"My brother had confided in me the day before he died that he had some concerns about his safety. He had heard some whispers but as we talked, he was able to convince himself that he was exaggerating the danger and when we left each other, he was in good spirits. The next day he was dead."

"I take it there was an investigation, wasn't there?"

"The authorities said they investigated. They said they had no reason to believe it was anything other than a tragic accident."

"Did you say anything about your brother not being an electrician?"

"No, I could not get involved. Langdan does not even know Sanjay was my brother. I need my job, especially now that I am responsible for feeding my brother's family as well as my own."

A new pleading look crossed Ram's face, expressing concern about whether Ben would keep his word about the confidentiality of this conversation. Ben made it clear he would tell no one. Ram continued.

"In fact, the police themselves questioned why Sanjay and Ranesh were there, but they turned it so that they speculated that my brother must have been there for some illegal reason, that he was plotting against the company or even against the government. They suggested that perhaps he sabotaged the transformer himself. And there is one more reason why they would not have investigated more fully."

Ram hesitated.

"And that is?"

"Four out of the five men were Muslim. You may not have noticed but we are a minority here in this city. We often don't have the same rights as the rest of the population."

"Thank you for telling me all this, Ram. You have my curiosity piqued now. I am going to ask some questions, but don't worry, I'll never let on I spoke with you about this matter."

"It was good to talk with someone about this. It has been a heavy load on my heart. Be careful, Mr. Ben. These men, I believe, can be very dangerous."

"I will, Ram."

The next day Ben met with Gill and Searles to update them on his progress. Williams had that day been loaded on a ship to be taken back to the States for medical treatment. As much as Ben detested Searles, he was now in charge and Ben felt obliged to give him periodic updates.

He outlined the results of his experiments and observations. Given Ben's experience with many non-scientists who want instant answers, he noted that the jute was still in the drying process and that it could not be hurried. He was collecting valuable information but he had at least two weeks before he could come to any solid conclusions. Gill seemed to understand but Searles expressed exasperation that there was nothing really to report.

At the end of their meeting, Ben recounted the chance meeting he had with Mr. Gandhi. He also summarized what Ram had told him but did not mention Ram by name, leaving the impression that it had all come from Gandhi. Gill did not react one way or the other.

"I've heard these rumors, too," he said, "and I learned a long time ago not to react to rumors. If they ever get beyond that, then we can figure out what to do."

Searles' reaction, on the other hand, was explosive.

"I would strongly recommend, Mr. Albert, that you not stick your nose where it does not belong! This incident has been thoroughly investigated by the authorities. Nobody needs you to be an amateur sleuth revisiting old issues and digging up skeletons that are best left buried!"

While Williams had been the senior officer on the trip, Ben often had the feeling that Searles was more plugged in to company politics. He appeared to have Andrews' ear more than Williams did. Williams was very good at his job but he could be somewhat clueless about what was happening behind the scenes at the company. Ben interpreted Searles' overreaction as an affirmation that perhaps there was more than what was contained in the official reports. Searles had obviously been told something about the "accident" that Landgan did not want made public. Ben responded to Searles that he would follow his recommendations and that he was just making small talk based on what he had heard. Searles harrumphed and walked out of the room, leaving Ben and Gill sitting there.

Ben went back to his lab. When he got there, a janitor was sweeping the floor. The Indian was of average height and build. His complexion was neither the darkest nor the lightest Ben had seen. He had a full beard, which looped back over each ear ultimately disappearing underneath a burgundy colored turban. Ben surmised he was a Sikh.

Ben sat down at his station and began to prepare some slides to view under the microscope. Every time he reached for the methylene blue to begin the staining process, he looked up at the Indian who by this time had segued to cleaning the windows. Finally Ben called out to him.

"Excuse me."

"Am I bothering you, sir? I can come back later to finish my work if that would be more convenient for you."

"No, no. Your work is fine. It doesn't bother me at all. I just have a couple of questions for you if that's alright."

"Certainly, sir."

"First, my name is Benjamin Albert. What's your name?"

"Singh, sir. Jasbinder Singh."

"It's pleasure to meet you, Mr. Singh."

Singh nodded in return.

"Mr. Singh, have you been with Langdan long?"

"About two years, Mr. Albert."

"Did you know any of the people who were killed in the accident a few months back?"

Singh looked wary but answered anyway.

"No sir. Two of them I had seen around but I did not know any of them personally."

"They say there was some problems in the city, some unrest, after the accident and the subsequent investigation."

"Yes, there was, but the police quickly calmed the situation. They..." his voice trailed off.

"You sound like you have some additional thoughts on what happened."

"No, nothing more."

"Okay. Thank you, Mr. Singh."

Ben watched for a few moments while the Sikh resumed cleaning the windows and then he returned to his own microscopy work.

At 9:30 that evening, there was a knock on the door of Ben's hotel room. He had just returned from dinner and was reading over his notes from the day. He had given Ram the evening off to be with his family so he answered the door himself. When he opened the door, Mr. Singh was there along with another Indian man. This man was about four inches shorter than Mr. Singh and muscularly built. Unlike Singh, he was clean shaven. He greeted Ben with a scowl.

"Mr. Singh. To what do I owe the pleasure at this hour of the night?"

Jasbinder Singh was apologetic.

"Mr. Albert, I beg your forgiveness for intruding upon you at this late hour, but it is important we talk to you. This is Mr. Supash Dutta. I was telling Mr. Dutta of our conversation earlier today and he insisted he had to talk to you immediately."

Dutta held up his hand, immediately silencing Singh. Ben invited the men into his room.

"My good friend Mr. Singh is correct; I am very curious as to why you, an American who works for Langdan Textiles, have shown such interest in the suspicious death of five Indians. He spoke of your sincerity. I also know that your bearer, Ramachander Parthathy, is the brother of one of the men killed and that you have been asking him similar questions."

Dutta paused for a second. He was trying to convey that he had eyes and ears everywhere. Ben had to admit he was impressed with the amount of reconnaissance this man was able to do on short notice. Dutta continued.

"I have come here this evening to see for myself what your intentions are in asking about this matter. Are you concerned that an injustice may have been perpetrated here? Are you simply curious? Or, have you been sent by Langdan textiles to entrap other Indians into implicating themselves and then finding themselves in jail or worse?"

"Mr. Dutta," Ben responded, "I admire your courage because if I were the latter, I certainly would not tell you so but would lead you on so that you would implicate yourself and ultimately you would find yourself in jail...or worse. I am not sure what I can say to convince you I am not a company man—at least not on this issue—but I am not. We were sent word by telegram about the accident, or rather deaths, prior to our arrival and I must confess that I did not even have the slightest bit of curiosity about it at that point. Accidents happen all the time, don't they? I didn't see any need for me to become in any way involved and I probably wouldn't have except for a conversation I had with a curious little man in a teahouse the other day. He mentioned the deaths and put them into a new light for me that piqued my curiosity. I've been asking questions ever since."

"A curious little man, Mr. Albert?" Dutta was obviously skeptical. He was the one who presumed to know all and, if there were a "curious little man" with information on the deaths, he would know about it.

"Yes, I never met anyone like him. He had a way of captivating your soul, and frankly I'm not even sure I have a soul. His name was Mohandas. Mohandas Gandhi."

Singh and Dutta both sat up ramrod straight at the mention of the name.

"You met Bapu? That's impossible!" They responded nearly in unison.

Ben did not like being called a liar or having his impeccable memory questioned.

"I don't know anything about Bapu; he did not introduce himself by that name. Rather, he introduced himself by the name I just said. He said he was in Calcutta for an Indian National

Committee Conference. Everybody had demands on him every minute of every day and he needed to be alone for a couple hours so he snuck out to get a pot of tea. He was wearing a ridiculous looking old-fashioned suit. The place was packed and he invited me to sit with him for a spell. We talked about a whole array of issues, but one of them was the Langdan accident and some suspicions that lingered about the causes or implications of the deaths."

The two men sat there dumbfounded. They had heard that Gandhi was coming for the conference but neither of them held out any hope that they could come within a mile of the man now that his fame was growing. Yet here was this white man—a man who had just arrived in Calcutta less than three months ago and had never even heard of Gandhi—who got to sit and share tea with the great man. The world was so unfair. Dutta offered clarification to Ben.

"Bapu means 'father'. He would not use it himself. Rather, it is an honorific title bestowed upon him by others out of love and respect."

Then Dutta turned reproachful.

"I am surprised that you had never heard of Mahatma Gandi. Mahatma is another title meaning 'Great Soul'. You really should do a better job of research before you go to a new country."

Ben smiled.

"That's exactly the admonition Mr. Gandhi gave me. I will take it to heart the next time I travel."

"You asked why I would come to you, sight unseen and not knowing you at all. You mention that I was putting myself at risk by doing so. Perhaps, but I have known Mr. Singh since we were children and I trust his judgment. He seemed to think you were sincere, as did Ram. Now that I have learned that Bapu saw enough goodness in you to confide in you; that is good enough for me. I believe you are interested in justice."

"What, Mr. Dutta, do you feel was unjust?"

Mr. Dutta paused for a second, not because he doubted his appraisal of Ben but more for dramatic effect.

"We have some evidence that casts doubt on the official version of the accident. We believe that one or more of these men were murdered by the company you work for."

"Have you presented this evidence to the authorities? I'm sure they are not as corrupt as you think and are interested in the truth."

Dutta smiled and shook his head.

"Ah, to be young and naïve once again. That would be nice. The authorities have the answer they want; they will not look favorably on anyone disrupting the peace with new theories or evidence. I do hope that you have heard of Amritsar, Mr. Albert."

"Yes, the massacre last year of hundreds of men, women and children by British soldiers."

"Very good, Mr. Albert," responded Dutta somewhat condescendingly, "The authorities had hard evidence of an atrocity and yet the commander, General Dyer, was sent back to England to what I believe was a hero's welcome. These are only five deaths—an inconsequential number to be sure—but we need to make the world understand that every life, Indian, White, Hindu, Muslim or whatever, is precious. We need to let them know about it, to let them know we are not going to allow this sort of thing to happen anymore without consequences. We plan to make an appeal to the Indian National Committee next week. It is heartening to know that Bapu is already aware of the case and is willing to petition on our behalf."

"What do you want of me?"

"We would like you to get as much information from inside the company as you can prior to our meeting with the Committee."

"You're asking that I spy on my own company?"

"In the interest of justice, yes."

Surprising himself, Ben did not outright decline the suggestion. Instead, he told the gentlemen that he would think it over and get back to them. They said they would drop by at the same time the following day. Dutta apologized for pressing him but time was of the essence. He said they had an ally on the Committee who was ready to present their case but he needed a bit more evidence to proceed. Dutta did not tell Ben who that person was.

The men rose as one, shaking hands and quietly acknowledging their goodbyes. As Ben let them out, he swore he could see the door to Searles' room closing, but he passed this off as a coincidence.

The following morning was hot and humid as Ben left the hotel for the laboratory. His walk brought him through the local produce market. The art of haggling was as alive and well as women dickered with the stall owners over the price of tomatoes and beans. As long as he was not involved in the negotiations, Ben enjoyed the squabbling and interplay. He had gotten quite adept at spotting who the master hagglers were; generally they were the merchants but an occasional wife could drive a hard bargain. The true experts were those merchants who could get the price they wanted but still make the customer feel like he or she had won. It was truly an art.

On previous trips through the market, he had focused on the squabbling, the interchange between merchant and customer. On this day, he looked beyond the stalls to the alleys in back of them. There he noted dozens of the poor, the destitute, hovering, hoping that some charity might be offered their way. Or perhaps, they were waiting to pounce on produce that was deemed unfit for sale and thrown out. He supposed they had always been there, lurking in the shadows; he just never saw them.

When he arrived at the office, his mind had shifted to thinking about the direction he was about to take. The official files for the entire company were stored in the room next to his lab. He generally worked later than most people so it would be very easy to rifle through the files to see if there was any information of note. He made up his mind; it was a decision he did not take lightly.

That night, Mr. Dutta arrived at Ben's door, this time alone.

"Mr. Singh had some family business he had to attend to so I am here alone," he noted but then he went right to the point, "Will you help us?"

Ben did not entirely trust Mr. Dutta. Not that he thought Dutta was up to anything underhanded but rather that he was not revealing everything he knew. Ben did not like operating this much in the dark on anything but in the end he decided to follow his instincts and agreed to help. He told Mr. Dutta he would not be able to do anything the following day as he was venturing out into the jute fields to take some samples but would look through the company files the following evening. That was all Dutta needed to hear as he headed back to the door. The meeting lasted less than two minutes.

Ben found the work in the field to be extremely rewarding. Mr. Tibbetts was unable to accompany him on this day, so he got himself an automobile, an antiquated Packard, to drive the twenty miles to his destination. Shifting gears with no right hand was a challenge, but he was able to manage.

What he liked most about the work in the field was the solitude. He always seemed to be at someone's disposal in the lab or the office. Out amongst the jute, he could be alone with his thoughts with no one or nothing to disturb him. He left at dawn and arrived at around nine in the morning. The jute was at a stage where it did not need any attention so there were not any field hands in the vicinity. After four hours, he gathered the data he needed. Sitting on the bank of the river, he ate the sandwich he had brought and then started the trip back. He arrived at his office at around four and spent the next three hours writing up his notes. Finally, he decided it was time to call it a day and headed back to his hotel to get cleaned up for dinner.

When he got up to his room he found Major Highsmith and two soldiers standing in the hallway.

"Major Highsmith. To what do I owe this unexpected pleasure?"

Seeing the major at his doorstep was hardly a pleasure to Ben, but it certainly was unexpected.

"Good evening, Mr. Albert," Highsmith responded somberly, "May we come in? I have some serious business to discuss with you."

"Why certainly," Ben responded as he unlocked the door. They all walked in. Ben invited them to sit down. Only the major accepted the invitation while the soldiers remained standing, assuming posts in front of the door as if they expected Ben to try and escape.

"Mr. Albert," the major began, "Are you acquainted with a Mr. Sanjit Rama? He is a member of the Indian National Committee."

"No, I'm not."

"Are you familiar with any member of the Indian National Committee?"

"Major, what is this all about?"

"Please just answer my questions, Mr. Albert."

"Okay. I did meet a gentleman by the name of Mr. Gandhi the other day."

"Gandhi? I find that highly unlikely. We would have known of such a meeting. Please do not lie to me, Mr. Albert."

"I am not lying. It was a chance encounter in a tea house, not a meeting."

Highsmith continued his line of questioning undeterred.

"Are you acquainted with a Mr. Supash Dutta?"

"Why yes. I met him two days ago and then again last night."

"Can you tell me the subject of your discussions with Mr. Dutta?"

"No, I cannot. I promised him that our discussions were in complete confidence."

"I see. No need to worry. My associates are in the process of taking Mr. Dutta's statement as we speak. I just thought you may want to get things off your chest before the hole you are in gets any deeper."

"I have absolutely no idea what you are talking about, Major. Has there been some trouble?"

"Yes, but I am the one asking the questions, Mr. Albert."

The two men stared at each other for a few seconds.

"Well, Major, ask your questions then."

"Where were you this afternoon around 1:00 to 1:30?"

"I was standing in among thousands of jute plants conducting some experiments."

"Is there anyone who can corroborate your whereabouts?"

"No, I drove out alone, worked by myself and drove back. There weren't even any workers in the fields."

"That's too bad because at around that time we received a report that a white man answering to your description—even down to the missing right hand I might add—was seen coming out of the residence where Sanjit Rama was staying. A half hour later we received a call from a servant in the house that he found Mr. Rama. He had been stabbed to death. Now the person who reported the white man with one hand also told us that he recognized Mr. Dutta in the same vicinity. As you probably know, Mr. Dutta is a known agitator in Calcutta. We have him in custody and we expect him to give us the entire story. You will only make it easier on yourself by doing the same."

"What the hell are you talking about? Are you accusing me of murder? I demand to know who said they saw me at the residence of this Mr. Rama when I was twenty miles away. This is preposterous."

"Sir, I am under no obligation to reveal my sources at this time. This will all come out at your trial."

At this point, Highsmith nodded to the two soldiers who began a systematic search of the hotel room. After about five minutes, one of the soldiers called to the major from the bathroom.

"Sir, you better come see this."

Highsmith went into the bathroom while the other soldier made sure Ben stayed firmly in his seat. When the major emerged, he was holding a beige Indian man's wrap stained with blood. From the wrap, he pulled an equally bloody ornate knife of about eight inches in length.

"Sergeant Willoughby, will you please manacle this man so we can take him to the station for the murder of Sanjit Rama."

"I've never seen those clothes or that knife in my life. I have no idea how they got in my room. You have to believe me!"

"I only believe my eyes. The servant told us that Mr. Rama was left half-naked. He should be able to identify this as Mr. Rama's, don't you think? Which was it? Did you want a souvenir of your kill, or was it easier to spirit away the knife in the wrap?"

"I tell you I've never seen this man, his clothes or that knife before. Why on earth would I want to kill him? I never laid eyes on him and had absolutely no reason."

"We'll figure all that out in good time. There are many white people who do not want the Indian National Committee to exist. Perhaps you're one of them. In any case, we have more than enough to place you under arrest. Lead him away, please."

32
Catherine

I've said it before and I'll say it again: nothing good ever comes from receiving a telegram. Usually they bring bad news: a death or some such tragedy. So when I opened the front door and there was a man with Western Union emblazoned on his breast, I immediately became wary. The man delivered the telegram, tipped his hat and was on his way.

The telegram was terse. I later learned that Ben could only send a maximum of seven words. It read: Arrested for murder. Innocent. Framed. Help. Ben

I read and re-read the seven words over dozens of times, trying to distill any further meaning out of the meager message, but nothing was forthcoming. All I knew was that he was arrested for murder. Whom was he accused of murdering? He said he was innocent, of this I had absolutely no doubt. Why did they believe he did it? He was framed. Who was framing him and why? He asked for my help. What can I do? Should I rush to India to be with him? How could I rush to India with a young baby to take care of? Is there anything I can do from here?

As I was sitting there staring off into space, lost and distraught, Molly walked into the room. Molly. I had not given any thought to how to break the news to her. When Ben first left on his trip, Molly had seemed her usual self, vital and energetic. As the months passed, however, she became increasingly lethargic. She had lost interest in many of the activities she had previously pursued. Finally, I forced her to go see a doctor. After examining her, the doctor told us that he believed there was a weakness in her heart. He said it was not entirely uncommon in someone her age; she had just turned 61 years old.

If she did indeed have a "weakness in her heart" how could I now tell her that her son, the very light of her life, her American Son, was in an Indian prison charged with a heinous crime. I decided not to tell her anything until I learned more. I folded the telegram, stuffed it in my pocket and painted on the pleasantest face I could muster and cheerily greeted her. She had heard the doorbell and asked who it was. I lied, telling her it was a solicitor that I summarily dismissed. So that she wouldn't ask anything more, I changed the subject and suggested it might be a good idea for us to take Harry for a walk. All of us could use a little fresh air I told her. She agreed and went to put on a jacket while I put Harry in his stroller.

When we returned, she said she was tired and would like to take a nap. I tucked both her and Harry in and then went to the telephone. I had to call Langdan Textiles to start getting some answers. The receptionist connected me to a Mr. Irving England in the company's legal department.

"Mrs. Albert, we have been in contact with our Calcutta office. Your husband is in serious trouble. We have hired a solicitor to assist him, but from what I have been told, the evidence is pretty conclusive."

"My husband is innocent. I know he is. Someone is framing him."

"That will all come out in the investigation, I am sure, Mrs. Albert. I must advise you that the person your husband is accused of killing was very popular throughout Calcutta. There will be much pressure for a speedy trial and a conviction."

Mr. England paused for a few seconds and then continued.

"Of course, Mrs. Albert, while we will assist in your husband's defense, we must be very careful that Langdan is kept at arms length throughout the process. I trust that you understand."

I understood perfectly. A few sarcastic responses raced through my mind but I decided I would just be wasting my breath. It was no use talking to this gentleman, especially over the telephone. I thanked him for the information and said goodbye. I knew what I needed to do. I had to go to Langdan Headquarters and discuss this face to face with someone who had the power to actually do something. I had to go and confront my father.

As I hung up the telephone, I was concocting the story I would tell Molly as to why I needed to be away for a few days. I also had to convince someone to take care of Harry and Molly while I was away.

I decided to tell her I had gotten word that an elderly aunt of my mother's passed away up in Boston. Since I was her only remaining kin, I had to travel there for a few days to take care of the estate. While I was up in the area, I would look in on our apartment to make sure nothing was amiss. I would also stop at Ben's office to take care of a few matters. All in all, this was not too far from the truth. My mother did have an Aunt Clara who lived just outside of Boston and had recently passed away. I was the only kin and had been notified, but there wasn't anything in the way of estate to worry about. I signed a few papers and mailed them back and that was that. The other two parts of the story, checking on our place and going to Langdan Textiles, were absolutely true.

I asked Ben's brother Robert to stay with Molly and Harry. He liked me well enough but I wasn't blood. If I asked him to do this for me, he might not have agreed but he would do absolutely anything for his baby brother. I put it to him in a way that he was doing this favor for Ben, not me.

I was reluctant to tell Robert the truth for fear that he would accidentally spill the beans to his mother about Ben being put into prison. Again, I resorted to a half true story. I told him that Ben had sent me a telegram (true) asking me to help him (true) in something involving the company (somewhat true) and I had to go to Boston for a few days to handle personally at company headquarters (again somewhat true). As soon as Robert heard that this was a request generated by Ben, he was practically packing his overnight bag.

I was sad that Molly did not feel up to seeing me off at the train. She was tired so much of the time. I kissed her and Harry goodbye and headed to the train station. The trip was uneventful but I got increasingly nervous and apprehensive as I closed in on South Station. I had no idea if my father would even agree to see me and, if he did, I had no clue what I would say to enlist his help.

Ben had told me that the office of Mr. Franklin T. Andrews, President of Langdan Textiles, was on the fourth floor so I did not even stop at the receptionist desk on the ground floor but went straight to the steps. The receptionist was filing her nails so she did not notice me scoot by.

On the fourth floor there was a middle-aged lady sitting at a desk in the outer office.

"May I help you?"

"I'd like to see Mr. Andrews please."

"Do you have an appointment?"

"No, my name is Catherine Albert. My husband is Benjamin Albert. It's vitally important that I speak to Mr. Andrews."

I could not detect any signs of recognition of my husband's name on the lady's face although I knew that to be impossible. By now Ben's name must have been gossiped about in every corner of the company.

"I'm very sorry, but Mr. Andrews left specific instructions not to be disturbed. If you would care to make an appointment, I could help you with that."

She paused for a second and then resumed.

"I'm also very sorry to hear about your husband. I met him once and he seemed like a very nice young man."

I knew I wasn't going to bull my way past the keeper at the gate so I tried a different approach.

"You're Mrs. Epstein, aren't you?"

"Why, yes. Do I know you?"

"No, but my mother, Lily Jackson, used to talk about you all the time."

Mrs. Epstein jumped up from her chair and threw her arms around me.

"You're Lily's daughter? Why of course you are. I can see the similarities. Your mother was my best friend when she worked here. We kept in touch for years after that but I'm afraid we haven't been too good about communicating in recent years. How is your mother doing?"

I now realized that I should have contacted Mrs. Epstein after my mother passed away but I did not want anything to do with Langdan Textiles or anything else associated with my father.

"My mother passed away about a year ago from the influenza. I'm sorry I didn't let you know."

Mrs. Epstein looked like all the air had been taken out of her as she settled back into her chair.

"Lily. Dead? Oh no. I am so very sorry. She was a wonderful lady. This is such a blow."

Tears were welling in her eyes as she thought about Lily Jackson, but then she recovered.

"You want to see Mr. Andrews?"

"Yes, I need to get more information on what happened to my husband. He could not have done what they charged him with. I called and spoke to Mr. Irving England. He wasn't much help, I'm afraid. Perhaps it was because I was trying to do it over the phone."

Mrs. Epstein rolled her eyes.

"Wouldn't have been any better in person. Irving's a nice guy but rather feckless, I'm afraid."

"I had gathered as much so I thought I would come up here and speak to Mr. Andrews himself."

"For Lily, anything. He's only doing some paperwork by himself right now so I will get you in."

"Thank you. But don't let him know I'm Lily's daughter. It's rather complicated."

Mrs. Epstein gave me a look like she understood completely and nodded. She went through the door and emerged a minute later.

"Mrs. Albert, Mr. Andrews will see you now."

Through her tears at the thought of my mother's death, she smiled as I went in.

I can't describe the mix of feelings I experienced as I walked through that door. Trepidation, anger, curiosity, loathing—they were all there in some measure. When I entered his office, he did not even extend me the courtesy of getting up from his desk to greet me. He wanted to make it clear I was intruding on his time and only out of his infinite beneficence was he able to grant me an audience. Instead, he sat there and waited until I neared and then he rose and extended his hand.

He did not recognize me. We had only laid eyes upon each other that one time at the funeral and even though I possessed a passing resemblance to my mother, I doubted that he would pick up on it. Much time had passed. Furthermore, the context of this meeting was not one in which he would have an inkling that this was his daughter standing in front of him. Still, though, I was prepared if he did recognize me.

He sat in his chair, scribbling a few notes on the pad in front of him, as if to emphasize how much I was disturbing his day.

"Mrs. Albert, let me first express my sympathy to you over the trouble your husband has gotten himself into. You must be beside yourself."

"Mr. Andrews, I am coming to you because I don't believe he did get himself into trouble. The telegram he sent me said he was innocent, that he was framed. And I believe him. I need your help in getting to the bottom of this."

"I know this must be very difficult for you. Ever since this unfortunate incident happened, I have been getting nearly hourly reports and from where I sit, the information seems rather conclusive that your husband is guilty. Sometimes people, even those to whom we are closest in the world, can at times be complete strangers to us. There could be any number of reasons why your husband could have snapped and done this. The pressures of work far away from home; a delayed trauma of his wartime service; an intense hatred of coloreds, which I understand he had. Any one of these could have caused him to snap."

I could not believe any of these things about Ben.

"Can I take a look at these reports you've received? I have only a seven word telegram to go on."

"Of course, my dear."

I physically recoiled at this bastard using this term of endearment in my direction.

"As I said, I'm sorry but there's really nothing else I can do."

"So you won't help me to find out the actual story here, to investigate this further?"

"No. As I mentioned, I have nothing to convince me that what is in the official report is anything but the truth. The company is providing your husband with legal representation to ensure that his rights are protected but I cannot in good conscience authorize anything more than that."

"When have you been accused of having a conscience?"

"I beg your pardon."

"You said you would not finance an investigation to prove my husband's innocence and to find out who framed him and how he was framed. However, in actuality you will be paying for it."

"If you are looking to somehow blackmail me, young lady, you will soon find yourself in a cell just like your husband's!"

"Oh, no blackmail will be necessary as you have already given me the funds to start my own investigation."

"Madam, please leave and take your lunacy with you!"

"I'm not crazy. Over the years I have never touched the generous trust fund you set up for me. Now, I will put that fund, which has grown substantially over the years, thank you very much, to a worthy use."

Slowly the truth began to dawn on him.

"Catherine? Is that you?"

"Yes, that is who I am. Daughter of Lily Jackson. If you would care to look on me with loathing like the first and only time you saw me, please feel free. This time I am not an impressionable thirteen year old starving for a father's attention. I can take it now and dish it back in equal measure."

He was still dazed.

"Lily's daughter? How is your mother?"

Even now, all these years later, he cannot take full responsibility. I'm your daughter too, you bastard!

"My mother is dead, but she might as well have died years ago for all you care."

"Dead? When? Why wasn't I informed? I had a right to know."

The news had hit him so hard that he seemed to have shrunk to about a third his size. For an instant, I almost had pity on him but his last statement changed my mind immediately.

"Right? You think you have any rights when it comes to my mother or me? You think that pouring money on us relieves you of the guilt that will forever stain your soul for abandoning your wife and baby daughter?"

Life was starting to come back into his face.

"Yes, I had a right. I loved Lily more than anything."

"You sure have a strange way of demonstrating your love. And it's reassuring after all these years to hear of the undying love you feel for this woman. It's so touching."

He looked up at me between his hands.

"You mother never told you, did she?"

"Tell me what?"

I had caught him off guard with news of my mother's death. It was not a position he liked to be in. He was the type of man who had to maintain and exert dominance over everybody. He knew he had information that he could now use to put me off guard and in turn put him back on top.

"That those many years ago you were not paying respects to your grandfather."

"I don't understand. What are you driving at?"

"That I'm not your father. If anything, I guess I would be your stepbrother."

"What?"

"What I am telling you is that you did not attend the funeral for your grandfather. Rather, you were paying your respects to your father. Oh yes, I loved your mother but she loved my father and bore him, not me, a child. After that, I sent the both of you away but I never forgot her or stopped loving her. Yes, I should have been informed that she died. I deserved that. It was my right. I can never forgive you for not letting me know. Now get out."

His eyes burned with hatred for me. I was floored by this revelation but I was not going to give him any satisfaction by reacting in any way. My eyes burned back at him as I turned and exited the room.

I thanked Mrs. Epstein for her help and for being a friend to my mother. I caught the next train back to New Brunswick.

33

The British colonial government did not want a repeat of the unrest and disturbance they had experienced in Calcutta after the Langdan accident so they moved to have an especially quick and very public trial. Langdan had hired a solicitor to manage Ben's defense, but this attorney was hardly given any time to conduct an investigation or to develop a workable defense strategy.

Sanjit Rama had indeed been a local hero. He raised himself up from the slums through education and hard work. He had been an ardent supporter of Indian rights and an advocate for the poor. He supported abolishment of the caste system and raising up of the untouchables in society. His death, just before the convening of the Indian National Committee conference, was a blow to the common Indian citizen in Calcutta and throughout the entire subcontinent.

The royal courtroom was packed as Ben was led in. His feet were shackled to his left hand. Although he had been allowed to shave and clean himself up, he looked disheveled and disreputable. His face was swollen with patches of blue from beatings to get him to confess and save the city from going through a trial. The crowd, which had already convicted him in their mind, was remarkably constrained and subdued as he was paraded to his seat.

Ben knew none of his traveling companions would be in attendance. Williams was halfway back to the States. Gill came to visit him once but said that he had been ordered back to Boston. Ben's solicitor, Mr. Hastings, had warned him that, while the company had retained him, Langdan had to maintain an arm's length relationship here. They could not run the risk of the business being adversely impacted by a negative outcome of the trial. Ben was on his own. Still, though, he would have liked to have had the support of Williams and Gill, men whom he regarded as friends.

The trial lasted only two days. Three judges in white wigs presided. Four men were called to testify. The first was Major Highsmith who talked about receiving the tip that a white man with no right hand had been seen fleeing the home where Mr. Rama was staying for the duration of the conference. The person who contacted Highsmith said that this person appeared very nervous and was acting suspiciously.

After Mr. Rama had been found dead, it was not difficult to track down Ben. There were not many one-handed white men walking the streets of Calcutta, the major informed the court. He described going to the hotel and confronting Ben in his room. He said that, in his trained opinion, Ben was acting nervous and suspicious especially when he ordered his men to search the room where they found the bloody wrap and knife. When these were produced as evidence for the court, there was an audible collective gasp throughout the courtroom followed by a period of murmuring and discussion amongst the observers. The judges quickly restored order. Mr. Hastings asked a few perfunctory questions of this witness after which Highsmith was dismissed.

The next witness was Mr. Rama's valet. His sole purpose was to identify the wrap presented in court as the one his employer was dressed in on the day he was murdered. Since wraps such as these are worn by millions of men throughout India, the valet was pressed to say why he was certain it was Mr. Rama's. He noted two features that made him certain. First, on the inside hem there was an embroidered symbol of a bird; it was the trademark of the tailor who made all of Mr. Rama's clothing. Second, Mr. Rama had a slight hunching of his left shoulder. Throughout his life, he had been very conscious of this deformity. To give the illusion that there was no abnormality, the tailor bunched up the cloth on the right shoulder. The valet was handed the bloody wrap and he demonstrated to the court where the bunching was located. Hastings had no questions for this witness.

After a short recess, the court called for the third witness to take the stand.

"Will Mr. Alexander Searles please come forward."

From the back of the room, Searles marched forward and took his place in the witness box. After all of the preliminaries were taken care of, the prosecutor got to the meat of his questioning.

"Mr. Searles, were you the person who contacted Major Highsmith, advising him that a person resembling Mr. Albert, the defendant, was, in the words of the major, fleeing the residence where Sanjit Rama was staying?"

"I was."

"Where were you when you saw this person?"

"I was in a café across the square having a cup of tea."

"You knew Mr. Albert prior to this case?"

"Yes, I did."

"Can you please describe to the court how you came to know Mr. Albert?"

"We had been traveling together for the past three months from Boston to Calcutta."

"So you would say that you have gotten to know the defendant rather well over that time?"

"Yes, I would say so. Even with the differences in our ages, interests and background, one cannot help develop some sort of a bond with a traveling companion, especially over an extended period of time."

"If you know Mr. Albert so well, why then would the major say that when you contacted him that you said you saw a man that fit Mr. Albert's description, even down to his missing right hand, rather than tell him directly that Mr. Albert was the man?

"Well, I've come to develop a fondness for the boy. I and my other traveling companions who are close in age to me took him under our wings as this was his first international business trip. I wanted to perform my civic duty to help keep public officials such as Mr. Rama safe, but I did not want to see the boy get into unnecessary trouble."

"Are you willing to state for the record that the person you saw was in fact Mr. Benjamin Albert rather than simply someone who resembled Mr. Albert?"

"I am"

Ben could not stand it anymore and he stood up.

"You lie! You know I was never near that place, you anti-Semitic bastard!"

Ben's attorney grabbed Ben by the arm and pulled him back into his seat while the presiding judge gaveled to proceedings back to order.

"The court will not tolerate outbursts like this. Any more and the defendant will be removed from the courtroom." Turning to the prosecutor, "You may proceed."

"Mr. Searles, did you know the deceased, Sanjit Rama?"

"I knew of him and knew where he was staying, but no, I had never met the poor man."

"If you did not know him, why would you know or even care where he lived?"

It was obvious that the prosecution and Searles had done a good job of rehearsing prior to the trial to answer any questions that may linger in the judges' minds.

"As Director for Government Relations for Langdan Textiles, it is my job to know such things. I can tell you who is important in local, regional, national and colonial government and politics. I know that there has been a great deal of unrest throughout Calcutta and I had to be aware of how that unrest occurs and how it is being handled by the authorities."

"That's very impressive, Mr. Searles."

"Thank you."

"Can you describe for the court what made you suspicious about Mr. Albert's behavior that day?"

"One of the things that I had learned during my travels with Mr. Albert was that he was a racist. He would constantly make remarks about the coloreds, into which he lumped all non-white people. Once we got into India, where the color of the skin of many people here is often as dark as the Negroes back home, his talk got more offensive and virulent. I realize I should not have jumped to conclusions, but when I saw him nervously hurrying from the residence, closely examining every Indian who walked by like he was trying to recognize them, I got concerned that he was looking to turn his rhetoric into actions."

"Can you give us a reason why he would be looking for Mr. Rama?"

"Mr. Rama was an advocate for Indians, especially the poor and down-trodden. He probably saw him as someone who could disrupt the natural order of things, namely that whites are superior and coloreds inferior."

"Is there anything else?"

"Well, yes, but it would be wild speculation on my part."

"Mr. Searles, I believe this court will decide what is relevant and what is speculation. Please proceed."

"I was told by someone who seemed to know that Mr. Albert boasted that, if he had the chance, he would make an attempt on the life of Mr. Gandhi as well."

The defense made an objection that this was speculative hearsay but the pronouncement had its effect. It took the police all they could handle to keep the crowd from setting upon Ben. It took the judges nearly ten minutes to finally restore order. Searles was dismissed and court was adjourned until the following day.

When the court resumed, the officers led Ben into the courtroom. It was obvious that he had been beaten over night. It was unclear to the court whether he had been beaten by the police or by fellow inmates. The presiding judge was incensed and ordered that the beatings stop and that Ben be kept from the rest of the general prison population.

Ben was called to the stand to present his defense. His story was exactly as he had told Major Highsmith. He was away all that day in the jute fields. He knew of no one who could corroborate his story. He had never met Mr. Rama in his life nor even knew who he was. He did admit to meeting Mr. Gandhi once in a teahouse and had a very congenial chat with him. In fact, Gandhi had opened his eyes on the plight of the everyday Indians. He had absolutely no idea how the bloody wrap and knife ended up in his hotel room. Lastly, he stated unequivocally that Mr. Searles was lying; why he was lying Ben did not know other than the fact that he hated Jews.

The court was dismissed while the judges debated Ben's fate.

34
Catherine

I felt so lost and alone as I rode the train back to New Brunswick. Even though I loathed and despised him my entire life, I still had the comfort of loathing and despising my father. Now he was just another man.

All this swirled around in my mind but what was even more distressing was that he was not going to help me free Ben. He wouldn't because he was involved somehow in the frame-up; I could see it in his eyes. I made a great show to him that I would pursue the investigation myself, but I didn't have a clue where to start. I needed a private investigator, but where could I find one who would go to India—to the ends of the earth if necessary—to help me?

I had to tell Molly what had happened. Regardless of how much it might hurt, it was not right for me to keep this news from her. I sat down with her as soon as I got home. Together, we would wait on pins and needles for any news from Ben. There were no letters or telegrams. Only silence.

A week passed, and then two. I ventured into New York to see as many private investigative agencies as I could find. Each of them was very sorry but they did not do any work out of the United States. At most, they would venture into Canada or Mexico but India was out of the question. I took the train home more dejected and despondent than I'd ever been in my life.

As I was walking up the sidewalk toward home, I noticed a tall fit man with a handlebar mustache about to knock on the door. He looked to be in his early forties.

"Can I help you?" I called out.

"Are you Mrs. Albert?"

"Yes, yes I am." I answered hesitantly.

"My name is Walter Jones. I've come to see you about your husband."

I let him in. The name sounded familiar and then it dawned on me.

"Are you Sergeant Jones?"

"Former sergeant, ma'am. I've been out of the service for a few years now."

"Please, have a seat. Can I get you anything?"

"No thank you. Let me get right to the point. Ben and I have kept in touch ever since the war. He sent me a letter from India. He asked me to contact you."

Jones handed the letter to me as he continued.

"As you can see in the letter, he asked that I come to you and offer my assistance."

I read the letter.

My dear Sergeant,

I am writing to request the largest favor one man can ask of another. I hope you will be willing and able to help me in this, my greatest hour of need.

As I told you the last time we corresponded over three months ago, my company sent me on a business trip to India. However, while here I was arrested and charged with a crime, a murder, I did not commit. Yesterday, the court concluded its trial and found me guilty. I have been sentenced to twenty years at hard labor.

You must believe me that I am innocent. I was framed. I need you to help me prove my innocence and get to the bottom of the story.

The first thing I need you to do is to go to my mother's house in New Brunswick, New Jersey (235 Commercial Avenue) and tell my wife, Catherine, what has happened to me. Tell her I have tried to write her many times but I doubt she has gotten any of my letters. I begged one of the guards to let me send her a letter. He said yes, but then laughed as he tore it into little pieces and threw it in my face. A second guard, one who I think believes that I am innocent, witnessed this and later told me to write another letter that he would be sure to post. Even in this hell hole there is an occasional kindness.

I ask you to be with Catherine when she reads this so you can help blunt the shock. She can also help you in the quest upon which I am unreasonably asking you to embark. Catherine is very capable and intelligent and can be your home base.

The person I believe you should start with is Alexander Searles, one of my traveling companions. He is Langdan's Director for Governmental Relations. If not the instigator for framing me, he is definitely complicit in its execution. His lies on the witness stand sealed my fate. I believe he headed back to Boston immediately after the trial. My two other traveling companions, Mr. Herbert Williams and Mr. Frederick Gill, may be able to give you some guidance, but as far as I know, they weren't involved and were ordered back to Boston before the trial began.

There are other people in India who can help you, but I am reluctant to put their names in writing for fear their health and safety might be jeopardized if this letter does not reach its intended destination. Should you agree to be so generous as to assist me, I am allowed one visitor per week and I will be able to discuss this with you in greater detail. I can tell you that my being arrested is directly related to an accident that occurred at the Langdan facility shortly before I arrived. Five people were killed in this incident. I was made aware of some facts that suggested it might not have been as much an accident as the official report stated. My troubles began after I started asking some questions about it. That's about all I can say right here.

Walter, If you do choose to help me (and believe me, I will never hold it against you if you cannot), please be very careful. I was naïve in whom I confided and too open with people with whom I should have been circumspect. Whoever is behind this is ruthless and will stop at nothing. In any case, whether you are able to help me or not, please share this letter with Catherine. I want her to know that I love her and Harry and my mother. I will never stop loving her and think of her every minute of every day and look forward to being in her arms again soon.

Your friend,

Ben

My tears were readily flowing with the last paragraph. Sergeant Jones put his hand on my shoulder. I looked up at his face and received a comforting and reassuring smile.

"Will you be able to help us?"

"Yes ma'am, that's why I'm here. I owe my life to that man. My first order of business was to come here. I'm on my way now to Boston to see what information I can get out of Mr. Searles."

The way he said this last statement made me wonder what methods he will use to extract information from Searles. Ben had told me that prior to becoming a sergeant in the army, Mr. Jones had been a New York City police office for ten years. I imagined he had a whole array of techniques at his disposal. I hoped he used every one of them on that bastard Searles.

"Please, call me Catherine. Thank you, sergeant."

He smiled and did not correct me for calling him sergeant. That is how he thought of himself.

"It's an honor to do something to repay Ben. As he warned, I am going to be especially careful so, for the indefinite future, I will be going by the name of William Jenkins, just in case Ben had told some people at Langdan about our relationship."

"That's very smart, Bill."

"I prefer Will."

It was clear that, once Sergeant Jones embarked on a course of action—in this case adopting a new persona—he dove in headfirst.

"Okay Will. Please keep in touch with me and let me know where I can wire money to you. I realize you feel you have a debt to pay but I also feel an obligation to cover your expenses. I have the money and someday I'll tell you its ironic source."

"Thank you Catherine. I live comfortably but my means are not unlimited. I wasn't going to ask, but I will gladly accept payment to help me along."

I did not want to respond to this because I sensed he was somewhat embarrassed.

"Would you like to join us for dinner. You're welcome to stay the night and get a fresh start in the morning."

"No thank you, Catherine. I have a long drive up to Boston. I prefer to get an immediate start so that I am at Searles' doorstep as soon as I can."

"Thank you again, sergeant."

He tipped his hat and headed off. It was the most confident I'd felt in weeks.

35

Before Jones went to visit Catherine, he had called Langdan to determine whether Searles had returned home to the Boston area. Pretending to be his uncle, he called the office and said he was going to be in town and wanted to visit with his nephew but had misplaced his address. The young secretary was very taken by Jones' old man voice. She was sorry but Mr. Searles was not due back for another couple of days. Even though it was against company policy, she gladly gave him Searles' home address. She agreed not to tell Mr. Searles that he had called. Jones wanted to surprise his nephew whom he had not seen in over three years.

He also called the offices of Williams and Gill. They were both in town. He would spend the next two days getting whatever information he could out of them. From what Ben had written him, both Williams and Gill seemed to be generally decent sorts who had no use for Searles. He did not imagine them to be much of a problem but still to everyone at Langdan, to be safe, he was Will Jenkins.

He first went to see Williams. His secretary said that he would not be able to see Mr. Williams without an appointment but when he had her tell him that Ben Albert had sent him, he was let right in.

"Mr. Williams, it's nice to meet you."

"How can I help you, Mr. Jenkins?"

Jones had toyed with interviewing Williams and Gill together but then thought better of it. If they had anything to hide, it would be easier to catch them in lies if they were separated. Together, they could compare notes.

"I am both a friend of Benjamin Albert and have been retained by him as a private investigator to uncover the truth."

"I am glad to hear that. I know in my heart that Ben was

incapable of doing what they said he did. I had to leave the country for medical reasons before the trial. I wanted to return, on my own time, to help him but it was made clear to me that my job was forfeit if I did. God forgive me. I wanted to help him but I can't afford to be without my job. I have four children and a sickly wife."

Williams looked truly distraught over not being able to help.

"Ben's a good man," he whimpered, "I don't know what happened. No one will give me a straight answer."

"Well, that's what I am here for, Mr. Williams. Someone framed Ben and God help whoever that was. How well do you know Mr. Searles?"

"Too well, I fear. He is a vindictive bigoted anti-Semite. If you were to tell me he was tied up in this, I would not at all be surprised."

"Ben wrote me that he lied on the stand. His lies sealed the conviction."

"He could very well have lied; I don't doubt it for a minute. But I doubt Searles would lie without being ordered to do so. He's the ultimate unimaginative company man. He's only nominally smart, and then only in a conniving, following-orders way. He's certainly not the brains behind any conspiracy that I believe you are looking for."

"How about Mr. Frederick Gill? Could he be involved in anything?

"Fred? No way. Gill is a happy-go-lucky type of guy who doesn't have a mean bone in his body. He and Ben got very close during our trip. You'll want to talk to him of course, but I doubt you get much information or background. He's not the deepest guy in the world; neither is he the most observant. I don't think he really grasped how much trouble Ben was in until he got back to Boston and the news trickled in to us."

"Thank you for your time, Mr. Williams. You've been most helpful."

"The best of luck to you, Mr. Jenkins. Ben's a good man who did nothing wrong. I hope you can prove his innocence and set him free. Can I ask you one favor?"

"Of course."

"When you see Ben, tell him how sorry I am that I was spineless and would not buck the company to go back and help him. It's a guilt I'll live with the rest of my life."

"I'll be sure to pass your regards on to him, Mr. Williams."

As Williams had predicted, Gill was not much help. Five minutes into the interview, Gill started to sob uncontrollably. Jones suspected that all he was going to get out of Gill was emotion, nothing more, so he thanked him and left. Gill was wiping his eyes and nose as Jones walked out the door.

That night, Jones parked across the street from Searles brownstone in Newton. It was an upscale neighborhood with many cars on the street so Jones' Oldsmobile blended in with the others. The street's gaslights gave off a little light, but his automobile was shrouded in darkness. He was able to hunker down so that none of the neighbors got suspicious of a man sitting in his car for hours on end.

Searles' home was dark; no movement could be detected. Jones had learned that Searles was unmarried and had no children. He wanted to get Searles alone so he had to proceed cautiously and made sure that there was no one else there once he got home.

At around 11:00, a taxi pulled up in front and after a few minutes a man, whom Jones assumed was Searles, got out. The driver helped him up with his bags and then drove off. Jones could see him through various windows, going about the business a person does after arriving at home from a long trip before retiring for the night. At around midnight, the lights went out and Searles retired. Jones started up the car and returned to his hotel six blocks away to get some sleep. Before retiring, he advised the young man at the front desk that he would be leaving very early in the morning. He settled his bill right then and advised the clerk he would leave the key at the desk before walking out.

The following morning at 5:00, Jones awakened. The first thing he did was to shave off his trademark handlebar mustache. He then put on a pair of wire frame glasses with clear lenses. He looked in the mirror and nodded, pleased he could not recognize himself. The young man was asleep in his chair when he came downstairs. He quietly left his key with a two dollar tip on the counter, careful not to disturb the slumbering clerk.

He parked his Olds in the same spot he had parked the night before and waited for Searles to emerge, which he did around 6:30. Jones was going to confront him but then had a better idea. It would be more advantageous to talk with the man when he returned from work in the evening. He would be tired and more willing to talk. He might also be more susceptible to having a glass of sherry to loosen his tongue.

At around 6:45 that evening, he saw Searles walking up the street. As he was turning the key in the lock on the front door, Jones walked up to him.

"Mr. Searles," Jones called out.

"Do I know you?"

"Not yet, but I would like a minute of your time."

Searles started to go inside but Jones grabbed him by the arm, preventing him from entering.

"See here, take your hands off of me or I will call for the police."

"Please do."

With that, Jones pulled out his old New York City police badge and waved it in front of Searles' face, too quickly for him to focus on the details on the badge but slow enough for it to impart its official message. To emphasize the effect, Jones made sure that his jacket opened just enough for Searles to get a good glimpse of the service revolver in its holster. It worked. Searles invited Jones in and closed the door after him. They sat down in the Victorian styled parlor. Jones noticed the well-stocked liquor cabinet off to the side.

"What can I do for you, officer?"

"Lieutenant. Lieutenant Williams Jenkins. It has been a long day. I was wondering if a drink of whiskey would be too much to ask."

"Not at all. I believe I will join you, but I'm a Scotch man myself."

He poured the drinks and sat back down. They clinked glasses and took a sip.

"Mr. Searles, I'm here to ask about Mr. Benjamin Albert."

"Albert? He's in jail in Calcutta, India. He was convicted for murder. What interest could a Boston policeman have in him?"

"I am part of the Joint International Inquiry Commission. You probably have heard of us. The commission was set up to make discreet inquiries whenever anybody is accused of a crime in another country. It's very informal, but sometimes various countries will exchange prisoners and we like to have information ahead of time. Because Mr. Albert is a resident in the Boston area, I have to ask some questions. Purely routine, I can assure you, and entirely confidential."

Searles puffed himself up in accordance with the importance that was being accorded him.

"Of course, I am always ready to perform my civic duty."

"Okay, let's begin. You are Frederick Searles, Director of Government Relations for Langdan Textiles, correct?"

"Yes, I am."

"I have here that you are an Episcopalian."

"Yes, that's correct. Is that relevant to your inquiry?"

"Probably not. I have no idea why they threw some of these questions in, but I always assume that this questionnaire was designed by much wiser minds than mine. In any case," Jones leaned over to Searles and said in a near whisper, "it's not my place to question. Do or die, you know. I bet Langdan has you do certain stupid things that don't make sense but you do them anyway, eh?"

"You don't know the half of it."

They clinked glasses once again and shared a laugh at the foolishness of bureaucracies.

"Do you happen to know the religion of Mr. Albert? Albert, that sounds like a good solid WASP name."

"No, as a matter of fact, he's Jewish."

"You sure? I hate it when they try to pass for us, don't you?"

"I certainly do."

"Well, this shouldn't take very long. I'm certainly not going to expend a lot of effort on a Hebe. He can just rot in India for all I care. Oh, excuse me for my bluntness. My father lost his grocery store when I was a kid to a greedy Jewish landlord. I'm afraid I'm not very impartial when it comes to their kind."

"You don't have to excuse yourself to me. I understand perfectly."

"Thank you for your understanding. I'll try to get through this as quickly as I can. My records indicate that you testified against Mr. Albert. Is that correct?"

"Yes, it is."

"And he was convicted of killing an Indian," again Jones sidled over to Searles in a conspiratorial manner, "I frankly don't see what all the fuss was. To paraphrase General Sheridan, 'The only good Indian is a dead Indian', eh? And in the process we put a Jew out of circulation. Not bad."

The two shared another laugh and raised their glasses for another drink. Jones continued.

"What can you tell me about Mr. Albert?"

"I was glad to do my part to convict the little prick. He thought he was so smart, so much smarter than the rest of us. I taught him a good lesson, I guess. I wonder how the damn cripple is doing at hard labor."

"He was a cripple? My records don't have that fact."

"Yeah, no right hand. Said he lost it in the war. Frankly, I bet he overused it counting his money."

Searles laughed at his own joke. Jones did everything he could to keep himself from pulling out his gun right there and shooting this bastard between the eyes but he joined in the laughter.

"Now, my notes indicate that you didn't actually see Albert stab the Indian, did you? You saw him emerge from the building after the deed. Is that correct?"

Searles looked around as if there were other people in the room.

"Don't worry, Mr. Searles," Jones said in a reassuring tone, "As I mentioned, this is an entirely confidential conversation. What you say or don't say will not be reported. I won't even take notes if that makes you feel easier. This will just provide some background for the committee, but I can assure you that this, as you called him, this little prick won't step a foot on American soil for many years to come, if he ever does."

Jones made sure to continually sip his drink, hoping that Searles would do the same. He readily complied. Jones asked if he might have another. Searles poured a fresh round for both of them.

Reassured and warmed by the Scotch he was drinking, Searles spoke freely.

"I actually did not see Albert anywhere near the house where that Indian was staying. I did go for a cup of tea at the café I said I was at, just in case the authorities asked around. I made sure to be real friendly with the waiter and gave him a nice tip so he would remember me. It was all unnecessary, though, as Major Highsmith was more than willing to take my word at face value. You see, he's of like mind as us, if you know what I mean."

Searles took another sip and winked at Jones.

"Major Highsmith? I take it he was in charge of the investigation."

"Yes, and he was in charge of "finding" the evidence."

Searles did the quotation marks with his fingers when he said the word finding and then giggled a little bit. Jones was pleased at how poorly Searles could hold his liquor. After only two glasses, his tongue was nice and loose. Searles got up to pour himself a third, offering one to Jones, who politely declined.

"This Indian, who was he?"

"He was some high placed swami in the Indian National Committee. He was nosing around in our affairs, digging up things after the accident."

"Accident?"

"Yes, just before we arrived, five Indians were killed when an electric generator exploded. There were some who were out to discredit Langdan by planting lies that it was no accident, that the men were murdered. This guy Rama was digging around and then when Albert for some reason started doing the same, it became obvious to the Director, Highsmith and me what had to be done."

Searles took another sip.

"Which Director is this that you are referring to? Williams? Gill?"

"Those guys? They're clueless. From the get-go. We shipped them out of India on the fastest boat we could find. No, Director Atherton, head of the Calcutta Branch of Langdan."

"Any idea then who actually killed the Indian?"

"Not a clue. Nor did I want to know. The only bad thing is that we never did find out how to solve the jute rot problem. The least Albert could do was to do his job before we arrested him."

Searles again laughed at his own cleverness.

"Well, Mr. Searles, I have taken up enough of your time. I will say my goodbyes now. You have been most helpful."

"Are you sure you don't want to stay for one more drink. I frankly don't get many visitors, especially like-minded ones."

"I'd love to stay, Mr. Searles, but I don't want to miss the last trolley to Roxbury to see my mother."

"Well, I certainly don't want to be accused of being responsible for keeping a man away from his dear Mom."

"Please be assured, Mr. Searles, that you will hear from me again in the future."

"I look forward to it."

The next day, Searles arrived to find that Mr. Andrews had called an emergency meeting of all Langdan Textile key managers. The meeting had just started when he walked in.

"Searles, you're late," bellowed Andrews, "sit down."

"Yes sir."

"This will be a very short meeting, gentlemen. I gathered you together to direct each and every one of you to contact me immediately if anybody approaches you or your employees asking anything—and I mean anything—about Benjamin Albert, the Calcutta office or anything remotely related to that situation. Failure to do so will result in immediate dismissal. Do I make myself clear."

Williams raised his hand.

"A Mr. William Jenkins came to my office the day before yesterday to ask about Ben."

"He came to see me as well," piped up Gill. Searles said nothing.

"And why didn't either of you advise me of this?"

"First of all, sir, you were not in town to tell. Second, it was only one minute ago that I even had an inkling that you wanted to be notified."

Andrews was seething but Williams remained calm.

"Did you ask him for any identification or what the purpose of his inquiries were?"

"He told me he was a friend of Ben's and that was enough for me. He wanted to know what happened to him. He was very concerned and was convinced his friend was innocent."

Williams held back that Mr. Jenkins had also identified himself as a private investigator.

"And what exactly did you tell him?"

"I told him all I know, which is next to nothing. As you may recall, Mr. Andrews, I had to return to Boston even before the trial began and was ordered not to go back."

"Don't use that tone with me, sir."

Williams said nothing in response but simply stared defiantly at his employer. Andrews turned to Gill.

"I suppose your story is the same."

"Yes sir, I also had no information to give him."

Andrews turned in his chair until his glare fell on Searles. In fact, all eyes were on Searles now.

"Well, Mr. Searles?"

"Yes, he came to my home last night. He is a lieutenant in the Boston Police Department; he showed me his badge and he was wearing a service revolver. He's also a member of the Joint International Inquiry Commission. He had some routine questions to ask. He was a very pleasant chap."

"The joint what?"

"Joint International Inquiry Commission. They're set up to facilitate any prisoner exchanges that two countries may want to do, but he assured me that Albert would never be exchanged. Still, though, he had to go through the formality of the official questioning."

Andrews got up from the table and walked over and opened the door.

"Mrs. Epstein, will you please call Detective O'Doul in the Boston Police Department. Tell him that you're calling for me. Ask him to locate Lieutenant William Jenkins as soon as possible. I need to talk with the lieutenant. Also tell the Detective that Jenkins is a member of the Joint International Inquiry Commission. I'd like some information on this commission. Interrupt us as soon as you have anything. Thank you."

Andrews returned to his seat and did not say a word. Searles began to speak but Andrews held up his hand. The entire group sat in silence for ten minutes until Mrs. Epstein knocked on the door and walked in.

"Mr. Andrews, Detective O'Doul checked the official records and there is no William Jenkins on the Boston Police Department. To verify, he called down to the personnel department in case Mr. Jenkins was a new hire. They had no record of him either. And in regards to the Joint International Inquiry Commission, he said there is no such thing. He checked with the office that makes appointments to various commissions, councils, task forces and the like and they never heard of this commission either. Will there be anything more, Mr. Andrews?"

"No, that's fine. Thank you very much, Mrs. Epstein."

Mrs. Epstein left and closed the door behind her. The meeting again descended into silence for another minute or so. Then suddenly Andrew slammed his fist on the table, startling everyone in the room.

"Damn it, Catherine! You want war; then war it is!"

As everyone sat there befuddled, wondering who Catherine was, Andrews regained his composure and spoke softly to the group.

"Thank you gentlemen. Everybody except Mr. Searles may leave. Mr. Searles, you are going to recite to me every single word spoken by both you and this Lieutenant Jenkins last night after which we will discuss whether you will continue to be employed by this firm."

As this meeting was commencing, the steamer *Navigator's Pride* was pulling out of Boston Harbor heading for Cherbourg, France. From there, Jones would get on a train for Marseilles where he would board another steamer that would take him the length of the Mediterranean through the Suez Canal and the Red Sea. Ultimately, he would get off at Bombay where he would board another train across the subcontinent of India to Calcutta. He despaired that the trip would take approximately two and a half weeks but it was the best he could do.

As promised, Catherine Albert had wired him $4,000 for his expenses. He knew all he had to do was to send a telegram and new funds would be wired to him anywhere in the world. He promised to himself not to be greedy and take advantage of the situation. He would stay in second class accommodations the entire trip. Taking Ben's admonition not to trust anyone very seriously, he would have Catherine wire the money to different names each time she sent it. Each name would have the same initials, W.J., but the names would be different. Searles was a dimwit but others at Langdan would undoubtedly be more clever and might have a way of searching Western Union's records for transfers to William Jenkins. All he had to do was to keep straight who he was at any given moment. Presently, he was Wilbur Jameson.

As the shoreline receded in the distance, Jones leaned on the rail smoking a cigarette. He felt the nubs of his mustache starting to reemerge. He could not believe how easy it had been to get information out of Searles. Jones was ready to pistol-whip the bastard and it would not have especially bothered him if he had. But he was generally a peaceable man and much preferred extracting what he needed through cleverness. He chuckled at the thought of the mess Searles was in right about now.

All he had gotten out of Searles, though, were a couple of names. The rest of the way would not be as easy. Pistol-whipping and other dubious methods he learned a long time ago as a police office would most likely be called upon but he had to be careful. As much as he liked Ben and owed to him, he did not want to end up in a filthy Indian jail himself.

He liked to have a feel of a place before planning how he would proceed but he did not know the lay of the land in Calcutta, having never been there before. Therefore, rather then spending his time laying out his plans, he decided to sit back and enjoy the trip. The only other time he had been on a steamer had been going to and from the war. There were no eligible females on that trip but this time was much different. He had already caught the eye of at least one comely lady. He did not think it would be overly difficult getting one or more of them into his bed before the excursion was over. That would be the only thing he would concentrate on over the next week or so.

36
Catherine

My world was in a shambles. The only bright spot was Harry; everybody remarked about how much he was growing, about how smart he was, about how good a disposition he had. I could find some solace there. I don't know what I would have done if he were crippled or slow or even just a wailing brat.

I wasn't performing my job properly and had made a few key mistakes in the books that cost Mr. Bress money. He was understanding, but for how long I couldn't say.

Molly initially took the news about Ben well, but then she retreated further into herself, sometimes staying in bed for whole days at a time. I wasn't feeling too great either. I was rundown with no energy; I had no appetite, but I couldn't allow myself to show this to others. I had to sally forth the best I could.

On the subject of Ben, the only things I had were the daily reports Sergeant Jones had provided me while he was in the United States. I wrote to Ben every day, but never received a response from him. I knew in my heart that he was writing me as often as he could but his letters were not being posted. Mr. Bress had theorized that probably his guards were Indian and, since Ben was a white man convicted of murdering a very popular Indian, one of their petty revenges was to keep letters from going out or coming in. I bought into this theory. It was better than all the alternatives that I could imagine: he was incapacitated or sick, he had given up hope and his despair would not allow him to pen any correspondence, he was filled with shame, or my worst thought, he was dead.

Sergeant Jones' telephone calls and telegrams gave me an illusion that we were doing something; we weren't just sitting around wringing our hands. However, now that he was at sea, I wouldn't get a report from him for at least a week. I sometimes wondered at the wisdom of counting on him. Perhaps I should have made the journey myself, but then I'd hear Harry stir or Molly come downstairs and I would come back to my senses. My responsibilities were right here.

I was nursing Harry when the telephone rang. After a bit of juggling, I answered. The woman identified herself as Mrs. Epstein, Franklin Andrews' secretary.

"Mrs. Albert, this is Hanna Epstein, we met each other when you were in Boston last month."

"Yes, Mrs. Epstein, how can I help you?"

I being was extremely brusque with her and my tone was not friendly in the least, but I couldn't help myself. Even though this lady had been a longtime friend of my mother's, I was not feeling charitable toward anybody associated with Langdan Textiles. Either Mrs. Epstein did not pick up on this over the telephone or she was being understanding as she continued.

"I was calling to warn you. I don't know any of the details but Mr. Andrews knows you are looking into your husband's incarceration. Please be very careful. Mr. Andrews can be a vindictive man without pity or compassion if you get on his wrong side. I just finished typing a letter to a private investigative firm he dictated. He's retaining them to investigate you. I fear he will try to blackmail you...or worse. He believes you hired William Jenkins to look into your husband's conviction. Mr. Jenkins was able to extract some information from Mr. Searles, our former Director of Governmental Relations. He testified against your husband."

"Mrs. Epstein, why are you telling me all this? Don't you report to Mr. Andrews?"

"Catherine," I was taken back a little at the informal use of my first name, "I was a close friend of your mother. Not only that, but my allegiance was always to his father—your father—not this man. He is a poor imitation of the man who used to sit in this office."

She knew? She knew who my real father was? She continued.

"Be very careful as to whom you tell anything. The company has used this investigative firm before. They're unscrupulous and will stop at nothing. There is definitely something Franklin Andrews wants to hide, perhaps having to do with the accident that killed five Indians. Watch your back and warn Mr. Jenkins, too."

"Thank you, Mrs. Epstein. You're most kind to call me like this."

"It's the least I can do. Your father was the most wonderful man I ever met. One day when this is all over, we'll have to get together so I can tell you all about him."

"I'd like that. Good-bye."

37

The old charm was still there, Jones mused as the train pulled into Calcutta's central train station. Over the course of the last two weeks, he was able to bed three different women, two of them less than half his age. Not a bad way to while away the hours but now it was time to get to work.

He had contacted Catherine when he got to Cherbourg and she told him about the conversation she had had with Andrews' secretary. He had heard of the private investigative firm, Dexter Applebee, and was aware of their reputation. They were indeed unscrupulous and resorted to many questionable tactics to get information they wanted. He would be on his guard but he had a distinct advantage. He knew who they were; they had no idea who he was. They were hunting around for a William Jenkins. They would especially be lost for some time since there was in fact a William Jenkins, P.I., based out of Hoboken, New Jersey. Jones figured they would waste a day or two checking him out. It was a bit unfair that they might rough him up a bit before discovering he was not the man they were looking for. Casualty of war.

Calcutta was a teeming, dirty city. You were either stepping over or around the poor with every step. At the beginning he gave some coins to a few wretched creatures out of compassion but soon realized he would be broke if he kept that up. He quickly inured himself to them.

He was not afraid of Langdan or their P.I.s but he knew he would have to be careful. He wanted to go and see Ben if for no other reason than to give Catherine a report on how he was doing. If he did this, however, his visit would be reported. Neither could he go to the authorities for the same reason.

He had read all the letters Ben sent to Catherine over the course of his trip to get some clues on other people he could contact. Three names stood out: a bearer called Ram, a Mr. Jasbinder Singh and Mr. Sanjit Dutta. These were the ones he would look for first. They would open other doors. They were three native Indians who believed that Ben was innocent. They were the best place to start.

He had reserved a room at the Great Eastern Hotel, the same hotel where Ben had stayed. Jones noted how progressive the hotel was, having an Indian native at the front counter.

"Hello, my name is Wilfred Jensen. I reserved a room."

"Yes, Mr. Jensen. I have your name right here. Welcome to the Great Eastern. We hope you enjoy your stay. We have you down for three nights but you may be staying longer. Is that correct?"

"Yes, that is correct. I was hoping to hire a bearer while I am here. A colleague of mine had one who he knew as Ram. He raved about this bearer and I was wondering if I could get him."

"Ram is generally saved for representatives of Langdan Textiles when they come to the hotel."

"Well, I am here on Langdan business. I perhaps forgot to mention that in my telegram securing the reservation."

"That is no problem at all, sir. I will have Ram go up to your room immediately."

"Thank you."

The room was on an upper floor with a magnificent view of the city and the river. Jones set about unpacking his bags when there was a knock on the door. Jones opened it to find a dark, slender Indian man standing there.

"You're Ram, I take it."

"Yes sir."

Ram noticed the open luggage on the bed.

"Please, sir, let me take care of unpacking for you."

"Please, come in."

Ram immediately set to pulling out and refolding clothes to put in drawers and on hangers for Jones. Jones watched him for a few minutes before speaking up.

"Ram, a friend of mine recently used you as his bearer and spoke very highly of you."

Without pausing in performing his folding duties, Ram responded.

"Who was that, sir?"

"Benjamin Albert."

Ram stopped folding and, though his back was to Jones, it was obvious the name struck a chord.

"I'm afraid you are mistaken, sir. I do not remember serving anyone by that name. We all look alike, or so I'm told."

"Ram, you don't have to be afraid. I'm here to find out what happened to Ben. I'm here to get at the truth."

"The truth, sir, is that because of Langdan Textiles, my brother is dead, your friend is in prison, a respected man named Mr. Rama is dead and another good man named Mr. Dutta is in prison. Those are the truths, sir, yet you ask me not to be afraid for me and my family?"

Jones could not argue with his logic.

"Well, we cannot bring the dead back to life but perhaps we can make sure they did not die in vain. Perhaps we can also free men who have been falsely imprisoned. I will do my utmost, Ram, to be discreet and not implicate you but I need your help. Help me avenge your brother and help my friend. Please."

Ram said nothing but after a short while he silently nodded his head.

"Mr. Ben had started asking questions about the death of five men at the Langdan factory. I do not believe that he ever discovered anything but he had met some men, Mr. Dutta being one of them, who he was helping gather some information proving that the death of the five men, including my brother, was not an accident as reported in the official report."

"You don't know what this information is or who the contact may be?"

"No, sir. Mr. Rama was killed and Mr. Dutta and Mr. Ben were arrested before any of this could be learned. Mr. Dutta is being held in solitary confinement and is not allowed visitors. I have heard that he is still alive, but I do not know for how long."

"I will just have to get in to see Mr. Dutta, won't I?"

"I do not see how that will be possible. An American asking to see Mr. Dutta will alarm the authorities. You will be arrested before you get within one hundred feet of Mr. Dutta."

"You're correct, Ram, but an English army officer will get in to see him, I should bloody wager."

Ram looked at him quizzically.

As he was checking in to his room, Jones had noticed down the hall an English army officer, a colonel, leaving his room. A smallish Indian man had preceded the colonel out of the room and then remained by the door when the colonel left.

Jones could not say how he felt about the idea of having a bearer, someone who would run errands, be a valet, clean up and do anything else that was asked of him. In general, one of the main duties of a bearer was to be available at a moment's notice during the day fulfill the whim of his, for lack of a better word, master.

"Ram, I noticed an Indian man down the hall. Is he a bearer, too?"

"Yes, that is Padmesh. He is a good friend of mine."

"Will he stay outside the door all day?"

"If his employer leaves for a meeting or for some other purpose that he does not want his bearer along, he will remain behind. If the employer trusts the bearer, the bearer will be allowed to spend the day inside the room. The colonel obviously does not trust Padmesh, so he waits in the hallway."

Ram gave Jones a 'that's the way it is' look and shrugged.

"Ram, I have to go out for awhile. I am expecting a trunk to arrive at the train station. Would you mind going to pick it up for me. It is rather heavy so do you think you could ask Padmesh to help you. Of course, you'll both be paid for your efforts."

"Very well, sir. Padmesh will enjoy the opportunity to get out rather than stay in the hallway for hours on end. I think retrieving your trunk will take at least two hours, maybe three. Is that not correct, sir?"

Ram smiled.

"Yes, I would say it's a three hour job."

"Yes, sir."

As soon as Ram left, taking Padmesh with him, Jones pulled out his tool kit and went to the colonel's room. He picked the lock in seconds, snuck in the room and went straight to the closet. As he had hoped, the colonel had two spare uniforms hanging there. He grabbed one of the uniforms, a pair of shoes and a hat and left as speedily as he had arrived. He neatly folded the clothing into a leather case he had and then headed out. Two blocks from the prison he ducked into an alleyway and changed into the uniform. Luckily, his size and build were similar to the colonel.

He then scouted the prison, hoping he could avoid entering through the main entrance. He noticed a door on the eastern side through which an occasional officer would enter or leave. He walked in to find a lone corporal at the desk who rose to attention as soon as he saw the colonel uniform. Jones assumed an arrogant pose and hoped the lad would not see through his over-the-top phony English accent.

"At ease, corporal. I'm here to see Sanjit Dutta. He's a prisoner here. I'd like to see him in an interrogation room so we can be alone. I do not want to be disturbed."

"But sir, I cannot let you see Dutta without signed orders."

"Listen son, I have to be on a bloody ship for London in two hours. It is of utmost importance that I speak to Mr. Dutta before I leave. If you feel a great need to have to check on me and I miss my opportunity to interview this man, then you should get very used to that chair. It will be as far as your career will go."

Jones folded his arms and waited for the corporal's decision, which only took about ten seconds.

"Very well, sir. Please follow me."

"Thank you. A wise decision on your part."

The corporal led the colonel down an ill-lit corridor and asked him to wait in a room. Jones was counting on the kid's nervousness and willingness to oblige a direct order from a colonel. Otherwise, if the corporal had second thoughts and went to his superiors, Jones could be in a lot of trouble. The boy did not disappoint as the door opened and an emaciated, bruised Indian man with a bushy beard and ragged clothes was led in.

"Thank you, corporal. Your attention to this matter will be reflected in my report. Please make sure no one interrupts me."

"Yes sir." Replied the corporal as he briskly strode away.

"Mr. Dutta, please have a seat."

Dutta wearily sat himself down, eyeing the colonel the entire time. He spoke first.

"Sir, I've told everything I know. Please, no more interrogation. Either kill me or let me go."

Dutta lowered his head. He raised it as Jones began to speak in his American accent.

"Mr. Dutta, I don't have much time. I am not a British colonel. I am an American. For your safety and mine I won't tell you my name, but what I can tell you is that Benjamin Albert is a friend of mine. I know that he is innocent and so are you. I have come to try and dig out the truth. I need your help."

Dutta still looked at the colonel with suspicion, expecting a trap.

"Please Mr. Dutta, I know you have no reason to trust me but that is exactly what I am asking you to do. I have known Ben Albert for ten years; he saved my life during the war. I am here to pay him back. Please, you must tell me what you know."

Finally Dutta spoke.

"I do not have any more information to give but there is someone who does have information."

Dutta looked Jones in the eyes one more time and decided to trust him, hoping against hope that he was not condemning another man to prison or death. He sighed

"You must see Lieutenant Arha Chakraborty. He is the Calcutta attaché to Major Highsmith. He is one of us. He has the information you seek."

Jones stood up.

"You keep yourself alive. I promise I will get to the bottom of this."

His colonel imitation was working so well that he was tempted to now go see Ben but time was running short. He called to the corporal and was escorted to the exit. Jones got back to the hotel two hours after he had left. He broke back into the colonel's room, put the clothes back on their hangars, hoping he had not soiled them too much, and returned to his room. A half hour later Ram returned.

"I am very sorry, sir. We went to the train station and spoke to the stationmaster but there was no record of your trunk arriving. He searched all over for it and made a few calls but it appears to have gotten lost."

"Well, thank you Ram. You and Padmesh did your best, I'm sure."

"I hope you had a profitable time while we were gone, sir."

"Yes, very profitable, very profitable indeed."

The two men exchanged a knowing glance.

38
Catherine

For someone who had never been one to venture far from home or to be involved in many activities, Molly had many friends and admirers. Everyday, a new person would drop by to pay his or her respects, to see if she had heard anything from Ben, to check on how she was feeling. Sol would venture down from Brooklyn a couple of times a week. It was obvious that he still carried a bit of a torch for her and would drop everything to do anything she asked of him. For this reason, I think she never asked for anything.

At least once a week, someone whom I did not know would arrive at our doorstep to pay respects to Molly. After being tipped off by Mrs. Epstein about Langdan hiring an unscrupulous private investigation firm, I became suspicious of everyone I didn't know. When these poor people arrived at our home, I would grill them on how they knew Molly, what their relationship with her was, etc. If their answers did not seem personal enough or otherwise did not pass my muster, I would politely advise them that Molly wasn't receiving visitors today. At first, I'd tell Molly the name of the person who came to call and she would be angry with me because he or she was in fact a longstanding friend. After awhile, I stopped telling her. I'm sure I sent away a number of well-meaning people, but I couldn't be too careful.

Our most frequent "visitor" was Edgar. He was the Western Union deliveryman. He came to the door so often that we were soon on a first name basis. "Hi Edgar, what do you have for me today?" I'd ask him. Sometimes we'd chat and he'd tell me about his two sons who were growing by leaps and bounds. I think I appreciated him because he was the only person who came to visit me, not Molly.

Sergeant Jones was wiring me constant updates on his

progress. Sometimes his messages would be rather obtuse and would take me a while to decipher. He was being careful. He hadn't yet gotten any breakthrough news, but he had gotten a new lead on someone he felt could provide that information. I could feel his excitement over the cold telegram I was holding in my hand.

Another constant source of telegrams that Edgar would deliver came from Mrs. Epstein, who now insisted I call her Hanna. I surmised that she did not have a telephone at home. Calling me from her office was too risky and the mails too slow so she started sending me telegrams. Mostly they contained things she heard around the office related to Ben or to India. By and large, the information she provided was worthless, consisting often of rumors she overheard at the water cooler, but I did everything I could to support her efforts. She was the one, after all, who tipped me off to the private investigators. I did not want her to get discouraged and then miss something that was actually vital. Plus, I enjoyed hearing from her. It gave me a connection to my mother.

I was thinking a lot about my mother during those days. I missed her terribly and I appreciated her more and more as time went on. At first I was angry with her that she had never told me who my real father was. I came to understand the difficult position she was in and how she handled being a single mother with dignity, grace and strength. I'm sure she didn't expect to die so young and would have told me in good time.

When I heard a knock on the door, I was in the middle of a reverie about my mother and for a split second my mind told me that perhaps it was she who was knocking. I quickly dismissed that thought and resigned myself to a pleasant chat with Edgar; he hadn't been by in a few days. Instead, when I opened the door it was Mr. Charney, Ben's grammar school teacher and longtime mentor and Molly's friend. I tried to hide my disappointment that it was another visitor for Molly as I invited him in.

"Mr. Charney, how nice of you to visit. Let me go get Molly for you."

"Actually, Catherine, it's you I'm here to see."

I must have looked puzzled as I invited him to sit down in the front parlor.

"I wanted to see you to apologize. Ever since I heard the news about Ben I've felt so helpless. I kept thinking there must be something I can do to help. Ben has been like a son to me his entire life but I've let him down when he needed me most."

"Mr. Charney, we all are feeling that way. There's not much any of us can do, I'm afraid. We're all pretty helpless here."

"Well, it suddenly dawned on me that there was something I could do. I was having dinner with my college roommate last night. His name is Dale Pearson. I don't know if Ben ever mentioned Dale to you. He's now the Rutgers Dean of Admissions. He worked hard to recruit Ben to Rutgers."

"I've heard the name, " I responded noncommittally.

"We were having dinner and were talking about Ben when it occurred to both of us at the same time that Dale's brother works for the State Department in DC. Not only that, but he is some sort of undersecretary in the Far East Section of the Department. Dale is going to call him today to see if there are any diplomatic routes we could pursue to help Ben. No promises, but I think at a minimum he'll be willing to place a few calls to the British Embassy. I think that the more people that start asking questions, the more scrutiny this injustice will receive and ultimately the truth will come out."

"I hope you're right, Mr. Charney. We need all the help we can get. Thank you and thank Mr. Pearson for his efforts."

Mr. Charney had some business to attend to so he asked me to convey his apologies to Molly that he could not see. He said he'd come back again soon to visit with her.

I did appreciate his efforts but I knew they'd be useless unless Sergeant Jones came up with some hard evidence clearing Ben. The diplomats would debate, and maybe even go so far as to lodge a formal protest but in the end it would be for naught. The English government would explain that Ben had been found guilty in a court of law; their hands were tied, especially if there were no new facts to present. Everything was riding on Jones.

While the sergeant's latest telegram sounded upbeat, my attitude was spiraling downward. From my perspective, he was bouncing from person to person. Maybe he was getting closer to the truth, maybe not. I preferred to believe that he knew what he was doing, but I didn't know this man from Adam. He could just be spinning his wheels like the rest of us. The difference was that we knew it, perhaps he didn't.

39

Jones was also getting impatient. He was tempted to kidnap Major Highsmith in the middle of the night and extract the truth out of the bastard by whatever means were necessary. In the end, he talked himself out of that course of action and continued on the more measured approach on which he had embarked. He had to be patient for a bit longer. Dutta had given him a name of someone who was nominally on the inside. From what he had learned about Highsmith, it was doubtful he shared confidences with too many people, but especially not with a native Indian. He had to figure a way to locate and identify Lieutenant Arha Chakraborty and then get him alone to see what he knew.

There was a café across the street from the police station. It would be a good spot to scope out the station without being too obvious. He saw numerous officers and civilians, both white and Indian, go in and out of the station, but none of them were majors. At around noon, he waved for the waiter so he could pay his bill when he saw a major emerge and head down the street. He was alone. He decided to make his move.

He located Highsmith's office on the directory. It was on the third or top floor. He went up and there was a white corporal sitting at a desk in the hallway outside his office.

"Major Highsmith, please."

"He's not here right now. You just missed him. He's gone for the rest of the day. You didn't have an appointment with him, did you?"

"No, no appointment, I'm afraid. I'd met him a couple of months ago. I was back in town and wanted to stop by and give him my regards."

"I can give him the message you stopped by if you like."

"That's very nice of you. Have we met before? You look vaguely familiar."

"I don't think so unless you've been in London recently. I just transferred here last week. I'm Corporal Richard Hazelton."

"It's a pleasure to meet you Richard, or rather Corporal Hazelton. Did you replace the Indian chap, whose name I can't remember—a Chakra something—who helped me out with some things back then. He was a lieutenant if I remember correctly."

"Lieutenant Chakraborty, yes, he's still here. I believe he's in. Would you like to see him?"

"Yes, I would."

"Who shall I tell him is calling?"

"How impolite of me. You provide me with your name and I do not do the same. My daddy back home would hit me upside the head for that unforgivable breach of protocol. I'm Albert Dutta."

Jones was somewhat chagrined to see the corporal writing the name down in the visitor log, but there was nothing he could do about it.

"How do you spell that, Mr. Dutta?"

"Call me Alby, everybody does. It's D-U-T-T-A. My actual name should have been Dutanofski but my grandfather had a bad stutter. It got even worse when he got nervous or upset. When he immigrated to America from Poland in '97, the agent asked him his name and all he could get out was Dutta. He even stuttered the 't' when they asked him to spell it. He didn't know whether a stutter was enough to bar admission to America so he stopped right there and that's what the agent wrote down. Been our family name ever since. That's probably way more than you wanted to know, corporal."

"Not at all. It's a great story. Far more interesting than my boring family history. Let me go get Lieutenant Chakraborty for you."

The corporal got up and walked down the hallway. Jones hoped the use of Dutta's name would be enough to intrigue the lieutenant to see him. A minute later the corporal returned with a light skinned Indian of medium height and build with slicked back black hair and neatly trimmed mustache.

"Mr. Dutta?"

"Lieutenant, I don't know if you remember me from when I was in Calcutta a short while back. You had helped me with some information on the Benjamin situation."

The lieutenant shot a nervous glance at the corporal who had returned to his desk. Jones had made a calculation that Ben's name would mean nothing to a low level soldier who had arrived only one week earlier. He was correct. Corporal Hazelton kept on with his paperwork and did not register any sign of recognizing the name.

"Of course, Mr. Dutta. How have you been? Please, won't you come back to my office? Thank you corporal."

The two men walked back to his office. Once inside, the lieutenant closed the door.

"Mr. Dutta, please have a seat and then you can tell me what your real name is."

"For your own protection, it's probably best you don't know. I was sent to prove that Benjamin Albert was framed and is innocent of the murder he's charged with."

"And why do you come to me, sir?"

"I was given your name by a mutual acquaintance."

"And who might that be?"

"Sanjit Dutta."

"When did you see Mr. Dutta?"

"Yesterday."

"You lie. Sanjit Dutta has been held in solitary confinement ever since he was arrested. He is not allowed visitors."

Jones turned on his English accent once again.

"An English colonel named Hyde-Whyte who threatens the poor corporal at the gate can get in to see him, I assure you. If you call the prison, I'm sure their logs will show such a visit at around 2:00."

Chakraborty said nothing and stared at Jones for a full minute. Then he spoke.

"I don't think that will be necessary. What did Mr. Dutta tell you?"

"That he told the authorities everything he knew, but still they kept wanting more. The one thing he did not reveal to them was your name. At the end, he finally said that he had nothing more but he knew of someone who may have what I'm looking for: you. He asked me to beg your forgiveness for providing your name to anyone, but he came to trust me and was at the end of his rope."

The lieutenant had gotten up from his chair and was staring out the window as Jones spoke.

"Oh, I forgive him. I am frankly surprised he had not given me up earlier. I admire his courage. Poor Sanjit. He is not cut out for this type of abuse and deprivation. Probably just seeing your face, anybody's face, was a tonic for him."

"Do you in fact have evidence that would exonerate both Mr. Dutta and Mr. Albert?"

Chakraborty was still staring out the window and remained silent as he considered his answer. Finally he spoke.

"Yes, yes I do."

"Why haven't you come forward with this evidence?"

"Come forward to whom, sir? As you can see if you walk around this building, the vast majority of officers are Englishmen. I am what you call window dressing. By giving me lieutenant's bars, they can point to the city, and brag how progressive they are, but I have no power or authority. However, being an officer does allow me access to places that other Indians do not have. I have been able to quietly gather this evidence but I have had to bide my time to make sure it gets in the right hands. Otherwise, I will end up in a cell beside Mr. Dutta and the evidence will be destroyed."

"Do you believe I possess, as you put it, the right hands?"

"I hope so, sir. I grew up among the English and know many honorable white people, but none here in this building or in the government. I am taking a leap of faith here but yes, I do believe you to be the man I am looking for."

40

Catherine

The sergeant's telegram was terse and to the point: BEING FOLLOWED. CHECK MAIL.

I didn't hear from him after that. Every day I would hope for Edgar to bring me another message, but the few times he came to the door they were messages of new rumors from Hanna Epstein. I checked the mail every morning, but day after day nothing of note was in the box.

Ben's letters used to take about two to three weeks to reach me so I knew I had awhile to wait. My mind raced with worry about what could have happened to Sergeant Jones. They were on to him. I hoped for the best but expected the worst. I felt responsible. If it weren't for me, he never would have started out on this expedition. Now he might be in prison or worse. I don't know if I could take having his death on my hands.

Two weeks to the day after I received his telegram, the letter came. I tore it open and a small key fell to the floor. I picked it up and began reading.

Dear Catherine,

If you get this letter but have not heard from me otherwise, then I am afraid that the burden must fall on you to pick up where I left off. In other words, you must hope for the best but assume the worst regarding my situation. You must come to Calcutta.

My final meeting provided me with the evidence I have been searching for. A man, whom I do not name out of fear for his safety, had amassed much evidence proving that Langdan Textiles was directly involved in the murder of five men and then covered it up as an accident; that Mr. Rama was murdered by agents who represented Langdan who then in turn framed your husband and another man, Mr. Dutta, for the murder; and that the local police and other government officials, led by a Major Highsmith, were complicit each step of the way.

Unfortunately, I sensed that I was being followed shortly after I attained the folder containing this evidence. I was able to give the men tracking me the slip, but I fear they will be on my trail again soon. I therefore have left Calcutta but I did not want to get caught with these materials on me. Before I left I was able go to the Great Occidental Bank of Calcutta. The key you find herein is for a safety deposit box at that bank. In that box is all the evidence you need to prove Ben's innocence. You must retrieve the folder and bring it to the proper authorities to help right this wrong.

Several words of instruction and caution. First, I left instructions at the bank that only two people are to have access to the box: me and Lydia Jones. Who is Lydia Jones, you ask; well, you are. That is the name you are to use on your trip. To obtain access to the box, you must provide identification proving that you are indeed Lydia Jones. For that, you must take the train into Manhattan and go to 235 Hudson Street, Suite 332. Ask to see Herman Jones. He is my uncle. Tell him who you are and that I sent you. I have sent him a letter already so he will be expecting you. He will prepare all the necessary paperwork to show the world you are Lydia Jones. Don't ask. If he chuckles a bit, it's understandable. That's my mother's name.

Also, trust only those close to you. Do not trust anyone else, especially Englishmen or other whites, in Calcutta. In fact, stay in Calcutta as short a period as possible. Grab the folder and get out. If you must stay a night, make sure you stay in an out-of-the-way, anonymous hotel. Under no circumstances are you to try and see Ben. Regardless of how tempted you are to go and provide him with solace and support, do not do it. Any attempt to visit him will be reported immediately and will ultimately harm both you and him.

Go to the American consulate in Delhi. Show them the evidence and tell them everything you know. Use your friend in the State Department. Catherine, be extra careful; I thought I was but still they were able to find me.

I will try to get in contact with you, if I can.
Jones

"If I can." Those words hung ominously in the air. The implications for Sergeant Jones were too frightening to think about.

Now, he was asking me to do the impossible. I'd always thought of myself as a modern, independent woman but the truth of it was that I have always been dependent on others: my mother, my "father" or at least his money, Mabel Smith Douglass, Ben, Molly, Sergeant Jones. One or more of them have always been there, my security blankets. Now, my husband's life depended on me traveling halfway around the world by myself. I started to shake with terror. I wouldn't even know where to begin.

I could come up with a thousand different reasons why I could not possibly make this trip. I had a young infant to look after. I had an ailing mother-in-law who counted on me. Mr. Bress's butcher shop needed my help to keep it running smoothly. I was just a woman; what he was asking of me was man's work.

I dropped onto my bed, burying my head in my covers. There were no tears, but, if I tried, I bet I could have mustered them in short order. I looked up and what caught my eye was a photograph of my mother on the end table. Her words came to me: 'You can do anything, Catherine. Nobody is going to live your life for you. Go out and live it yourself.' I smiled at her and thanked her for once again having confidence in me. I pulled myself together and got up. I went up to Molly's room. She was dressed, but sitting on her bed.

"Hi Molly."

"Hello, my darling. How are you today?"

"I'm not well, Molly. I have some news to tell you. I have to leave. I have to go to India to help Ben. I'm going to be gone at least a month. I'm going to speak to Robert and Sol and Mr. Charney to help you and to take care of Harry. It'll all be alright."

Molly looked up at me with pleading eyes.

"The man who helps you, he helps you no more?"

"He's done all he can, Molly. It's up to me now."

Molly considered this and then stood up.

"Is good then; you go. We take care of Harry. You go bring my

American son home where he belong."

Tears were in her eyes as she held out her arms. I walked into them and held her close. My eyes were welling as well.

"You be careful, my daughter. You be careful."

"I will, Molly. I'll be around a few more days. I have to make travel arrangements and take care of a few other things."

My first task was to head into New York. I located Sergeant Jones' uncle Herman. His office was a mess. Papers, newspapers, photographs were strewn everywhere. Any available flat surface— the desk, the file cabinet, a long table off to the side—were piled high and appeared as though they'd not been cleaned in years.

When I arrived, the door was unlocked but no one was there. I called out and soon I heard some commotion from an adjoining room. Eventually the door opened and a five foot nothing chubby old man with thin white combed-back hair shuffled through. He must have been at least eighty.

"Lydia Jones?" he asked me.

When I told him yes, he indicated that I follow him into the back. As he shuffled slowly along with me in tow, I thought of the sergeant's line that his uncle may chuckle a bit about the use of his mother's name. This man had not chuckled in many years, I thought.

By contrast to the front office, the back room was immaculate. To the right was a darkroom for developing photographs. A camera aimed at a stiff-backed wooden chair in front of a white screen was set up in the middle. A drafting table was on the left. Not a piece of paper, or anything else for that matter, was out of place. Without a word, he motioned for me to sit in the chair. The next thing I knew, a flash of light blinded me.

"Please wait in the outer office," he advised me.

I moved a pile of papers off of the only seat and sat down. An hour later, Herman Jones emerged and cleared off a section of the desk, placing the documents he had just created in the temporary clearing. He handed me a pen.

"Sign here, here and here, Lydia Jones."

He had repeated my name to ensure that I did not

absentmindedly sign Catherine Albert. After I did as he directed, he put the documents in my hand and turned away, heading back through the door.

"How much do I owe you, Mr. Jones?"

In response, he simply waved his right hand and continued on, closing the door after him. I departed and headed back to New Brunswick wondering what kind of strange world I was entering into.

My next destination was to talk to Mr. Charney. I needed him not only to look in on Molly and Harry but I also wanted to use his connection to the State Department. Hopefully, I would be able to use him to facilitate my travel arrangements and to ensure that any visas or other paperwork I needed were taken care of. I also wanted to put him on notice that I may be appealing to him to help get the evidence, whatever it was, into the correct hands to free Ben.

It all came together a lot easier than I thought. I was soon steaming out of New York Harbor into the unknown. Rather than switch back and forth between steamer, train and automobile, Gary Pearson was able to use his State Department contacts and get me a diplomatic excursion on a steamer that went from New York to Bombay with only a one night stopover in Marseille to refuel and re-provision. It would have all been quite exciting if Ben were with me and if I weren't scared most of the time.

I had no idea if anyone was following me or not. I couldn't worry about that at this point in time. I surveyed my fellow passengers each time I passed but no one seemed out of the ordinary or overly interested in me. After a bit, I decided not to look anymore. There wasn't much I could do if I were being trailed; I might as well just sit back.

I could not understand how sailors went out on the sea for months on end; every way you looked was water. I needed solid land beneath my feet. It occurred to me that I was quickly learning all the things I was not cut out for: a spy, a sailor. I was sure I would learn of others as I went along.

The trip across the Atlantic was somewhat rough but for the

most part uneventful. It did not take me long to miss terribly my little boy, especially after getting acquainted with a young family who were heading to Marseille to visit relatives. The daughter, Maria, was about Harry's age. I enjoyed her company, she was so pretty and well behaved but she also made me feel guilty about leaving my son behind. More than once I had toyed with the idea of bringing him along on this voyage but the sergeant's words about how careful I had to be—and the associated message of how much danger I could be in—kept appearing before my eyes. I could not risk exposing Harry to any hint of danger if I could help it. I had to make this trip alone.

A couple of the deck hands were very nice, probably hoping they could strike up a romance with a young woman traveling alone. I flirted with them a little, I must admit. It felt good to have someone show a little attention to me that way. I had to be careful that it did not go too far or that I gave them more license than I wanted them to have.

When we finally reached port in Marseille, most everyone, even those who were going on with me, got off the ship. I remained aboard. I had to remind myself that I was not on a pleasure cruise; I had a mission that I could not jeopardize. However, I do have to say that the sights and sounds of Marseille, at least what I could see and hear from my window and from the deck, were tantalizing. I could hear a French accordion playing a rather mournful rendition of Lili Marlene as I sat reading on deck.

The captain had let most of the crew have the night off to go into the city and he invited me, as the only other person onboard the ship, to join him for dinner. At first I was skeptical and a little leery of his intentions, but I really could not refuse. I couldn't afford to alienate anyone on this trip and I had to spend another five days on his ship before we reached Bombay.

I got more nervous when I arrived at his quarters to join him for the dinner. White linens, a silver candelabra and cut crystal enhanced my feeling that this man was expecting more out of the evening than I was willing to provide him.

"Mrs. Jones. How wonderful of you to join me." The captain said in greeting as he opened the door.

I did have to say that Captain Harris really looked the part. He had the bearing and appearance you would expect in a sea captain: handsome with a neatly trimmed beard flecked with gray; tall and trim and supremely confident. This only increased my trepidation about what he may be expecting.

"I have a special treat in store for us tonight. There is one particular restaurant in Marseille that makes the best bouillabaisse in the entire world. Every single time I dock in this city I go to this restaurant to savor this magical culinary invention. Have you ever had bouillabaisse?"

I responded that I hadn't.

"Ah, then this will indeed be a special evening. I've been to this establishment so often over the years and have sent so many of my passengers there to eat that they always do the bouillabaisse up extra special for me. They are not in the business of putting together orders to be carried out, but for me they have done so on those occasions that I am forced to remain with the ship. Since I heard that you were not going to be venturing out, I thought this to be a perfect occasion to dine in and get to know you better."

I was getting more anxious by the second. I wouldn't have been surprised if I were perspiring profusely even thought the room was entirely comfortable with a nice cool Mediterranean breeze coming in through he window.

"Can I offer you something to drink? I'm going to pour myself a cold glass of white Burgundy. Can I offer you the same?"

I nodded yes, too nervous to speak at this point. I could have refused, knowing that he was trying to ply me with alcohol, but I did not want to refuse or agitate him, which could have been even worse for me.

"The meal should be arriving momentarily. I sent my first mate, Mr. Wheeler, to pick up the bouillabaisse. Since it is made to order, it takes a bit of time, but it is well worth the wait."

At this point I was on the verge of excusing myself claiming I was ill, but then his next sentence made me glad I kept my mouth shut.

"I hope you don't mind but I've asked Mr. Wheeler to join us for dinner. It isn't proper for me to be alone with you now, but it certainly would be out of the question for this to continue into dinner. Plus, you won't believe the amount of food they will have given to Mr. Wheeler. It would be virtually impossible for two people to eat so much."

I silently breathed a sigh of relief.

"Why captain," I responded, "I can't imagine I would feel anything but safe in the company of a man of your character."

"You're just lucky you didn't meet me before my Emily took me in tow and made an honest man of me."

"Emily's your wife, I take it."

"Yes, my lovely bride and the mother of my son, Ernest."

He went to his dresser to show me the picture of his wife and son. They were quite attractive.

"It must be tough being away from them for so long at a time."

"I just have to truly savor the short times we have together."

"That's quite poetic of you, captain."

He said nothing, but just smiled a shy smile. He was so masculine and charming right then and there. It was a good thing that there was a knock on the door at that moment. For all my nervousness and plans to run away, if he had grabbed me at that moment, I might not have been able to resist.

The captain was correct; there was enough food to feed six people. And it was absolutely delicious. Fish and shellfish of every variety imaginable were piled high on wooden trays. You took what you wanted for your bowl and then poured the most flavorful broth I've ever tasted over it.

During out meal, we each spoke about our families and our lives. Captain Harris had grown up in Boston but the sea was really his home, having run away to crew a ship when he was only fifteen. Mr. Wheeler was a boyhood friend of the captain but had for years gone in another direction. He also had run off when he was only fifteen and joined a circus. He did all sorts of jobs: clown, high wire, animal trainer, emcee. One day he was walking down the streets of Norfolk, Virginia when who should he meet but his old friend, who was now the captain of a freight steamer. The captain was at that moment without a first mate and offered him the job on the spot. Wheeler didn't have to think a moment before he accepted the offer. That was a decade ago. Captain Harris had piloted two different ships, including the present one, since then. The only stipulation he had when accepting each job was that Mr. Wheeler be hired, too.

My life story sounded so boring after their tales, but they seemed fascinated. They had never really had a full conversation with a college-educated woman before. I was surprised each of them proclaimed that, if they had to one thing differently, they would have done more schooling. Both said they felt inadequate when talking to college-educated men. I told them that was utter hogwash. First of all, I pointed out how eloquent both of them were without a college education. Secondly, I repeated highlights of the life experiences they had that an educated businessman could never hope to duplicate. They appreciated my reasoning.

"So, Mrs. Jones," Mr. Wheeler asked, "What is it that would bring you all alone half-way around the world, away from your son and everything that is familiar to you?"

I thought of Sergeant Jones's admonition to trust nobody, but I knew I could not live that way. I had to talk to someone. In addition, I assumed I was safe going under the Lydia Jones moniker.

"My husband is in prison in Calcutta. He was framed for a murder he did not commit. I'm going to prove his innocence and set him free."

They were too stunned to speak for several moments.

"In Calcutta? It's a tough city. Bombay is no piece of cake either. I take it you've never been to India before, correct?"

"No, I never have, but I don't have a choice. A man who was helping me has done all he can. I have to take over where he left off."

"How do you plan to get from Bombay to Calcutta?"

"I'm going to take a train."

Both men shared a knowing glance and then excused

themselves for a moment. They exited the captain's quarters, leaving me alone, perplexed as to what they were discussing. A few minutes later they walked back in. The captain, with a look of resolve on his face, spoke.

"Lydia," he stopped himself, "I hope you don't mind me calling you by your first name."

I told him I didn't mind in the least.

"Mr. Wheeler and I discussed it and we cannot permit you, a white woman traveling by herself, to make her way across India."

I started to protest but the Captain held up his hand so I let him continue.

"India is no better, no worse, than any other place. In fact, I have always found the Indian people to be generous and warm hearted. But just the logistics of a woman, unfamiliar with the country and its customs, traveling alone are mind boggling."

I must have had a look on my face that implied that I didn't think it could be all that difficult so the captain went into detail.

"Well, first of all, good luck finding a train that will bring you straight from Bombay to Calcutta. You'll find yourself crisscrossing over the whole damn subcontinent trying to find the right connections. Second, you'll inevitably find yourself stranded when one or more of those trains break down. We are not talking the most modern or well-maintained equipment in the world here. Third, unless you buy first class tickets, you'll find yourself standing mashed up against a host of loud, foul smelling people. Some of those trains are so packed that people ride on top of them. Fourth, although England is in charge of the country, don't assume everyone speaks English. And many who do pretend they don't to the whites, all in the interest of national pride. Where was I? Oh yes, fifth, there has been recent waves of nationalism and independence that sometimes erupt into violence, especially after the Amritsar massacre last year. As a woman alone, you would be an easy mark for someone trying to make a political point, never mind every bandit riding the rails. I could go on, but I believe you get my point."

I did. I was completely intimidated but I had no choice. I had to press on regardless of what these men said. I was also somewhat indignant over the automatic assumption made by these two men I'd only just met that I was a helpless female incapable of accomplishing what I had set out to do. I had to demonstrate otherwise so I assumed a defiant pose and responded.

"I'm afraid you two gentlemen have absolutely no say over what I do or don't do. I will press on whether you like it or not."

I was about to storm out of the room when the captain held up his hand once again. I was amazed at how commanding a presence he could be and I sat back down and shut my mouth. He smiled.

"Lydia, we aren't telling you all this to scare you. We fully realize that you are on a mission from which you won't be—nor should you be—deterred. We are not suggesting that you turn back. What we are proposing is that Mr. Wheeler accompany you. We've discussed it. I will try get by without Mr. Wheeler's estimable services for a couple of weeks. All we would ask is that you cover his expenses during this time. Neither he nor I are rich men."

"I can't ask this of you."

"I don't recall you asking, my dear."

"I don't know what to say. We've only just met yet you provide me with such a generous offer."

"You haven't said as much, but we sense there are dangers to your safety other than the trip itself, which are themselves considerable. I don't know if I could live with myself if I let you go on your own and then found out that something happened. Mr. Wheeler will take good care of you."

So, it was settled. I was ignoring each and every warning Sergeant Jones had given me. I should have steadfastly refused the offer, but I was so nervous about the rest of the trip that it came as a relief and I gratefully accepted.

The next three days were as beautiful as the Mediterranean could offer. Before I knew it we were entering the Suez Canal. After hearing stories of how beautiful and how highly engineered the Panama Canal was, I expected the Suez to be similar but I found it to be a major disappointment. There were no locks, just a long, straight and narrow finger of water through the most desolate land you could imagine. I couldn't wait to get back to open water. After traversing the length of the Red Sea, we skirted the Arabian peninsula for a straight shot across the Arabian Sea to Bombay.

The shoreline of India appeared on the horizon; my heart started beating fast. I still had over 1,000 miles to go, but just to finally be approaching the same country that Ben was in gave me feelings of hope and anticipation.

As the ship docked, I stood at the railing and looked out at the wharf. It was abuzz with activity as the land crew scurried about, making preparations for unloading the vessel of its passengers and cargo. I was struck at the paucity of white faces among the people scurrying about. It would be the first time in my life that I would be in the minority and I must admit I was not comfortable about this fact.

Mr. Wheeler walked up beside me. As if he could read my thoughts, he spoke to me.

"A different world, isn't it?"

"Yes indeed, Mr. Wheeler."

"Please, since we're going to be traveling companions for some time, call me Stan. You go by Lydia, not Lyddie or something like that, correct?"

I had to keep telling myself that I was Lydia Jones, not Catherine Albert.

"Yes, a bit formal I must admit but it's just always been that way."

We looked out on the wharf scene for a while without saying anything.

"Stan, I must thank you again for this. As you said, it is a different world, much different than the one in which I'm comfortable. I'd have plowed ahead on my own but it's much preferable having along someone such as yourself who has much more experience in the world. You know India well?"

"Both Bombay and Calcutta have been ports of call on a number of occasions. One time our ship needed some work after our propeller got damaged on a whale that got too close. We limped into Calcutta. It took us three weeks to get a replacement so the captain and I went on a trip into the interior to see some of the sights. It's an amazing country and people. I must say, this is my first cross-country excursion, so it will be somewhat of a new experience for me as well.

"I do believe there are train tracks that go straight across the country connecting the two cities but we'll probably have to change trains at least once. You said that you will need to head to Delhi after Calcutta. Hopefully there are tracks heading there as well but don't worry, I'll get you there if we have to ride elephants part of the way."

He smiled as if joking, but I sensed a part of him was serious. We very may well have to ride on an elephant before this was over.

I thanked the captain for all his kindnesses and we were on our way. Expecting that we were going to have to ride in an oxen-drawn carriage to get to the train station, I was pleasantly surprised when we hopped on a modern electric tramway that passed by the port. Within fifteen minutes, we were at the train station.

As we alighted from the tram, we were met by hundreds of men, all dressed in white linen shirts and pants and sandals. They were walking silently and solemnly in rows of five along the street in front of the station. At the front was a small man clad in a white serape and sandals. He had extremely close-cropped dark but graying hair and rounded rim glasses. Being somewhat shorter than nearly everyone else in the entourage, his strides were longer and more purposeful than the rest but I had the feeling that whatever pace he chose, the others would naturally fall behind him.

"What do you think is going on here, Stan?"

While I stood there transfixed at the spectacle, Mr. Wheeler's attention was focused on arranging our bags to bring them into the station. He looked up when I spoke.

"That? That's Gandhi. He's making quite a name for himself trying to kick the Brits out of India. He's organized marches and demonstrations all over the country, pushing for justice and rights for native Indians. He espouses a doctrine of non-violence that drives the Brits crazy. Armed rebellions they can fight, put down and then claim the moral high ground because they were attacked. They don't quite know how to react to demonstrations like this because, if and when they respond with force, they end up with a black eye that gets blacker and blacker. We probably should move along before the British army arrives to disperse the crowd and arrest Mr. Gandhi yet again."

I was shocked at perhaps being in the presence of the man who had inadvertently set Ben's wheel of madness in motion.

"Gandhi? Mohandas Gandhi?"

"I believe that's his name but he goes by other titles: Mahatma, which means Holy One and Bapu, which means father.

I was increasingly impressed by Mr. Wheeler's breadth of knowledge. As he started for the front door of the station, I shouted out.

"Mr. Gandhi! Because of you, my husband is in prison."

I did not want it to come out as blatantly accusatory as it did, but I also wanted to get his attention. It did. It also got the attention of about a half dozen other men who immediately jumped in front of Gandhi to protect him from a perceived threat. I could see Gandhi quizzically eying me between the two taller men who had jumped in front of him. He put his hands on the shoulders of the two men and told them he would be quite safe. The men parted like the Red Sea and Gandhi walked through to me.

"My dear woman, the only person I can recollect being responsible for sending to prison is myself."

The men around him started to laugh but when he noticed how distraught I was he held up a hand and the laughing stopped.

"Come," he said as he motioned to a nearby bench, "let's sit for awhile so you can tell me what I did and how I can make amends."

We sat down. Gandhi spoke a few words to another man who appeared to be his main lieutenant and within minutes, all of the hundreds of men sat down in the street where they stood. I looked around for Stan, but he had proceeded into the station to get our train tickets while I spoke with Mr. Gandhi.

"Mr. Gandhi, thank you for talking to me. My name is Catherine Albert. My husband is Benjamin Albert. He is in prison, falsely accused of murdering Mr. Sanjit Rama."

"Ah, yes. I am very familiar with that case. Mr. Rama was a very close friend of mine. I miss him dearly. If I remember correctly, the murder weapon and Mr. Rama's wrap with his blood on it were found in your husband's hotel room. There was also a witness who placed your husband at Mr. Rama's residence at the time of the murder. Guilt seemed pretty clear to the judges in the case. I still do not understand how this has any relationship to me."

"My husband was framed. One witness has already been shown to be a liar. I am on my way to Calcutta to gather evidence that will prove his innocence. You enter the picture because he never would have been in a position where he would have been framed if it weren't for a conversation he had with you. Actually, it was a conversation that changed his life, and I'm not talking about prison, I'm talking about the effect you had on his spirit."

Gandhi looked confused but let me go on.

"I don't know if you remember him, but when you were in Calcutta about four months ago, you were in a crowded tea house and invited my husband to join you for a pot of tea."

"Wait, that was your husband? I never made the connection. Of course, now I remember. He did tell me his name was Benjamin. We had a nice long talk."

"Yes, and his next three or four letters to me were all about you and the conversation you had. I could tell that something about him had changed. All of a sudden, and pardon me if I offend you, sir, but he no longer referred to Indians as 'colored'. He said he started to get to know the person who was working for him, his bearer he called him. But one thing he also started to do was to ask some questions about an accident at the Langdan Mill in which five men died. I believe you had talked about it when you met. Even though he had heard about it when he arrived, he didn't do anything or ask any questions until you planted the seeds in his mind, and in his heart."

"Oh dear, I remember your husband well and I could see a

goodness in him but also a naiveté. If I had made the connection, I would have known that the man they had accused of killing Mr. Rama was incapable of such a crime."

"Believe me, Mr. Gandhi, I am not telling you all this because I hold you responsible. You are right, Ben is a good man but he had always worn blinders about people who were different from him, especially those of a different color. You helped remove those blinders and made him a better person. No, the ones responsible are at Langdan Textile and the corrupt government in Calcutta."

"You say you have evidence that can set him free?"

"I believe so. A man had been helping me and wrote me that he was given a whole folder of documents and pictures that prove his innocence. Before he could do anything with the documents, though, he thought he was being followed by agents working for Langdan, parties whom he believed would stop at nothing. He could not risk them catching him with the evidence on him so he put it into a bank safety deposit box and sent me the key. I don't know if he's been captured or if he's alive or dead at this point.

"I'm simply looking to anybody who can possibly help me and when we stumbled on your march I had to find a way to talk to you. I am so sorry about publicly accusing you the way I did, but I had to get your attention."

Gandhi chuckled.

"Yes, it did do that; it did do that indeed. The question is, what can we do now?"

"Well, I plan to go to retrieve the documents in Calcutta and go to the American consulate in Delhi. I was told not to trust anyone in Calcutta."

"That is very wise advice and a fine plan of action. I am trying to think of something I can do to help. As you may know, I am not overly popular with the British administrators throughout the country. As a matter of fact, I would not be surprised if I were to be arrested within the hour for blocking traffic in front of a train station. A direct appeal by me would be of little help and may in fact hurt your cause."

He paused and pondered deep in thought for a few seconds but then his face brightened.

"Ah yes, I know what I can do. Yes, yes. I have a friend, a young American journalist, who has become very interested in our cause here in India. He is a very good man. He files reports with both American and foreign wire services. His name is Mark Weston. He is here in Bombay with us right now. I will tell him of your husband's plight. I'm sure he will recognize a good news story when he hears it. I think you will need his help. My prediction is that the American consulate will be sympathetic to your plea but will tell you they are helpless and cannot interfere with the judicial workings of another country. Public pressure and outcry that will result from a news article may convince them otherwise. It will help us as well. We have long been concerned about official English corruption in Calcutta. This will shine a light to expose that corruption. The English have an expression that we would be killing two birds with one stone."

"Americans use it as well."

"Very good. I will ask Mr. Weston to meet you at the American consulate in Delhi in say eight days. Will that give you enough time?"

"Yes, I think so. I believe the train takes three days to get to Calcutta. I plan on getting in and getting out of the city as immediately as I can but it may take me a day or more to catch a train to Delhi and then that's another couple of days."

"Good, I will arrange it. He will be there at noon a week from tomorrow. He is your average American with medium length brown hair and glasses."

"I don't know how to thank you Mr. Gandhi."

"Anything that advances justice is all the thanks I need."

I left Mr. Gandhi and headed into the train station. Stan was standing there, looking at his watch.

"I was about to come out and get you. The train leaves in five minutes. We have to hurry down to the tracks. What did you and Gandhi talk about?"

"He had met my husband once. I thought he might be able to help me."

"Can he?"

For some reason, even though I had been so upfront with Stan and the captain, I was reluctant to mention that he was going to have a journalist assist me.

"He's going to ask around, but he's fully aware that, when it comes to the British government here in India, he's persona non gratis. I'm still on my own, with your help of course."

I could see Stan eying me closely but he said no more and we boarded the train.

Luckily, Stan was able to secure a private first class compartment. It was rather cramped and the upholstery was a bit tattered, but compared with the rest of the accommodations on the train, we were in the lap of luxury.

The best part of the trip was getting to know Stan. Between his years with the circus and those at sea, he was full of stories. The characters he had met, the things he had done, the places he had seen, they all provided grist for his tales. And, he was a wonderful storyteller. Numerous times I was bent over in laughter as he told about the exploits of a lion tamer or getting in and out of a jam in a Liverpool pub or a brief affair he had with a tattooed lady. He must have thought me quite boring whenever I spoke, but he never let on as much.

I would occasionally look out the window at the Indian countryside. I was hoping to see an elephant or a tiger or a mongoose, any of the exotic Indian wildlife I'd heard and read about since I was a little girl. Alas, none were to be seen. Maybe we didn't go through areas where they lived or maybe the loud train engine and horn scared them off. I did observe some of the small villages we rumbled through. The sights were both mesmerizing and at times disgusting as I witnessed the condition in which some people existed, at least those who lived near the train tracks.

We pulled into one small city, where we laid over for a couple of hours while the train took on coal and water. The conductor told us we could get out and stretch our legs if we wanted. It was a densely populated town and it was squalid, dirty, noisy and malodorous. Naked children and scantily clad adults were everywhere. Holy cattle and heavily laden bullock carts—and the substantial contributions each made on the pavement—made traffic through the narrow main street difficult so we made our way back to the train.

By some sort of miracle, the train arrived in Calcutta precisely on schedule, at around 5:00 in the evening. It was too late for the bank so we had to find a place to spend the night. I told Stan of the sergeant's admonition to stay away from the larger hotels. Stan knew an out of the way hostelry where he had stayed a few years back. It was a small cheap place, but very clean. He also knew of a restaurant in that area that served a wonderfully spicy lamb vindaloo.

The next morning precisely at 9:00, we found ourselves at the Occidental Bank and Trust. They were just opening the doors as we arrived. I went to the bank manager and advised him that I needed access to safety deposit box number 311. He dug the records for the safe deposit boxes out of a drawer, and found that two people were allowed access: Walther Jenkins and Lydia Jones. I produced my passport identifying me as Lydia and we walked into the vault together. He left me alone there while I opened the box.

Inside was a thick manila envelope. The wiser part of me said to simply grab the envelope and depart for Delhi as quickly as I could. Instead, I pulled out the contents and laid them on the table. I started to go through the different documents, taking care to keep them in order along with the notes that had been affixed to each piece of evidence.

First, there was a photograph of a dead Indian, blood all over his head, neck and chest. There was a note on the back that read: This is a picture of Sanjit Rama, taken an hour before his body was taken for cremation. Note the well-known mole on his left cheek, indicating that this photograph accurately depicts Mr. Rama's right and left sides. Note that there are seven stabbing wounds, all on the left side of Mr. Rama's chest and neck.

I turned the photograph back over. The note had gone on to explain the implications of this revelation but I didn't need to read further. The picture virtually proved that Mr. Rama was killed by a right-handed person, at least someone with a right hand. It would have been extremely difficult if not impossible for Ben to have committed the murder.

Without even looking at the remaining documents, my heart was pounding out of my chest. I was also extremely bitter and upset. Why wasn't this piece of evidence provided to the trial? I told myself that I had to look forward. The goal was to get Ben out of jail; recriminations toward those who were at fault could come later. I went on to the next item.

It was a legal looking one-page document. It was a notarized affidavit, written in both English and Sanskrit, of a statement by a resident of Chakdaha where the jute fields were located. It was a statement of a local resident who swore that he saw Ben in his car and on foot in the fields at the time of the murder. The affidavit noted that, while the resident had not seen many automobiles in his lifetime, he loves cars and noted the make and the model of the automobile. There was a notation attached to the affidavit that Chakdaha was a twenty mile drive from Calcutta so that even if the time of death were off, it would have been impossible for Ben to be in Calcutta when Mr. Rama was killed.

The next set of documents was a sort of diary, consisting of around forty sheets of paper with dated handwritten entries. A note on the top indicated that the documents were taken from Major Highsmith's desk and were purported to be in his handwriting. The writer of the note postulated that the Major had recorded all of his meetings with Langdan officials because he did not trust them and, if anything went wrong, he had no doubt they would sell him out to save themselves. If he went down, he was surely going to bring Langdan down with him.

I leafed through the forty pages. The first dates were about a month before Ben arrived. The entries described the trouble the company was having with two Indians who were organizing workers at the mill and agitating for improved wages and working conditions. They needed to be "taken care of." A later entry noted that the "deed was done" and that Langdan had an old electric transformer that they needed to replace anyway that could conveniently be put to use to "cover up." To his credit, Highsmith did express a modicum of regret about the fate of the three other innocent men who had inadvertently gotten entangled in the mess and also got "taken care of" but he noted, c'est la guerre.

I skipped to around the date that Ben arrived. There was an entry about a meeting Highsmith had with Mr. Searles of Langdan who was complaining about his Jewish traveling companion, wishing there was some way to "put him in his place." Highsmith obviously thought he was being witty by writing that "his place was in the morgue" but there was nothing he could do about that, not at the moment anyway. Highsmith noted he had met the Jew at an official reception but did not know of his lineage until after the fact. He castigated himself for not being more careful but also took the Jew to task for trying to pass with a normal surname like Albert.

I went to a month later and noted that Highsmith wrote about this Jew who was asking all sorts of questions around the company about the death of the five Indians. There was fear that he might actually stumble on some answers. Something had to be done. By now, the word Jew was never written without some sort of derogatory adjective. The word "dirty" was most prevalent by as time went on, the adjectives became more expletive and inflammatory.

Finally, it was noted that certain "Indian agitators" were arriving in Calcutta for the Indian National Committee conference. These agitators (one in particular was cited but not named) had also raised questions on the deaths and would certainly pursue his inquiries. It was then that someone came up with the idea of "killing two birds with one stone" to eliminate the agitator and frame the Jew in one fell swoop. I thought to myself about the irony that I had recently heard the exact same phrase by Mr. Gandhi on the same issue but in an entirely different context.

The rest of the entries had to do with the trial, with the handpicked attorney representing Ben and with how justice had been served by putting the Jew away for a long time in Calcutta's hell-hole of a prison. Although he himself would have preferred hanging the Jew, putting him away where "he would be mistreated by the Indian guards who believed he had killed one of their heroes provided some sort of poetic justice."

The final entry, which was dated about three weeks ago, was a note that he had received word from Langdan that I was launching my own investigation. He was going to be watching out for me or anyone who represented me. My mind went to Sergeant Jones, wondering if Highsmith had tracked him down.

I went on to the next piece of evidence, also taken from Highsmith's desk. It was a bank receipt acknowledging that £10,000 was transferred to his account in the very bank I was now sitting. The funds originated from Langdan; that did not surprise me. What nearly knocked me out of my seat was that the transfer was authorized by none other than Franklin Andrews himself. That bastard was in on this plot, and knew even when I spoke with him.

The last piece was a notarized statement by an employee of the hotel that, on the day of the murder, she had observed Major Highsmith and two of his men enter into Ben's room at the hotel. This occurred about three hours prior to when Ben returned from the jute fields. She stated that she had mentioned all this to hotel management but was ordered, on fear of losing her job, not to tell this to anyone.

There were a couple more pieces of paper in the envelope. These seemed of no consequence as I stuffed everything back into the envelope. I put the box back in place and locked it. I walked out and found Stan sitting in the lobby.

"Was everything you needed there?"

"Everything and more," I exclaimed. I could hardly control my excitement, but I knew my job was only half done.

"Let's get back to the train station and figure out how we get to Delhi," he said, "I know a short cut."

I eagerly followed Stan out of the bank and onto a side street. As we weaved our way through the city, first through busy markets and then through deserted alleys, I began to wonder if Stan knew where he was going. His short cut seemed to be taking longer to get to the station than it did to come from there. I soon found out he knew exactly where he was taking me.

We turned the corner onto an alley that smelled terribly and had no people. We had gone about fifty feet when I asked:

"Stan, do we really have to go this way? It stinks."

He was ahead of me and when he turned around a pistol was in his hand.

"Yes, I'm afraid we did have to come here, Catherine."

I stared at him, too stunned to speak.

"That's your real name, isn't it? Catherine Albert. We've known all along."

I didn't say anything. He looked around at the dreary and foul surroundings.

"This is one of those alleys that people throw their toilet waste out their windows, so no one uses it. You'll notice there are no doors and the windows are sealed tight with shutters to keep out the smell. People generally throw their waste out early in the morning so we won't be disturbed. You're lucky it hadn't rained in awhile but you won't have to worry about the smell for much longer."

"Stan, please."

"You think the captain and I decided to accompany you out of the goodness of out hearts? You really are one naïve women, Catherine. Langdan had you followed up to the dock of our boat and then paid us handsomely to do the rest. I'll take that envelope off your hands, if you please."

I handed it over to him; I had no other choice.

"Now I really am sorry to have to do this. I really am. I kinda liked the time we spent together. Actually, the captain wanted you left alive. He's such a soft-hearted sort. I just can't have you following us. You're naïve but I have to admire your persistence. Goodbye, Catherine."

He raised the gun and aimed it at me. A shot rang out, reverberating back and forth in the narrow alleyway. I had braced myself for the pain of the shot, but I felt none. I looked at Stan and soon a rivulet of blood dripped from a corner of his mouth. A few seconds later, he crumpled forward into a heap on the ground. I looked up from his body and saw Sergeant Jones striding toward me.

"You couldn't heed my advice to trust no one, could you?"

His voice was stern but as soon as I rushed to him and buried my sobbing face into his chest, he softened.

"There, there. Catherine. It's okay. You're safe now."

He gently patted my back as he comforted me. He let me cry for a minute more and then bent down and picked up the envelope where Stan had dropped it. Luckily, it fell into one of the few dry spots in the alley. Jones looked down on Stan's body.

"He got what he deserved. Let's go Catherine. We still have work to do."

I pulled myself together and we headed out for the train.

41

Molly had willed herself better. She had to, for Catherine and Benjamin and Harry's sakes. Mr. Charney and Sol and Robert each stopped by periodically to check on her and do some errands, but she did not need constant care anymore.

She was alone when the doorbell rang and she opened it to find Edgar, the Western Union deliveryman, holding a telegram for her. She thanked him and ripped it open.

Molly, Have evidence proving Ben innocent. Must get it to proper authorities. Could not see Ben, but hope to soon. Out of touch for another week. Love to you and Harry. Catherine.

She read it and thought it was good news but was unsure of her English. When Robert came over in the afternoon, she asked him to look it over.

"Yes, Mama, this is good news. Perhaps this means Benjamin can be set free soon."

Molly felt the best she had in months. She felt so well that she asked Robert to take her out to do some food shopping. She then made a big dinner for the two of them, the type of cooking she used to put together.

When Edgar arrived the next day with another telegram, she assumed that this was good news as well. She didn't even notice that it was addressed to Catherine, not her, as she opened the envelope. She tried to read it but a number of the words like regret and cholera were completely strange to her so she put it away. She expected Mr. Charney to drop by later in the day. She would surprise him with dinner and ask him to read it to her.

When Mr. Charney arrived, he was delighted to find Molly in such good spirits. He also welcomed the smell of brisket slowly cooking in the oven. Molly showed him the first telegram she had received the day before.

"This is wonderful news, Molly. If I'm reading Catherine's words correctly, she has all she needs to set Ben free. Maybe they can come home together."

"Yes, I hope. I receive second telegram today. You read and tell what it says, yes?"

"Of course, Molly."

She dug the telegram out of the pocket in her dress and handed it to Mr. Charney. He unfolded it, took one glance at it and then had to sit down.

"Oh no," he gasped, "Good God, no."

"Mr. Charney, it is not good?"

Mr. Charney looked up at her with a lost expression on his face.

"No Molly. It is not good; not good at all. You better sit down."

"Please tell me. Please read."

Mr. Charney took a deep breath to compose himself.

"The telegram is addressed to Catherine. It says," he paused again as tears choked out his words, "it says: *Dear Mrs. Albert, We regret to inform you that your husband, Benjamin Albert, succumbed to an especially virulent strain of cholera early this morning after the disease swept through the prison. He died peacefully. Please be assured that we did everything we could to save your husband's life. In order to halt the further spread of the disease, it was necessary to cremate the body. We will send you his ashes. We are very sorry for your loss.*

Quinton Farnsworth, Prison Administrator"

Neither said anything for a minute. Many of the words like 'succumbed' and 'cholera' Molly did not know, but the part she understood clearly she repeated back to Mr. Charney.

"He died peacefully."

Mr. Charney reached over and took her hand, patting it gently.

"He was innocent," she stated, "He not to be there in first place. I never forgive."

Mr. Charney agreed, but decided not to respond in kind. That would only intensify the bitterness in the room.

"We have to get word to Catherine. I will go see my friend, Mr. Pearson. He can contact his brother in the State Department who can send a message to the American Consulate in Delhi. That's where you said she's heading next. Isn't that correct, Molly?"

Molly nodded in reply, not looking up from the floor.

"I will go get Robert to stay with you while I'm gone."

Again, Molly nodded but said nothing. Mr. Charney headed out the front door.

42

Catherine

As with our train from Bombay to Calcutta, luck was with us and there was a train leaving for Delhi an hour after we arrived at the station. We secured first class tickets for a compartment that we shared with a middle-aged British couple who were making a grand tour of the colonies. Like me, it was her first trip away from home.

After Sergeant Jones saved me, I was still tempted to disregard his advice and go to the prison to see Ben. I was so burning to see him, even in the horrendous conditions he was in. The sergeant gently pointed out to me that the best way to help Ben was to get these documents into the hands of the proper authorities. He was gentlemanly enough not to point out how badly events had turned when I went my own way before, but he made it clear as to the best way he thought we should proceed. I reluctantly conceded and we boarded the train.

Mr. and Mrs. Doolittle, the couple, were delightful. While she had been home raising six children, he had traveled all over the world on business, which coincidentally happened to be textiles. He was familiar with Langdan, and quite frankly did not have a very high opinion of the company or its chief officer, Franklin Andrews. He found them to be a corporate bully that did little to advance the textile trade as a whole. They were solely interested in maximizing their own profits regardless of the cost to the industry. He was very plain spoken about his distaste for Langdan's policies as they related to its workers. He had once visited the Langdan facility in Dundee, Scotland, the burlap capital of the world and found the conditions to be appalling.

At one point, Mr. Doolittle apologized to me for being so blunt, especially with my husband in their employ. I assured him that I had the same feelings for Langdan that he had. Certain that he had not offended me, he continued.

We arrived in Delhi three days later. We said our goodbyes to the Doolittles and headed straight to the American Consulate. Mr. Gandhi's friend the reporter was not due to meet with us until the following day so we went straight up to the ambassador's office. I was surprised that the secretary in the outer office knew my name and told me the ambassador was expecting me. I was wondering if Mr. Pearson's brother had made calls to pave the way. I was exultant at the possibility that things were going to work out. Perhaps we would not need the reporter after all.

We walked into the office and a stocky but fit, silver haired man in his fifties got up from his desk.

"Mrs. Albert," he said as we shook hands, "I'm Lester McCormick, United States Ambassador to India."

He turned to Sergeant Jones who introduced himself as William Jenkins, playing the game all the way to the end.

"Won't you please have a seat? I understand you have been traveling for the past few days and have not been able to communicate with the outside world."

I wasn't sure what our traveling had to do with anything so I said nothing. The Ambassador fidgeted and looked generally uncomfortable.

"I don't know any delicate way to put this so I'll have to just come out and tell you. I've received word that your husband died of cholera in prison. I'm very sorry."

I didn't believe him at first.

"No, this can't be. It can't be."

I clutched the bag holding the evidence I thought would free him close to my chest.

"I'm afraid it's true."

"When, when did this happen?" I weakly asked.

"Four days ago, I believe. The prison sent a telegram to you in the States. Your family contacted me through the State Department. They knew you were headed here. I am so sorry to be the bearer of such unhappy news."

After that the room began to swirl around. The next thing I knew I was lying on the couch in the Ambassador's office while Sergeant Jones held a cold rag on my forehead. I sat up and stared at the Ambassador.

"My husband, an American citizen, was framed and arrested on false pretenses. I know appeals were made to the State Department to intervene and ensure he was treated fairly, yet you did nothing to help him. Now he's dead."

"We cannot interfere in the judicial affairs of another country."

"That's a load of bull and you know it. You could have done more. You still can do something. You can clear my husband's name. I have evidence of his innocence."

"I am sorry for your loss; I really am. But at this point since your husband is dead it would not be a prudent use of my resources to pursue this any further. India, with the wave of nationalist fervor that is sweeping the subcontinent, has the potential to become a powder keg at any moment. Pursuing this case further would only serve to open wounds that were only recently closed. It is in our country's best interest for us to stay focused on larger issues."

We argued for another half hour. In the end, I saw that I was not going to get anywhere and I asked him a simple question.

"Can I at least see my husband to say goodbye?"

"I am sorry, Mrs. Albert, but I've been advised that your husband's body has been cremated. They had to do it to stem the spread of the disease. His ashes are being shipped to your home."

I had been amazed that, other than the initial fainting spell, I was able to maintain my composure. But this news sent me over the edge as I burst into uncontrollable sobs. Sergeant Jones took my hand and I looked up into his face. His eyes were moist as well.

"Come along, Catherine. There's nothing more for us here. At least now we know how little our country regards its war heroes."

As I got up to join the sergeant heading for the door, the ambassador felt the need to respond.

"That's not fair, Mr. Jenkins. We have an international situation we have to consider."

Sergeant Jones only glared back at him in return as we exited. Once outside in the fresh air, I had somewhat regained my composure.

"Thank you for all you've done, Sergeant. Ben truly had a good friend. Now, I just want to get back to my son. He and Ben's mother are going to need me more than ever."

"I don't think we're done yet, Catherine. I say we stay one more day and see this reporter. You say he's supposed to arrive here at noon tomorrow?"

"That's what Mr. Gandhi said, and he seemed pretty confident that his friend will show."

"I understand your desire to leave this place, but if we can't get the government to act, perhaps the press will. It's too late to save Ben but we can clear his name. Perhaps we can use this reporter to get the word out and bring the people who are responsible to justice. There's also an Indian man, Mr. Dutta, who was unjustly arrested. Perhaps we can help set him free. Let's stay one more day."

"Okay. One more day won't make a difference."

We returned to the consulate the next day and, as promised, a man in his mid thirties with wavy brown hair and wire-frame glasses who fit Mr. Gandhi's description was standing by the front entrance. He was casually reading a newspaper.

"Mr. Weston?" I cautiously asked as we approached.

"Yes. Mrs. Albert, I presume."

"Yes, call me Catherine. This is Wil"

The sergeant extended his hand, interrupting me mid-word.

"Walter Jones. I've read a number of your articles and bylines over the past couple of years, Mr. Weston. Very impressive. It's a pleasure to meet you."

I was glad to see that he was through with the cloak and dagger approach, using his real name. I was also taken by his attention to the niceties of human interaction. It wasn't an attribute I would have ascribed to Sergeant Jones.

"Thank you, and please call me Mark. How about we go to a café I know of near here so we can talk?"

We walked to this dingy little place that was busy, but not overly crowded. We found a table in the corner.

"Thank you so much for agreeing to meet with us, Mark."

"Well, first of all, I would do anything Bapu asks, I have that much respect and admiration for the man."

"Bapu?" I asked.

"Yes, it means father. It's an honorary title that Mohandas Gandhi earns every single day. I know it doesn't make me sound like an objective journalist, but when it comes to him, I'm not one. Anyway, when he laid out for me the background, the objective journalist in me smelled a story, and a good one. Bapu has been after me to write a story exposing both the official corruption in Calcutta and the excessive influence that Western business interests have in exploiting that corruption. We all knew it was happening but I've never been presented with solid enough leads or concrete enough facts to write a story. Until now. I have the general background but please fill in the holes and show me what you have."

The sergeant and I laid out the entire story in detail for him from beginning to end. We went through each item of documentation, answering any questions he had. When he asked about how we came upon Major Highsmth's journal and how we knew it was authentic, Sergeant Jones directed him to the Indian lieutenant who had taken them from Highsmith's desk. But he gave him Lieutenant Chakraborty's name only after he made Mark swear that the Indian's identity would never be revealed. Otherwise, his job—and not to mention his life—could be in jeopardy. Mark readily agreed. I got the sense that as a journalist he had to constantly agree to terms such as this to get to the truth.

At the end, Mark said that he was definitely going to write a story. He couldn't guarantee that his editors would push it or that papers would publish it, but he thought it was too good a story for it not to run. He said that he doubted that they could hold Ben much longer after it ran. We told him that Ben had died.

"I'm so sorry. I didn't know. But I hope you pardon my journalistic insensitivity when I say that his death may even help the story get a bigger run than otherwise. I can highlight it as an ultimate injustice that was perpetrated."

He saw from my expression that I did think he was insensitively using my husband's death to increase the sales of his story.

"Catherine, I am truly sorry about your husband's death. It is important that the people responsible for his death be exposed for what they are. His death—and his life—could be used to weed out this corruption and improve a great many lives."

I smiled at the thought that Ben would be remembered in the way he just described. I nodded my assent.

43

Mark Weston knew a good story when he stumbled upon one, and this was a good story. He had enough to write a strong article on the basis of what he collected from Catherine Albert and Walter Jones, but he had a sense that what he had been presented thus far was only the tip of the iceberg. He intended on digging much deeper to see what else he could uncover.

His first task was to go to Calcutta. There he surreptitiously interviewed Lieutenant Chakraborty to corroborate the pieces of the puzzle attributed to him. When he asked about Major Highsmith, he was advised that the major had unexpectedly returned to England on "personal matters." He then went and interviewed the man who swore he saw Ben in the fields that day and the hotel attendant who witnessed Highsmith enter Ben's room that day, probably to hide the knife and bloodied garment. Everything that Catherine and Walter had told him was being corroborated to the letter. However, he could not get anyone either in the Calcutta government or at the Langdan mill to give him the time of day.

Mark had scheduled a vacation to the States starting two weeks after he met with Catherine. He was going to visit his family in Maryland, but he decided to first make a side trip to the Langdan Textiles Boston headquarters. Catherine had shown him one document, on which the company president himself had been implicated. He was sure there must be more. It was definitely worth a couple days of his time to investigate.

He arrived at Langdan and went straight to Franklin Andrews' office.

"Good morning. May I help you?" Mrs. Epstein asked him in greeting as he walked through the door.

"Good morning. I'd like to see Mr. Andrews. My name is Mark

Weston. I'm with Westbrook News Service."

"A reporter? I've always found that world fascinating."

"It can be at times, but like anything else, it can also just be a job."

"Well, unfortunately Mr. Andrews is out of the state right now. He won't be back until next week. If you like, I can get a message to him and have him contact you."

"That would be very kind of you."

"Can I give Mr. Andrews some indication of what you want to talk to him about?"

"I'm doing a story on the death of Benjamin Albert, whom I believe used to work for Langdan."

An icy silence descended on the room. Mrs. Epstein finally spoke.

"That was such a tragedy. I only met Mr. Albert once, but I knew even from those brief acquaintances that he was incapable of doing what they accused him of. Now, he's dead. How is his wife, Catherine, holding up? I was very close to her mother."

Mark was sensing an opening here.

"She's doing as well as can be expected. I believe she's back home now in New Jersey. She wants some answers on what happened to her husband; she wants whoever was responsible to be held accountable."

Again, there was silence. But this time he could tell it was because Mrs. Epstein was thinking hard, considering options.

"Mr. Weston, are you going to be around for awhile?"

"I'm heading home to Maryland tomorrow afternoon."

"That will be perfect. I see no need to bother Mr. Andrews. Can you come back here tomorrow morning?"

"Yes, I can."

When he arrived at 10:00 the next morning, Mrs. Epstein handed him a six-inch thick accordion folder crammed with files, journals and ledgers.

"I think this will provide you with the answers you seek. All this has to stop. I stood idly by for years, but the death of Ben was the last straw. Maybe I can sleep again. If you talk to Catherine, tell her

I'm so sorry. If I had spoken out years ago, perhaps Ben would be alive today."

"Thank you Mrs. Epstein."

Mark started plowing through the folder as soon as he found his seat on the train but nothing seemed to jump out at him. The documents were arranged chronologically. They involved many of the far-flung holdings of Langdan Textiles: mills in Thailand, Indonesia, Dundee, Canada, and the United States. There were many memoranda and copies of letters sent to Dexter Applebee Security of Landover, Maryland. Since nothing was really catching his eye, he put the folder away and enjoyed the scenery racing by.

When he arrived at his home in Baltimore he pulled the folder back out. For no special reason, this time he started from the most recent files and worked back. The first item that drew his eye was a cancelled check to Dexter Applebee with a notation of "Rama". A similar check from a few weeks earlier had a notation of "Guru", the name of one of the five men killed in the Calcutta accident. He leafed through all of the checks, each one had a similar notation.

The bureau often used Fred Goliscevsky, a librarian who worked at Georgetown University, to perform background research. Mark called Fred and recited the list of names from the checks, the date the checks were written, and Mark's best guess as to the appropriate country.

Two hours later, Fred called Mark back.

"Mark, I'm gonna feel guilty billing the bureau for this one, it was so easy. But don't think that's gonna stop me sending you my bill."

Mark laughed.

"I expected no less, Fred. Whaddya got?"

"Each of the names were of guys who died not long after the dates you gave me. Three of 'em died in accidents, two were the subject of foul play. None of the murders was solved, at least at the time the deaths were reported anyway. All were well-known enough in their respective countries to get mention in their local papers. Most of them seemed to be involved in labor movements of one form or another. That's what made the job so easy. I'll make notations of where I found these articles and send you the list. Is there anything more you need on this?"

"No, Fred. And believe me, you've earned whatever you charge us."

Mark now went back to the correspondence that did not make much sense before but now became crystal clear. The first letters and memoranda were very oblique in their references and intent but as time went on, they became more obvious and blatant. Instead of using the phrase 'take care of' he now used terms like 'eliminate.' Now that he had the context, the letters made perfect sense now.

Mark believed he was observing pure, unadulterated arrogance at work here. These people all died in "accidents" similar to the five men in Calcutta.

He had to find out more about this Dexter Applebee Security. He dug his old Model T out of his garage and set out for Landover. The address on all the correspondence to this firm was 11 Mechanic Street. After asking two people who had no idea where Mechanic Street was, he got himself a street map of the city. He searched it over and over several times and final found the street, a dead end no more than a block long at the far eastern end of town. When he got there, he found a vacant lot in amongst four dilapidated and boarded up houses. He calculated that 11 Mechanic Street would have been where the vacant lot was. It looked as if there had not been a building on this site for at least a decade, maybe more. The address was a sham.

He felt he had all he needed to put together a story. He was taking on Langdan Textiles, one of the biggest companies of its kind in the world, so he knew he had to get his story approved up and down the chain of command, but he had his documentation. It was a good story; he knew that. Despite how powerful the adversary, a story as good as this one would run. Furthermore, he knew it would have an impact.

44
Catherine

It felt so good to have Harry back in my arms. When I opened the door, Molly was in the living room holding him. She looked up at me with tears in her eyes as she handed him to me.

"I tell him about his papa, how good a man he was. I tell him his mama return soon, she is good woman, too."

"Thank you, Molly. How are you holding up?"

She said nothing as she stood up and gave me a big hug. We cried into each other until Harry started to cry because we both were starting to smother him in between us. We looked down at him and couldn't help but smile at the bundle of life writhing in my arms. I put him on the floor and let him crawl around.

For the next week, I moped around the house, doing nothing. I kept telling myself that I had to carry on, to pick myself up and be productive again. I could be pretty sure that Mr. Bress had allowed his finances to become a mess once again. I could dive back into that job with no problem. I needed to push myself for Harry and Molly if not for my own well-being. I could not find the energy, however.

When the doorbell rang, it startled me out of my reverie. It made me wonder how Edgar was doing. I could use him at the door gushing about his sons. Instead, it was the mailman with a special delivery envelope for me. I signed for it and thanked the man. As I was opening the envelope, I noticed it was from Westbrook News Service. In it was a copy of the News World Tribune, one of the papers that carried Mark Weston's articles. Attached to the paper was a note from Mark.

Dear Catherine,
I'm not sure whether you've had a chance to see this, but I filed

my story and it has run in over fifty papers worldwide. On the attached paper, it even ran on the front page, below the fold mind you, but still front page. I have already received calls from the State Department, the United States Attorney General's office and the District Attorney of Boston as well as telegrams from the British government, both in India and in England. Each has expressed a desire to interview me about this case. As I feel that I have a journalistic obligation to protect my sources, I would like your permission to share information with them. Perhaps justice can finally be obtained for your husband.

I am heading back to India next Tuesday and will be hooking up with Mr. Gandhi again. Please try to get back to me with your instructions on how you would like to proceed before then. I await your response.

Sincerely,

Mark Weston

I yelled to Molly that I was running down to the Western Union office and would be back in a half hour or so. When I walked in, Edgar was behind the counter. He gave me a big smile and welcome back. He extended his condolences.

I grabbed a piece of paper and jotted down a response to Mark giving him my absolute permission to talk with whomever he felt necessary to get the story out and to finally make someone accountable. I told him I would be happy to participate in any interviews if he needed me. Edgar clicked away, sending my message along into the electrical ether. People in authority were finally listening to Ben's story. I couldn't believe how consumed I was with a desire for revenge on the man I held most responsible for the tragic turn in our lives: Franklin Andrews. For some reason though, men like that seem to always land their feet regardless of how reprehensible their deeds may be. I resolved to put all thoughts of him behind me and get on with my life.

As I predicted, in the few short months I was away, Mr. Bress had fallen back into bad habits. His business sorely needed attention and I dove back in. The work provided a great diversion from my troubles. I was working my way through his books as Harry played with one of his toys beside me when the doorbell rang. I hoped it was another letter from Mark giving me an update on things. I was also curious whether he had joined up with Mr. Gandhi yet.

When I opened the door, it was not the postman with a letter or Edgar with a telegram but there stood Sergeant Jones. I threw my arms around him in greeting, which startled him somewhat as our relationship had always been on the formal rather than the familiar side. I could tell he struggled with calling me Catherine as I had insisted, preferring to use the stiffer appellation of Mrs. Albert. He never corrected me or asked me to call him Walter, so I still referred to him as Sergeant even after all this time and traveling together.

After we came back together from India, Sergeant Jones saw me home all the way to my door. But after we said goodbye, I frankly thought I'd never see him again. We each had our own lives to live and the primary connection we had to each other—Ben— was gone. I expected a yearly Christmas card and perhaps a letter now and then, but that would be about it. I told him that, by saving my life, he should feel that he had repaid in full any debt he felt he owed to Ben for saving his life in the war. The sergeant nodded at my logic.

So I was surprised to see him standing at my doorstep. He offered up the lame 'I was in the area' explanation, but something in my head told me that he had made a special trip just to see me. Nor did I mind it when he said he was going to be in town for a little bit, again because the job demanded it. When I asked him what the job was, he stammered something about a security job for the city, but I could tell he was lying. I just smiled.

He came in and had lunch with Molly and me while we caught up on events. He had been traveling and hadn't seen the news article. Rather than looking at the positives of the article that perhaps it may force justice to finally be achieved for Ben death or perhaps it may serve as a catalyst to make long overdue changes in a corrupt government in Calcutta, the sergeant frowned. He didn't say anything until Molly left the room.

"Catherine, over the years Langdan had been pretty ruthless to get its way. Now that this article is out there and they have district attorneys and the State Department and everyone else nosing into their affairs, there's no telling what they may resort to. Desperate people often do desperate things. They are not going to simply fade away. You need to be careful."

I generally found the sergeant's pragmatic approach to everything he faced to be a strong and admirable quality, but in this case I found it to be annoying. This article was the first positive thing in my life after months of horror. Despite the fact that the horror was still continuing in my life because I'd lost my husband, I could go on because I saw that there might be a possibility that the people responsible for Ben's death may be brought to justice. Now, the sergeant points out the negatives in even that.

"Sergeant, don't you believe in justice?"

"I believe in life, Catherine. There are many unfair and unjust things in the world; this would get added to the list. Justice is not going to bring Ben back. I frankly could do without hearing of Langdan ever again in my life and it's not a priority for me whether they get their just desserts. And while it may help advance Mr. Gandhi's goals for his country, I could care less about the cause of the Indian people. Don't think Langdan won't come after you."

"You give them too much credit, sergeant."

"And you sell them way too short. Despite your failure in judgment regarding the ship captain and his friend, I admire the way you can take care of yourself. However, you are a woman and now you have no one to look out for you. Your mother-in-law seems like a very nice woman, but I somehow doubt her protection skills are up to the task."

"Sergeant, I can take care of myself and my family quite well, thank you. I appreciate your concern but I think it would be best if you left now."

The sergeant nodded, rose and left without a word. As the words were escaping my mouth, I regretted saying them. I really did not want him to leave but his condescending attitude made me so angry. This time, I truly did despair of ever hearing from him again.

When the doorbell rang the next day, I hoped it was he. I opened the door and standing there was Franklin Andrews. As soon as the door was open a crack, he burst in, pushing me back, almost onto the floor.

"Get out of here this minute or I'll call the police!" I exclaimed.

"I don't think so," He calmly retorted as he pulled a revolver from his jacket pocket.

"Mrs. Albert," he continued, "You have succeeded in ruining me. Since that scandalous article ran, half of my clients have backed out on their contracts. I am being investigated by at least four government agencies on three continents. All because you and that damn husband of yours could not keep your noses where they belonged."

His eyes were shifting back and forth, not really focusing on anything. It was only ten in the morning, but I could smell alcohol on his breath. His hand shook, not from nervousness but from pure excitement. Why had I sent Sergeant Jones away? It was too much to hope for that he would show up in the nick of time as he had in Calcutta. Andrews wasn't done yet.

"I know I'm going down but I'm not going alone. I already took care of that bitch Epstein. She was another of my father's whores, just like your mother. Did you know that?"

I gasped as I thought of poor Mrs. Epstein. She was such a good woman, my mother's best friend. I had to calm him down or he would have shot me right then and there.

"What do you want, Mr. Andrews?"

"So formal, little Catherine? We're brother and sister after all. What I want is for you to no longer bother me, or anyone else for that matter, ever again."

I wanted to keep him talking but I could not think of a single thing to say to the man that had single handedly ruined my life from beginning to end. He obviously did not have much to say himself as he lifted the gun and aimed it at my head.

I was expecting to be dead any minute when the door from the kitchen burst open and through it flew Molly, a cast iron frying pan in her hand.

"You leave my daughter alone!" she cried with the vehemence of a tigress protecting her cubs.

"Molly, don't!" I screamed.

She was initially able to surprise Andrews as she stormed across the room. It did not take him long to recover, however, as he wheeled around toward her. He fired wildly in the direction of the onrushing middle-aged woman but not before she swung the heavy skillet in a wild wide arc towards the intruder's head.

Instinctively, Andrews flinched and turned his head. As a result, the edge of skillet landed square on his adam's apple causing a sickening and unnatural crunching sound as it crushed his larynx. He dropped his firearm and grabbed his throat as he attempted to force his windpipe open. He tried gasping for air, but none came. He looked to me for help, but I only spared him the briefest of glances as I turned my attention to the woman I loved.

Despite the close range, I originally thought that the bullet missed Molly. Molly stood triumphantly over Andrews but then she turned towards me. That's when I saw the blood. The bullet had caught her flush in the chest. I ran to her as she stumbled in my direction.

She fell into my arms.

"Catherine, my darling, I love you."

She closed her eyes and died. Not long after, Franklin Andrews ceased thrashing about as he died, too.

"Molly, I love you, too." I cried as I held her close.

I don't know how long I sat there on the floor holding her, rocking back and forth. The first thing I remembered was Mr. Charney rushing in through the slightly open front door. Through the fog in my brain I could make out his cry of anguish as he kneeled down to hold both of us. I irrationally felt sorry that he got Molly's blood all over his nice jacket. Finally, he gently pried my arms away and laid her down on the carpet a short distance away. I remained sitting on the floor as he laid her out. He checked her pulse, but I knew it was a futile gesture; she had long since passed away. He then went over to check on Andrews. To my astonishment and relief, Molly's frying pan blow had been true and severe.

Mr. Charney helped me to my feet and led me to the kitchen to get me away from the carnage. At that point I was so pliant he could have left me anywhere. He tenderly placed me in one of the wooden chairs around the kitchen table and then put some water on the stove to make some tea. Then he went in the other room to call the police.

I could hear someone else come in through the front door and ask Mr. Charney where I was. Sergeant Jones walked into the kitchen. Without saying a word, he went to the sink, filled a bowl with soapy water and proceeded to wash the smeared blood off of me. I was surprised at how delicate this often gruff and direct man could be as he tenderly wiped off Molly's blood. At one point he kneeled in front of me and looked up to see me gazing down upon him. Our eyes met and, though I knew the proper thing would be for me to look away, I kept looking into his eyes. It was he who eventually averted his gaze as he returned to cleaning me up.

45

The police came, took statements, and then left. The mortician came, took the bodies of Molly and Andrews, and then left. The house on Commercial Avenue was quiet again.

When interviewed, staff and managers at Langdan Textiles in Boston noted that Franklin Andrews had always been a bit of a strange bird but he had gotten even more erratic over the past few months. His behavior became especially troublesome after the article came out. As one by one the company's clients cancelled their contracts, Andrews became suspicious of everybody. In a three-month period, eight of his top executives, including Mr. Williams and Mr. Gill, either quit or were fired. Numerous overseas executives and managers were also let go.

After Mrs. Epstein went through Andrews' personal files and extracted the documents she would provide to Mark Weston as the final pieces for his article, she packed up her desk never to return. Three days later, the article ran and within the next week the phone calls and telegrams calling for inquiries started to pour in.

Andrews did not even notice that Mrs. Epstein had left. Neither had he noticed that his personal files had been pillaged. When the article broke, he decided to burn his personal files. When he went to look for them, they were not there. Now it became clear to him how numerous pieces of sensitive information found their way into the news piece. He knew exactly who was to blame.

He left the office that night determined to exact his revenge. Mrs. Epstein's body was found a week later in a marshy area up around Lynn.

46
Catherine

I couldn't live in New Brunswick after Molly died; there were too many memories. Robert had finally met a nice woman and they were married. They now lived in the house. Harry and I had to start fresh so we moved back into my mother's old house in Westfield. The only memories I had here were the pleasant ones of my youth.

Harry started school and shows signs of having his father's intellect and personality. Only time will tell what kind of man he will become, but I have high hopes.

Two years after Franklin Andrews died, I received a special delivery letter from Langdan Textiles. This was curious because the only address they had for me was the one in New Brunswick. I had not filled out a form advising the postal service where I was moving but my guess is that they went to Edgar, who had a way of finding out things. In any case, they found me and delivered the letter.

It was only one page but I had to read it over at least a dozen times before I fully grasped what it was saying. I was being advised that I was the sole owner of Langdan Textiles. After Andrews died, the company had been held in some sort of legal term, whose name I'm sure I can't remember, until the details of ownership got sorted out.

Since its creation in the mid-1800s, Langdan had always been a family-owned corporation. After the elder Mr. Andrews passed away, the ownership of the company naturally passed on to his son, Franklin. Since he had no known siblings and no offspring, a battle for ownership and control of the company developed after his death. Then, as the court was going through his papers, the original will of the elder Mr. Andrews appeared and on it, I was named as the next in line.

I had lived much of my life under the false impression that Franklin Andrews, Jr. was my father. Then I found out that my real father was in fact Franklin Andrews, Sr. but I believed he had no idea that I existed. I assumed that Junior had kicked my pregnant mother back to New Jersey without informing his father that he had a daughter. Mrs. Epstein had told me that my true father was indeed aware of my existence. Now, I learned that not only did he know of my existence but he had put me down by name in his will as his heir in the event of the demise of his son.

After the international scandal brought to light by Mark Weston's news article, Langdan slipped almost to the point of oblivion. It was only Andrews' death that ultimately saved it. The few remaining company executives were able to point at the corpse of their former company president and say to the world: 'He did it! He was the one responsible for all the bad stuff Langdan had ever done! We're the new Langdan! Come back!' And come back they did. Feed companies and other concerns that shipped bulk product needed quality burlap bags to ship their products. They fled out of principal, but could now claim they were returning for the same reason. They didn't fool anyone, though. The real reason they were coming back was because they needed the bags.

I had to admire the managers who stuck it out and saved the company, my company. But I did not like their attitudes toward me. After the will was found, it took the court six months to track me down. Then the upper management spent the following six months in court contesting the will. In the end, the court said that the will was valid. I owned Langdan Textiles and was their boss. Still, they did not concede entirely because accompanying the letter of concession was an offer to buy the company from me for an "amount to be negotiated."

I had no intention of running a corporation, nor did I have any illusion that I had the ability to do so, but I certainly was not going to be bullied out of what was rightfully mine. I had no intention of letting go any of the men who had saved he company from extinction, but I also did not want them in ultimate control of it either. I had to come up with someone that I thought could do the job but would not be too objectionable to this group. Then it occurred to me. I would find and hire Herbert Williams, Ben's traveling companion and mentor. Ben raved about Williams, both as a businessman and as a man. I would make him president of the company.

The first thing I had to do was to find Herb Williams. I assumed he had gone to work for one of Langdan's competitors, but which one? I had done enough sleuthing to last a lifetime but I knew someone who could easily hunt him down for me.

After the police had left and the undertakers took away the bodies, Sergeant Jones stayed with me. I had expected a similar type of relay for me as I had arranged to look in on Molly and Harry when I went to India. Sol had gotten older, but was still spry and would come to New Brunswick at least once a week. Mr. Charney was such a dear and would have traveled to Westfield every day to see that we were okay. In the end, it wasn't necessary. Sergeant Jones moved into the spare room and was there all day and night. When I asked him about work, he cryptically answered that he was between jobs. He said he was where he needed to be and that was it.

We eventually fell into a rhythm together that was very comforting. When I needed something, inevitably it turned up for me. About a week after Molly's death, I felt as though the world was crashing down on me. I was sitting in the kitchen and I picked up one of Molly's old worn wooden spoons, the one with a big chip out of it. They were so beat up that I once asked Molly if she would like me to buy her a new set of spoons. She said no, it would be like giving up on an old friend. She said that over the years the spoons had formed to her hands and she didn't think she had the patience, time or energy to break in a new set.

Well, I picked up her spoon to stir some soup and the memories all flooded over me. My eyes started to water and by the time I sat down, I was in full cry. I had thought that Sergeant Jones had gone for a walk but before I knew it, without a word there was a hand patting my shoulder. I knew this man would be there for me whenever I needed him. When I decided to move to Westfield, I asked the sergeant if he would like to move in with me there. He indicated that he would.

After I received the letter from Langdan, three things came to mind regarding the sergeant. First, since his profession was private investigation, it was only natural that I ask him to locate Herb Williams for me. He characteristically accepted this assignment with a nod. Second, I wanted to make sure that nothing like the corruption and wrong-doings that occurred under Franklin Andrews ever happened again so I asked the sergeant if he would be my director of security and international operations. He would review the operations of each of our plants and make sure that everything was above board and that the people employed at our facilities were being treated fairly. With his innate sense of honor, I knew he would be the perfect man for the job.

He said he was intrigued by this offer. He had resumed his private investigation business but I sensed that his primary occupation was looking after me. As a result, he would only have an occasional client, just enough to pay the bills but no more. I think he felt a sense of guilt that he did not arrive in time to save Molly. He didn't want such a thing to happen again so he stayed close to home. I didn't mind the attention but I could easily see that this was not a proper life for him. Further, the disgust he felt for the clients he did get—a husband who suspects his wife of cheating, a boss who suspects an employee of giving company secrets to a competitor—was palpable. He needed something important to do with his life.

He was intrigued but he did not jump at the opportunity, probably because it would take him away from me for long stretches of time. He had to know that I was perfectly safe now. I think he was afraid that he would lose me, or that I would forget about him and move on if he weren't here, physically present in my life. I had the perfect solution to that concern.

"Sergeant, I told you I had three offers to make you. You've heard the first two, but I need to tell you that those offers are only valid if you accept the third."

He looked at me quizzically.

"Sergeant Jones, I want you to marry me."

Sergeant Jones was not a man of many words, but he was even more speechless than usual. Finally he spoke.

"But Catherine, I'm nearly twenty years older than you."

"It turned out that my father was in his sixties when I was born. We Jackson women have a thing for far older men, it turns out."

"Won't people talk?"

"Let them. The amount of time we spend together, I think most of my neighbors assume that we have an amorous relationship already."

"Oh Catherine, I'm so sorry. It never occurred to me that I've been responsible for any discredit that people may apply to you."

"Well, let's fix that, shall we?"

"But Catherine, what would Ben say?"

"He'd say that he's been dead nearly three years now. He'd say it was time I moved on and lived my life. He'd say that there couldn't be better hands for me to be in than yours. Yes, Ben would be very happy. Sergeant, are you trying to tell me that you don't want to marry me?"

"Catherine, there is nothing more that I want in the entire world. I've always been a relatively simple man. I've had aspirations but I've always accepted my lot and whatever comes my way. I'm just having trouble believing that something this wonderful could happen to me. To use our Indian connection for a second, marrying you would be like achieving nirvana, and I'm sure I'm not worthy of such a blessing."

"Sergeant, that is perhaps the nicest compliment that anyone has ever bestowed upon me. So, once you sort it out in your mind, do you think there's a chance that you would say yes and marry me?"

He smiled down on me.

"Yes, Catherine, I love you more than life itself. I will marry you."

So, the sergeant set out to accomplish each of the three tasks presented to him. Locating Herbert Williams was the simplest of the three. He was indeed working for a competitor of Langdan, Brunswick Textiles. After he was fired by Langdan, Franklin Andrews spread throughout the textile world some scurrilous stories impugning Mr. Williams' character. Combined with the need to find a job quickly to support a wife and four kids, he settled for a position far beneath his abilities. When I took the trip up to Boston to meet with him, he was anxious to leave Brunswick, but at the same time he was incredulous and skeptical of the offer I was making him.

"Mrs. Albert, I don't know if I'm the best candidate for the position you're offering me, President and Chief Operating Officer for Langdan Textiles."

"Mr. Williams, I should show you some of the letters Ben wrote to me from his trip to India. It's almost embarrassing the way he raved about you and about your character. And he wasn't just viewing you as a friend that he wrote such things; he saw you as a top-flight manager who was capable of doing anything you set your mind to. That's the kind of man I see overseeing the operations of this business."

Williams looked downcast.

"Some friend I was. I abandoned Ben when he needed me most."

"Mr. Williams. That was a situation in which there were no winners. I received a letter from the British provisional government in India apologizing for their role in allowing the affair to go on the way it did. A friend of mine in the State Department said such an admission was practically unheard of. They ended the letter by stating that if there was anything I needed, please let them know. I wrote them and told them to bring my husband back; until such time that they did that, I would never forgive them. I will hold them more than responsible to the day I die but you, Mr. Williams, were put in an untenable position. If you had stood up it only would have hurt yourself without helping Ben one bit. Believe me, if I held you in the least bit responsible, I would not be here today. Instead, I am going to rely on my husband's judgment of character and offer you this job."

"Thank you Mrs. Albert. I accept."

As I expected, the sergeant dove into his second task of upgrading the professionalism of Langdan worldwide with enthusiasm and dedication. He was to report to only two people, Mr. Williams and me. He immediately made a world tour of all of the company's facilities, starting with the Calcutta operation. Within a matter of weeks, he had weeded out what he referred to as managerial deadwood and made a number of other changes. One of the most profound changes he made was to install a native Indian in a key management position, one with real responsibility. This was practically unheard of for most concerns throughout India. He made similar changes in other Langdan plants in the rest of the world.

He would make this world tour every two years to check on the operations and make sure the changes were still in place and whether any further changes were needed. On his second trip to Calcutta, he was approached by a smallish Indian man with glasses dressed in a white flowing serape and sandals. The sergeant recognized him immediately as Gandhi.

"Mr. Jones, I presume," Gandhi said in greeting, "your reputation precedes you here to Calcutta."

"Mr. Gandhi," the sergeant responded as they shook hands, " your reputation precedes you throughout the world. It is an honor to meet you."

"The honor is mine, sir. The changes you have put in place here have been nothing short of miraculous. Of course, you know I won't rest until Indians have control of their own fate and their own economy, but in the meantime improvements such as the ones put in place here are most welcome."

"It is only the right thing to do, sir."

"Yes, you are right, but sometimes it takes an unjust death to make people do the right thing. I have seen death in my lifetime, and I am afraid I will see much more before I'm through on this earth. Much of it has been pointless and leads to nothing. Benjamin Albert's death is not one of those. You and Mrs. Albert can take pride in knowing the good things to which his death has led. Please give Mrs. Albert my fondest regards when you see her next."

"I will sir. Thank you and good luck in your quest."

With that, Mahatma Gandhi strolled away.

The sergeant dove into his third task with equal enthusiasm and dedication. We were married shortly after he returned from his first tour. Harry was presented with a brother, Benjamin, about a year later. A year and a half after that, his sister was born. We named her Molly-Lileth after both of my mothers.

A short while after he had turned six, Harry walked up to me. He seemed confused about something.

"Mama, how come some people call Daddy Walter but you call him Sergeant?"

"Sometimes people can be called different things, but it doesn't change who they are. I call you 'honey' and 'my American son' sometimes, but your name is still Harry, isn't it?"

"Yes, I guess so."

He still looked confused.

"Daddy was born with the name Walter; Sergeant was a title he earned. It was what he was called when I first met him and that is what I've continued to call him out of respect."

I patted the sofa and had him climb up beside me.

"You wait here a second, okay? I'll be right back."

I got up and went to the desk in my office. I pulled a black tin box out of the top right drawer and returned to sit back down beside Harry. I opened the box and extracted the dollar that Harry's namesake had left for Ben those many years ago. I handed Harry the dollar bill, telling him he had to be very careful with it.

"I want to tell you a story. This story is about the man you're named after and about the woman who looked after you early in your life and about the man she called her American Son."

Purchase other Black Rose Writing titles at www.blackrosewriting.com/books

and use promo code PRINT to receive a 20% discount.